Joyner's Dream

Joyner's Dream

A novel by

SYLVIA TYSON

HARPER
PERENNIAL

Joyner's Dream
Copyright © 2011 by Sylvia Tyson.
All rights reserved.

Published by Harper Perennial, an imprint of HarperCollins Publishers Ltd.

Originally published in Canada in an original trade paperback edition
by HarperCollins Publishers Ltd: 2011
This Harper Perennial trade paperback edition: 2012

HarperCollins books may be purchased for educational, business,
or sales promotional use through our Special Markets Department.

HarperCollins Publishers Ltd
2 Bloor Street East, 20th Floor
Toronto, Ontario, Canada
M4W 1A8

www.harpercollins.ca

Library and Archives Canada Cataloguing in Publication

Tyson, Sylvia, 1940–
Joyner's dream / Sylvia Tyson.

ISBN 978-1-55468-496-0

I. Title.
PS8639.Y88J69 2012   C813'.6   C2011-905870-7

Printed and bound in the United States
RRD 9 8 7 6 5 4 3 2 1

To Timothy Findley
for his friendship and inspiration

Contents

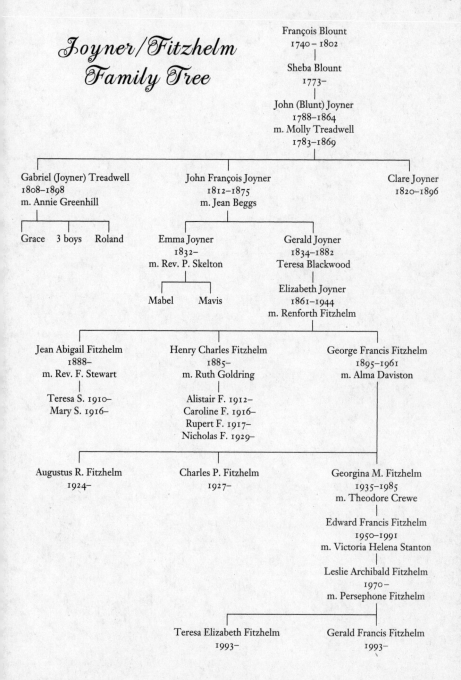

Joyner/Fitzhelm Family Tree

François Blount
1740 – 1802

Sheba Blount
1773–

John (Blunt) Joyner
1788–1864
m. Molly Treadwell
1783–1869

Gabriel (Joyner) Treadwell
1808–1898
m. Annie Greenhill

Grace   3 boys   Roland

John François Joyner
1812–1875
m. Jean Beggs

Emma Joyner
1832–
m. Rev. P. Skelton

Mabel   Mavis

Gerald Joyner
1834–1882
Teresa Blackwood

Elizabeth Joyner
1861–1944
m. Renforth Fitzhelm

Clare Joyner
1820–1896

Jean Abigail Fitzhelm
1888–
m. Rev. F. Stewart

Teresa S. 1910–
Mary S. 1916–

Henry Charles Fitzhelm
1885–
m. Ruth Goldring

Alistair F. 1912–
Caroline F. 1916–
Rupert F. 1917–
Nicholas F. 1929–

George Francis Fitzhelm
1895–1961
m. Alma Daviston

Augustus R. Fitzhelm
1924–

Charles P. Fitzhelm
1927–

Georgina M. Fitzhelm
1935–1985
m. Theodore Crewe

Edward Francis Fitzhelm
1950–1991
m. Victoria Helena Stanton

Leslie Archibald Fitzhelm
1970–
m. Persephone Fitzhelm

Teresa Elizabeth Fitzhelm
1993–

Gerald Francis Fitzhelm
1993–

Prologue

*L*et me introduce myself. My name is Leslie Archibald Fitzhelm, although, following the disappearance of my father when I was eight, Stanton is the name I was raised with.

Since this is part of my contribution to the family journal, a brief history of who I was.

I was born in 1970 in the village of Stanton, now swallowed up by the northern sprawl of Toronto but founded by my maternal-two-times great-grandfather, the original Archibald Stanton, in 1876. Having secured an ideal river site, he built from local stone a modern grist and flour mill with adjoining grain, feed and general store. He'd have been right at home in today's world of multiplexes, for he then built an Anglican church with attached meeting hall and schoolroom, and two facing rows of semidetached cottages for his employees. This generated Stanton Builders, later to become Stanton Construction, sold before I was born but often proprietarily spoken of by Aunt Rachel and Aunt Sarah.

Four years later he built, from the same blue-grey stone, Stanton House, foursquare on a bluff overlooking the river and the town, as a wedding present for his bride, Amelia Fitch. It was liberally decorated with green gingerbread, unexpectedly topped with a red tile roof, and at the peak, dead in the centre, a large hexagonal cupola with windows on all sides so he could survey his fiefdom unimpeded. This was crowned by a dragon weathervane imported from England, I was told, at considerable expense.

The new mill was not greeted with enthusiasm by everyone, particularly the owners and employees of other local mills, and the aunts often related the story of how, over seventy years later, my grandmother's wedding dress was ruined by the tobacco-tinged spittle of an old woman who declared that Stanton money was stained with the blood and sweat of honest working men. Their indignation was as fresh as if it had happened yesterday.

I've kept only two of the Stanton family photographs. The first is of my grandparents' wedding in 1946, my grandfather Isaac, newly returned from the war, looking older than his twenty-nine years, very stiff and solemn in his high collar and dark suit, holding the hand of my grandmother Eleanor, a frail, pretty, dark-haired girl of eighteen, overshadowed by the elaborateness of the ill-fated dress. On either side of them stand Isaac's two spinster sisters, Rachel and Sarah. My wife, Persy, calls it "Canadian Gothic." Within two years Eleanor was dead of the breech birth which my mother, Victoria, survived, and five years later the still-grieving Isaac was the victim of an influenza epidemic, leaving my mother in the custody of his sisters.

The second is of my parents' wedding in 1969. Until I was twenty, it was the only picture I had of my father. I've inherited his even features and his distinctive hands with their long fingers and spatulate tips. My mother is beautiful in her honeymoon suit, her dark hair sculpted into a rigid bouffant piled with sausage curls, her delicate face shadowed by chronic illness. My parents are flanked by the two sisters from the first photo, older by some twenty-two years, tightly permed and corseted, wearing the expensively dowdy dresses

and elaborate hats common to women of their station and generation in the late sixties. "Arbus redux," Persy calls it.

All other memorabilia rests with the Stanton Historical Society,
founded by Aunt Rachel and housed in the old Stanton-built firehall,
which is now the local library.

My parents met when my father was sent by his firm to conduct
an assessment of the Stanton properties and to discuss the estate with
Aunt Rachel. My mother would never have been allowed to date any
of the village boys as the Stantons were of that breed of small-town
aristocrats who only marry one another, but as Aunt Sarah confided
to me in later years, before Alzheimer's had fully claimed her, my
father, though not personally known to them, was descended from
English aristocracy on one side and old Toronto money on the other.
It was good enough for the aunts, who actively encouraged the union
and eagerly awaited the birth of a son and heir—me.

My childhood was one of moderate privilege straitjacketed
by Victorian sensibility. My father's lineage notwithstanding, there
were things Stantons simply did not do. Not the usual paranoia over
what the neighbours would think, but rather the firm conviction that
Stantons were responsible for setting the community standard for
proper behaviour.

My mother had rheumatic fever as a child, which weakened her
heart and left her vulnerable to a variety of illnesses, though I firmly
believe she'd have lived a much healthier, happier life if she hadn't
been constantly reminded by the aunts how fragile she was. Beyond
a quick hug and kiss at bedtime, the fear that I might inadvertently
pass on some infection discouraged much physical contact. I loved
her, but from a distance.

Most of my affection was focused on my father. He loved to
roughhouse, laugh and tell silly jokes, taught me how to play chess
and do card tricks, and read to me at bedtime, books sometimes a
little over my head but carefully explained: *Treasure Island, Two Years*

Before the Mast, the stories of Will James, and toward the end, passages from an old kid-bound edition of *Gulliver's Travels* under its original title, *Travels into Several Remote Nations of the World*. I would drift off to sleep with visions of cowboys and giants and sailing ships.

He also wrote and illustrated little storybooks for me, with characters like Wally the Walleye and Terence the Trout. My father was an avid still and fly fisherman, meticulously hand-tying all his flies, hand-shaping his lures, then reproducing them with ink and watercolours in a small notebook. We spent many Saturday mornings in our aluminum boat among the reeds in the river above the long idle mill, where he'd entertain me with hilariously absurd lectures on the psychology of fish, or we'd drive in his old Volvo to some fast-moving stream, don our waders, and he'd instruct me in the intricacies of fly fishing. These are my happiest childhood memories.

I attended the local public school, but was discouraged by the aunts from socializing or joining in sports. The fact that I was a Stanton and had a girl's name branded me as a stuck-up little bastard and a pansy. My one friend was another outcast, the son of the preacher for the newly built Jehovah's Witness meeting hall. We were both denied TV and shared a secret passion for comic books, which we read and hid under the trailer his family lived in while their house was being built. He was awed by Stanton House. I dreamed of living in a trailer.

Rachel and Sarah were pillars of the church and the bane of the choir director's life, vying for solos with their shaky sopranos, although it was my mother who had a sweet, true voice. They alternated as presidents of the altar guild and the quilting society, chief organizers of bazaars, jumble sales and church suppers. Rachel dominated the school board and the village council. Sarah was her second in command and constant shadow. If Rachel said "Under no circumstances," Sarah immediately echoed "No circumstances." They were unchallenged, even by my father. That was just the way it was.

With all these obligations the aunts were seldom home during the day. My mother rested in the afternoons, and as my father commuted to Toronto and didn't get home 'til dinnertime, I occupied myself after school doing my homework at the oilcloth-covered kitchen table, and sharing milk and cookies with Mrs. Jensen, our housekeeper and cook, and her battle-scarred marmalade tomcat, Duke, only tolerated by the aunts because he was a ferocious mouser. Any dreams of having a dog were dashed. Rachel declared them filthy, flea-ridden beasts, and that was the end of that. Persy says I've more than made up for it with our current menagerie.

At dinner, under the watchful eyes of primitive portraits of Archibald and Amelia Stanton, I'd report on the progress of my schoolwork and my father would make vague comments about his work, while my mother and the aunts dissected the intricacies of local politics and gossiped in a genteel and disapproving way. They limited themselves to ladylike portions, while my father and I, being the men of the family, were allowed seconds. This was a struggle for my mother, who loved anything starchy or sweet, and I remember my father giving me a wink, then slipping spoonfuls of mashed potatoes and gravy or rice pudding onto her plate when he thought the aunts weren't watching. We never dined out, so an occasional secret trip to McDonald's with my father was a highly anticipated treat. And so things continued until the summer my father disappeared.

Perhaps if I'd been older I'd have sensed some tension, but I was as self-absorbed as most eight-year-olds, and secure in the predictable routine of life at Stanton House. For almost as long as I could remember my parents had had separate bedrooms, so this was normal to me. No one ever raised their voices or quarrelled, and if there was less conversation than usual around that time I didn't notice, for I was to spend the month of August at a dude ranch in Alberta, living in a bunkhouse and learning to be a cowboy with twenty other young greenhorns—although I knew I'd have the Will James advantage. My father said it would be good for me, and surprisingly the aunts agreed. I couldn't wait to fly by myself on an airplane, and was embarrassed and impatient to pull away from my father's last hug to join the other boys. I barely remembered to turn and wave to him.

It was a glorious month, free of all the Stanton baggage. The friendly, communal chaos of the bunkhouse, trail rides, campfires, eating beans and bacon for breakfast—everything was new and exotic to me. I discovered a natural seat and affinity for horses, and returned home strong, tanned and more self-confident than I'd ever been.

Rachel met me at the airport, in the old Buick Town Car driven by Mrs. Jensen's husband, Ole, our chauffeur and handyman. When I asked for my father, she said we'd talk about it when we got home. I wasn't bothered by her lack of response, and happily prattled on about my amazing summer, even hinting against all odds that I'd like to have a horse.

As we stepped out of the August heat and into the cool darkness of the hallway with its smell of lemon oil and floor wax, the grandfather clock struck the quarter-hour. I dropped my duffle bag and headed for the kitchen and Mrs. Jensen, but Rachel caught my shoulder and steered me to the parlour. I was told to sit on a chair facing my mother and the aunts on the Victorian settee. I searched my mother's face for any hint of what was happening, but she dipped her head and wouldn't look at me.

Rachel said, "You're going to have to be very brave, and a real little man. Your father has gone away and he's not coming back. You'll no longer bear his name. You'll be Leslie Archibald Stanton from now on. There will be no further discussion. The subject is closed."

"Closed," echoed Sarah, then added that she hoped I'd be ready to buckle down to work when school started.

I waited for my mother to say something, anything.

"Oh Leslie, I'm so sorry," she sobbed, and fled from the room in tears.

I looked down at the blue Chinese carpet with its islands, bridges and pagodas. My father had joked that the two figures on the humpbacked bridge were fishing for carp, and they must have a pretty good catch after all these years. I willed myself to be with them, and if anything more was said, I didn't hear it.

I was finally excused, and somehow found my way to the kitchen where Mrs. Jensen gathered me in her arms. Dry-eyed, unable to speak, I might have stayed like that forever if Sarah hadn't sent me to my room to unpack, saying Mrs. Jensen had work to do.

The days that followed were a fog of bewilderment and misery. When Mrs. Jensen had come to work on the Monday after my departure, I learned, my father was gone. She'd been ordered to air out his room, strip the bed, and dispose of anything of his she found. She'd discovered his old grey cardigan hanging in his basement workshop, and saved it for me. I took it to bed with me every night, the smell and feel of it comforting me as I read and reread our favourite books, imagining his voice. The ones my father had made for me were gone. A clandestine search of the house yielded no clues and only three tangible things: one of his flies, a mayfly, caught on a piece of carpet in the mudroom, the picture from my parents' wedding in a box of old photographs, and in the attic, my paternal great-grandfather's violin, dusty and forgotten in its case. I hid everything in the back of my wardrobe.

I was told my mother was ill again and not to be disturbed. Attempts to sneak into her room were intercepted and punished. The only thing that brought me a little solace was that Duke, the cat, slipped into my room to sleep with me at night. He wasn't affectionate, and had never shown any interest in me before except as a source of treats, but from that first night until he died several years later he was my companion, slipping down the back stairs to the kitchen each morning before dawn.

I sank for the first time into the state I now know intimately as depression. Back then I had no idea what was happening to me. I was a prisoner in my own skin, incapable of leaving my room and my bed, but when I slept I had recurring dreams of voices taunting me as I wandered endlessly through a nightmare version of the abandoned mill, knowing my father was there somewhere but unable to find him.

The aunts displayed the typical small-town reaction to any hint of mental illness and put it about that I was suffering from tick fever picked up on my holiday. As sunk as I was in my misery I sensed that my passivity gave me a kind of power. All ambitions for me as the heir and conservator of the Stanton legacy were stymied by an eight-year-old's refusal to eat, speak or leave his room. I even started to wet the bed, which, to my secret satisfaction, horrified the aunts, but I stopped when I saw how much work it made for Mrs. Jensen. Attempts to call me Archie were met with stony silence.

I missed over ten weeks of school and had to be tutored to catch up. Prompted by fears of some public episode and the resulting gossip, it was decided that someone as delicate and unstable as I was would do better at a nearby private school, and though I was a day boy not a boarder, it was liberating. I joined the chess club, the debating club, played baseball and soccer, and even joined the music program to learn to play my violin, anything to prolong my hours at school and escape Stanton House.

A visionary teacher who had an IBM PC persuaded the school to buy one, and started a computer club. We played Dungeons and Dragons, and Space Invaders, tame by today's standards but pretty exciting back then. I savoured small rebellions: missing my bus so I could watch TV at a classmate's house, smuggling tapes and a cassette player home in my backpack to listen to music under the covers at night, inventing rehearsals, study groups and class trips so I could go to see *Star Wars* (four times) and *Star Trek: The Motion Picture* (twice).

Like the others you'll meet in this journal I've promised myself to be absolutely honest, so I'll confess one other symptom of my unhappiness then. I started to steal, sometimes money for my covert activities, but mainly to cause annoyance and anxiety to the aunts, things like reading glasses, embroidery scissors, an address book. I became quite devious, and once even staged a break-in when I knew the safety deposit box had been brought home for an insurance evaluation of the family jewellery. That time it was an old diamond brooch and the police were called in. I stored my loot in a biscuit tin which I hid under a loose board in the attic floor. I stopped as suddenly as I'd started when my mother died, and had forgotten about it until I began writing this account. The box remained in its hiding place next to my comic book collection until recently when I revealed it to my children.

In all those years I never asked about my father, although I once plucked up the courage to phone his old firm. I was told no one of that name was currently employed by them and that they no longer represented the Stanton estate. Over time the pain subsided to a dull ache.

My father had never treated my mother as an invalid and could always make her laugh, coaxing her out into the garden to watch us play croquet or to join us for picnics by the river. After he disappeared she complained constantly of pains in her joints and chest, seldom leaving her room. The doctor came more frequently and I was restricted to short, supervised visits, quickly learning to limit conversation to neutral subjects as any upset would have her wheezing and calling for her inhaler. Bouts of pneumonia grew longer and more debilitating, and I was fifteen when her heart finally stopped beating forever. She was only thirty-six.

If her death were not enough to push me over the edge again, the grisly ritual of her open coffin in the parlour clinched it. The smell of lilies still makes me nauseous. Through the whole ordeal I clung to the hope that my father would suddenly appear and take me away, but when he didn't I had to accept that he must be dead as well.

I began to sense a sort of smug satisfaction in Rachel, as if she expected and even welcomed another breakdown, and as I recovered I recognized my feelings of bleakness were not the product of a fevered imagination, but firmly rooted in reality. I wasn't back in school a week before Rachel summoned me to the parlour and laid out her plans for me.

When I graduated I was to attend divinity school at Trinity College with the purpose of replacing the aging rector of Saint Luke's, the Stanton-built Anglican church. I felt like a vulture whenever I encountered him. In time, I'm sure, Rachel would have found me a suitable girl to marry. It's easy to say I should have asserted myself, but openly confronting Rachel wasn't an option. As she constantly reminded me, if it weren't for her and Sarah I'd have no one. I was financially dependent and mentally unstable, unfit for anything.

"No backbone at all," she once declared. "Just like your parents."

"Like your parents," said Sarah.

At that moment I felt a jolt of pure hatred like an electric shock, which scared the hell out of me. I forced my fists to unclench, knowing that if I followed my gut I'd be playing right into Rachel's hands. She was right. I couldn't leave . . . but I could escape.

I presented the case that with my history of nerves and university entrance looming I needed absolute, uninterrupted privacy to concentrate on my studies. The cupola at the top of the house was simply an empty, dusty space with a panoramic view, but it had been a refuge when I lost my father, and it would become so again. Rachel's bad knees and high blood pressure would discourage her from climbing the stairs.

Ole Jensen and his son, Harry, weatherized the place. Phone and power lines were installed in anticipation of the computer and printer I so desperately wanted. Fortunately Rachel's ignorance of anything technical allowed me to convince her that a computer was little more than a glorified typewriter and crucial to my studies, though she balked at the cost. I dismantled the workbench from my father's basement workshop to build rough bookshelves, then added an old armchair, a carpet and a table to use as a desk. A simple bolt on the trap door guaranteed glorious isolation, a place to read or study or practise my violin in peace. The violin was a bone of contention with Rachel, who insisted that piano or organ would be more appropriate for an aspiring clergyman, but I knew her opposition had little to do with the instrument itself, rather that she saw it as some lingering vestige of my father's influence.

One of my schoolmates got a new stereo system, and gave me his boom box. The speakers were for classical music, but the headphones vibrated with rock stations and the compilation tapes friends made me from their record collections. I liked Springsteen and Mellencamp and Prince, but loved Brits like the Eurythmics, Dire Straits, Robert Palmer, and once almost got caught singing and dancing to "Red, Red Wine" by UB40. Rachel heard the noise and tackled the stairs. When her pounding finally penetrated my headphones, I lifted the trap door to find her red-faced and wheezing, demanding to know what all that thumping and caterwauling was.

"Calisthenics," I said.

By this time, Sarah was showing signs of the dementia that would finally overtake her. She'd often mistake me for her brother Isaac, and was so guileless and confiding that at times I almost liked her. As she diminished, Rachel grew stronger.

I barely spoke to either of them at breakfast and dinner, but in my tower I communicated with my schoolmates, played cutthroat chess with opponents in Russia and China, researched exotic destinations. I even picked up some interesting information about sex, having nothing firsthand to go by (Persy says I should rephrase that). I fantasized about travel, not to the Caribbean or the Greek Islands, but to the times and places in my growing collection of travel literature, from Samuel Johnson's *A Journey to the Western Islands of Scotland* and Charles Doughty's *Travels in Arabia Deserta* to Bruce Chatwin's *Songlines* and *In Patagonia*, which reminded me of my old childhood acquaintance, Lemuel Gulliver. That book had disappeared with my father.

At university I was bright enough, but unmotivated, and drifted along doing only what was necessary to maintain my point average. With an endless bus ride to and from Toronto each day, my extracurricular activities were reduced to nonexistence. University acquaintances were not welcome at Stanton House, and when a girl I liked offered me a lift home, she was met by Rachel with such icy politeness she never spoke to me again. It was like being suspended in some sort of limbo, waiting for God knows what to shake me out of it.

Persy says I'd have rebelled eventually, but I'll never know, because on February the 21st of that year, 1991, an official-looking letter was hand-delivered to me as I left one of my lectures. It was from a Lester Fairplay Junior of the Dickensian-sounding law firm of Fairplay, Fairplay and Honeywell, and stated that if I would make an appointment at my earliest convenience he had some information which might be to my advantage. I was intrigued, and arranged to meet with him the following day at four.

Lester Fairplay, a short, stocky, sandy-haired man of about forty in a rumpled suit with a crooked bow tie, greeted me warmly and ushered me into a book-lined corner office with large windows overlooking a high-rise canyon, and cluttered with precarious stacks of files. We sat in comfortable wing chairs as the receptionist served us coffee.

"I'm delighted to finally meet you, Leslie. Ridiculous name for a law firm, I know. I'm it, you see. My father retired some years ago, and Honeywell's been dead for almost twenty. Forget Mr. Fairplay or Lester, call me Junior. Everyone does."

I replied that with the difference in our ages I didn't know if I could bring myself to call him Junior, and would he settle for Les.

He laughed and said, "You have your father's sense of humour."

The room suddenly shifted. I felt the coffee cup slipping from my fingers, and my lunch rising to my throat.

"Are you okay?" he said anxiously. "Let me get you some brandy."

When he handed it to me, I gulped it down like water.

"Please, I've heard nothing about my father since I was eight. Is he alive? Where is he? Can I see him?"

"Oh, he's alive—and most anxious to see you. Wants to explain everything himself, but in his defence I feel it's only fair to tell you that under the terms of the separation he was barred from all contact with you and your mother. There was a restraining order that would have resulted in his arrest. The only concession I could negotiate was that he be allowed to write to you. He was puzzled, then deeply saddened when you didn't reply. He's now very ill, and asked me to make one last effort to communicate with you on his behalf."

I assured Junior that as far as I knew my father had simply disappeared. I knew nothing of any separation agreement, had never received even one letter. I was desperate to see him. Junior said he'd arrange it and pick me up at eight the next morning.

I had an hour-long bus ride to think about what I'd learned, and was seething by the time I reached Stanton House. Rachel was waiting for me at the front door complaining about my lack of consideration in being late for dinner, saying I'd have to eat it cold in the kitchen.

When she finally actually looked at me, she said, "Why are you staring at me like that? What's wrong with you?"

"Where are my father's letters?" I could see the alarm in her eyes as they nervously flicked upward. In her room, then. She hadn't destroyed them.

"I don't know what you're talking about. You're having another of your spells. I'm calling the doctor."

"No more doctors, no more lies. I want my father's letters. Give them to me or I'll tear your room apart piece by piece until I find them."

She stood with her arms crossed, blocking the stairway, but I shoved her aside and ran up the steps. It was the first time I'd ever openly confronted her about anything, and certainly the first time she could have perceived me as a full-grown, potentially threatening adult. I threw open the door to her bedroom with a satisfying crash as she puffed up the stairs after me, saying how dare I lay hands on her, how dare I enter her room without her permission. I started yanking out drawers, dumping the contents onto the floor.

"Stop it! Stop it this instant! There's no excuse for this barbaric behaviour."

I started on the closet.

"All right! All right! That's enough! They're here—" On her dresser was one of those portable Victorian secretaries that look like brass-bound wooden boxes. "I only did it for your own good. God knows what vicious nonsense he filled them with."

I grabbed the box and raced up two more flights to my tower, slamming and bolting the trap door behind me.

There were close to a hundred letters in bundles secured with elastic bands, unopened, addressed to me in my father's spiky hand-writing. They were all about me. Did I still read our old books (titles of books he thought I might like), did I still enjoy fishing, was I still having trouble with math? He'd learned about my trans-fer to private school from an old classmate who was a teacher there, and had sent him money to cover the cost of sports equipment and other little extras I'd always assumed Rachel had relented on. He'd even risked sitting in the back of the auditorium when our band played its first concert, but left when he spotted my mother and the aunts. He said it devastated him to see my mother looking so pale and sad, and when he learned of her death his words were so anguished I could barely continue to read. The last letter, dated six months earlier, said his health was failing and he prayed I'd answer as it was his greatest wish to see me once more. I thought my heart would burst.

I ignored Rachel's repeated pounding and threats, and when I heard the doctor's voice I calmly assured him that I was neither violent nor suicidal, suggesting he offer his sedative to Rachel.

The last interruption was around midnight, a desperate voice whispering, "Oh Leslie, you have to apologize. I've never seen her like this. She's pacing back and forth in her room like a madwoman, talking to herself. She's so angry and I'm so frightened. I don't know what she'll do."

"Go to bed, Sarah," I said. "It will all sort itself out in the morning."

At some point I dozed off, lying on the floor surrounded by the letters, and awakened around five in the morning, clear-headed and focused.

Slipping down to my bedroom in stockinged feet, I pulled out my backpack and duffle bag, stuffed the letters and some clothes into them, and carried them down the back stairs through the kitchen to the mudroom. I made two more trips for my computer and printer, moved everything out to the front gate where Junior was to pick me up, then sat down on the front steps to wait. It was bitter cold and Rachel found me shivering there when she came down in her housecoat to retrieve the newspaper.

"Well," she said, "if you're ready to apologize we'll say no more about it, but I won't tolerate any more outbursts."

"You won't have to tolerate anything about me. I'm leaving."

I was suddenly bulletproof. Nothing penetrated. She was still railing at me when Junior pulled up to the gate. I loaded my belongings into the back of his car, and her final words were aimed at my back.

"If you go you go for good! I'll cut you off! I'll make sure you never see a cent of my . . . of Stanton money!"

"What the hell was that about?" said Junior as we drove off, and the enormity of what I'd done suddenly hit me.

"Seems I'm homeless and broke," I replied. "Guess I'm going to need a job and a place to live."

He chuckled and said, "We'll work something out."

I turned to take one last look at the village, and Stanton House sitting above it all. No regrets, only overwhelming relief. My heartbeat gradually dropped to normal as I related the events of the previous night. Having a listener helped put it all in perspective, and I was actually able to laugh a little.

But Junior sobered me by saying, "I don't want to add any more drama to your life right now, but you need to prepare yourself. Your father's illness has altered him drastically. I won't sugar-coat it. He has lung cancer."

I was so distracted by this news I barely noticed that we'd been heading not into Toronto, but east into the countryside, and only registered our surroundings when the car stopped at a security checkpoint set in a high, intimidating barrier of metal fencing and razor wire banked with piles of grey snow. We were entering a prison.

"This is a relatively new medium-security facility," he continued. "The infirmary in maximum was pretty antiquated and since your father needed full-time care and could hardly be considered a security risk, I managed to get him transferred here. Frankly, he's dying."

I'd prepared myself for him to be ill, but finding him in a place like this and learning that I was going to lose him all over again was staggering.

"This is crazy! What could he possibly have done?"

"I defended him on a charge of armed robbery with violence. He was innocent, of course. Unfortunately the two others charged were juveniles, and there was a gun. His appeals have been denied. He's now in the fifth year of a ten-year sentence. There's a parole hearing pending, and he'd probably have gotten it, but it makes no difference now. The anticipation of seeing you has rallied him, but don't be deceived. It won't last."

"How long do we have?"

"Perhaps as little as a month, possibly two or three. It's impossible to tell."

"There must be something we can do. Can we get him moved to a real hospital?"

"No point. He was diagnosed too late. It's down to pain management and quality of life. The facilities here are pretty basic, but he's relatively comfortable. The whole process of getting him moved would mean a hearing. It would take a lot out of him and probably shorten the time you have left together. That's the most important thing to him now. You need to be strong for his sake, and be guided by his wishes."

We passed through various checkpoints. The staff was familiar with Junior and barely glanced at the contents of his briefcase. My identity verified, I was patted down and my ballpoint pen and keys removed.

The smell of mingled sweat and urine, cigarette smoke and disinfectant was pervasive as we were escorted down a long featureless hallway. There was some attempt to make the infirmary more cheerful—blue paint instead of institutional beige with travel posters pasted to the walls between the high safety-glassed windows. Half a dozen men in metal beds watched with undisguised curiosity as we passed. At the end of the ward by the matron's office was one more bed obscured by a privacy drape. As we rounded it I saw him for the first time in thirteen years.

My first thought was that this wizened grey-faced man was not, could not be, my father, but when he smiled and said, "Hi, Twig! Hi, Junior!" it couldn't have been anyone else. Whenever the aunts would launch into one of their lectures on the illustrious Stanton family tree, my father would joke that I was the last twig on it, and needed to grow some before I could bear the full load of their expectations.

"C'mon, Twig, let's get out of here," he'd say. "The tree can do without you for a while."

He gestured for me to sit, put on his familiar wire-rimmed glasses, took both my hands in his, and for a few moments we simply stared at each other.

"My God," he finally said. "You're a young man! I guess I'd pictured you the same as when I saw you last."

It wasn't that the years had disappeared, but rather that they didn't matter. When he asked if I could forgive him, I tearfully assured him there was nothing to forgive. I described my confrontation with Rachel. He told me how he'd been arrested when he tried to attend my mother's funeral. So much to talk about and time passed quickly, but as we approached the subject of his present circumstances he winced and started to cough. It suddenly hit me what a tremendous effort it must have been for him to sit up and talk as long as he had, and that the apparatus by his bed was for oxygen.

I adjusted his pillows and hugged him, saying this was only the first of many visits. I watched through the glass of the matron's office as Junior took some papers from his briefcase and my father signed them. The matron informed me that a compassionate visitor's pass would allow more frequent visits.

I was lost in thought during the long silent drive to Toronto, but as we reached the outskirts the practicalities of my situation caught up with me.

"Where are we going?" I asked.

"Your father owns a house near the university. There's plenty of room for you and it'll be handy for school." It hit me then that my university days were over. "I know it's already been a full day for you, but it's not over. There's someone waiting to meet you. His name is Teddy Crewe."

As we pulled up to the neat little Victorian house on a downtown side street, I had a blinding flash of memory. I'd been there before. I was four, going on five, for I know I was to start school shortly and I was excited to be going with my mother and the aunts to meet my grandmother for the first time. It was also the last.

This magical creature had opened the door, with a halo of red-gold curls, wearing a long, floating rainbow-coloured dress, unlike any grandmother I'd ever seen. I sat beside her on a sofa crowded with cushions as she hugged and kissed me, feeding me chocolates and ginger ale. Enveloped in an intoxicating scent, a blend of some exotic perfume, cigarette smoke and alcohol, I was enchanted. Rachel, however, was not. She was scandalized by something I have no memory of, and hustled us out of the house with no goodbyes.

This time it was Teddy Crewe who met us, in a navy blazer and grey flannels, beautifully tailored, but looking as if they belonged to a slightly larger man. He'd have been close to seventy then, with a mane of silver hair and a boney patrician face.

"Leslie, what a pleasure to see you again! Just call me Teddy. Technically I'm your grandfather, but that makes me feel so old. I don't know if you remember your grandmother."

I told him what I did remember, and he gestured toward an arresting nude portrait over the fireplace.

"That's her. The artist was in love with her, of course, everyone was. It's still hard to believe she's gone."

Teddy was off and running. I hardly had to say a word.

"We were Rosedale brats, friends from the cradle. She was so charming and funny, an actress you know, sang and danced beautifully.

When I started my career as a writer and director she was my ingenue, my muse. She had her dark side I grant you, moody, self-centred, promiscuous, but being her oldest friend and gay I was spared most of the dramatics."

"But you were married?" I asked.

"Well, she got pregnant, you see. Never would say who the father was. Mine had heard some nasty rumours about me, so the nuptials were a great relief to both our families."

"My father never talked about you."

"Sadly, Gina was completely missing whatever gene it is that makes a woman a mother. Loved the appearance of motherhood, but simply lacked the instinct. I did discover in myself some capacity to be a father and Eddie became the son I was never likely to have, although in retrospect I'm afraid we both let him down rather badly in that department.

"He left here for good after a flaming row with Gina. Well, that's to say it was a row on his side. Fighting with Gina was like fighting smoke. We didn't see much of him after that. We weren't invited to his wedding, and only learned about you when your mother and those two old harpies brought you here to meet us. Now that was an epic clash of lifestyles, a total train wreck . . . but what am I thinking, rattling on like this. You must be exhausted. I'll put you in Gina's room. It's a bit frou-frou, but I think you'll be comfortable. I'll call you for dinner around eight and we'll work out the domestic details then."

As I said goodbye to Junior, he handed me an envelope containing a cheque and a note from my father saying that this should take care of any expenses until further arrangements could be made. Teddy then showed me to a second-floor bedroom decorated in a riot of chintzes and still smelling faintly of tobacco and that same exotic scent I remembered from all those years ago. As I lay down my head was swimming, and I sank immediately into a long dreamless sleep.

My life became focused on the visits with my father. I'd never learned to drive, so if Junior couldn't take me then Teddy would deliver me in my father's old Volvo. The time was short: that brief window between when he'd just had his medication and wasn't quite lucid, and when the effects were wearing off and the pain was returning. I bought a Walkman to record our conversations and left it with him because it had a radio receiver and he said listening to music would help him sleep. I joked about his keeping it so close beside him under the covers, but he reminded me that this was, after all, a prison and things had a way of disappearing. As the tape rolled we filled in the missing years, and transported ourselves to other, happier times. I laughed more in those few weeks than I had in all the time he'd been gone. We celebrated his fortieth birthday and my twenty-first with a cake baked in the prison kitchen, and I gave him a copy of Brautigan's *Trout Fishing in America* I'd found in a second-hand bookstore.

About three weeks into this routine Teddy had a visitor. He described him as a weaselly little man in a cheap suit who claimed to be a private inquiry agent seeking information on the whereabouts of a certain Leslie Archibald Stanton who might be calling himself Leslie Fitzhelm.

Teddy had thoroughly enjoyed himself. Pretending to be a company-starved, doddery old man, he invited him in and sat him down with a generous measure of Scotch, saying how exciting it was to meet a real detective and how could he be of assistance. The man said he'd been retained by a Miss Rachel Stanton, who was gravely concerned about her dear nephew whom she'd raised from an infant and who'd suddenly disappeared with no explanation some weeks before. He showed Teddy an old photo of me attached to a copy of a missing person's report Rachel had filed with the Toronto Police Department stating that I had a history of mental illness and might be a danger to myself and others. He stressed that Miss Stanton's only concern was for my care and safety. Teddy confirmed that he was indeed my grandfather, and that sadly there'd been a rift in the family and he hadn't seen me since I was a child, but if I got in touch he'd certainly let him know.

When Junior checked with the police they told him the same thing they'd told Rachel, that I was of age and if I chose to disappear it was hardly a police matter. His take was that she was trying to have me declared incompetent. I tried to laugh it off, saying she'd have a hard time proving it if she couldn't find me. With Junior and Teddy in my corner I wasn't that worried about a confrontation, but it did bother me. I started using the back door in case the "weasel" was watching the place.

We had just over seven weeks together.

I won't tell my father's story here. His words have their own place in this journal.

In the early morning of Wednesday, April 24th, 1991, I received a call from the warden saying that my father had died during the night, and would I come as soon as possible. I called Junior and he picked me up. On arrival we learned that he hadn't simply passed away in his sleep. He'd taken a massive overdose of barbiturates, probably traded with one of the trustees for the Walkman. The obvious concern was that I might hold the administration responsible and take legal action, but he'd left a brief "To whom it may concern" letter saying that he was of sound mind and solely responsible for his actions, and I didn't challenge it. He'd grown progressively weaker, his breathing more laboured, his voice failing, his lucid periods fewer and shorter. We'd agreed not to place him on life support when the time came. He'd made his decision and, devastating as it was, I accepted it.

I saw him for the last time in the prison mortuary. I mechanically signed all the paperwork Junior put in front of me, and sorted through his belongings. His glasses, a faded photo of me as a child, jazz and classical music cassettes, a few sketches, some paperbacks, his Saint Christopher medal and wedding ring, everything fit into a big brown envelope. The Walkman, of course, was gone, but it didn't matter—I had my tapes.

Tucked between the pages of the dog-eared copy of *Trout Fishing in America* was a letter in shaky handwriting which I read sitting in the infirmary on his empty bed.

April 23, 1991

My dear son,

I deeply regret the pain this will cause you, but I find I can't face the prospect of lingering on in some half-life. I'm so grateful we were able to spend these few weeks together.

Whatever I have comes to you, and Junior will explain all that, but there is one last thing. In my old room on the third floor of the house you'll find my legacy to you, a wooden chest handed down in our family for almost two hundred years. Press the carved rosettes on the lower corners to release a hidden drawer containing several items, the most precious of which is the family journal, a private history both ordinary and extraordinary. I hope you'll experience the same excitement and pleasure I did in discovering who you are and where you come from.

If I have one wish for you, it's that you'll have the courage to do what I never could. Discard your old life. Pursue some amazing adventure and know that through you it will be my adventure too.

Always with you, your loving father,
Edward Francis Fitzhelm

We drove silently back to the house. Junior squeezed my shoulder and said he'd be in touch about funeral arrangements and my father's will. Then he and Teddy watched anxiously as I climbed the steps to my father's old room on the third floor.

It was a long, slant-roofed loft with windows at both ends. Model airplanes hung from the ceiling; a dusty train set sat on the floor in one corner, his fishing gear in another. There were stacks of boxes and crowded bookshelves. The narrow bed was neatly made up, and on every surface were shells and fossils, pieces of driftwood and odd bits of mechanical things, as if the boy had left one day and never come back.

In the middle of the room sat a beautifully inlaid wooden casket with a domed lid. It was about two and a half feet long, over a foot wide and deep, and gave off a soft glow in the muted light of the room. I lifted the lid to find an empty cavity in the shape of a violin, lined with worn purple velvet, the bow still in place. I then opened the secret drawer to reveal a series of objects in various wrappings. The first was in a brightly patterned kerchief. Tears pricked my eyes. It was the same one he'd always worn around his neck when we went fishing, and contained the little storybooks he'd made for me. *Gulliver's Travels* was wrapped in tissue paper. The third object, in stained chamois, was a man's gold pocket watch, the case embossed with the classical figures of Venus and Adonis. When I opened the back there was an inscription that read, *Gerry and Tess—Come what may.* The fourth was a jeweller's box containing a beautiful little star ruby and diamond ring, barely big enough for a child's finger, and a single large pearl set with sapphires in a pendant. At the bottom was a sheaf of handwritten pages which appeared to be a letter, and two yellowed sheets of musical notation entitled "Joyner's Dream." This left the final object folded in brittle black silk—a book about two inches thick, bound in worn brown kid and bearing in faded gold the title *Saint Nicholas of Myra—Instructions to His Knights.* I lay down on my father's old bed and started to read.

(What follows is my transcript of the journal. Where I've discovered letters pressed between the pages, I've included them in context, and I have added my grandmother Gina's letter to my father and his taped conversations with me. L.A.F.)

Chapter 1

JOHN JOYNER (1788–1864)

It is my father's wish that I should set down these events, as he can neither read nor write, and wishes to leave an account of his life so that some part of him will remain in the world and in the memory of those who follow. Although I have somewhat tempered his rough-spokenness, I have endeavoured to record him faithfully, and to in no way alter his intent. Here, then, are my father's words. —FRANK JOYNER, 1863

I was born plain John Blunt, in 1788. My mother's name was Sheba, chose by her mother after a queen in the Bible. Of my father I have no sure knowledge, as my mother would not name him. She was but fifteen when she whelped me. It was a painful birthing as she oft-reminded me, and she had no more after that, for which she both blessed and cursed me, according to her mood. We lodged with my grandfather in the hayloft above the stables for the Inn at Kingsfold on the old London Southampton Road.

Of my grandfather's early life and family I know little, save that he had been François Blount, a sailor on a French frigate who had deserted his ship in Southampton, for his eyes, which finally failed him altogether, had begun to dim, and he knew his days as a sailor were numbered. At first he spoke no English, and had nothing in this world save the clothes on his back and the fiddle he had won at a game of dice from a Norwegian sailor. It is a wondrous instrument of dark golden colour and bright, sweet tone, carved about the head in the likeness of a bearded apostle or saint. My grandfather had been popular among his sailor comrades, for he had only to hear a melody once through to have it forever in his memory. Once ashore, he sustained himself by playing in the dockside alehouses.

It was in Southampton he met and married my grandmother, a maid of all work in the house of an uncle in the hemp trade. She was already carrying my mother when she received a message to return to the family farm nigh to Kingsfold to keep house, as her brother's wife was heavy with their fifth child, sickly, and unable to carry out her duties.

My grandfather, being a half-blind and penniless foreigner with no living beyond his fiddle, was not welcome in the house. Within the year, his brother-in-law left him no choice but to find his own lodgings, leaving his wife and infant daughter with her family.

In the years that followed, my grandfather, called Blind France, became well known hereabouts. He played most nights for travellers at the inn, at the square on market day, and was in great demand for dances, fairs and weddings, performing all the popular tunes, "The Parson's Nag," "Poacher's Dream," "Mrs. Everly's Fancy," melodies I was weaned on, and learned to play in my turn. I never met anyone who knew so many tunes as he.

Father and daughter were reunited when she appeared at his lodgings already swelling with me in her belly. She had been ordered to leave the house of her uncle who had declared her morals loose and her behaviour uncontrollable. He further declared he would not have such wantonness and wickedness dwelling in his house with his children, but the bitterness of her reproaches regarding his monstrous hypocrisy left me little doubt as to the truth of my begetting. The upshot was that I, like our Lord, was born in a stable, although it is here all likeness ends.

Of my early years, there is little to say. By seven or eight, I was making myself useful feeding and watering the horses, and accompanying my grandfather to the market when he played, passing 'round the cup for him. He was a stern man, my grandfather, but even-tempered with it, and if I sometimes took a cuff on the ear, you can wager I'd earned it. I learned very early to obey him without question for there was always sound reason behind it.

My mother found a place as a serving maid in the alehouse of the inn. She was a great favourite with the patrons, as she would joke and laugh with them in a saucy way, singing naughty songs and dancing with great abandon and gaiety. I thought my mother the handsomest woman I had ever seen. She was tall for a woman and slim, but with a full bosom and hips, shining hair and eyes of a light brown washed with gold. I have no doubt it was her resemblance to my mother that first drew me to my Molly, though in temperament they could not have been more different, for Molly is as constant and calm as a clear summer day, while my mother was changeable as the weather and the seasons. It was not until Molly and I were married that I ceased to have dreams of being held in my mother's arms, though in waking hours those moments were rare enough, for my mother, known by most for her amiable nature and high spirits, could suddenly sink into the depths of black despair. At these times, she would lie for days on her pallet, her eyes dull and her body listless. I learned as a child to sleep still and silent, for in this state the least noise or movement could send her into fits of weeping and tearing at her hair and clothes, complaining bitterly that we were all whispering against her and wished her dead. I found these times baffling and terrifying, but my grandfather would gruffly assure me that he had seen it all before, and it would pass.

Life went on neither better nor worse, until I was twelve or thereabouts.

There is a night I will remember, as clear as yesterday, until my death. I had spent that day helping to move provisions into the kitchen, for there was a great celebration for the new century and the inn was overflowing with revellers. I was weary and had gone to my bed early, but slept fitful. It was just on midnight, for I heard twelve strikes of the church bell, with a great roar of voices from the inn and a rousing toast to King George III, him that later was said to be mad. I was on the edge of sleep again when my mother appeared in a fever of excitement and shook me awake. She said I must help her collect her belongings, for she was to be married that night to a sergeant of the local regiment which was shortly departing to battle against the French emperor, Napoleon. She would join a company of women who followed the troops and reunite with her husband when they reached their destination, which place she did not know. She was wild with anticipation at the prospect.

I had seen her in this state before, and knew there was no reasoning with her, but I feared for her safety when the fever cooled and she found herself tied to a brute some twenty years her senior, and in a foreign country far from all that was safe and familiar to her. I begged to come with her, but she claimed he insisted she come single, and I must not spoil her chances, as she was nigh thirty and could no longer rely on her face and figure to support her. I wept, and asked what would become of me.

Her last words to me were, "You are most a man now, Johnny, and don't need your mammy. Your grandda and you must do for each other." With that, she hugged me fiercely, kissed me on the mouth and departed.

I never saw her or heard of her again.

I had no time to mourn her, for it was shortly discovered she had taken with her two silver mugs and a set of spoons left to the innkeeper's wife by her mother, and which were her pride and joy. The innkeeper, a good fellow but wishing to keep peace in his house, said he must put us out of our lodgings, and we were fortunate this was all, for his wife would have had us gaoled. So ended my first life, and began the second.

My grandfather and I spent three nights sleeping rough and fiddling on the High Street through the day until we came afoul of the beggars' guild, a collection of ruffians who, in those times, wheedled pennies from travellers with piteous looks and rattling of cups. They took issue with us, claiming that Blind France and his brat collected the lion's share of the coin, leaving too little for them. My grandfather stoutly refused to share our takings, saying they were righteously earned by honest work. Their leader, a hulking club-footed fellow, attacked him with his stick, and urged his scurvy band to follow suit. My grandfather tossed me the fiddle and yelled that I should run and not look back. As always I obeyed, but I am still filled with shame that I did nothing to save him, old and blind, from the terrible beating that followed, for when I ventured from my hiding place to find him senseless and bleeding, he looked barely human.

I do not know what would have become of us had we not been approached by a certain Mr. Abel Jolly, who said that he might take us in if we were agreeable to what he called a mutually profitable proposition. He led us to a decaying cottage on the edge of town, where we made the acquaintance of his pregnant wife and his six children who rose like stair steps to greet us. We sat down to a meal of salty turnip soup thickened with stale bread, and were grateful for every spoonful.

Our host proceeded to make himself known to us, saying, "You'll find me both Abel and Jolly by name, and by nature."

And indeed he was the most clever and cheerful man I have ever met, unlike his wife, who complained of her aches and pains and the harshness of her life from morning to night.

He further told us in his joking way, "I was formerly the proprietor of a small carnival, but retired from the game for reason of health, that reason being my threatened horse-whipping at the hands of some angry citizens who claimed they had been swindled by the Wheel of Fortune. I considered it wise to decamp before I suffered the same fortune as the unfortunate Wheel."

The only remains of the family's former life were Jock, the monkey, who sat at table and ate as daintily as any of us, and a gay-painted caravan which became sleeping quarters for my grandfather and me, the cottage being already full to bursting with Jollys.

As I was soon to discover, everything Abel Jolly put his hand to was for him a game of sorts, and he shortly revealed why he wished to recruit us. He told us straight that the crowds Blind France drew 'round him were bread and ale to him, for necessity had made him an accomplished pickpocket.

"I immediately spied the possibilities of a lucrative partnership," he said, "for you, good sir, can simply play your fiddle as you have always done, and with a little coaching, this boy, obviously a nimble and clever lad, will be my new apprentice."

My grandfather was reluctant, but the beating had caved in his ribs causing him sharp pain and making him short of breath, and he recognized we would not last long as vagabonds.

Jolly took me in hand, saying what a pleasure it would be to have such a willing and clever pupil. His second son Ewan, he said, was quick but not quite old enough, and William, his eldest, had been a great disappointment for he was a thick and clumsy lout—which phrase seemed to amuse the family mightily, including William himself. Jolly had contrived a simpler game for William and his sister Sal. The pair would wait in the hedgerow by the side of the high road until a private carriage approached. William would throw himself under the horses' feet, burst a bladder of pig's blood, and lie still and bleeding as Sal came screeching and wailing to his side declaring he was the only support of herself and their widowed mother. Ladies in the coaches were especially sympathetic, and we often had meat in the soup as a result of their bounty. William was jokingly called Willie Wreck.

Our game then, was this. My grandfather was now accompanied to market by Jolly's daughter, Maeve, a pretty little maiden of about ten years. She would dance while Blind France played, and when the tune ended, Jock the monkey would dart out with cup in hand to collect the coppers, biting each one as he placed it in the cup to the merriment of the crowd. Jolly would spy a likely mark and point him out to me. I would run headlong into the fellow as if I were a high-spirited boy larking with my friends, and in the process relieve him of his purse and watch. I was instructed never to apologize nor curse nor pause in any way in my flight, as this would only make me more memorable when the theft was discovered, and Jolly had a variety of caps and jackets to alter my appearance. I became so clever at this, the loss was never discovered during the act. I was clear from the outset that I would not approach ladies in this manner, but he made no difficulty about this, saying it was the gentlemen who carried the coin. He also impressed upon me that we must not be greedy, as this too would draw attention to our game. We never singled out more than two prospects each market day, one in mid-morning and one in the early afternoon as people were departing, and so we prevailed, and in a modest way we prospered.

My grandfather's health steadily declined and his breathing became so laboured he could only sleep sitting up. Each fit of coughing stained his kerchief with a pink froth. With the coming of winter it was evident that he would not see spring, and it was late in January that he painfully breathed his last. His great gift to me was his fiddle and the music I could bring forth from it. He could not have done better by me were he ten times a rich man, and I mourn him still.

I now took his place with Maeve in the market, as Ewan, who had sprung up in the last year, was thought old enough and skilled enough to replace me. It was a relief to me for I had reached a size and age where I feared my actions might be taken as an attack, and not as simple boyish fun. It gave me some comfort also to know that some part of my grandfather lived on in me, and that, like him, I could bring pleasure to the listener.

It was at this time that I first laid eyes on my Molly.

Truthfully, I thought I had seen a ghost, for the woman I spied across the market was so like my mother as I first remembered her that I froze in the midst of playing "The Dancing Mare," and Maeve and Jock were left to gather what coin they could from the dwindling crowd as I hastily wrapped my fiddle in its sack and pushed my way through the market. On closer view she was both like and unlike, being not so tall as my mother, her hair as bright as a new copper penny and her eyes like plump brown raisins. She had also such an expression of happiness and content as was never seen on my mother's face, and which made her even more beautiful to me. She says she recalls seeing a handsome lad of about fifteen gawking at her as if he had taken leave of his wits, and who turned cherry red and stuttered when she spoke to him.

In the weeks that followed, we became fast friends. I would be waiting when she arrived at the market in her little donkey cart. I would water the beast and tether him on the green, then help her to provision the stall. She had a fine variety of foods from her father's farm; cheese and curd, eggs, fresh baked bread, honey and preserves, and seasonal fruits and vegetables. She also concocted simple cures from the herbs from her garden, and from roots, berries and bark gathered in the surrounding countryside, rendered into teas, tinctures, poultices and salves as learned from her mother, and was often called upon for her cures and midwifery.

Molly was one of four daughters of Master Thomas Treadwell, a skilled builder, cabinetmaker and locksmith much in demand throughout the district. He owned a small freehold and workshop convenient to the town. His wife had died some years previous, leaving Molly, the eldest, to manage the household and raise her three sisters. She was twenty, five years my senior, and yet we seemed equals from the outset. There is only one secret I have ever held back from Molly, and although she has not always approved of my actions, she has never judged me. I found myself openly telling her of my mother and grandfather, and my life with the Jollys. Although there were those I cared for, I had never before had a bosom friend, and in all these years since, I have never needed another.

It was in June of that year, 1803, that Molly arrived at the market in a state of some excitement. She said she had something of great importance to tell me, but that it would keep 'til the stall was provisioned. This done, she gave me my breakfast of bread and cheese, and delivered her news.

"My father's long-time journeyman is old and ailing and wishes to retire to live with his sister. My father, though hale enough, finds he no longer has the strength of his youth and, having no sons, thinks to take on an apprentice. I have put you forward as a likely prospect, saying you are young and strong and have shown yourself, in my view, to be a clever and capable fellow. I beg forgiveness for any liberty I may have taken on your part, but I believed from our conversations that you might be ready for a change."

I found myself of two minds. The narrow bounds of apprenticeship were very different from the rough, free sort of life I had always known, and I was not sure I would take to it, but then there was Molly, for whose sake I would chance anything. I promised to think on it, crossed the market to join Maeve and Jock, and began to play in a sort of trance.

I had first to speak to Jolly, for I owed much to the family and was truly fond of them. That afternoon I took him aside and told him of my situation. He understood, perhaps better than I, what I was wrestling with, and said I must do what was best for me. He further said the family was thinking of moving on, as their activities had begun to attract the attention of the authorities. I joked that perhaps it was a matter of his health once again, and we laughed heartily at that. We parted on the best of terms and I returned to help Molly load up the cart and make the short journey to her father's house.

Master Thomas Treadwell proved to be quite a different proposition from his daughter. He was a big burly man, blunt in his manner, and quickly made it known that as much as he valued his daughter's good opinion, he had some knowledge of my history, and some doubts as to whether I would suit. He was, he said, willing to chance it on her say-so providing I would agree to certain conditions.

In his own words, "You will take a new name of your own choosing, forswear all your old associations and apply yourself wholeheartedly to your new situation. You will sleep in the workshop at night and take your meals in the kitchen with the family. You must obey me without question in all things, and seek my permission regarding any action you might consider. In return I will teach you all the skills of an honest trade, you will have your bed and board, and will yourself be paid the apprentice fee, having no father to receive it on your behalf."

Having decided beforehand to take his offer I accepted his terms, making only two requests, the first that I be allowed to accompany Molly on market day and play my fiddle, the other that I could say my goodbyes to the Jollys when they departed. He allowed that though some considered the fiddle to be an instrument of the devil, he was not of this opinion, and he would not begrudge me the few coppers I earned at the market.

"Of course you must bid your friends farewell," he reasoned, "for it will make a clean cut from your old life, and a tight join with the new."

They departed some three weeks later. Jolly had found a sway-backed old nag to pull the caravan, and the family was loading it up in cheerful chaos. They would go to London, for Jolly believed that Maeve would make their fortune there with her singing and dancing, as even at twelve she was a startling beauty. Willie was to stay behind, having met a girl he would not leave. I solemnly shook hands with Jolly, kissed the wailing baby thrust at me by Mrs. Jolly, and embraced Maeve, who had become a little sister to me. I told her to be good and to take care of herself. She winked at me through her tears saying she would be as good as need be. As they left, some part of me left with them, for they had been my family those three years.

So ended the second and began my third life.

The Treadwell farm sat on twenty acres with a mature orchard and large vegetable garden but was otherwise dedicated to hay and grains. There was a solid two-storey stone house and several outbuildings surrounding a cobblestone courtyard. These were the workshop and the curing shed for fine woods, the smithy where the hinges, handles and locks were forged, the stables, and the poultry run.

My new sleeping quarters were as good as a palace to me. The workshop was a long low building attached to the end of the house against the kitchen chimney. There was a small fireplace with no lack of fuel, and I slept warm and dry for the first time in my life. Molly provided me with a comfortable pallet filled with sweet-smelling wood shavings, a thick woollen blanket, a big bucket of water and soap to wash myself, a razor and a piece of mirror to shave in, a comb, and a new shirt and trousers. I later built a rough wooden box to hold my fiddle, which was my only belonging.

Thomas Treadwell was a demanding but fair and patient master, and I pride myself that I was quick to learn and to apply my new skills. I thought hard on the matter of a name, and settled on one of the first skills I attempted, that of a joiner. I could as easily have been Turner or Sawyer, but there was some rhythm and music in John Joyner, and so it was John Joyner I became.

It was an orderly and comfortable life I now lived, working with Master Thomas most days, sharing meals at the long kitchen table with him and Molly and her youngest sister, Rose, the other two sisters, Martha and Meg, being in service. I helped Molly with the garden and the chickens, and as agreed, accompanied her to market once a week. Sundays were a day of rest. We attended morning prayer at the Church of Saint Stephen by the Falls, then spent the remains of the day as pleased us. In the winter we would sit companionably by the kitchen fire, where I would play my fiddle as Molly finished a bit of mending, and Master Thomas carved some piece of detail for a cabinet or dressing table. In fine weather, I would go poaching with the unspoken approval of Master Thomas, returning with a couple of rabbits or a nice fat eel to add to the variety of the table. I was content, and missed little of my former existence.

Life continued in this way until I was in my eighteenth year.

Molly and I had grown steadily more devoted, and it was our greatest wish to wed. The urgency became even greater when Molly announced to me that she was with child. It fell to me to broach the matter to Master Thomas. After a long and sleepless night I determined to speak with him first thing after breakfast.

As he entered the shop I asked leave to speak with him on a matter of great import, told him of Molly's condition, and said with an air of some defiance that as much as we hoped for his approval, we would wed with or without his blessing, for our only wish was to be together.

Again he surprised me, for he laughed out loud, saying, "I had wondered how long it would take you to screw up your courage. Having fathered four daughters, I easily recognized Molly's condition. I have no desire to remarry, and to lose both my housekeeper and my apprentice would turn the place upside down. You have my consent provided you agree first to continue as my journeyman rather than my apprentice; secondly that you accept that not being of my blood, you will never be my heir; and finally that this child if it is a boy, or your first son thereafter, will become my heir both in name and in property."

I begged leave to speak with Molly.

Master Thomas's offer was on the face of it fair, even generous, yet I was reluctant to agree and could not explain my uneasiness. I had no family name to preserve, and the child would be our son in all but that, with his living and that of his children secured. Molly felt a similar unease but, like me, could not put tongue to it, so we gave Master Thomas the answer he desired, and were wed forthwith. Some six months later, third day of October, year of our Lord 1808, Thomas Gabriel Treadwell was born, and was so christened by Father Basil in front of the great stone altar at Saint Stephen by the Falls. Thus began our life as a family.

From the beginning there was a bond between Gabe and his grandfather. Molly said he spoiled the boy beyond reason, and from the moment he could walk he followed his grandfather everywhere. Even in appearance they were alike, fair and ruddy and big-boned, and though he called me Father, it was his grandfather he looked to in all things.

On the tenth of January, 1812, our second son was born, and christened François Joyner in honour of my grandfather. This is my son Frank, who preserves these words for me.

Master Thomas was never unkind or unfair to Frank, but his preference for Gabe was apparent at all times. I, on the other hand, favoured Frank. Molly, of course, had no favourites. Frank was like his mother in appearance, but even from a babe displayed the clever, splay-fingered hands I had inherited from my grandfather. Though he does not have a natural ease for playing music, he has a great love for the fiddle, and through practice has come to play it quite well. In his nature he is sweet-tempered and generous, but always inclined to take things too hard, and to carry a burden of blame for anything that goes amiss.

Once Frank was weaned, the two boys shared a bed and were fast friends, untouched by any preference on our part, and so things continued until Frank was in his ninth year.

Molly and I grew ever more certain that Frank was meant for a different sort of life from his brother. He was never still, constantly questioning and tinkering, unlike Gabe who was an uncurious and placid boy. We agreed that both should be schooled. Father Basil, the priest at Saint Stephen, instructed a small class of boys twice a week at the manse, and I asked if he would take on our lads though we had little to pay him with. He agreed to do so in return for some much-needed repairs to the church. Master Thomas grumbled that the boys would get above themselves, and that I was needed at home, but Molly prevailed, saying it was God's work I would be doing, and a little learning would do no harm. She further argued he had no right to stand in Frank's way, as only Gabe would inherit.

Gabe quickly showed himself to be no scholar, but as Frank progressed, Master Thomas saw the benefit of having someone in the family who could read and write and, more importantly, do sums. Before long, Frank was keeping a record of work contracted, work completed, moneys owed and moneys paid. He grew much interested in fine veneers, parquetry, marquetry and scrollwork, and used the occasion of our work in the big houses hereabouts to make note of the furnishings and finishes. I relied on him for much of the fine work on the pieces I crafted, for like my grandfather's, my eyes had weakened with time, and I dreaded the day when they might fail me altogether.

The flaw in our agreement with Master Thomas was now quite clear, for if I could not afford Frank the means to make his own way, he would remain a journeyman like myself, labouring for his grand-father or his brother until he died.

It is here that the fourth, and hitherto secret, part of my life begins, which only Frank has ever known.

It was quite innocent in its beginnings. Molly's three sisters were now all in service, and having contrived to have the same half-day, every third Sunday afternoon of the month they gathered in the kitchen for tea and gossip after church. It was clear that the men were not welcome, and we had our separate ways of filling the time. In fair weather I would go fishing, but if it were stormy, I had con-structed a comfortable couch from the sacks of flour and grain in the cellar, and would retire there for a pint, a pipe and a doze, for my Molly made the finest cider in the county.

I was so employed one stormy Sunday when I heard female voices as clear as if they were in the room with me. The mystery was easily found out. My couch lay close to the shaft for the platform and pulley we used to move supplies between the kitchen and cellar. The hatches had been carelessly left open, and by some trick of sound, the women's voices were carried down the shaft to my ear. I thought it would be a great joke to repeat some of the conversation to Molly when we retired that night, and so I set myself to listen.

Little Rose was then in the employ of a prosperous wine and spirits merchant whose wife had died in Rose's first year of service. He had married with unseemly haste less than a year later, and to a young woman barely four years older than his only child, a daughter named Lily. The new wife brought her own lady's maid, and so Rose, as well as performing her duties as a housemaid, saw to Miss Lily.

The girl had been crushed by her mother's death, and shocked by her father's hasty remarriage and her new stepmother's determina-tion to remove any trace of her mother. All the former lady's belong-ings had been disposed of except her jewellery, which was locked away, she said, for safekeeping. The exception was a handsome locket given by the mother to her daughter in her last days, which was in the form of an ivory medallion painted with the lady's likeness set in gold and surrounded with seed pearls. In the back was a lock of the lady's hair preserved beneath a crystal, and it hung on a velvet ribbon. This then was the girl's only memento save a dress of lavender silk which Rose had rescued from the rag and bone man. Miss Lily wore the locket at all times excepting leaving it on her bedside table while she slept, and her stepmother took it as a great affront, complaining to all that it was a morbid and tasteless piece of work, and not fit for a young girl.

Life in the house was thus made unpleasant for everyone save the master, who either did not notice or chose not to, and there was much heated discussion in the kitchen, and great sympathy for the poor little miss. There was therefore a considerable to-do when the locket went missing from the girl's bedside. All the servants were closely questioned, and it was feared that one of them would be accused and dismissed, Rose being the most likely. None had a doubt but it was the new mistress who was responsible, and there was talk of a sleeping potion in the girl's warm milk at bedtime, for cook had found a grey muck in the bottom of the cup when she rinsed it. There was naught the servants could do but let matters take their course, and though she was kept on at Miss Lily's tearful pleading, the cloud of suspicion over poor little Rose made her very unhappy indeed.

She was saying, "Miss Lily has taken to her bed and refuses to stir from her room, seeing none but me. The master says she will soon get over it, but I can see she's wasting away, and looks like a little shadow with none of her former colour or humour."

I found myself quite stirred up on Rose's behalf, and oddly touched by the story of a girl whose face I had never seen. I thought on it a great deal over the next few days, and came to believe I might have it in my power to remedy the situation.

In my years of working with Master Thomas, we had plied our trade in most of the fine houses in the district. It was then the fashion to have false panels, cleverly hidden drawers and disguised cupboards to hide valuables, and the wine merchant's house was no exception. Five years previous the former mistress had requested that I devise a sliding panel in the surround of her sitting-room fireplace concealing a locked hidey-hole for her jewels. I had, therefore, good reason to believe that whatever the new mistress might wish to conceal would likely reside there. I began to think how I might gain access to it, and formed a daring plan.

I was quite often abroad in the night with my poaching, so my absence would not be remarked on, especially as Molly was then heavy and uncomfortable with our daughter, Clare, and I was sleeping away from her. The wine merchant's house was at some remove from others in the locality and heavily treed, allowing me to approach it unobserved. As for entry, it was no challenge, for had I not manufactured many catches and locks after Master Thomas's designs, and did I not have my master keys?

I stitched up a pair of black sheepskin slippers to silence my boots and tied a dark kerchief 'round my neck to pull up over the whiteness of my face. I had some concern for the dogs, then recalled Rose saying they were kept in the stables as the lady would not have them in the house. I briefly thought to fortify my courage with drink, but recalled Jolly's words: "I'm as fond of a pint as the next man, but drink thickens the mind and the fingers, and many a bold venture has been unhorsed at a crucial point by the pressing need of a piss."

With heart thumping so hard I feared the sound of it might betray me, I slipped into the house and up the back stairs, keeping to the edges of the steps so that the creaking of the boards would not give me away. Entering the lady's sitting room, and lighting a candle stub brought for the purpose, I slid aside the secret panel. As I opened the safe box, the click of the lock sounded to me as loud as a cannon, but no one stirred. By the flickering light, I could see several velvet boxes and wash-leather pouches, and thought I might have to examine them all—until I spied the locket in question tossed carelessly on top of a bundle of letters. I took the letters as well, for although I can neither read nor write beyond my own name, I reasoned that hidden away in this manner they might not be from her husband or family, and if they were, no harm done. I closed the hidey-hole, doused the candle and tippy-toed my way to Miss Lily's bedroom, which location I knew from my former work. I cracked open the door, and having satisfied myself from her breathing that she was asleep, felt for a level surface just inside, and left the locket and the letters to be found in the morning. I barely remember the journey home, and I slept dreamlessly.

It was nearly two weeks later that I learned the outcome of my night's work. I had retired to my couch in the cellar in wait for the conversation to come, and, sure enough, Rose could barely contain herself as she spilled the news to her three sisters.

"The most mysterious thing has happened. A fortnight ago Miss Lily completely recovered from her indisposition, and so suddenly and in such a way it was like a miracle, with no hint as to the cause save that she has her locket once more. She ate a hearty breakfast and chattered to me throughout her bath and toilet as if she would never stop, then held me back from my household duties to alter her mother's dress so that she might wear it at dinner that evening. I feared the consequences for both of us, but she would not be reasoned with.

"I was assisting at table when Miss Lily appeared wearing the locket and her mother's lavender silk. Her father and stepmother were already seated and supping their soup, for she was not expected, and I had to hastily set a place. Her father said he was pleased at her recovery and hoped there would be no more childish nonsense, and she replied, 'What was lost has been found amidst some old corres-

pondence, and if it goes missing again I shall know where to look.'
The mistress turned quite pale and silent, though the master seemed
unaware. Miss Lily said she had been invited to a house party the following weekend, and had a mind to wear her mother's pearls if her
stepmother would be so good as to make them available to her. The
master said, of course she should have them, and the lady, for once,
made no argument. The servants are all agog and none can venture
an explanation, although much nodding and winking has been aimed
at me."

I was fairly hugging myself to keep from laughing out loud, for
I had no doubt that any sound I made would carry as clearly to them
as their words to me. I then dozed off, and did not waken 'til I heard
Molly call me to supper.

I had made considerable progress in the repairs at Saint Stephen, replacing any of the old wood affected by dry rot or worms,
tightening the door and window frames against the weather. Master Thomas would sometimes join his efforts with mine, and we
would work together in companionable silence save "hand me that"
or "steady this," even replacing such slates on the roof as had been
cracked by the frost.

It was at this time I spoke to Father Basil on a matter I had been
turning over in my mind. I wished to carve a series of saints' heads to
adorn the ends of the pews at Saint Stephen. Father Basil balked at
first, saying it might be taken for popery, and that this was an English
church, but I argued it would be as inspiring for the faithful to have
the names and faces of the saints on constant view as it would be for
me to carve them. He relented, and I set to work.

Frank drew up the sketches for me, carefully printing the names
so that I could carve them correctly. I began with a large figure of
the first martyr, Saint Stephen himself, to stand by the door with his
hand raised in blessing, turning next to the heads of the Apostles,
each with name and symbol to identify him, then on to other saints

as suggested by Father Basil. For the family pew at the back where we sat each Sunday I needed no such guide, as I intended to carve a likeness of the noble head on my fiddle, and to name it Saint Nicholas after Saint Nicholas of Myra, saint of repentant thieves, as thanks for his intercession. It is one of my finer works, and I smile to myself whenever I see it.

I have always found that such work as is natural and easy to the hand frees the mind, and while I was engaged in this task my mind returned to the night I had retrieved the locket and I began to see other possibilities. I will admit the adventure was no small part of it, but I had also a strong desire to secure Frank's future. My repentance fell by the wayside as I prepared to go on the game once again.

Through Molly and her sisters and the gossip of the market I easily learned of the comings and goings and events among the local gentry. The opportunities were rich, but caution ruled me for I now had much to lose.

For my second adventure I settled on a local bachelor of about nine and twenty years. He lived with his grandmother, a wealthy old lady both bedridden and deaf. The fellow was a drunkard and a gambler, and I reasoned that if I chose a night when he had gambled successfully, his drunkenness would cloud his memory, and he might not miss that portion of his winnings I intended to relieve him of.

On such a night I shadowed him home, and set myself to wait until the house went dark. As I stealthily climbed the stairs, I could hear his thundering snores even through the thickness of the door. He had fallen into bed fully clothed save for his waistcoat and boots, the window and bed curtains still open and the moon illuminating the room and bathing his slack face. He had carelessly tossed the contents of his pockets on the dresser. I left behind his watch and enough cash to dispel suspicion and was congratulating myself on the ease of my efforts, when I heard the old lady yell out.

"Kitty, quick girl, the commode!"

I froze to the spot, for the snores had suddenly ceased, but the fellow never opened his eyes, only turned over, and the thunder soon resumed. I fled from the house as if my shirttails were on fire.

My night's work had gained me just under two guineas, and my only regret was that I had no one to share my victory with, for this act would exceed even Molly's tolerance. In the days following I fashioned a hiding place under one of the paving stones in the cellar floor, and over time added to the contents on at least a dozen occasions.

One of my few acquaintances beyond the family was a man called Ezekiel Cooper. Zeke was a Gypsy, and patriarch of a large family who, though still camping in caravans in the old way, had forsaken the travelling life to take up the free tenancy offered by the D'Ursey family for whom they broke and trained young horses. The Coopers were known to have a magical hand with the beasts, and Zeke's sons, Aaron and Jacob, were much in demand, having largely overcome the ill will which plagues their tribe. Zeke used our forge to hammer out the shoes he used to correct the gaits of young horses, and we had formed a bond through music, for he played the fiddle, as did most of the Cooper men, and we spent many an evening swapping melodies. It was through his son Jacob I met a peddler named Barker who would give me coin and no questions asked for any small objects of value I picked up on my midnight rambles.

Our daughter, Clare, named for the lady Saint, was born in the spring of 1820. Although she was small it was a difficult birth, for Molly had lost one child and was a little past her prime for childbearing, and we felt that Clare would be our last. She could not have been more different from our sons. She never truly cried as other babes do, making fretful little noises rather than the lusty yells of the two boys at that age. Even as she grew she was so tiny and timid that I called her my mouse, but she was a sweet and affectionate girl, and much loved by us all.

Around this time a most singular thing happened. It was market day. The morning had passed uneventfully, and we had just finished our noon meal. Molly was nursing Clare, and I was playing a spirited version of one of my grandfather's melodies called "Bring the Glad Tidings," when an elegant lady approached me and dropped a handful of silver in the cup. I thanked her nicely, but did not look up, for I had learned not to take too much notice of the ladies since there might be some gentleman to take offence.

She lingered, and when the tune ended she said, "Don't you know me, Johnny? It's Maeve," and so it was.

A breath could have blown me over, such was my surprise. In truth, she was a sight to gladden the eye, for her childish prettiness had blossomed into true beauty, and her dress, though cut of rich stuff, was both modest and tasteful. I shouted to Molly to look who was here, and I would have hugged her but she looked so grand. She said she had much to tell me. Molly bid us be off for our gossip and she'd hear about it all later. We sat in the shade of a tree, and both started to talk at once. She insisted I speak first, then related a story which delighted me.

Upon leaving Kingsfold, the Jollys had indeed gone to London, where they shared lodgings with a troupe of acrobats. Maeve was trained to walk the tightrope and proved to have a natural bent for it. This became quite an attraction as she would dance on the rope and sing also. At fourteen she was approached by a man who devised entertainments for music halls, and he easily found a place for her. From her very first performance she was a great favourite, for along with her golden curls and her rosy lips and cheeks she displayed an elegant figure in her tights. She received many a proposal from gentlemen in the crowd, often generous, none respectable, but her father kept a close eye so that she was not compromised.

It was in this way that she met her husband, Arthur. She was then about seventeen, and the support of the whole family. She said she would never have thought to marry such a man, for though wealthy he was neither young nor handsome; however, he came to see her every night, and behaved in such a gentlemanly way that she was soon won over. She said he was the kindest, most agreeable man in the world who had gladly taken on the whole Jolly tribe. Her parents now lived in a pretty cottage on his country estate, and her brothers and sisters had been given a good start in life, Ewan being a clerk in a solicitor's office, Sal happily married, and the younger Jollies being variously educated. Abel Jolly was now a proud gardener who bragged of his roses and vegetable marrows. Mrs. Jolly had embraced the opportunity to become a permanent invalid with a maidservant to wait on her, though she was in fact in a rosy state of health. Maeve had two little girls, high hopes of a boy, and said she had never been happier, for her husband was truly the best of men, and she believed she had been an excellent wife to him. It was a coach to Portsmouth and a boat to France for shopping in Paris that had brought her here on her return, seeking her brother, William.

I had sad news regarding William. Willie Wreck had continued to ply his game assisted by the girl he married, but had taken to drink and lost his agility. On one dreadful occasion he had misjudged his fall, and both his legs had been crushed below the knee by the wheels of a London-bound carriage. Any recompense for this tragedy was quickly spent and he was soon reduced to pushing himself along on a sort of platform with wheels, and begging on the High Street. His drinking became ever more habitual, and he turned abusive to his wife and children and increasingly reckless and rude in his person. He then devised for himself a new game, which was to roll down the cobblestones of the High Street with a great clatter and "whoop" and to scoop up coins from the caps and bowls of the other beggars, disappearing 'round the corner to some hiding place until the furor had quieted and he could buy some rum to drink himself senseless.

The beggars' guild took swift and terrible action, and Willie Wreck was found floating face down in the River Bliss.

I told Maeve where to find his poor widow and children, and taking tearful but most affectionate leave of me, with promises to give my best wishes to her parents, she went to rescue them. I was sorry to part with her on such a sad note, but most happy to hear of her good fortune and that of the Jolly family.

When Frank reached his sixteenth year, I judged it time to speak with him regarding his prospects. I doubted it was a subject to which he had given much thought, for though a man in appearance, he was still young, and unlike myself had never met the crueller side of life.

On a fine Sunday after church, we went fishing. We spent a pleasant afternoon in each other's company, and as we ate the simple meal Molly had provided, I asked if working for his grandfather and brother at a journeyman's wage was all that he saw for himself. I pressed him also as to what he desired if chance allowed. He admitted to dreams of his own workshop to carry out the elegant designs in his drawings, and refine the fancy inlays and rich veneers he so seldom got to apply in his grandfather's employ. He allowed that through his lessons with Father Basil there had grown in him a great love for books, and that nothing so moved and excited him as lingering in the libraries of the great houses as we worked, examining the spines of the volumes with their rich leather bindings and gold lettering, and imagining their contents. He longed for a library of his own, but knew full well he would never have the means nor position.

Things had always been easy and open between us, so I had no fear of revealing my secret. He knew little of my life before marrying his mother, save that I had been raised by my grandfather. I told him of my mother, Sheba, of being reduced to begging in the street, and the solution provided by Jolly. He was gape-mouthed at my exploits, though I took pains not to glorify my daring, and was careful to point out the consequences of discovery. It was only then I put it to him that he might join with me to fatten what I had already gathered for him, making it clear the decision was his alone, and should he decide against it, nought more would be said. We returned home with our catch, and for the next few days he seemed lost in thought.

By the Sunday following, I could see he had reached some resolve.

Molly had asked me to build another storage rack for apples in the root cellar, thus allowing us to speak unobserved. At first we worked silently, completing the task as if our four hands were guided by one mind, then Frank stepped away and unburdened himself. He had, he said, grave concerns about the venture, for though he now desperately desired what he had formerly only dreamed of, he had never been dishonest or devious beyond the usual boyish pranks and poaching, and feared any attempt at deception would be instantly found out. I assured him he would soon learn to assume the open and honest countenance that was the thief's greatest ally. It was simply a matter of learning new skills, and in this I could guide him.

He raised questions of morality that would only be satisfied if he believed some good had been achieved. He had, it seemed, been greatly affected by my telling of the adventure of the locket and further by some tales he had read. I warned him against romantic notions, for though he might shy at the word, we would be thieves and better off with baser motives; however, he would not be swayed. I therefore bargained that we would do good when opportunity allowed, and take care to bring no physical harm to those we encountered. We shook hands on it, and agreed to keep our eyes and ears open for the first opportunity.

I have urged Frank to add his story to mine, and so I will not rob him of the opportunity to recount his first experience as thief and adventurer. Enough to say it was the first of several, and in time we collected enough coin to secure him a modest house and workshop, at which point our excursions ceased, my repentance was resurrected and I settled into the fifth and final part of my life as a respectable journeyman and patriarch, my lawless years behind me.

I have had Frank read to me what he has written, and although I have twitted him for making me seem such a learned fellow, I know it is just his way with the words. The account is true enough as it stands, and I am well satisfied.

At the time of this writing, I have reached my seventy-fifth year. Master Thomas is long dead, though fondly remembered. Molly and I live a quiet life in our little cottage close by the old house now occupied by Gabe and his Annie so that Molly can be nearby to help with the children. I am a grandfather and great-grandfather several times over, Gabe and Annie having five children and Frank two. Sadly, Frank lost his wife, Jean, in childbirth when his children were still young, and he has never remarried. His work as a craftsman has been far more rewarding than his efforts either as a fiddler or as a thief, and he has become so lettered that he can easily record these words for me.

Of all the grandchildren, much as I love them, I will admit I favour Frank's son, Gerry, for we are the most like. I have twice had the instruction of him, first on the fiddle, as solace for the motherless boy whose father was too sunk in his own grief to comfort him, and the second when as a young man his wild ways would have made an outlaw of him had I not taught him in a more prudent brand of thievery. He is a patchwork of the family, with the dark curling hair and clever hands of my grandfather, Blind France, as I first remember him, and also his precious gift of music, which is so strong that I have only to play a tune once for him to know it, play it and add his own flourishes. He has his grandfather Thomas Treadwell's tall sturdy build, and his mother Jean's blue eyes, but alas, he has inherited my mother Sheba's unquiet mind. His road in life has been a rocky one, and I know not how it will fall out, but it is to him I bequeath Old Nick, my beloved fiddle, although I know it pains Frank to hear it, for he has long desired it. It is only recently Frank brought Gerry's daughter Beth to see us. She appeared two years ago from nowhere, and not one of us can guess who the mother might be. She is a little bit of a thing, pretty as a flower, and I have chided Gerry for his neglect of her, for having once acknowledged her, he seems to have no thought for her at all. Gabe's Annie has taken against her for being a bastard, and were it not for Frank, I do not know what would become of her.

We have had a good life, Molly and me. Little Clare never showed an inclination to marry, but prefers to live quietly at home with us, sustained by her faith. She is a great comfort to us in our old age.

For a time I had a pair of spectacles which allowed me to do a little carving, but my eyes have nearly failed me now, and although Gabe still patiently allows me to fumble about in the workshop, I know he would rather I sat by the fire and played my fiddle.

I no longer play the lively tunes of my youth, but favour the slow, sad airs. Of late, I have taken to playing one of my grandfather's melodies, a song from his childhood he said was the saddest he knew, called "La Fee du Roy," which he sang in French, concerning the beautiful daughter of a king who meets a handsome knight while walking in her garden. They become lovers against the wish of her father, who has promised her in marriage to a prince of Spain. The king, in anger, slays the two young lovers, who die in each other's arms. I regret I never learned the words. As I play it, I see my grandfather's face, and other familiar faces of my youth, although I can no longer clearly distinguish the features of those dear ones around me now.

I hope that I will be remembered as neither a good nor a bad man, but as one who loved his family and worked toward their betterment. I know I shall have much to answer for when I come before my Maker, but I trust that Saint Nicholas will intercede for me.

Here ends my father's account of his life, although he lived on for another year. My mother lives still with my sister Clare, and as of this writing is in good health, as are we all. — FRANK JOYNER

Chapter 2

JOHN FRANÇOIS JOYNER (1812–1875)

In 1864, my father, John Joyner, died peacefully in his sleep at the age of seventy-six, surrounded by his loving family, who mourn him still.

It is now almost twelve years later that I, Frank Joyner, pick up my pen to fulfill both my father's wishes and my own in continuing this history, for my health is failing, my will to live has long since fled, and my one desire is to be joined once more with my darling Jean, who was so cruelly taken from me while still in the bloom of her youth.

My father's wish was that succeeding generations should know him. As for myself, having been a diligent and enthusiastic collector of books since first I learned to read, it seems to me that there exists an overabundance of tales chronicling the lives of the high and mighty in which ordinary folk like us serve only as colourful backdrop, comic bumpkins or faithful retainers. It is therefore my hope to reveal the drama and dignity of ordinary lives through those events which are most personal to me. It is never intended for the world at large, but rather for my family and their descendants. I have manufactured for this purpose a handsome volume with a sturdy leather binding and pages of the finest vellum, wherein I write these words following those of my father previously entered, and modelling myself somewhat after Charles Dickens, and another author I have only just discovered called Thomas Hardy, whose work so perfectly reflects my own views.

It was my intention to leave it untitled, but having once entered my library to find my cretinous son-in-law perusing it, I resolved to take more care, and have deeply embossed the spine and face in gold leaf with the title *Saint Nicholas of Myra—Instructions to His Knights*, and placed it with similar titles, sermons and religious tracts in the belief that the very ponderousness of the subject matter will discourage the casual reader. It is also a continuation of my father's little joke, as he once told me that thieves were sometimes called the knights of St. Nicholas.

Until my father's revelations, I had no knowledge of the bargain struck between my grandfather and my parents. It was natural to me that Gabe and my grandfather, being so similar in appearance and nature, would be drawn to each other, and that Gabe as the eldest would certainly be his heir. We were never rivals, and I have fond memories of the parry and thrust of our wooden swords as we played at being King Arthur's knights in the courtyard. We still share a fraternal bond that is beyond kinship or friendship.

Of my early life there is little to add, save that it was patterned and ruled by the seasons and the demands of our trade. We were not dependent on the marketplace for our daily bread, nor any other needs for that matter, since our land and livelihood provided all. I knew nothing of the difficulties my parents had overcome in securing an education for me, but I am forever grateful for the advantages and pleasures it has afforded me.

Let me relate here a brief history of the town of Kingsfold, and the Church of Saint Stephen by the Falls as told to me by my teacher and mentor, Father Basil.

Somewhere at the beginning of time, the little valley in which the town rests split across its middle so that one half remained at its original elevation and the other dropped to a depth of about the height of ten men, creating a fold in the landscape and revealing a rocky face over which fell the River Bliss, becoming the falls at Saint Stephen.

The legend is that some ancient king, wounded in battle, prayed to Saint Stephen the martyr to intercede for him that he might be delivered from his enemies. Saint Stephen appeared to him in a vision, and parted the falls to expose a small grotto, where he concealed himself until he heard a party of his own men approach, then revealed himself as in a miracle stepping forth from the water. Inspired, his army fought on to victory, and the king decreed that a stone altar be built on the rocky outcrop above the falls in honour of the saint.

Some centuries later the first Lord D'Ursey constructed a church of the same stone that had been transported for the foundations of his house. It was built around the ancient altar, and intended to serve both as a burial vault for his family, and as a place of worship for the people of Kingsfold, the town that had sprung up in the vicinity to build and to serve the great house. Father Basil was twelfth in the progression of priests at Saint Stephen.

Outside of my family, Father Basil was and remains my most enduring influence. He was a firm believer in God's creation, but with such an inquiring mind that I think his faith and his intellect were locked in constant battle. Although the Bible was my first schoolbook, and continues to be a source of wisdom and consolation for me, the good father also introduced me to the immortal words of Milton and Donne and Bunyan, and through him I formed my lifelong fascination with books, which goes beyond the contents to include the richness of the cover and the bindings, the heft and the feel, the fineness of the paper and the print, and even the smell of the paper and ink. I have many interests, but books are my one, my only, obsession.

On that fateful day when my father revealed his secret, I found within myself a maelstrom of contradiction. It contravened everything I had been taught both at home and in the church, but I, being young, was drawn to tales of heroic action and adventure, of chances taken against great odds and to great ends. My father warned against ambitions of becoming some latter-day Robin Hood, saying it was a sure path to the gaol or the gallows. We therefore arrived at a compromise to create a tithe against whatever we took, and to distribute it amongst those we found most in need.

My initiation into my new profession came about through a confluence of circumstances centred around D'Ursey Court, known locally as the Willows, commissioned in 1593 by Sir William D'Ursey, employing a local architect named Richard Trent. It is a most handsome dwelling, situated on a hillside well back from the River Bliss, which is its primary view, and fronted by a small ornamental lake containing an island folly, and bordered with the giant weeping willows which give the house its name. I have always found it intriguing that when you stand at a distance, through some trick of the builder, the design of the facade causes the house to look much smaller than it is.

The D'Urseys were similarly self-effacing, being an old but minor titled family, never rich, ambitious or aristocratic enough to attract either the pleasure or displeasure of the court. Their fortunes had steadily diminished, and when the last heir, Major Charles D'Ursey, died without issue during the first Kaffir War, his aged parents sold up the London house and retired in sorrow to the Willows to be cared for by their daughter, Lady Agatha.

I knew her as Miss Aggie, a maiden lady in her seventies, much reduced in circumstances and burdened with this graceful but shabby and unmanageable house, and mounting debt. She had little option but to sell and retire to the dower house. She wished to retain certain paintings and favourite furnishings, and my grandfather, knowing of my love for old furniture, gave me the task of reducing the size while maintaining something of the original grace and proportion of furniture better suited to the spacious rooms and high ceilings of the Willows. She never complained of the decline in her fortunes and treated me as an equal, urging me to take home whatever pieces of exotic wood resulted from my reductions. It was from these that I fashioned the first of the intricate puzzle boxes with their secret catches and drawers that later became one of my specialties.

By contrast, the purchaser, Mr. Albert Blige, was a thoroughly pompous and unpleasant individual, with a highly jumped-up view of his own importance, having made his fortune in the manufacture and import of textiles. His wife was not so intolerable excepting she had little experience in the ways of wealth, privilege and the subsequent treatment of servants, and the only original staff remaining were my aunt Meg, a superb cook who brooked no interference with her kitchen, the kitchen maids solely ruled by Aunt Meg, her husband Gervis Slane, the groundskeeper, and their youngest son Tom, who assisted him. All the other house servants were city girls recruited from the ranks of the workers in Blige's textile factory, with the exception of Everidge, the butler, who had been hired through a London agency.

Mrs. Blige had a horror of being spied upon at night, and so Blige had hired us to build a separate wing at the back of the house. It was a modern and practical but exceedingly ugly addition of his own design, with rooms for the servants above, and new stables and housing for his coaches on the ground floor using the stone foundations of the graceful seventeenth-century stables which had been demolished for the purpose.

Mr. and Mrs. Blige resided in Southampton during the week, leaving the main house unoccupied, and returned on weekends with large parties of business acquaintances and their wives.

All this intelligence came to us through my mother and Aunt Meg, but our plan did not begin to take form until my aunt Martha made the acquaintance of Everidge the butler while visiting Meg in the kitchen of the Willows, where he would often sit of an evening complaining of the indignity of being required to act as both butler and housekeeper, and the impossibility of turning untrained, cheeky city girls into competent housemaids. It was his intention to resign before the year was up.

Aunt Martha was a recent widow, having married her employer, a publican some twenty years her senior who had expired from overindulgence in his own spirits and an excess of my aunt's excellent cooking. Her brother-in-law, feeling that the public house and other properties should be his by right if not by law, had become at first a clumsy then an increasingly aggressive suitor. Her solution was to find another husband, and she set her sights on Everidge. My father opined that we could move things along by robbing the Willows, likely assuring Everidge's dismissal, or at the least speeding his resignation.

The final element was one of injustice. The Cooper tribe, in return for the breaking and training of young horses, had been granted free tenancy to a small wooded glade on the River Bliss by Miss Aggie's grandfather. Jake Cooper, the youngest son of my father's old friend Ezekiel, had been unfairly detained, and awaited judgment for theft on the say-so of Mr. Blige, who having no interest in horses save as the engines for his carriage, wished to rid himself of undesirable tenants. Although Jake was hardly blameless in other ways, his only crime in this instance had been to wait too long to claim his own property, two saddles stored during Miss Aggie's time in an outbuilding at the Willows. When he could produce no proof of ownership Jake was arrested, and the family evicted. There was some outrage in the district, for the Coopers' skills were much valued, and Jake greatly in demand within the horse community, but nothing could be done. Mr. Blige was wealthy and influential, and being new to the county had little regard for the sensibilities of his neighbours. My qualms were satisfied. We would proceed.

The occasion of our adventure was to be the Feast of Saint Stephen. It is the custom hereabouts to celebrate Christmas Day quietly with church and family, and to have a great community feast on the twenty-sixth day of December, Saint Stephen's Day. Father Basil once told me that this event had replaced a much earlier pagan festival known for the roasting of wild boar, and the wearing of animal horns as a prelude to much consumption of strong spirits, and lewd and lascivious dancing. The only remnants of this former revel are the roasting of several domestic pigs, rosy-cheeked children in masks, and of course much consumption of strong spirits, with the dancing being more and more sedate in manner.

The climax of the celebration is the dramatic entrance of an archaic personage called the Old Horse, a sort of hobby-horse figure who chases the young women and rears up, threatening to cover them with his huge ragged hoop skirt. The local belief is that this ensures fertility, so the maidens all run before him laughing and screaming while some married women wishing to conceive contrive to be caught. The Cooper men, having the command of several instruments among them, would provide the music, with everyone singing,

> *"Old Horse, Old Horse,*
> *Seek the maiden's laughter.*
> *Ups his nose, and down she goes,*
> *And the children follows after."*

Then the Horse disappears into the night scattering sweets behind him for the little ones. Gabe and I secretly believed it was our grandfather who inhabited the creature, but could never discover the trappings.

To return to our plot, my father said that a simple plan swiftly executed was best, and our plan was simplicity itself, greatly aided by circumstance.

Mr. and Mrs. Blige were to depart for Southampton six days before Christmas with the intention of returning the day before the New Year with a large company for an extravagant party. Blige had hired a horse and cart to take the housemaids to their families in the city for the same period, and Meg and her family would spend Christmas with us at home, leaving Everidge in charge of the Willows. Everidge, however, had accepted with alacrity Aunt Martha's invitation to spend the holiday with her, so the place would stand empty. The Saint Stephen's Day feast would continue into the small hours of the morning, and with a bit of luck, our activities would not be discovered 'til some time the following day.

We were blessed with clear cold weather, and little snow. My father and I put in an early appearance at the feast, taking turns playing with the Coopers and making a show of becoming highly inebriated. With the excuse of sleeping it off for a bit, we slipped away to a horse and cart we had secreted among some trees about half a mile from the festivities, and proceeded with all possible haste to the Willows. We drove well past the long drive to the house so that we could leave a well-defined track in the frosted grass showing we had entered from the south across the grounds rather than north by road from the village. Although there was no difficulty in entering the house undetected, we elected to make it look like a clumsy entry by smashing a pane of glass in the library doors, and overturning chairs as if we could not find our way in the dark.

We planned to take only the most portable and saleable of items, silverware, candlesticks and picture frames, and whatever jewellery Mrs. Blige had left behind. I, however, could not fight the temptation to linger in the library on our way out, for although Blige had no taste for such things, Miss Aggie had told me that her family were great readers and collectors of books, and over time had amassed many fine volumes which had remained with the house. I had no time to peruse titles and simply scooped up as many of the old and richly bound books as I could carry. My father was not pleased, saying it would make our activities appear as something more than simple theft, but I ventured that a local thief would have no interest in such things. Haste became my ally and I was allowed to keep my prizes.

We returned by the same route, dropping one piece of inferior silver on the road south, circling back to leave our treasure hidden in the ruins of a deserted cottage, and appearing again at the feast scarcely more than two hours after we had left it, just in time to join in for the Old Horse. No one seemed to have noted our absence, and we ate and drank, played and danced 'til well into the morning hours. Recovering from my initial apprehension, I became highly exhilarated by the experience, and for the first and last time in my life got so staggeringly drunk that my father, against my vehement protestations, dragged me home and put me to bed, informing me the next day that I had displayed an alarming inclination to confide our secret to the whole assembly.

We heard numerous stories of the furor raised by our adventure. Aunt Meg reported that Mr. Blige threatened dire consequences, and that Mrs. Blige was hysterical, "vicious barbarians" and "murdered in our beds" being the most repeated phrases. She declared she would not stay in the house another day. The Coopers were closely questioned, but there was no doubt regarding their presence at the feast, and nothing came of it. The local authorities, having no love for Mr. Blige, attributed the robbery to experienced thieves, most likely from outside the district.

Everidge resigned before Blige could dismiss him for his truancy, thus granting Aunt Martha her wish. The house was immediately put up for sale.

Aunt Meg and Uncle Gervis remained as caretakers, and good cooks being more precious than rubies, they were retained by the new owner, Colonel Bliss, a descendant of the same old county family for whom the river was named. He was an ardent sportsman and horseman with a passion for racing, who welcomed the return of the Coopers. Jake was restored to the bosom of his family, as there was no further cause to detain him.

I faced a dilemma regarding my precious cache of books, for left where they were they might suffer from the damp and the depredations of mice, but if I brought them home my mother would certainly question me as to their source. I finally told her they had been loaned to me by Father Basil and prayed she would not think to ask him. It pained me to deceive her, but I was now committed to my lawless path and its guilty pleasures.

The rest of our booty remained in its hiding place until Barker and his son appeared with their caravan full of pots and pans, ribbons and trimmings, and other sundries for the ladies. We met in the ruins of the cottage, and old Barker and my father bargained endlessly, exhibiting considerable enjoyment in the process, while his son Victor and I listened and learned. Transaction completed, the Barkers went on their way, and my father and I returned home well satisfied with our proceeds.

My mother was often sought for her home remedies, as many of our neighbours found the fees of a doctor beyond their reach. She was also a midwife, and rumoured by some to be a witch, though it was never spoken aloud within our hearing. I shared her interest in botanicals, and, as is my habit, recorded the names, descriptions, habitat and medicinal properties of each plant accompanied by a rough drawing, so that I would remember them. I found account ledgers to be ideal for the purpose, having sturdy covers and large blank pages. I later acquired a young lady's paintbox on one of our excursions, thus adding colour to my representations.

When I finally came to examine my prizes, I discovered that I was now the owner of two magnificent volumes on anatomy published during the previous century by a man called Bernhard Siegfried Albinus and titled *Tables of the Skeleton and Muscles of the Human Body*, and *Tables of the Human Bones*. The language was beyond me, and I dared not apply to Father Basil for the meaning, but they were illustrated with engravings of such artistry that all horror of the dead was dissipated, and I was struck by the elegant lines and perfect joins of the human frame, like a piece of finely balanced furniture.

It was through my study of these drawings that I became a bone-setter, at first with injured animals, but of necessity treating my first human subject when a stable lad from a neighbouring house was viciously kicked by a horse, and carried into our kitchen with a broken shinbone. We laid him out on the table and my mother dosed him with opium. I could feel it was a clean break, the skin bruised but not broken, and the bone with the flexibility of youth knitted quickly once I had set it. In time it was as if he were never injured. Word spread, and from thence forward my newfound skill was often called upon.

It was at this time that Father Basil delivered a fiery sermon on the subject of the two Scottish murderers, Hare and Burke, saying that grave-robbing alone was an abomination, but to murder sixteen souls, then sell the bodies to be desecrated in the service of science was beyond redemption, being a sin against both God and nature. He deplored that the anatomist, Dr. Knox, in soliciting human corpses for his medical students, had knowingly rewarded these monsters for their crimes, and had himself been neither accused nor convicted. Although I could naught but agree with my revered teacher, there was still some dark part of me which understood the doctor's thirst for knowledge, but I digress, and besides I have documented all these things in my notes and drawings.

As for my criminal career, my father and I carried out perhaps a dozen more forays over the next three years. Though none yielded so rich a reward as the Willows, the collection of coin grew steadily, as did my collection of books, but I was not sorry to abandon the endeavour, for it seemed my particular gifts included neither thievery nor musicianship despite my father's patient instruction in both. Still, just as thievery would provide me with the means to make a good start in life, so music, however laboriously learned, was a source of much joy to me.

I knew that when I moved from home, I would not have my father's fiddle to hand, and so I set about building one for myself. I studied his instrument from every angle, making measurements, calculations and drawings, going so far as to invent a way to reflect sunlight into the interior through the use of mirrors so that I could view the construction. Even the glue was my own invention, being a refinement of the carpenter's glue used in my grandfather's shop with fine sawdust mixed in to bind it. The formula is in my notes.

Once I had collected and seasoned and shaped the woods I needed for my new instrument, it took me two years to build it, and though it is plainer than my father's fiddle and darker in colour, I am not displeased with the results. The tone is deeper and more melancholy than the original, with a certain reedy vibration to it. In my pride, I burned my initials and the date into the inside of the back panel. I have built several other fine instruments since then, but it is to this first creation I always return.

I also taught myself to read and write simple musical notation, aided by a copy of the published melodies of Playford, the famous dancing master. As I had previously heard many of the tunes, I could apply them to notes on the page. It increased my repertoire far beyond what my memory would have allowed me, and enabled me to make note of the tunes that came to me from my father and great-grandfather, so that over time I amassed quite a fine collection.

I must reveal here a secret that has festered in my memory all these years. It concerns Gabe and me and our little sister, Clare, and

I only tell it now because I know we will all be past caring by the time it is read.

It would have been in 1830, for the country was still mourning the death of King George IV, and preparing for the coronation of his successor King William. The village of Kingsfold was a small market town of about two thousand souls, little touched by the world at large, for the passengers in the coaches on the London–Southampton highway stayed close to the inn, taking scant interest in the narrow winding streets of the town. We had all heard tales of the violence and lawlessness of London, but London was as far removed from us as any great capital in the world, and we were therefore slow to recognize such corruption in our midst.

There had gathered in the town a group of young men, a year or so younger than myself, who having no gainful employment roamed the streets at all hours, bullying and extorting money from those weaker than themselves. Under their leader, a certain Charlie Beggs, their boldness increased as they met little or no opposition, for they chose their victims well.

It was our habit to accompany our parents to the market, and for Gabe and me to go off with friends, leaving Clare with our mother. Though almost twelve at the time, and showing the first signs of becoming a woman, Clare was quite shy and childlike, and, despite urging to become more independent, seldom left our mother's side. On this occasion, Gabe and I returned to the stall to find our mother in a state of agitation, for Clare had been missing for the better part of an hour, and our father had gone to seek her. We joined in the search, and it was only by chance that we turned down a narrow alley, and were stunned by a scene that burns in my memory to this day.

Little Clare lay on her back in the mud, her barely formed breasts exposed and her skirts pushed up around her thighs. Between her legs knelt the rampant figure of Charlie Beggs, while 'round them stood his cohorts urging him on and awaiting their turn.

I had heard the term "seeing red," but never fully understood it until that moment, when a veil of blood fell over my eyes, reason fled, and I could as easily have killed anyone who came into my way as swatting a fly. I scarcely remember the sequence of events, save that Gabe went in with his fists, whilst I grabbed up a stout club from a pile of kindling. We laid into them with a cold, purposeful, silent fury I have never experienced since that day, and had bloodied them all by the time the cowards ran from us.

Gabe then knelt down and cradled Clare in his arms, saying I must run to fetch our mother.

But Clare roused herself to cry, "No! You must tell no one. The shame is mine alone. I was lured away by a peddler's ribbons and laces."

When we protested that the blame was not hers, she begged our silence, saying she feared what violence our father and grandfather might commit should they hear of it, and that the stain of murder, however provoked, must not fall on our family for her sake. There was a strength and resolve in her that we had never seen before, and we were both swayed by it. She then swore us to secrecy, which vow I have kept until this moment.

I returned to the market mumbling some story of Clare having fallen and muddied her clothes, while Gabe carried her home to wash and change. And change she did, for she was never again the happy, loving Clare we had known. Previously devout, she became morbidly religious, embracing the austere habits of the lady saint for whom she was named. She ate barely enough to stay alive, her clothes hanging on her like those of a scarecrow, her former curls rigidly confined in a knot at the back of her head, and her breasts bound so tightly as to hinder her breathing. I think had the opportunity existed, she would have taken the veil. As it was, she made quite sure that no man would ever gaze on her with desire again. My mother, greatly alarmed at these changes, questioned us closely, but we held to our oath, although I have often had cause to regret it.

We had not seen the last of Charlie Beggs.

His mother, Mary, came to us once a week to help with the washing and mending. We called her one of my mother's wounded birds, for Mary's husband Herbert was a violent drunkard, and she had oft born signs of his attentions. My mother, therefore, paid her with firewood, wholesome food and outgrown clothes for her three children, for if there was coin in the house, he would have it for drink. Herbert Beggs had suddenly disappeared sometime the previous year, and excepting his wife, no one seemed to mourn or miss him. My father declared that of course he was dead, having undoubtedly come up against a more violent and devious brute than himself. The family was certainly no worse off, but it seemed that young Charlie was hell-bent for following in his father's footsteps.

This was brought home to us one bitter winter evening the following year. We had just finished our meal and I was reading by the firelight when we heard a thump at the kitchen door, and a woman's voice calling out for my mother. When we opened the door, Mary Beggs fell into the room with a young girl in her arms, and a younger one still clinging to her skirts.

"I beg your help, Missus. I fear her arm is broke, and her head busted. It were that Charlie."

I lifted the limp body onto the table, and beheld for the first time my darling Jean. She was, at that time, about fourteen, tall, but too thin and too pale. Still, there was an ethereal beauty to her, with her thick golden hair matted about her face and shoulders like Jason's fleece, and one tender breast exposed by a rent in her blouse. Immediately my attentions were claimed by the gash on her temple, and the unnatural angle of her right arm. I quickly determined that the arm had been wrenched from its socket at the shoulder, and that the long bone of the forearm was snapped. I asked my mother to give her something for the pain, for I would have to manipulate her shoulder back into place, but my mother said with the blow to the head she must not be allowed to slip away. As I looked at Jean, eyes the blue-grey colour of a storm cloud opened and locked with mine, she spoke to me for the first time.

"Do it," she said.

I stiffened my resolve, and with one brutal twist returned her shoulder to its socket. She swooned and I took the opportunity to fit the bone of her delicate forearm together, and bind it. My mother revived her by holding to her face a cloth saturated with spirits of ammonia, then bathed the cut on her temple and stitched it up with silk. We sat her up, and I strapped her arm to her body. My mother then urged her to her feet, saying that she must walk, and for the space of about an hour they moved about the kitchen, my mother supporting her weight. Although it seemed cruel, I did not protest, for I had learned to trust my mother's judgment.

Mary Beggs huddled by the fire clutching the little one, Flora, in her arms, and brokenly the whole sad story came out. Charlie had come home that night in a state of drunken unreason, and demanded food and money.

Mary told us, "The only food in the house was porridge, and there was no money to be had. He broke into a rage and struck me on the jaw with his fist. He would have struck again, only Jean flew at him to save me. He twisted her arm and flung her across the room. Her poor head hit the door frame with a dreadful sound, and she fell to the floor like a rag doll. He turned again to me and said I had best come up with something, or little Flora would be next." Mary then gave to him the only thing of value left in the house, her gold wedding band, and he lurched off into the night leaving a string of curses behind him.

Clare listened rigid and white-faced, finally running from the kitchen. I followed her up the steps, and found her kneeling beside her bed in desperate prayer. When I put out my hand to comfort her, she shrank from me as if I had burned her, and I had no recourse but to withdraw.

In my absence, Gabe had returned home from courting Annie Greenhill, and was told what had occurred. Our eyes met, and we stepped out into the courtyard, Gabe declaring that we should have finished what we started, and that Charlie Beggs wasn't fit to live. My father and grandfather joined us, and we conferred, our breath rising like smoke in the chill air. We agreed we must find the villain, but it was in the matter of punishment we disagreed. Gabe and I in the heat of our youth, and with the bond of our previous encounter, pronounced ourselves ready to kill him, and my grandfather swore he was not too old to thrash him to within an inch of his life, but my father counselled that corpses were not so easily disposed of, and that there were other ways for a man to disappear. We found no quarrel with his plan, and set out on our search.

The Beggses' wretched cottage was empty, the door open and the hearth cold. We proceeded to a hellhole of a public house in Kingsfold called the Beggar's Rest, which Charlie was known to frequent. My father found him slumped and glassy-eyed at a table, having consumed whatever his mother's ring had afforded him. He coaxed Charlie out into the street, saying he had a nice bottle of rum they could share, and Charlie, being buffleheaded with drink, willingly followed him. He had sufficient of his wits about him to be alarmed when he saw Gabe and me, but by then we had him. We returned to the Beggses' cottage, where Gabe and I kept watch over him for the rest of that bitter cold night. Torn between our comfort and Charlie's discomfort, we rekindled the fire and roughly secured him in the farthest corner of the room.

My father returned in the morning with the cart, and we loaded the bound, belligerent and now painfully sober Charlie Beggs onto the back of it. I took the reins, while my father had a conversation with Charlie regarding his future, or lack thereof.

In my father's grim words, "Charlie, my lad, as I see it you have but two choices. You can take King William's shilling and sign up with the recruiting sergeant, or else we will cheerfully murder you, butcher you and feed you to the hogs. Either way you will disappear, for should you balk at the first choice, we will certainly carry out the second."

Gabe punctuated my father's words with sharp blows to the ribs and gut, not wishing to present a damaged face to the sergeant.

Charlie, thick-headed though he was, could not deny the force of the argument. The recruiting sergeant was a hard and practical man who did not question the circumstances surrounding this reluctant recruit, and so I printed out Charlie's name, and he scrawled his X beside it. The sergeant took him in charge, and with a wink to my father assured Charlie that it was within his authority to shoot deserters should such an action be contemplated. The shilling my father pocketed for Mary Beggs.

We returned home to find Mary and the two girls snug in the workshop, where they had spent a peaceful night. I examined Jean and found nothing amiss. My father told Mary that, in a fit of remorse, young Charlie had decided to go for a soldier, and that he'd sent his shilling as some small recompense for the pain he had caused, promising more when he had it. Mary seemed pitifully willing to believe it (and over time, with the small yearly sum my father and I allotted her in his name, she endowed him with almost saintly attributes). My mother and I then drove the three of them back to their cottage with food and firewood to last for several days.

As for myself, I could not keep my thoughts from returning to Jean.

The year that followed was one of change and turmoil. That spring Gabe and his Annie were married by Father Basil at Saint Stephen. They had been sweethearts since childhood, and both families welcomed the union. Indeed, Annie's parents, being prosperous farmers, had endowed their only daughter with so many goods that my mother was hard-pressed to find room for them all, and the feast that followed was long remembered.

With the funds my father and I had amassed I secured a modest house convenient to Kingsfold. It had a sound roof and a good dry cellar with plenty of room for my living quarters, and a long low shed, well suited to my cabinetmaking. I began to build a steady custom.

In the heat of August, my grandfather, Thomas Treadwell, died while moving some oak planks into the curing shed. He dropped the planks, clutched his chest and fell to the ground, being instantly dead. He had always been so hale and strong that we thought he would outlive us all. My mother pronounced that Annie must now become mistress in her own house, and so we set about building a cottage on the family property for my parents and Clare.

I was by then a frequent visitor to the Beggses' cottage, doing all those things which a husband and son had never done: chopping firewood, repairing the thatch, tightening the doors and windows, clearing the chimney, and filling the chinks in the stone walls. Jean and I had eyes only for each other, but took care not to meet out of her mother's sight, for she was barely fifteen. Her mother might have turned a blind eye, but I was a most serious young man with honourable intentions and wished to establish myself before I took such a step as marriage, and Jean being so young, I wanted her to be sure of her own mind.

She had recovered save for stiffness in her shoulder, and a scar on her temple. The hair my mother had shaved away for the stitching had lost its colour, making a silver streak against the gold. Easier circumstances had added bloom to her complexion, and roundness to her body, and I was as much in love as a man could be.

The family approved of my choice with but one exception, that being my sister-in-law, Annie. I have no quarrel with her, for she has been a good wife to Gabe, but she is overfond of what she calls "speaking her mind."

Upon my announcement of the wedding day at a family supper, she declared, "I, for one, think you can do far better for yourself than the daughter of a drunkard and a skivvy who cannot bring one penny portion to the union."

In the silence that followed, I could feel the heat rise to my face, further enflamed by the sight of Clare nodding her agreement. I would have replied in a most intemperate manner had Gabe not slammed his tankard on the table, saying that as the rest of the family did not hold her view, she had best hold her tongue. From the pursing of her lips and narrowing of her eyes I had no doubt that poor Gabe would have an earful when he went to his bed that night.

Jean and I were married at Saint Stephen by Father Basil early in the spring of 1832, a simple ceremony with only family and close friends. I was twenty, and she was two weeks past her sixteenth birthday. For just over a dozen years I believe we were the happiest pair on earth.

Our daughter Emma was born in December of that year, three days before Christmas, a plump, contented baby. Jean had been covered by the Old Horse the previous year, and claimed Emma as the result, though I ventured I might have had some part in it.

Two years later, in the fall of 1834, our son Gerald was born. It was a difficult birth, for Jean was narrow through her hips, and he was a large infant, having somehow turned in the womb. It took my mother some time to stop the bleeding, and she warned that the damage might make future births a dangerous undertaking.

Jean seemed well contented as my wife and the mother of our children. I continued to prosper, having the added custom of fine finishing of my brother's work, and keeping accounts for him and other tradesmen, and I thought myself well situated for the rest of my life.

Emma, from the time she could walk, wanted nothing more than to be a wife and mother, and mimicked Jean in everything, yet it was Gerry who was his mother's darling. I tutored him from the time he was four, but beyond the rudiments of reading and writing he was an indifferent student. He chafed also at working with me in the shop, and could not wait to be out of doors and rambling with the dog. The only time he was still was when his grandfather played the fiddle. I attempted to teach him to read music, but he had no more patience for notes upon the page than he had for the written word, and angrily declared that music was for the ear, not the eye.

The beginning of our downfall was a joyous occasion.

Jean's little sister, Flora, had been a housemaid at the Willows for some three years, having secured the position through Aunt Meg. Flora and Tom Slane, Meg's youngest, had formed an attachment, and were to marry. The wedding took place on the most beautiful of summer days. The bride wore a dress of larkspur blue, with a garland of daisies in her hair. Jean wore wine-coloured velvet, and a string of garnets with gold beads which had been my wedding gift to her. She was still, after a dozen years, the most beautiful woman I had ever seen.

We went to our bed that night as if we too were newly wed. As I was about to pull away from her, she locked herself to me, and would not let go until I was spent. I chided her, reminding her that we had agreed to have no more children, but she started to weep, and confessed that what she wanted more than anything in this world was to bear one more child. It was the only time we ever quarrelled. I begged her to cleanse herself, but she refused, saying that I must not deny her this one thing. Truthfully, I could never deny her anything, and so against all my best judgment, I agreed.

Within the month, it was apparent she was with child, and she showed every sign of robust health for most of her time, but suddenly in her seventh month she started to bleed and to suffer severe spasms. I sent Emma to fetch my mother, and she in turn sent my father to find the doctor, for she said she feared this birth would be beyond her skill.

By the time the doctor arrived, Jean had died in my embrace. The infant, a girl, had been delivered in a profusion of precious blood, and survived only long enough to be baptised as Helen by Father Basil so that she could be buried in her mother's arms. My mother wrapped the tiny body in the little woollen blanket she had made in expectation of her, and dressed Jean for the last time in her wine-coloured velvet. I placed the garnets about her neck, but Emma begged that she be allowed to have them in memory of her mother, and I had not the heart to refuse. I kissed my darling for the last time, consigned her to the earth, and within the year had marked her resting place with a stone carved with the words of John Milton—*"Flesh of flesh, bone of my bone thou art, and from thy state mine shall never be parted, bliss or woe."*

The days that followed were bleak and empty and endless, a sort of death for me as well. I buried myself deeply in my work and my books. I had recently acquired a collection of poems by William Blake, and in challenging my teaching and taxing my comprehension, they allowed me to defer my melancholy for a time. I was a ghostly presence at meals, not caring what I ate. My lamp burned until morning, for I dared not sleep, not in fear of my dreams, which were full of blissful reunion, but rather for the inevitable cruel awakening and the despair that followed.

My mother finally took me to task, saying she could stay with us no longer, that Emma was too young and too grief-stricken to take on her mother's responsibilities and that in the absence of any discipline from me, Gerry was running wild with a pack of young ruffians. She sent my sister Clare to manage the household for as long as she was needed. Clare remained with us for near five years.

My father took Gerry in hand, instructing him on the fiddle and teaching him all the old tunes. Before long he had far outstripped anything either of us might have taught him, playing the fiddle in the same headlong fashion that characterized everything he did.

It was some months before I emerged from my grief sufficiently to discover that Emma had taken Clare as a model in her mother's place. The two of them perceived themselves as martyrs pitted against the godlessness of the world at large, and Gerry and myself in particular. Gerry dealt with this by absenting himself as much as possible, and I found myself shrouded in an atmosphere of pious disapproval whenever I ventured out of my workshop. No trace of our former happy existence remained.

Some years previous, my sister Clare had become disaffected by the comfortable ritual offered by Father Basil and the Church of Saint Stephen, and had allied herself with a certain Right Reverend Percival Skelton, pastor of the Church of the Children of the True Path which he had founded. The creed of this congregation of about one hundred misguided souls was to deny oneself all worldly pleasure in the pursuit of an equally bleak existence in heaven. I was no stranger to the Bible, having been weaned on it, and had often returned to it as a salve for my sorrow, but this fellow's constant carping on the darkest of the Revelations brought to my mind William Blake's "Everlasting Gospel" and the words "Both read the Bible day and night, / But thou read'st black where I read white." Through Clare, Emma had accepted these preachings unquestioning, and fairly worshipped the man himself. It should therefore have come as no surprise when she announced that he had asked her to marry him and she had accepted.

I was outraged, for she was barely fifteen and the fellow was over thirty, but I would have been wiser to have kept my head, for my anger only hardened her resolve and caused her to say some monstrous things; that Gerry and I were godless and beyond redemption, that Gerry and his music were the spawn of Satan, and finally that I was no better than a murderer, for I had murdered her mother with my lust. I was shocked into speechlessness, knowing that these were Clare's words issuing from my daughter's lips, but damning myself by my silence, for some part of me believed it true. I belatedly asserted some authority by forbidding her to marry before she turned sixteen.

The situation deteriorated further when I returned home on the eve of Emma's sixteenth birthday to find her, Clare and the Right Reverend Skelton virtually looting the place. Emma declared she was only collecting her mother's things, which she had a perfect right to. I put a forceful stop to it, and my anger was further inflamed when her affianced, who had never had the decency to speak with me regarding his intentions toward my daughter, had the effrontery to offer me his and God's forgiveness with such an air of superiority and sanctimony that I had him by the scruff of the neck and the seat of his trousers and would have thrown him bodily from the house had not Clare and Emma intervened.

Despite my mother's pleas, both Gerry and I refused to attend the wedding. It was one of the last times we agreed on any subject. For a time, our intransigence put a severe strain on family relations, but as the Right Reverend's strictures increasingly became so inclusive and so oppressive as to throw a pall over any occasion, the family became more sympathetic to us. In the end, excepting Clare, none of us cared to see much of Emma and her husband, and I mourned the loss of my sweet sunny little girl as if she had died with her mother and sister.

Gerry was then fourteen, and the two of us settled into bachelor life. I hired a woman from the village to keep house and cook for us. We were seldom together except at meals, and then it seemed only to argue or to sit in hostile silence. Excepting his childhood friend, Jake Cooper's son Joseph, Gerry seemed to be drawn to bad company like a dog to spoiled meat. He had always appeared older than his age, being a tall, handsome, well-set-up lad. He was reputed to have a great deal of charm, but I never experienced it. My period of abdication had taken its toll, and attempts to discipline him were useless. Coupled with this was the fact he had only to look at me with his mother's stormy eyes, and all the heat of anger would drain from me.

In truth, Gerry has always been a conundrum to me, having all the kindness and patience in the world for dumb animals, and none at all for his fellow man. He seems driven not by maliciousness or meanness of spirit, but rather by some personal devil over which he has little control, and pays for his excesses in those periods of deep gloom that overcome him from time to time. My father feared he had passed to Gerry the taint of his own mother, Sheba.

Knowing that Gerry would reject any influence of mine, it was my father I turned to when his behaviour became so wild and so destructive I feared he would end his life in prison, or on the gallows. His respect and love for his grandfather prevailed, and it was with great relief that I began to see a difference in his behaviour, for he began to display a concentration and sense of purpose which had hitherto been absent in him.

I was never made privy to his early exploits as a thief, but often cautioned him against the blatant display of his newfound prosperity. He believed, as is the way of youth, that he was immortal and impervious to the forces that range against the rest of us, too bold and too clever to be caught out. I had further to censure him regarding his shameful exploits with women, for he was the subject of constant gossip, and I am thankful that no outraged father came forward to claim him as a son-in-law, for that would have been a dire solution for all concerned.

Throughout Gerry's life there has been one true and shining thing, and that is the music which runs like a golden thread through the heart of all his turmoil. From the age of five he was fascinated by the fiddle, and gave me no peace until I had built for him one that his small hands could hold. His lifelong friendship with Jos Cooper is based in large part on their mutual love of music, horses and dogs.

Jos plays the fiddle also, but has an innate understanding of any stringed instrument, and indeed of any instrument at all, playing the lute, Italian mandolin, flute, and penny whistle with equal facility, and the two of them are great favourites at dancing parties and seasonal celebrations. Had Gerry been able to make a livelihood of it, things might have unfolded quite differently.

By the time he was in his twenties, Gerry and I had softened a little toward each other, and when he was sober, we were almost companionable. For a time, there was a certain cheerful preoccupation in him, and though he said nothing, I guessed he had at last met someone he cared for. I knew also that something disastrous had occurred some time later when he barricaded himself in his room with a cask of brandy, refusing to emerge even for food, and playing the same melancholy Gypsy melodies over and over. This funk lasted until the cask was empty, at which time he resumed his former reckless and dissolute ways.

It was no more than five months later that I was engaged with a young boy who had fallen from a tree. His father had rushed him to me, fearing his wrist was broken. It transpired that he had nothing worse than a bad sprain, and a bump on the head that would blacken his eyes for a few days. I bound the offending limb and, having ascertained that his pupils were normal, dispatched him with a dose of laudanum to take with milk at bedtime. I had just bade them goodbye when a plump, fair-haired young woman with a swaddled infant in her arms presented herself at the door, saying that she was Miss Nancy Bell, and that she had a message for Master Gerald Joyner. I offered to relay it, as he was away from home, but she replied it was for his ears alone, and she would wait. I installed her in the kitchen, where she set about nursing the child, and I went back to my work.

Gerry arrived home some two hours later, and I heard raised voices from the kitchen. When I questioned him, he said there was no doubt the child was his, and if this was not acceptable to me, he would find other lodgings for the three of them. I said that of course they must stay, and so, in 1861, I first set eyes on my grand-daughter, Beth, who solemnly observed me as well. She was then an infant of about six weeks, tiny but robust, her hair like rosewood, a mass of dark curls with glints of red, her eyes still the opaque blue of an infant.

I sought to question Gerry further, but he stormed from the house, saddled his horse and rode off, not to be seen for several days. He returned in the company of his friend Jos, who had found him dazed and delirious at the door of his cottage. He had taken him in, but found him beyond any help he could offer. Nancy Bell and I nursed him through the worst of his fever, but as he recovered, he became more and more withdrawn.

My initial thought had been that both the woman and child were some of Gerry's chickens come home to roost, for she had cer-tainly born a child, but Nancy said that she had simply been engaged as a wet nurse. When I asked about the mother, she replied that she could say nothing on the subject, having given her word, and this was as much as I ever elicited from her on the subject.

In all other things she proved to be a most open and honest person, and over time became an essential part of the household, for she stayed on long past Beth's weaning, and indeed is with us still. She quickly took over the running of the house, and we were almost a family again, save that Gerry was drinking to even greater excess, becoming ever more distant and morose as the days passed. Having once acknowledged the child, he barely noted her existence, and it was for me to arrange her baptism through the grace of my old friend and mentor, Father Basil, who, most sadly, died shortly thereafter, may he rest in eternal peace.

The human heart is a mystery to me. Perhaps if I could dis-mantle it and examine it as I would any other intriguing puzzle, its intricacies would become more clear. Beth adored her father. From the time she could walk she followed him like a pup, and like a pup, the more he rejected her, the more persistent she was in her affection. I do not doubt she loved me, and Nancy Bell was a mother to her in every way but flesh, but her attachment to her father was so transparent and so painful to watch that my heart bled for her.

My parents and Gabe easily accepted Beth, although Gabe's wife Annie had taken against Gerry when he was a boy as a bad influence on her own sons, and Beth's illegitimacy extended this prejudice to her. Clare's disapproval was a given. Emma and her husband came once to the house, she to gloat over her brother's perceived shame, and to crow over the perfection of her own two daughters, and he to confront me regarding what he called Emma's rightful marriage portion. The visit was brief. I discovered Skelton pawing through my library and in the act of examining this account of my father's confessions. Again I ushered him from the house amidst threats of God's wrath, which I would certainly have endured more easily than another confrontation with this pair.

When my father died, Gerry again closeted himself in his room, this time with the wonderful instrument he had inherited, playing out his grief hour after hour until he fell into drunken sleep, only to repeat the cycle the next day and the next. I have often thought that fiddle to be the only thing in this world he truly loves.

I chose to honour my father's memory by building a domed casket of rare woods and intricate inlays, fitted with velvet inside as a case for the fiddle, with a concealed drawer built into the bottom large enough to receive copies of the melodies I had preserved so that the instrument and its music would rest together. My apprentice by then was Gabe's youngest boy, Roland, and his work can be seen on the back of the casket.

Beth would have been close to three at that time, and it is sad that she cannot have much memory of my father. Her subsequent visits to my mother were coloured by Annie's prejudice and the pious disapproval of Clare. She therefore grew up little used to the company of other children, and spoke and behaved much as an adult.

I took great pleasure in being a grandfather, and by the time Beth was four we had settled quite happily into the roles of student and teacher. She is an extremely intelligent and curious child, absorbing any and all information like blotting paper, but beyond her retention, her comprehension is likewise remarkable. She is a natural mimic, and I have had to guard my tongue, or hear some less-than-creditable phrase of mine echoed in every inflection by her childish voice. She soon found that this amused her father, and it pains me to see her become a little clown in his presence. As for music, although she has a sweet true voice, and loves to dance, she has never shown the least inclination to play an instrument, and though I take care not to show it, this is a disappointment. She has, however, learned both to read and to write music, which accomplishment pleases me greatly.

Nancy Bell remains a constant in our lives, and is devoted to Beth. True to her word, there has never been a hint as to her employer's identity, but it must be a person of some wealth and position, as once a year Nancy takes a coach to London, returning with her wages and some extravagant gift for the child.

Several years passed with little change.

I did not comprehend the true depth of Gerry's moral deterioration until early in Beth's ninth year when Nancy came to me one morning in a state of great anxiety, saying she could barely rouse the girl from her bed, and that she seemed pale and exhausted. This was most unusual, as Beth was habitually a cheerful and early riser. I instructed Nancy to make a large mug of hot tea with a good quantity of milk and honey to fortify the child's blood, and gradually wakened her with gentle words and touches. She did not seem to be ill or out of sorts, in fact she finally stretched herself, catlike, and favoured me with a beatific smile. She said that she and her father had been on a great adventure, and was about to tell me of it when she recalled it was to be a secret between them. I was shocked to the core by the implications I drew from this, but not wishing to press her further, I made speed to pound on Gerry's door to ask him what he thought he had been up to. He too had been deep in sleep and was most abusive about my interruption of it, but I, thinking the worst, was not to be deterred. When he realized what I was implying he barked with laughter.

"Don't worry yourself on that account. I have no need or desire to satisfy myself with a child. I've merely acquainted her with her Joyner birthright, and enlisted her as my apprentice, dressed up as a boy. She's as agile as a monkey, sharp with it, and can easily gain access through openings that I could never attempt." It seems they had made their first run the previous night, and he had been well pleased with the result.

Although relieved that my worst suspicions were unfounded, I was temporarily speechless at his callousness, then erupted in a torrent of recriminations that recounted every misstep he had made since childhood. He listened, silent and stone-faced, and finally replied that, as he was so obviously unwelcome here he would seek other accommodations for himself and his daughter.

Inevitably I capitulated, for my granddaughter was now the one bright presence in my life, and I could not bear to lose her. I sputtered a few inconsequent warnings to Gerry about the grave danger he was putting her in, but he replied it was time the brat made herself useful, and bid me good day, slamming and bolting his chamber door in my face.

I was tormented as to what action I could take. Gerry in this mood was intractable, and he would continue to take Beth out on these ventures until she grew too big to be of use. My only recourse was to teach her some means of safeguarding herself, and in the months that followed I had her recount to me the details of each "adventure" so that I could instruct her as to her best defence if things went awry. She is as adept in this as in all her studies, but my fervent prayers go with her on each occasion. Following my advice, she has started to amass a collection of small but valuable items which she can easily hide on her person during the course of the robbery, and which her father knows nothing of, for I have been ailing and fear that if I were gone and he were apprehended she would be left alone and destitute.

She sometimes returns with books for me, having little discrimination as to what she takes, but rather being influenced by the colour of the binding or the brightness of the gold in the titles. I thus have come into possession of some dismal self-published books of poetry, an exquisitely bound and illuminated compendium of the hours of the saints, and best of all, a fine kid-bound edition of Jonathan Swift's remarkable *Travels into Several Remote Nations of the World*. The story of Gulliver's fabulous travels has become a great favourite. At first I censored it somewhat, but soon realized this was a fruitless exercise, as the child can read as well as I.

On one occasion she accompanied me to the Willows when I delivered a linen press I had built for the colonel's lady, Mrs. Bliss, and when that good lady discovered the child could read, she gave her *Alice's Adventures in Wonderland* and *Through the Looking-Glass*, saying her own daughters had outgrown them. I will say this man Dodgson is a very clever fellow, and I enjoyed them nearly as much as did Beth.

I must record here a most singular experience that occurred around this time. It was my habit to tally accounts before I retired. I found that the rows of figures could send me to Morpheus more quickly than any potion I could concoct, and often fell asleep at my desk with my head upon the ledger. On this occasion, Jean came to me once again in a dream, and we lay together as we had all those years ago. In the midst of this bliss, I heard a melody as whole and pure as a prayer. My eyes flew open, and I groped for pen and paper to write it down before it escaped me. It is the most lovely, slow air, and is my Jean through and through. Having longed all my life for that mystical moment when inspiration transcended intellect, it was a blessing to have it come to me at the point when I had all but given up the hope, and in such a glorious way.

I had been doing another job of work at the Willows, and the colonel's lady kindly gave me the previous year's editions of a publication called *Tinsleys' Magazine*, containing chapters of a novel called *A Pair of Blue Eyes* by a man called Thomas Hardy. His writing immediately engaged me, and having since learned that he is both fiddler and builder following his father and grandfather, I feel a strong kinship. I knew that no other title would do for my Jean's melody, and I have placed "A Pair of Blue Eyes" with the other manuscripts which are my legacy to my son and granddaughter.

I have little more to say. I have lately noticed a shortness of breath, and a pinching in my chest which tincture of foxglove relieves for a time, but I have no doubt I shall leave this world in the same way as did my grandfather, Thomas Treadwell. To this end, I have instructed that my tools and notes on the design and building of furniture should go to my nephew Roland Treadwell, for I see in him much of my skill and love for the trade. The house will go to Gerry, but I have charged Beth with being the keeper of the remaining notes, my musical manuscripts, my precious books, and my fiddle, for I know that she will treasure them and keep them safe.

I pray for my son and my daughter that they may eventually find some peace and happiness in this life, as I do not suppose they will find it in the next. I pray also for Beth, and hope that I have instilled in her the skills she will need to survive in this world, for she has been my only joy in these last years. As for myself, I grow impatient to join my darling Jean in the churchyard at Saint Stephen, that we may lie close together as we did that first time when the heat of our bodies would have melted all the snows of winter.

Chapter 3

GERALD JOYNER (1834–1882)

My father, Frank Joyner, died in September of 1875, and rests with my mother in the churchyard of Saint Stephen. May he find more joy in the dead than he did in the living.

In his last days, he handed me this journal with the charge that I should add the events of my own life to those of himself and my grandfather, and to pass it on to Beth when the time came. I have always been a man of action rather than words, unlike my father for whom there were never words enough; however, now that my own life is coming to an end, I will honour his request by adding my scrawl to these pages with the assurance that I will be brief.

The people I have truly cared for in this life can be counted on the fingers of one hand; my sainted mother and my grandfather, both long dead, my lifelong friend Jos Cooper, who remains true despite the different paths we have followed, and my lovely, wicked Tess, whom I shall never see again.

My mother lives in my memory as a shining angel who was torn from me, leaving a wound that has never healed. My grandfather, unlike my father's softened account of him, was an unrepentant old scoundrel 'til the day he died, and if his tales to me were true, greatly enjoyed his escapades, suffering not a whit of conscience. We had much in common, for he gifted me with the two skills at which I could excel, music and thievery, and at his end left to me my most precious possession, Old Nick, my fiddle.

Jos Cooper has been my boon companion since we were chicks. Everything I know of horses and dogs, and much regarding music, I learned with him at the hands of his father and grandfather. I know that I have but to ask, and he will answer, and when I have burnt the candle too long and too brightly and am snuffed out by my old enemy, melancholy, I can always ease my pain with those wild melodies we first played together by firelight in the Gypsy encampment by the River Bliss.

Of Tess I will speak later.

I will not fill these pages with the excesses of my youth, save to say that I early formed the habit of absenting myself from my father's house whenever possible to avoid the constant preaching of my sister and aunt, roaming the village and the countryside with rough companions, and it is here and here alone I will confess I once killed a man.

I was just turned sixteen, and thought I would try my hand at being a highwayman. Having purchased a pair of handsome pistols from Victor Barker, I believed myself quite the bold fellow. I had in mind the son of a local squire, a soft, lazy, superior-acting fellow of a type I despise. It was his habit twice weekly to visit his slut, departing in the early hours of the morning in a highly drunken state. Surely nothing would be easier than to rob him at gunpoint, leaving him fuddled and horseless by the roadside.

Events unfolded quite differently.

I sat in a copse of trees for what seemed an endless time, shivering in my thin coat and breeches, my little mare, Jenny, skittish from the inactivity. I had disguised myself with a kerchief to cover my nose and mouth, and a cap to pull down over my eyes. At last I heard the hooves of his horse and spurred forth. It makes me squirm to recall that I loudly commanded him to "stand and deliver." He greeted this with the curse it deserved and pulled out his own pistol, pointing it at me with a wavering arm. I scarce remember firing my weapon, and as good or bad luck would have it, hit him square in the forehead, having never so much as cocked the thing before. He fell from his horse like a sack of barley. His animal scarcely flinched. My Jenny, however, was panicked, as was I, and we rode off as if the very devil were after us, without a thought for the fat purse I had left behind. I had at least the presence of mind to throw the pistols into the river, but left poor Jenny in the stable still saddled, lathered and shivering, with no blanket to cover her.

I quaked in my bed for the rest of the night, expecting a pounding on the door at any moment, and when I finally dropped into a fitful sleep, and the pounding came, it was my angry father wanting to know what I thought I was about, leaving the mare in such a pitiful state, and for that I was truly ashamed.

I spent several anxious days, and was much relieved when I heard that someone had been taken in charge. He was some sort of tramp who had obviously come upon the carcass and helped himself, being caught dead to rights with the fellow's jacket, watch and pistol. I certainly had no intention of coming forward, and the poor devil was hung.

I must now speak of Tess, who, excepting my mother, is the only woman I have ever truly loved.

Jos and I with two other players were quite in demand for local dances and weddings, with occasional employment at the big houses in the district if they wished for something a little more rustic. It was in such a way we found ourselves playing at a costumed ball at a house known as Belfountain owned by a family called Skedding. The theme of the ball was after the revels of the French court at Versailles, with the costumes representing that unlikely view of yokels and shepherdesses and such. Jos and I laughed ourselves silly when we pictured these ladies and gentlemen trying to herd sheep.

Such gatherings were heaven-sent for spying out possibilities for my other activities, although I already had some knowledge of the place through one of the housemaids, May, a plump, cheerful and willing girl I had a fondness for.

We were putting the dancers through their paces with a lurching comic jig called "Two Left Feet" when I spied a handsome bosom upon which rested a magnificent ruby pendant like a great drop of blood surrounded by diamonds. Save for her fine figure and small stature, I could not tell much more about the lady's appearance as she was masked, and her hair elaborately curled and powdered, but as she lingered nearby, I was aware of being examined and not found wanting. The rest of the evening passed without incident, but the ruby pendant lodged in my memory, and I was determined to have it.

The festivities ended in the small hours of the morning, and as we left I stole a moment with May. We arranged to meet in the kitchen garden the following evening.

May was a simple, unsuspicious girl, happy to prattle on about the personages at the ball, and I learned that the pendant was the property of Lady Teresa Blackwood, the recent young bride of "some grand sort of sailor" who was currently at sea. The Skeddings were cousins of his, and Lady Teresa was residing with them until he should return. The gossip among the servants was that she had been "brought up very wild," and in his absence her husband, "who was ever so old, and had a fine London house and a large estate in Derbyshire," wished to remove her from the temptations of London society. May did not personally attend her, but tidied for her.

"She is moody," she said, "but not unkind, and has such lovely things as are better suited to salons and balls and truly wasted here in the country. I feel quite sorry for her, as there are no ladies of her own age and station to keep her company, and her maid is a dried-up old spinster hired locally by the husband."

I ended our assignation in the potting shed with the promise of more attentions to come, and the crucial information that the house retired early, with everyone well abed by eleven. It seemed there were better pickings here than I had imagined.

I returned some nights later, leaving Jenny by the wall of the kitchen garden, tied loose to leave no impediment to a speedy retreat. I had unlatched a pantry window upon leaving the ball in hopes the kitchen staff would overlook it, and so they had. Fitting soft slippers over my riding boots, I entered the house. Through May's gossip I had a pretty fair notion of the upper floors, and the location of the lady's bedchamber and dressing room. May had said she was not in the least careful, and left her fine things scattered about as if they were trifles.

I found my way to the dressing room, guided by a small spirit lantern devised by my father, shuttered on all sides save one which was lensed, and mirrored within so as to cast a strong, narrow beam of light. It could be quickly snuffed, and had been useful on many occasions. The curtains were closed, and the room black as pitch. I aimed my lantern toward the dressing table, upon which various valuable trinkets were strewn. I pocketed them, though none was the prize I sought. I was rifling through one of the drawers when I heard a slight sound, became aware of a light other than my own, and turned to see an extraordinary sight.

The source of the light was a branched candlestick held by a small white hand, and in the other hand a little pistol aimed at my belly. As my eyes travelled upward, I saw an ivory bosom upon which rested the very jewel I sought, burning as if with its own fire, and above that, a coldly smiling elfin face surrounded by curls of the deepest copper. In height, she would barely have reached my shoulder. I later discovered that she had magical eyes that changed from grey to green to gold, depending on her mood. She spoke.

"Sir, I warn you I am no blushing maiden. If you move so much as a finger, you'll find I am an excellent shot, and will not hesitate."

I here experienced such a rush of feelings as I can scarcely describe. Certainly alarm was uppermost, for her hand was steady, and I believed her absolutely, but a certain part of my anatomy reacted perversely by coming to full attention.

"Remove your cap and kerchief, and let me see what I have here."

I most carefully did as she asked, although as my wits returned, I took heart that she had as yet shown no inclination either to shoot me or to raise the household.

"Ah, the handsome fiddler from our bucolic ball. I wondered if I should see you again. Well, sir, what's your name then?"

Her voice was musical, a high soft drawl with no shrillness in it, like the cooing of a dove. I was so struck that I did not answer, and she repeated her question. I said I was Gerald Joyner for I saw little to gain in lying, then applied myself to charming her, in part because this had been my salvation in the past, but also because I was completely bewitched, and wished to know more of her. I made no excuses, carefully placing the pocketed items back on the dressing table, but declared that I was driven by curiosity about the beautiful lady who had gazed so frankly at me as I played.

I was intrigued that although she accepted my compliment as her due, she was in no way deceived into dropping her guard. She bade me sit down, for which I was grateful as it somewhat disguised my obvious state. She declared herself weary of her kind but tiresome hosts, and craving some conversation outside their conventions. With a knowing little smile, she said I might rise or fall depending upon my eloquence. Placing the candlestick on a table, she sat opposite me in her white bed gown of muslin and lace, the ruby glowing in the cleft of her bosom, the pistol never once shifting from its target.

I then faced a thorough interrogation, throughout which I was aware of being toyed with, but rather than being angered, I was spurred by it, and held nothing back. I was no stranger to the attraction between men and women, but this was something stronger, more compelling, and there was a thickness in the air between us that one could almost touch.

Finally she laid down her pistol, picked up her candlestick and said, "Come, Mister Joyner. It is time we were joined in bed."

I must have sat there gaping, for she laughed like a tinkling of bells and took hold of my wrist, pulling me up out of the chair and through the door to her chamber. She stripped off her nightgown, revealing the body of a miniature Venus, her bush as red as her hair, the ruby still glowing between her lovely breasts. I hastily shed my own garments, aware of the danger, but beyond all caution.

We sank into her bed, and I breathed in the scent of her body and hair, a sweet mixture of roses and almonds. She was a lusty and demanding lover, with no pretense at coyness, unlike any other woman I have known. We coupled three times in as many hours, and as the first light of dawn showed itself, she pulled away from me, saying that she must see me safely from the house, for she was beginning to imagine great possibilities for us. Opening the window she showed me a stout trellis covered with vines, and after a final long embrace I climbed lightly to the ground, feeling that I could as easily have floated.

We had agreed to meet early in the morning, two days hence. She said it was her habit to ride at this hour, and no one would mark her absence.

I spent those days in an agony of anticipation, for she filled both my waking thoughts and my dreams. Like any lovesick fool, I twice rode close by Belfountain hoping to catch a glimpse of her, but in vain.

When that morning finally came, I arose early and spent unaccustomed time on my appearance, departing the house shaved and brushed and dressed in my best.

Our meeting place was a neglected barn on the edge of the estate, with concealment for our horses, and plenty of sweet-smelling hay stored there against the winter. Once again we came to each other's arms as if we were the only two lovers on the earth. When finally we rested, she began to tell me something of herself.

Her name had been Teresa Riddell. Her mother had died in childbirth when she was six, and her father was a navy lieutenant more often away than at home who finally met his end in China, a victim of dysentery. This left herself and two younger brothers in the care of their grandfather, a retired navy man settled near Dover in an isolated, windswept house with an unimpeded view of the ocean. She spoke fondly of those days of freedom, rambling and shooting with her brothers in the open countryside, and being their equal in the schoolroom when the local schoolmaster came to tutor them.

All this changed in her sixteenth year with the death of her grandfather.

At the funeral a certain Commander Nelson Blackwood introduced himself to the three orphans, saying he had been their father's commanding officer, and that in memory of him he had agreed to become their guardian. He soon secured places at a good public school for her brothers as preparation for the naval academy, and Tess was dispatched to the Misses Blanding's School for Girls, where she would learn to be a lady. She had been quite taken with Commander Blackwood despite his age, for he seemed most kind and gallant, and cut a fine figure in his uniform. He visited her on several occasions during her time at school, raising some envy among her classmates. She found the other girls hopelessly timid and conventional, and more than once her guardian was called upon regarding matters of deportment and discipline.

Upon her eighteenth birthday, Commander Blackwood came to see her on quite another matter. He said he was soon to be called back to China in defence of the tea trade, and he feared for her future should some misfortune befall him. His solution was that they should marry so that she and her brothers would be safely provided for.

"I saw no objection," she said, "for he was a dashing fellow, wealthy and titled, and I do not come into my inheritance from my mother for three more years. I also harboured the romantic notion that I might travel with him as some other navy wives did, and that I would thus experience some of the exotic places I had only read about."

Once married, however, his true character emerged and he became very stern and controlling, saying he had no intention of exposing his wife and the future mother of his children to the rough manners of English sailors, and the filth and pestilence of foreign ports. She would reside with his cousins, the Skeddings, until his return, and so there she rested, "marooned" as she said.

I now come back to the ruby. It was his wedding gift to her, presented to him by an Indian maharajah in gratitude for the safe transport and delivery of his son to an English boarding school. It was valued in the thousands, and she wore it at all times, for although it was a symbol of her subjugation, the thought of its value comforted her in her exile.

As for me, the only jewel I now coveted was Tess herself.

It was at our next meeting that she revealed her plans to me. As I have stated, she found her hosts stodgy and tiresome, and she longed for some excitement and fun. She claimed also to be in desperate need of money, for her husband kept her woefully short of it. The solution, she said, was to join me in my exploits. I was horrified, and protested that this was no schoolgirl lark, and the consequences of discovery would be dire, but she pleaded and cajoled, and I, the love-sick fool, was persuaded. To this day, I do not know how I could have followed her lead in such a blind, headlong fashion. My grandfather had instilled in me some measure of calculation, but suddenly all caution was lost, and I was caught up in such a whirlwind of intrigue, excitement and danger, with lust as the driving force, that I would have dared anything for her. She had only to think of a thing, and we would do it.

We next met four nights later at midnight. I waited with Jenny in the shelter of the hedgerow while she descended the vines outside her window dressed in boy's riding breeches and jacket, which she had discovered packed away in the attics of the house. Her flaming hair was similarly disguised under a cap, and she had tied a silk kerchief 'round her neck to be pulled up over her face. I easily hoisted her up on the saddle behind me, for she was no weight at all, and was alarmed to discover that she had tucked her pistol into the waist of her breeches where I could feel it pressing against my back. I protested that we were thieves, not murderers, and convinced her to leave it in the fork of a tree where we could collect it on our return. It was as well it were left behind, for such was her nervousness that she started at every shadow, and we would certainly have roused the countryside had she fired.

Our destination was the quite new and undistinguished country house of a London solicitor named Grantly. Tess was often invited to teas, dinners and dances hereabouts, and had considerable knowledge of the local gentry, their houses, habits and possessions. On one such occasion, her doting host, Mr. Grantly, had confided to her that the two little Florentine figures of Venus and Adonis which she had so admired were not gilt as she had supposed, but in fact solid gold, acquired by his parents some years before on their grand tour of Europe. We intended to have them, and at the same time to take several other valuable items which Tess had spied.

I slipped the latch on one of the dining room windows, and hoisted Tess over the sill. She quickly secured the items we desired, and

passed them to me to be wrapped in chamois so that they would make
no noise nor be damaged in my saddlebags. She then exited as she had
entered, dropping into the saddle behind me. I could feel her heart
pumping wildly against me as we rode, and we spent a fevered hour
together in the barn before we parted beneath her bedroom window.

Over the succeeding months we made several such expeditions,
always returning to the barn where we would fall into each other's
arms, the thrill of our adventures sweetening our lovemaking. On one
such occasion she said family legend had it that one of her ancestors
had been a lady-in-waiting to the court of King Henry the Eighth,
and had borne him a child "on the wrong side of the blanket," as she
put it. If fate had made it a boy, she said, she'd be royalty today, but
as it was a girl, the lady had to be content with a modest dowry and
a hasty marriage. It was then she jokingly said if she had a child and
it were a boy, she would name him Henry, and if a girl, Elizabeth.

Our final adventure was that of Mrs. Montfort's pearls.

Herbert Montfort was a brewery baron, Montfort's Pale Ale and
Cream Ale being the source of his considerable fortune. Although
the Montforts were new to the county and to society in general, their
wealth overcame most social barriers, and they were well known for
their lavish entertainments, and the illustrious personalities that
attended them. Tess said the ballroom rivalled the Trianon for gild-
ing, and the dining room could seat thirty. My mouth fairly watered
at the thought of all that silver, but this was not our quarry.

The pearls, called the Tears of Kashmir, were formerly the
property of a maharani, and consisted of three long matched
strands with elaborate diamond stations and clasp, each pearl the
size of the end of my little finger. It was an ill-kept secret that
Mr. Montfort had had a replica made which his wife wore on most
occasions, but for certain events he would collect the true pearls
from his London bank. At this time, they were to host a dinner for
a member of parliament, with all the local worthies invited. Tess

had this news from Mrs. Skedding, who was greatly excited at the prospect of seeing the fabled necklace at first hand.

Having been invited as a weekend guest, Tess set about gathering information regarding the plan of the house and the domestic arrangements of the hosts. She easily ingratiated herself with Mrs. Montfort—Lucy—calling on her several times in the guise of a new young wife seeking marital advice from an older and more experienced one. My grandfather would have heartily approved of her scheme, which though risky, was simple in the extreme. She discovered that Mr. and Mrs. Montfort slept apart, reportedly because he snored as loud as a trumpet. She learned also that the necklace in its velvet pouch would be collected and locked away in Montfort's library safe once Lucy Montfort had retired for the night, and so her opportunity would be brief.

She secured the replica from Lucy's dressing room early in the day while that lady was engaged in consultations over the dinner arrangements. At the end of the evening, she begged leave to speak to her hostess on a personal matter which was vexing her, and was invited to join her in her dressing room for an intimate chat before bedtime. She then feigned a sudden faintness, and while Lucy was fetching brandy, she spilled the true pearls from their pouch, and substituted the replica, slipping her prize into a deep pocket she had sewn into the seam of her dressing gown. Bidding Lucy good-night, she hastened to her room, and signalled to me with a candle passed back and forth at the window. She tied the pearls into a handkerchief, dropped them to where I waited on the ground below, blew me a kiss, then went off to her bed.

Tess thought it likely the theft would be discovered and the alarm raised almost at once, but it wasn't 'til almost a fortnight after the pouch had been returned to Herbert Montfort's London bank that Lucy discovered the replica was missing and informed her husband, who lost no time in concluding that the original might be compromised.

By this time I had been to London to see the Barkers. Victor Barker and his son, Adam, were away about their business, and I dealt with the youngest daughter, Sarah. Despite her youth, any thought that she might be easier to bargain with than her father was soon dispelled, for she declared that the pearls were too recognizable, and would have to be reworked into several different pieces at considerable expense. She offered me less than a third of their value, and I was obliged to take it, but I had her hold back one of the pearls in order to set it in a neckpiece so that I could give it to Tess as a token.

When next we met, and I gave Tess her share of the takings, she flew into a fury.

"By God," she said. "You are such a gullible fool! Of the three of us, Sarah Barker is by far the better thief!"

This was a different Tess than I had ever seen, and it still pains me to think of the cruel things she said. I began to suspect that whatever my feelings for her might be, hers must be of quite a different nature. She mounted her horse and galloped off without a backward glance, leaving me in confusion and misery, but with still some vain hope that she might relent.

It was some endless, miserable weeks later that a note from Tess was delivered to me by a small boy. I tore it open to read that she regretted her harsh words, and she requested that I meet her in the morning three days hence, as she had a most pressing matter to discuss with me. My heart leapt to my throat, and it never occurred to me to refuse. Not wishing to compromise her by a note from me, I gave the boy half a crown and instructed him to tell her, and her alone, that I had read and understood her message.

The pearl, handsomely set with gold and sapphires on a velvet ribbon, was retrieved from Sarah Barker on a mad dash to London and now rested in my breast pocket in anticipation of our reunion. I set out with a light heart.

We embraced as if we had never parted, and although I would not have thought it possible, our union was more passionate than any previous. When at last we rested, I gave her my gift, and she swore it would never leave her throat. There was a long moment of silence between us, then she imparted her news. The words wound me still.

"You must believe above all things in my love for you. Our separation has been a torment, but I must now make a heart-rending decision. It is made even more painful as for these six months I have been carrying a child that is most certainly yours."

Any joy I might have felt at this was dispelled by her next words.

"I leave in the morning to arrange for my lying-in away from the prying eyes of my husband's relations, for I can no longer conceal my condition. I have received a letter from my husband saying that he is to return to England in a few months' time. It is my intention to repair to our London house in anticipation of his return, and I pray that I can bear our child, and find a safe haven for it before he returns, for it is my intention to honour my marriage vows and to henceforth be his wife in all ways."

I desperately protested that I would care and provide for her and the child, but she said she had had much time to consider her options, and there were obligations which she could not ignore.

"The lives and careers of my two brothers are in my husband's hands, and I cannot be responsible for a scandal that would bring about their ruin as well as my own," she declared.

I raged at her, calling her every kind of vile thing that came to my tongue. She did not return my rage, but only stood unflinching with tears flooding her eyes, and her final words to me were that if I struck her dead on the spot it was no more than she deserved, and it would relieve her of the terrible burden of doing what she knew she must do. She then mounted her horse and departed, plunging me into a deep well of despair.

It was Jenny who brought me home, for I don't recall anything of the journey. When I later revived enough to go unsaddle her and rub her down, I found that I had already done so with no memory of it.

I became a walking dead man, cut off from all human emotion save a cold impotent fury. Eventually I returned to my former bad companions and habits, but driven by a new recklessness. After comparing Montfort's Ale to horse piss, I reduced a local public house to wreckage, and was roundly beaten by the landlord's sons, adding one more to a growing list of establishments where I was no longer welcome. I confined my lust to married women, where no declarations of love were expected or given, and I don't doubt that more than one local gent has a cuckoo of mine in his nest.

My only moments of peace were in those times when Jos would come with his mandolin or guitar to talk of the innocent adventures of our youth and play the old songs once again. I might eventually have regained some semblance of my former carefree life, but Tess had one more blow to deliver.

It was in January of 1861, some three or four months later, that I returned home to find Nancy Bell in the kitchen with the infant Beth. She handed me a letter, saying she had been given to understand that I was the father of the baby girl, that she had been engaged by Lady Teresa Blackwood to be her wet nurse and to care for her, and that she would await my instructions once I had read the letter.

I was outraged. Not only was Tess saddling me with the brat and her keeper, she insulted me with a paltry twenty pounds a year for her upkeep. I stormed from the kitchen, encountering my father as I headed for the stables. I allowed to him that the child was mine, and that he could go to blazes if he expected any excuses or explanations. He seemed pitifully willing to welcome her, which suited me well enough, as it saved me the trouble and expense of finding new lodgings. I thought my head would split apart as I fled the house, and I was lost for three days before I turned up on Jos's doorstep.

(I include here the text of the letter from Lady Teresa Blackwood as found, much creased and handled, between the pages of the journal. L.A.F.)

To My Beloved King of Thieves,

This is to introduce Miss Nancy Bell who has in her care our daughter, Mary Elizabeth. I pray that you can put aside any quarrel with me, and take Beth into your heart and home, for she is the pure and innocent issue of our love.

Do not trouble yourself about wages for Nancy, for I will bear that cost, and I will further provide a sum of money per annum for Beth's upkeep. I would wish to make it more, but I do not come into my inheritance for another year and some months, and must, until then, account for every penny. In the event that you refuse to take her in, I shall attempt to make some other arrangement, but I found that I could not bear to think of our child at the mercy of strangers.

Nancy carries two mementos for you; my pistol for which I will have no further need, and a gold watch, its case embossed with the images of Venus and Adonis, and which I have inscribed so that you may remember our brilliant but all-too-brief liaison. You must believe me when I say that what I do now I do solely out of duty, and that you are the first, and I believe the only man I shall ever have truly loved.

Tess, Your Bandit Queen

The succeeding days, months, years ran together with little to distinguish them. Desperately needing money, I resumed my nocturnal rides. On a visit to the Barkers, I read in a London paper that Commander Blackwood and his lady had removed to the quiet of their country estate in Derbyshire following the birth of their first child, a son named Edward Alexander Henry. That occasioned another violent drinking spree, and another dark spiral.

As Beth grew she appeared more like her mother in every way save colouring, for her hair was almost as dark as mine with only glints of her mother's copper. She was fortunate in her grandfather, for her father could not bear the sight of her, and it bedevilled me that the more I shunned her the more she sought my company. I have always been quick to anger, and she has received more than her share of the rough side of my tongue.

When my poor old Jenny went lame, I had not the heart to put her down, but only pastured her where I could see her enjoying her rest. Jos was now married, and his father's second as head groom and trainer for the racing stable at the Willows. He found me a spirited stallion called Ulysses, a handsome black brute and difficult to manage, but after I covered his nose and eyes with my jacket a few times he accepted my smell and my authority, and I could handle him with little difficulty. Being well matched in temper, we suited each other, and together with Rex, my hound, we made many a wild run.

In Beth's eighth year, I began to see she might be useful to me. I softened my manner and found her a more than willing accomplice. She was clever and agile as a boy, and in fact seemed more comfortable in boy's clothing than in girl's. Once she donned her disguise, and blackened her face with soot, my discomfort with her was eased. I did suffer a sharp pang of memory when I pulled her up on the saddle behind me, and her arms tightened 'round my waist, but I hardened my heart and forced my thoughts back to the task at hand.

My father burst into my room the next morning, and if his blustering about incest hadn't been so laughable I might have been more careful with my response. As it was, he came closer to striking me than he had ever done when I was a boy. Taller than he by some six inches, and much stronger as well, I could easily have bested him, but instead backed him down with the threat of Beth's removal, for

I knew he loved her dearly and would not easily let her go. I further salted the wound by reminding him it was he who had introduced me to my profession through my grandfather, and he could have no quarrel if I chose to enlist my daughter.

Nancy Bell had become a permanent part of our lives, carrying out everything necessary to the daily running of the household. I found her handsome enough, but never was one to force my attentions on the unwilling. She regarded me with stiff disapproval, but never openly opposed me, slyly carrying her complaints to my father. She was as fiercely devoted to Beth as any mother, and, I believe, truly thought of her as her own child. Once a year she took a coach to London to collect her wages, returning two days later with an extravagant gift for Beth and the yearly sum for her upkeep. At first the gifts were childish, dolls and picture books and sweets, but as Beth grew the gifts matured as well, a set of silver-backed brushes and mirror, and a gold locket which I later sold, and on one occasion a box of finely milled soaps with the scent of roses and almonds which caused me to put my fist through a door panel. Never once did I gain any word of Tess from these journeys, and although she claimed it as a condition of her employment, I think it secretly pleased Nancy to withhold it.

My father continued to reproach me, but Beth herself was so determined to continue, he had to satisfy himself with schooling her for the enterprise. She had a natural ease with the workings of all kinds of locks and catches, and there was no place she could not gain entry to.

My father died when Beth was thirteen. My sister Emma and her cowardly cur of a husband came sniffing around with their two lumpish daughters to see what they could gain, but I soon sent them packing. I had to halt our runs, for Beth was so brought down as to be useless. In truth, she was fast becoming a woman, and now nearly matched her mother in figure as well as face. This alone might have altered my course of action, but fate stepped in.

I had spent a wild night carousing with some like-minded companions, and was riding home well after midnight. Ulysses lived to run, and I usually gave him his head, for I too loved the thrill of a full gallop through the moonlit countryside. We were about a mile from home when we encountered a low stone wall and were set to clear it, when a fox darted out from the bushes and Ulysses swerved, coming down with a crash on his side, my left leg trapped under him. I knew that something dreadful had happened, for he could not rise, and was screaming with pain. Being trapped I could do nothing, and his thrashing put me in a most dangerous position. His cries finally attracted the attention of a poacher by the name of Wilkins. I begged him to put my poor old boy out of his agony before assisting me. It took three shots to the head to dispatch him. Wilkins then used his rifle stock as a lever to free my leg. My brave Ulysses had broken a foreleg, but even worse, had been pierced through the side by a jagged tree trunk. My own leg was smashed beyond saving. Perhaps if my father had been alive he could have patched me up, but the local surgeon was not equal to the task, and it was evident that at best I would walk with a stick to the end of my days.

My constant pain could only be dulled by opium. I soon found I could not do without it, and so became an addict as well as a drunkard. At thirty-eight, my career as a thief was ended. I faced a future with little choice beyond playing for pennies on the street like my ancestor Blind France. Though I fought the darkness, it crept over me as surely as day into night. Once more I buried myself in my room, with Old Nick and brandy as my sole companions, emerging only when hunger drove me to take in whatever food was left outside the door. I would sometimes find Beth sleeping there on the floor with my dog Rex, whose tail would thump hopefully.

Jos sought to encourage me, offering to find me a place at the Willows, but knowing my uncertain temper as I do, I refused to put his livelihood at risk.

It was Nancy's wages that kept food on the table through this time, although my cousin Gracie brought fruit and vegetables weekly at the urging of Uncle Gabe. She and Nancy became fast friends, and it was Gracie who finally stormed the door of my room, giving me as thorough a tongue-lashing as I have ever had, and saying that even if I were at death's door it would not warrant this kind of tiptoeing about. She looked so comical, sputtering and shaking like a hen in the rain, that I had my first good laugh in an age—but as always, it was music that saved me.

The voices in my head were crowded out by melodies that begged to be played. Beth, sensing a change, fetched Jos. The result was three short pieces, a slow air called "The Downcast Lover," a lively melody called "Roll of the Dice" and a galloping sort of tune called "Rakehelly," which joined together in one long piece I called "Joyner's Dream." I later discovered that Beth wrote it down as we played it, and added it to my father's manuscripts, where it lies still.

Seeing that with this turn in my spirits I would need to get about, Jos found me a new mount, a big strong bay gelding named Nicodemus. He had none of Ulysses' fire, but was a much easier ride for my damaged leg, and on his back I could, for a time, almost forget the pain and oppression of my affliction.

Once roused from my funk, I sorely needed a new source of income, but did not begin to form a plan until Nancy returned from her annual visit to London with her gift for Beth, a handsome dress of velvet, modestly cut but displaying her budding figure to excellent advantage, its russet colour bringing out the reddish glints in her hair, and the rosiness of her complexion. With her hair pulled up, she looked quite the fine young lady.

I recalled a young fellow of my acquaintance called Julian Bendick, well favoured as to appearance, and having had all the social advantages, but a thorough bad lot who made his living as a card sharp. It struck me that if I could enlist him to teach Beth some of his skills, I would have the makings of a first-class gambling establishment.

Upon my father's death his cabinetmaking tools and notes went to my cousin Roland. I made no protest when he came to collect them from the workshop, for they were of little value to me, and left empty a long, low, snug building, separate from the house and ideal for my purpose. There was a stone fireplace to warm us through the winter, and the workbench would serve nicely as a sideboard for the nightly supply of bread, cheese and sausage, and the jugs of cider and ale that would keep our patrons' bellies satisfied, and their rumps at the gaming table.

Clever Beth easily mastered Julian's bag of tricks, and invented some of her own. She readily adopted the plummy accents of some of our more refined patrons, and they felt quite at ease with her. With both of them at cards and myself at the dice, I soon had three tables running at a nice profit. I hired an ex-army sergeant, Billy Crake, to be our doorkeeper, and a strong arm or back whenever it was needed. We worked out a series of signals to identify whether a patron was an easy mark, a difficult customer, or someone influential who should be allowed to win a bit by way of a bribe. Beth became quite practised at the give and take of clever compliments, and had little difficulty in turning aside unwanted attentions, so that I had no need to play the outraged father. That is, until Nancy informed me that Julian Bendick's attentions to Beth had progressed to a most intimate state.

I must have been blind not to see which way that wind was blowing. The last thing I needed was another brat on my hands, and I dispatched Master Bendick with a clip on the ear and a warning as to what would happen to his privates if he opened his mouth to the wrong party.

That was the only time I ever had the full support and gratitude of Nancy Bell. She had been opposed to the enterprise from the outset, but Beth had talked her 'round, saying we must feed ourselves somehow, and she would be safe under our watchful eyes. Like her mother, she had a very winning way with her, did Beth, amusing us all with her clever impersonations, and singing popular airs in her sweet voice when Jos and I would play.

During this time a significant chain of events occurred. It concerned two men, Ted Enderby and Robert Clithering.

Enderby was a cooper, overfond of the contents of his barrels. He had begun to make a drunken nuisance of himself, running up losses he could not sustain, lecherously pawing my daughter, and insulting other players. Billy Crake had several times seen him from the premises in a none-too-gentle fashion, and on a final occasion, when he had overturned a gaming table then dropped his trousers to piss in a spittoon, I barred him from returning. He threatened revenge, but I dismissed it as drink-addled raving.

Robert Clithering was a reeve of the village. He had a reputation as a highly moral but fair man, and a sensible voice in village affairs. It would therefore have been a surprise to see him in my establishment, had I not had forewarning from a very reliable source, for I had taken affectionate leave of his wife some hours previous. Stella Clithering and I enjoyed an arrangement of some duration, she being a ripe and ready jade some years her husband's junior. She informed me that Ted Enderby had made a bitter complaint to the council regarding shady practices in my establishment, and demanded I be shut down. She had urged her husband to spy out for himself how the land lay, then made haste to warn me of his plan.

On that night, he arrived around nine of the clock, leaving two men at arms concealed outside in the bushes. Even if I had not known his intentions, I would have guessed something afoot from his barely suppressed air of intrigue. I clapped him on the right shoulder by way of greeting, and as a signal to Beth that this was one of our privileged patrons. She applied herself to gently flattering him, and allowing him to win, little by little throughout the evening, a modest sum. It was difficult to accomplish, for he was an abominable player, but it had the desired effect of convincing him that the proceedings were honest, and he departed at midnight satisfied that he had done his duty. It was a bitter night, and Nancy Bell had done her part by delivering steaming mugs of sweet tea laced with butter and rum to the two men at arms, saying, wasn't it a pity that it was no longer safe for a gentleman to be abroad on his own.

Ted Enderby was discredited, and looked quite the fool. His dissipation increased until eventually he lost his livelihood, becoming ever more bitter and resentful. To my lasting regret, I had vastly underestimated the virulence of his enmity.

By this time my health was failing, and at times I was hardpressed to rouse myself for the evening's work. We had completed another unremarkable night, and I had just sunk gratefully into my bed when Rex began to bark urgently. As I roused myself and struggled into my clothing I became aware of an unusual glow, and could hear the frantic whinnying of Nicodemus in his stall. I soon saw that my gaming house was well aflame and the stables now threatened, and I ran to rescue Nicodemus. He was so panicked I had to blindfold him to calm him and move him away from the flames.

Billy Crake had been dossing down on the old workbench at night, but had escaped before the smoke overcame him, and with Beth and Nancy we quickly doused the end of the building nearest the house with buckets of water to prevent the further spread of the flames, but we could save little else. It was later reported that Ted Enderby had been seen in the area, but nothing could be proved. Our happy enterprise was at an end.

Thinking that we were secured for life, I had put nothing by. My black mood, along with my physical infirmities confined me to my bed, and I was forced at last to borrow against the house. My body was bloated, my joints were swollen, my hands shook, and I was bedevilled by lurid nightmares. Food was like a knife in my gut, and I could not even piss without crying out, a sad by-product of my amorous adventures and the poison employed to cure it. The doctor was useless, only shaking his head gravely, and I alternated between constant pain and the floating dream-world of opiates.

I thought it was a dream as well that I roused myself in the dark, one bitter, rainy January morning, dressed, wrapped up Old Nick, and made my way to what remained of the stables, for I was sure I heard music, the wild strains of "Fox Run" drifting down the river, and I felt a great urgency to discover the source. I somehow summoned up the strength to saddle Nicodemus, and, whistling up Rex, set off on one last ride.

It was Beth who found me, following the sound of Rex's howls. She had only discovered that I was not in my bed when Nicodemus returned, riderless, to the yard, and she set off on his back to seek me. She found me unconscious and sodden on the ground by the firepit of the long-abandoned Gypsy encampment, clutching Old Nick to my breast with faithful Rex by my side.

I spent several weeks hovering on the brink of death, suddenly awakening with vivid clarity only a fortnight ago. The pain still dogs me, but at some remove, and I will use this respite to fulfill my father's request, for I do not doubt my reprieve will be brief.

It is God's little joke that since the body which has always served me so well is failing, it is words that must serve me now. When I reflect I can see how I have spent much of my life railing against things I could not change; my mother's death, my father's part in it, the loss of Tess, the cruel accident that crippled me. If my father's account is true, my mother was the tragic victim of her own longing, and my father a man like any other man. No more can I blame Tess, for there are some things once said that cannot be unsaid—and why would she put her fate into the hands of a man who could summon up every foul phrase to call her a whore, but never one word to say he loved her?

Beth, you have always been a good and clever girl, and a better daughter than I have deserved. You could not have known the source of my discontent and your forgiveness is too much to ask for, but perhaps this account will offer you some understanding. I request one last thing of you, that you will say farewell to Jos for me, and deliver to him my horse Nicodemus and my old dog Rex. As the house is forfeit, my only legacies to you are this journal, my gold watch and Old Nick, my fiddle. I hope you will keep him safe by you for my sake. With your sharp wit and handsome appearance I know you will make your way in the world, and that you will provide me with a fitting epitaph.

I make no further excuses or apologies. My life has been a wild and glorious ride for the most part. Some might say I am taking the coward's way out, but my mind fails along with my body, and that I cannot bear. I must finally put a stop to the pain, and this endless bickering of voices in my head, and so I will say goodbye if not farewell.

Chapter 4

BETH JOYNER (1861–1944)

In the early hours of this morning, my father, Gerald Thomas
Joyner, died by his own hand. He was forty-eight. I can write no
more, for my hand shakes so that I can barely hold the pen, and
there is much to do.
—MARY ELIZABETH JOYNER, MARCH 15, 1882

FALLOWFIELD COTTAGE, DERBYSHIRE, 1917

There's a fine spray of blood, once red now rust, that lies over
my father's last words, taking me back to that night as clearly
as if it were yesterday. It was not until three years later when I was
secure in my own house that I could bring myself to read that page
again, as well as the others in this journal, and not until now, thirty
years later, that I've read them again to add my own story, for my
son, George, embarks on a new life in a new country, and this journal
will go with him.

The events surrounding my father's death are still etched in my memory. I recall that on the morning of the previous day a picture of the Mother and Child, which hung by the kitchen fire, fell with a great crash, and Nan said, "That means a death," but I thought little of it at the time, for she was given to these pronouncements. At dusk that evening a coven of noisy crows gathered in the trees at the end of the lane, and Rex, my father's dog, grew restless, wanting out, then in, then out again. When finally we refused to let him in again, he set up a howling in the yard, and Nan said we'd have to quiet him or we'd surely have words with the neighbours.

When I was awakened by the shot, my first thought was that it was some poacher come too near the house, and my second that it was Ted Enderby up to some further mischief, but it was too loud and too close, and I knew in my heart there was but one place the report could have come from. The means of my father's death was the small pistol that had rested on his desktop for as long as I could remember, and was the only gun he would have in the house. I'm sure his intention was a clean shot to the temple, but the weapon had lain so long unused that it had become corroded, and the barrel had burst, leaving little to recognize of that once-handsome face.

I fell into a faint, and came back to consciousness on my bed with Nan applying cold cloths to my forehead. Against her protests I returned to my father's room, for I'd seen my name in his handwriting on the last pages of the book by his bed, and knew I must read those final words. Nan had thrown a covering over him, and I sat by his shrouded body as I read, the metallic smell of his blood tainting the air.

Having taken in his instructions, I prepared to carry them out.

Nan, ever practical, said she wouldn't be shook from her know, and her know told her the bailiff would be in the house before my father's body was cold. I didn't argue, for she was more often right than wrong. I saddled Nicodemus, whistled up Rex, and we set off to find Jos Cooper, first to deliver the horse and dog as my father had wished, and second to seek his aid to save from the bailiff those few items of value we had left.

Jos in his sorrow remained a true friend. We returned to the house, and loaded his cart with my grandfather's books, notebooks and musical manuscripts, the little chest of valuables I'd collected during my brief career as a thief, and Old Nick in his domed casket, this journal and my father's gold watch stowed safely in the secret drawer. I insisted Jos have Grandda's fiddle, saying he would surely have wanted him to have it, and it would please me to think of him playing it. We shook on it, then he departed, saying he had a safe snug place to store our things 'til I should call for them. My final task was to inform Grandda Gabe and the rest of the family.

The word was well out by evening, and as predicted the bailiff appeared early the next morning. His name was Butcher, a stout amiable man, ill-suited to his unpleasant task. He said my old acquaintance, Mr. Clithering, had asked to be remembered to me, and instructed him to show the utmost kindness and courtesy in view of my bereavement. Nan established him in the kitchen with a mug of tea, some soda bread and our last bit of cheese, and they became quite cozy over the next few days.

As his death was kindly judged an accident rather than a suicide, my father was laid to rest beside his mother, father and infant sister in the churchyard at Saint Stephen. Sergeant Crake helped Grandda Gabe and the verger to dig the grave. He would leave right after the burial to go to his sister in Sheffield. Grandda Gabe had built the coffin, and would erect a simple stone inscribed with my father's name and the dates of his birth and death, also recording his passing in the family bible. Under the disapproving eye of Grandma Annie, he gave me a little purse, saying he hoped it would tide me over 'til I found my feet, and that I would turn to him if I were in difficulty.

There were more mourners than expected given my father's reputation. All the Treadwells, my great-aunt Clare, Jos Cooper and his family, and Aunt Emma Skelton with her husband and two daughters, attended, but none excepting the Skeltons came back to the house, I suspect not wishing to embarrass me that there was no food or drink on offer. Aunt Emma claimed there were still things of her mother's she was entitled to, and I told her she was free to battle with the bailiff. She greedily eyed my only piece of jewellery, Grandma Jean's little gold-set cameo that Grandda had given me, but stopped short of demanding it. The mother and two daughters were stuffed like sausages into their sombre silk dresses, and Nan declared she was reminded of the words from the psalms about "people enclosed in their own fat." They bustled off to see what they could scrounge, leaving me in the parlour with the Reverend Skelton.

He immediately moved to my side, and placed a moist hand on my knee, declaring that he grieved with me for my loss, and felt it his Christian duty to offer me refuge in his household. He said I'd be a great help to my aunt Emma now that the girls were married, and that after a suitable time of mourning, during which any gossip about my reputation might die down, he'd find me a respectable man to marry. His meaning was clear enough. At twenty he considered me an old maid with no protector, no prospects, and in no position to bargain. At best I'd be an unpaid servant in his house, at worst I would be at his mercy, and I resolved that I'd sooner cut my own throat than spend one night under his roof. Mastering my temper, I said sweetly that although I was grateful for his generous offer, I had a kind lady patron who had found me a nursemaid's position, and I would take this opportunity to make my own way, that being the only lie I could conjure up at the time. He reluctantly removed his hand, shouted up his wife and daughters, and they departed, triumphantly carrying off some kitchen cutlery, the old flowered carpet from the parlour and the threadbare quilt from my bed.

The question of my future was troubling. I turned to Nan for advice.

"Of course, we must go to London and see your mother. She will know what to do," she said, but I move too far ahead in my story, and must go back to the beginning.

My earliest memory is from the age of two. Grandda had taken me to visit Great-grandma and Great-grandda Joyner, at their little cottage. It was a hot summer afternoon, the trees heavy with apples, the air smelling of windfalls and new-mown hay. We sat out of doors with the bees buzzing drunkenly around us, and Great-grandda, nearly blind and confined to a chair with rheumatism in his hips, raised Old Nick and began to play.

I've never been able to keep my feet still when there is music, and this music was magical, starting off slowly then moving faster and faster to end in a long, sweeping flourish. I started to dance in my childish way, spinning like a top, to finally collapse in a heap, dizzy and breathless. Everyone was laughing, and I was the happy centre of their attention. We heard a loud clattering of pots from the kitchen, and I remember Great-grandda saying it was Aunt Clare showing her disapproval, and that she could never tolerate anyone having a good time, especially on a Sunday. Great-grandma hugged and kissed me, and gave me barley sugar to take home. Great-grandda died not long after that.

My father is still the handsomest man I have ever seen. Even today my judgment of a man's appearance is influenced by my memory of him in his prime. My son George is very like him in appearance as well as nature. Much has been said in these pages of my feelings toward him. I can't truly say that I loved him, for love should be mutual, but I was deeply fascinated by him. My childish attempts to amuse him were simply to make him smile, for when he did, his face would soften and lighten as if there were a sun inside him struggling to shine out. I came to think of him as Lucifer, the dark angel. Romantic nonsense, I know, but it was how I felt.

"That's what comes of reading bad poetry," my grandda would have said. He could disassemble a piece of ill-constructed writing as easily as an ill-constructed chair, though the chair was generally the better for it. I spent many hours with him in his workshop where he would patiently explain to me whatever he was doing, from carving a piece of intricate inlay, to plotting the inner workings of a lock or a clock, to adding up the lines of figures in his ledgers, or transcribing a new piece of music, and in the evenings by the kitchen fire he would play the fiddle or read to me. I grew accustomed to running to his apothecary cupboard to fetch whatever he needed to treat a colicky baby or a broken bone. He taught me to love books and words and music, to trust my own eyes and ears, and not to be blinded by sentimentality which he said was a sad substitute for true emotion. I agree, although I admit to a perverse taste for it which I try to confine to popular songs and novels. My favourite books were *Pride and Prejudice* and *Jane Eyre*, both of which I read many times and at much too early an age. Heathcliff was too like my father for me to embrace the gothic gloom of *Wuthering Heights*. I also adored Lewis Carroll's *Alice*, with whom I felt a great kinship regarding the incomprehensibility of adult behaviour.

Neither my father nor Nan ever spoke of my mother, and Grandda knew as little as I, or I'm sure he'd have told me. I had all sorts of fancies about her, that she'd died in some tragic way, or that she was some grand lady and I was her dark secret; odd how close that was to the truth. I suppose I didn't really miss her, because I had Nan.

Nan, like the air I breathe, has always been there, nurse and mother, friend and confidante, and for a time I chose to believe she was my mother. In appearance she is a portrait of nature, with apple cheeks, periwinkle eyes and wheat-gold hair now gone silver.

I can always count on her to take me down a peg or two with a bit of her homespun wisdom whenever I get too far above myself. As the youngest of a large family, I was last in line for my cousins' cast-offs. Nan was a fine cook and housekeeper, but an indifferent seamstress, and took little interest in appearances so long as I was neatly and cleanly dressed. I therefore eagerly devoured every description of the ladies' dresses in my books, and have an abiding passion for elegant clothing.

Although the Bible was my first schoolbook, we didn't regularly attend Saint Stephen, as no clergyman could ever measure up to Father Basil in Grandda's estimation, but we appeared at Christmas and Easter services, the Saint Stephen's Day celebration, and the endless marriages, christenings and burials of the Treadwell family. I had a special fondness for Great-grandda's carving of Saint Nicholas, which differed from the head of Old Nick only in that there was the barest hint of a smile about the mouth.

By the time I was five, it had been announced that the new railroad would bypass Kingsfold to cross the river at Fenton-on-Bliss. Grandda Gabe and Roland were among the builders who constructed the new bridge and train station. With its completion, the number of horse-drawn coaches on the old London–Southampton road slowed to a trickle, the contents mainly goods rather than passengers. Many of the merchants and tradesmen had already removed to Fenton, and market day was a much smaller, more local affair than in my great-grandma's time. The village was settling into becoming the quiet backwater it remains today.

With the railway came London's newly rich seeking property for country homes, and my grandda and grandda Gabe were very much in demand for the building, finishing and furnishing of them, so although we lived simply, we were quite prosperous. It wasn't 'til after Grandda died that I had any notion of what it was like to be poor.

It was always feast or famine with my father. When he had money it flowed through his fingers like water. When he didn't, he would roll through the house like a thundercloud until he subsided into melancholy and withdrew to his room. When he emerged, weeks later, haggard and unshaven, there would be a certain glint in his eye, and within days, he would be his old confident self, handsome and vital and ready for some new venture. The source of his income was a mystery to me until, when I was nine, he decided I should join him. I didn't know what to make of his suddenly eyeing me as if I were some promising piece of horseflesh, but I was a willing recruit. I gloried in the freedom of my boy's clothing, and the memory of those midnight rides still thrills me, clinging to his waist, my face buried in his back, the feel and the smell of him as we galloped through the darkness.

He'd instruct me how to enter a premises and where to admit him. How he came by this intelligence I don't know, though I once overheard Nan in the kitchen with cousin Gracie refer to him as "the housemaid's dream," and even at that age I had no doubt as to her meaning. I'd first find some small safe place to hide should our presence be discovered, then admit my father, and as he went about his business, I'd scout the parlour and dining room for some small valuable object like a silver snuff box or card case which I could conceal in the back waistband of my trousers, for if my father detected anything, he'd have it from me. Although their value was not great, I loved glass paperweights, and if I saw a pretty one, I'd have to have it. My greatest prize was a set of silver apostle spoons. I also stole books for Grandda, for my father took no notice of them. Grandda's favourite was Jonathan Swift's *Travels into Several Remote Nations of the World*, but he was tolerant and quite humorous about what he considered my more inferior acquisitions such as *The Poetical Works of Mrs. Hemans*. Between my ninth and twelfth birthdays we robbed at least two dozen houses. Grandda made me a little wooden chest for my treasures, which we concealed under a false floor in the linen cupboard.

Grandda's death was not unexpected. He'd complained for days of tiredness, shortness of breath, and pain and tightness in his chest, and none of his usual remedies brought him relief. It was his habit to work late into the night, and sleep on a pallet on the floor of his workshop rather than disturb the house in the early hours. It was there that Nan found him, and she said he had such a look of peace on his face, it was as if the weight of years had been lifted from him.

I was inconsolable, holding his hand, weeping and rocking by his side until Nan pulled me away. My father disappeared, leaving Nan and me to inform the family and deal with the arrangements. This, however, allowed me to hide the most treasured of Grandda's belongings, for once it occurred to him, I knew my father would sell the lot.

I remember little of the day of the funeral. Grandda Gabe, looking suddenly very old, had chiselled the year in the allotted space on the stone where Grandda had carved his own name and the date of his birth beside my grandmother's so many years ago. My father appeared very late, and hung back in the crowd like some curious bystander.

I couldn't bear it when Cousin Roland came to empty the workshop. My father made little difficulty about the tools and the woodworking ledgers as they were of no value to him, but the large store of fine woods in the seasoning shed was another matter, and he told Roland he'd have to pay or it would be used for firewood. I think Roland was prepared for some such demand, for he gave my father cash on the spot and left with everything.

I became like a ghost in the house, wandering from room to room, barely eating what Nan put in front of me, automatically carrying out my household duties. Because Grandda had left a little money, and there were several pieces of good furniture to be sold, my father did not immediately intrude upon my grief, but I had little doubt that before long I'd be donning my trousers and blacking my face again.

Fate, however, intervened in a most cruel way.

I was then in my fourteenth year, and was out early, feeding the hens, gathering the eggs, and conducting my morning duel with the rooster who considered it his duty to attack my ankles with a great cackling and flapping of wings. It was a daily dance with us.

My father had been absent overnight, which was not unusual. It was unusual, however, to see Grandda Gabe and Roland pull up to the kitchen door, as their relations with my father were less than cordial. I happily ran to greet them, but as I drew closer, I could see their faces were very grave, and Grandda Gabe said I must prepare myself for a great shock. Roland pulled back the corner of a canvas in the back of the cart to reveal my father's face, very pinched and grey. I first thought he was dead, but he stirred and groaned. Roland pulled back the covering further to reveal my father's left leg, wrapped in bloody bandages and resting in a sort of shallow wooden trough they had devised to prevent it from being jarred by the motion of the cart. I cried out for Nan, and the four of us transported him to his bedroom on an improvised litter.

Grandda Gabe reported that Wilkins, the poacher, had come pounding at the door in the early hours of the morning. They carried my father into the kitchen of the old house and laid him out on the table 'til the doctor should come. He was delirious with pain, and fighting them the whole time, but the doctor quieted him with a dose of opium.

The news was bad. At best he would walk with a crutch or cane for the rest of his life, and if infection set in he might well lose the leg altogether. Roland gave me a little pot of the opium, saying that the doctor had recommended my father take it twice a day in sweet tea to mask the bitter taste. Grandda Gabe and he then departed, saying they would return to help with the chores, and that Gracie would come by whenever she could.

My father's convalescence was hell on earth for all concerned, for he was an impossible invalid, fighting every attempt to aid him and railing against the fates for bringing him to this sorry pass. He spat out the tea and demanded real drink, which I believe he truly needed for he'd never in my memory passed a day without it. Our solution was to dose him three times a day with opium-laced rum, as this brought some measure of relief for him and some respite for us. I searched my grandfather's apothecary cupboard and found enough of the substance there to see him through the worst of the pain, for what the doctor had provided lasted barely three days. One of Jos Cooper's old aunties provided a further supply, and once the poppies had budded, I manufactured more from the instructions in Grandda's notes. I blame myself for my father's addiction. It was easier to keep him in a dreamlike state than to wrestle with him when he struggled to get out of bed in search of spirits, damaging his leg further in the effort. Gracie's visits were a blessing, as at first he sweated copiously with fever, and Nan and I alone could not move him to change the bed linen. By some miracle there was little infection.

It was some three or four months later that he was finally able to move about, aided by a stick Grandda Gabe had carved out of a stout tree branch. He used it 'til the day he died, when I packed it away with my other belongings, and I have it still.

My father might have gone mad altogether and us along with him if Jos had not come calling with his mandolin, coaxing him to play all the old tunes. This allowed me to commit to paper several of his compositions, including his favourite, "Joyner's Dream," which, in the absence of any other likeness, always brings him back to me. He slept much better on those nights, and was more calm in his manner, but the true turning point was when Jos delivered Nicodemus, for he became my father's legs. I'd always hated Ulysses, an

evil-natured beast whom none but my father could approach. Nicodemus was as even- and sweet-tempered as Ulysses was intractable,
and I never had an uneasy moment when my father was abroad on
his back.

With our former activities at an end, and my father showing
no sign of seeking an alternative, we soon found ourselves in tight
circumstances, but poverty in the country is not such a terrible state,
for at least one doesn't starve or lack for firewood. We had chickens
and eggs, milk from our old cow, and vegetables from the garden.
Nan assisted Gracie at the market once a week, and would return
with flour, cheese, honey and other necessities. Jos would fall by with
a rabbit or duck or fresh-caught fish, all cleaned and dressed. In season, there were fruits and berries, and we would put up preserves to
store in the cellar with the apples and root vegetables for the winter.
Nan had a little money put by, and we might have gone on in this
way almost indefinitely, but our lives were to take yet another turn.

Shortly before my fifteenth birthday, Nan left for her annual
journey to London. All I knew of these trips was that she stayed with
an aunt and uncle who owned the small hotel where Nan had been
employed as a maid before delivering me to Kingsfold. She always
returned with a gift for me. On this occasion it was my very first
new dress, and what a dress it was, two pieces with a full skirt and a
jacket with boned bodice, jet buttons up the front, jet trimmings at
the neck and sleeves, and made of the most beautiful russet velvet. I'd
filled out considerably that year, and was not yet comfortable with
my bosom and hips, but the dress changed that. Nan pinned up my
hair in a sort of topknot, and I looked like a real lady. I ran proudly
to show my father.

The last time he'd examined me in such a speculative manner,
I'd become a thief's apprentice, and so my exuberance was quickly
tempered with some reservation. He said nothing, but was in a most
pensive mood for the rest of the day, and that evening mounted

Nicodemus and rode off with a great air of purpose. He returned at breakfast in the company of a young man he introduced as Julian Bendick. The introduction was typical of him.

"Beth, my girl, this is Mr. Bendick. He is to be your tutor. I think I may say this is an important step in your practical education."

He then left Mr. Bendick and me to take the measure of each other. I now realize that Julian could not have been much more than twenty at the time, though he seemed much older, with an air of world-weariness and sophistication. He was the antithesis of my father, for he was well spoken and fine-featured, with silky blond hair, grey eyes and a slim physique. If he was a little short in stature it didn't matter, for I myself was never to exceed five foot. His clothes were not new, but of stylish cut and good cloth, and he presented a most romantic figure to an impressionable young girl.

My father's intention was to make a gambling establishment of Grandda's workshop, and Julian, having perfected his cardsharping abilities through three public schools and two failed years of university, was to be his dealer. I would be schooled to preside over a second table, and a third table for dice would be manned by my father. Julian's gentlemanly appearance served us well. He was expert at identifying local sports with money in their pockets, striking up an acquaintance and steering them to our tables. They naively saw him as being of their own class and therefore trustworthy. He was an accomplished cardsharp but extremely lazy, for he'd sooner use marked cards than depend on his mental or manual dexterity, and a marked deck was seldom in play for more than an hour before some suspicious player would demand fresh cards.

I spent most mornings perfecting my new skills, and soon mastered all the games and most of Julian's tricks, shuffling and manipulating the cards with ease, but I was never able to properly palm cards, for although I had inherited my grandfather's clever hands, mine were small like those of a child, and the cards too large. Julian

warned that seasoned gamblers were suspicious of everyone, and
would be on the watch for any chicanery. I learned to create diver-
sions, and to employ the sleeves of my dress, keeping my hands in
full sight, but what eventually served me best was an infallible memory for cards played and an instinctive grasp of odds. One simple
tool that aided me during this time was a mug of black tea, not to
drink, but to reflect on its surface the identity of cards dealt over it.

My father's contention was that a pretty young face and figure would serve to distract all but the most dedicated gamblers, and
he further improved the house's chances by providing a moderate
amount of food and a great deal of drink. He called it a gentlemen's
club, and charged the members a small monthly fee, reasoning that
this not only defrayed his expenses, but also kept out the riff-raff and
deflected the attention of the authorities. He hired Billy Crake as a
sergeant-at-arms, and to help with any heavy work, which was just
as well, for Julian, having been born proud, was useless about the
house, always assuming that Nan or I should bring him this or that,
and complaining if he were so much as asked to fetch firewood, and
he was terrified at any hint of violence.

Let me make it clear that what transpired between Julian and
myself was initiated as well as terminated by me.

I'd grown up close enough to the farmyard to be familiar with
the simple act of procreation. What I did not understand was what
happened between a man and a woman to inspire the romantic stories and poems I so dearly loved to read, and my curiosity overtook
me. I'd shunned the clumsy advances of local boys, but took Julian's
languid form of speech and manner to be the earmarks of a gentleman, and chose him to initiate me into the mysteries of adult inter-
course. The clandestine nature of our trysts seemed at first romantic
and exciting, but in truth I was soon heartily tired of Mr. Bendick,
for the perfunctory nature of his lovemaking was a great disappointment and I was fast coming to the conclusion that the flowery poetry

I so admired was little more than a blandishment invented by men to convince women to lie with them, much in the way that the peacocks at the Willows puffed themselves up and spread their tail feathers for the hens.

Nan had never taken to Julian, saying she had more use for his room than his company. She was therefore satisfactorily alarmed when I tearfully revealed I'd been taken advantage of. She informed my father, who threw Julian out of the house with some explicit threats as to what would happen to his jewels should he show his face again, and that was the end of that.

I became very popular among our "gentlemen" but felt safe under the watchful eyes of dear Sergeant Crake who had appointed himself my personal protector. The signals we established became second nature, and if I detected a malcontent, a cheat or a knee pressed to mine, I had only to give a nod, and the gentleman in question would become aware of the hulking figure of the sergeant at his shoulder. Committed gamblers appeared most nights, while others favoured a particular night to gather with comrades, as many of our gentlemen preferred to fraternize with their own class. My talent for mimicry was useful there, for I easily slipped into any manner of speech.

Jos and my father would often resin up and play rollicking dance tunes, and it became a gathering place for musicians. One of our gentlemen had a fine tenor voice, and another a passable baritone. I was easily persuaded to sing as well. My own taste was for love songs and sad ballads, but the favourites in the house were those with comic verses like "The Drunkard's Prayer," or the naughty lyrics of "My Darling Evelynda":

> *I'll set a course so straight and true*
> *Nor wind nor waves can hinder*
> *My harbour lies between the thighs*
> *Of my darling Evelynda*

Wouldn't some of the good people who know me now be shocked to hear that?

Grandda's lessons in musical notation became useful when my father acquired a handsome pianoforte as payment for gambling debts, and similarly engaged a local music master to instruct me. I found I had some natural ability for it, and with practice was soon able to provide modest accompaniment.

Any childish awe or admiration for my father had long since faded into an amused and tolerant resignation. I had moreover learned to assert myself, being after all my father's daughter. My lovely dress had barely survived six months of constant wear as the velvet became permeated with sweat and tobacco smoke, the stitches would no longer hold, and the sleeves grew worn from constant rubbing against the table. I confronted my father about money for clothing, arguing that my appearance was critical to the success of his enterprise. None of what was generated at the table came to Nan or me beyond what was absolutely necessary for the household, and my father was not easily persuaded, but finally relented. I engaged a dressmaker to make two serviceable serge skirts in dove grey and moss green with matching jackets after the style of Queen Victoria, trimmed with black braid, and also a half-dozen modest blouses of fine Indian cotton with tucked fronts and lace insets. The dressmaker protested that the cut wasn't fashionable and the colours were too drab for one so young, but practicality prevailed.

So life continued until the dreadful fire, which consumed all my father's hopes and schemes, along with my lovely pianoforte. He went into permanent decline, the fact of his disability being compounded by the effects of habitual drink, addiction to opiates, and syphilis. His features and figure had grossly coarsened, and his temper grew even more uncertain. Toward the end, he was barely able to rise from his bed to relieve himself, and slept much of the time.

It's always been my greatest fear that I would inherit my father's demons. I've shunned alcohol and maintained an iron grip on my emotions, and I believe my efforts have been successful, though Nan says I sometimes go broody and can't be reasoned with. I feel, however, that this has prevented me from experiencing fully the deeper feelings, and in this way, my father rules me still. I believe too it has caused me to be unsympathetic toward my son, George, when he exhibits any signs of my father's weaknesses.

I am firm in the belief that my father's suicide was his second attempt, and that the first took place on a bitter cold, rainy morning early that same year. I was the first awake, and had gone to the kitchen to build up the fire and put on the kettle. I saw from the window that Nicodemus, fully saddled with his head and reins hanging down, stood wet and shivering in the icy yard. In my father's room, I found signs of violent activity, bedcovers on the floor, a chair overturned, cupboards and drawers gaping open, and Old Nick's casket empty, but no sign of my father. Nan and I searched the yard and the ruins of the stables with no result. We tried to imagine where his tortured mind would take him, and concluded he would either have gone to town in search of drink, or to seek out Jos Cooper. Praying the latter was the case, I mounted Nicodemus, and set off for the Willows. I was riding along the riverbank when I heard Rex's deep-throated baying, and followed the sound to the old Gypsy encampment, where I found my father lying soaked and still on the ground, the faithful old dog close by him, and Old Nick, miraculously undamaged, clutched to his breast under his cloak. Having determined that his heart was still beating, I rode on to seek Jos, and we brought him home.

He was delirious with a raging fever and chills, hanging between life and death for some weeks. I was finally heartened to see him rally, weak but clear-eyed, as the first signs of spring appeared. His ordeal seemed to have left him more peaceful and thoughtful, and I had hopes that our lives might change for the better, but it is here that I must return to the beginning of my story, and my account of his death.

"Of course we must go to London and see your mother. She will know what to do," Nan had said.

I cannot describe my confusion, for I'd thought myself an orphan. Nan said we were all orphans if we lived long enough, but it hadn't come to that. She then revealed my mother's identity, defending her long silence and saying it must remain the deepest of secrets. I was first angry, then had a flood of questions, but Nan put an end to any further talk, saying we must prepare to leave at once. We'd already received the order to vacate and what contents remained in the house were shortly to be sold at auction. She packed our clothing in my father's old carpetbag under the watchful eye of Butcher the bailiff, while I retrieved from Jos some items from my little chest of treasures. Grandda Gabe's money would get us to London, but we'd have nothing to sustain us once there. I intended to make the Barkers' pawnshop my first destination.

Cousin Roland kindly drove us to the train station in Fenton, and he and Gracie saw us off. It saddened me to leave behind all that was familiar, but I looked forward to the adventure with great anticipation.

It was my first train journey, and I don't recall it with any pleasure, for we were crowded into a steaming, airless carriage with rude men, and harried women with screaming children, all with more bundles and baskets than they could possibly manage, and all jostling for more room. Nan and I managed to squeeze ourselves into a seat, bumping knees with a garrulous and deaf old woman and an enormous man who reeked of drink and snuff, and constantly hawked and spat into a cup. I suppose we should have been grateful for his fastidiousness. Other than the deafening noise of the wheels and the rocking of the carriage, I had no real sense of travelling from one place to another, for the steam on the windows obscured the view.

After seemingly endless stops and starts we finally emerged into the grey drizzle of our first afternoon in London, rumpled and cross, and covered in soot and cinders.

Nor was my first view of London promising, and I have since had little reason to alter my opinion. The sheer weight of humanity was overwhelming, and as Nan said, they all looked like they were going home to murder somebody. We had no money to waste on a carriage and were obliged to walk to the hotel in the rain, our heavy carpetbag between us growing heavier by the minute. We must have presented quite a sight to Nan's aunt Eva as we stood dispirited and dripping on the flagstones of her spotless kitchen floor.

It was called Graham's Hotel, a modest establishment serving mainly commercial travellers. Eva's husband, Bert Graham, had inherited it from his father. He'd started there as a boot boy, knew the running of it from the bottom up, and had met and married Eva when she was employed there as a cook. We were installed in the box room that was Nan's room when she visited. As it was past midday and the travellers off about their business, I luxuriated for the better part of an hour in the big high-backed tin bath. It was a great improvement on the wooden tub and dipper we'd had in the kitchen at home, and created in me an enduring love for long hot soaks. Restored, I joined Nan and Eva for a substantial tea in the kitchen.

Eva knew all about me and my mother, although the origin of that knowledge was not then revealed. Nan insisted we go to my mother's house and present ourselves at the kitchen door as she had always done, but I wished to exercise some tact, as I doubted Lady Blackwood would take kindly to the unannounced appearance of an illegitimate daughter. I laboured over my brief missive well into the evening, trying to strike a balance between my desperate desire to see her, and my fear that she might not wish to know me. It was addressed to Lady Teresa Blackwood, Windward House, 10 Covington Square.

Dear Madam,

*I regret to inform you of the tragic death of my father, Gerald
Thomas Joyner, and to further inform you that I am presently
residing at Graham's Hotel on Sutton Street should you wish to
contact me.*

Respectfully yours,
Mary Elizabeth Joyner

Despite her protests, I made Nan promise that she would simply deliver the note.

I next sought out the Barkers. I'd assumed their shop would be
a shabby affair on some squalid side street, but was surprised to discover an elegant facade on a busy thoroughfare with gold lettering
proclaiming that it was "Barker and Son, Fine Silver." I entered,
introduced myself, and enquired for Mr. Victor or Mr. Adam Barker,
only to be told by the rather superior-looking clerk that Mr. Victor
was deceased, and that Mr. Adam was presently attending an auction
in Edinburgh. He asked doubtfully if there were anyone else who
could assist me. I then asked for Miss Sarah Barker, and was told
that I must mean Mrs. Green. He sent to the back of the shop a boy
who returned and whispered in his ear. The clerk gave me a rather
startled look, then ushered me through a baize-covered door into a
crowded office, and announced me to a formidable lady seated at a
cluttered rolltop desk.

She'd have been just under forty then, tall and severely featured,
with piercing blue eyes, and dressed in black from head to toe, her
fair hair covered with heavy netting. Her only adornment was a gold
wedding band, and a jeweller's loupe on a black cord around her
neck. I boldly informed her that I was the daughter of the late Gerald Joyner and that I had reason to believe she had some knowledge

and acquaintance of my family. She stiffened slightly, then asked in her deep voice what she might do for me. Sensing this was a ticklish situation, I said that following my father's death I'd found myself in a delicate position, and was obliged to sell some valuable items I had in my possession. She softened slightly toward me, and I wondered if this were another of my father's conquests.

But she surprised me by saying,"Your father was a very hard man. It cannot have been easy being his daughter."

In that moment was born a recognition and kinship between us, which we share to this day, and I have often had reason to be grateful for her friendship and advice.

She asked if I'd care to take a cup of tea in her private room above. We mounted the narrow steps to an airy whitewashed chamber in marked contrast to the dark crowded premises below. We sat in a bay window overlooking the street, and in the hour that followed, I opened my heart to her and she to me, for surprisingly we had much in common.

She recounted to me the days when she, only sixteen, was left on her own for weeks at a time to run the shop and bargain with the dregs of society for their ill-gotten goods, and how her father in death had overlooked her to leave everything to her brother, Adam. If she had not married, she said, she'd have been left dependent on her brother's dubious charity.

As for my treasures, she told me that largely through her efforts Barker and Son was now a legitimate enterprise, and the provenance of my items less than savoury, but that she still had a few contacts from the old days and would see what she could do. She took what I had on offer with the exception of two miniatures painted on ivory, which I had taken because the lady looked a little like me, and the gentleman reminded me of my grandfather. She said they were of negligible value and I might as well keep them. They served in my subsequent life as portraits of my parents, and are still on display in my sitting room. The advance she offered was most welcome, for Nan and I were nearly at the end of our meagre resources.

Our meeting had taken up most of the morning, and I hurried back to Graham's to be greeted by Nan with an envelope in rich vellum, sealed with an imposing crest. I tore it open to read that Lady Blackwood would be pleased to receive Miss Elizabeth Joyner at Windward House for tea at four o'clock the following afternoon.

I presented myself at the front door of Windward House just as some church bell sounded four. I was dressed in my carefully brushed and pressed moss-coloured serge with much-mended gloves and a hat borrowed from Eva Graham, my heart beating as though it would jump from my breast. It was not the grand mansion I had envisioned, but one of a row of handsome Regency fronts situated on a quiet, tree-shaded cul-de-sac. The bell was answered by a neat young parlourmaid who curtsied and conducted me down the marble-floored hallway and through the door of a lovely golden sitting room with glass-paned doors overlooking a sunlit garden.

At first I couldn't see the lady properly, for the sun was at her back, but as I drew closer we were both struck speechless, for standing opposite her was like standing before an antique mirror in which the silvering has become a little seamed and tarnished. Our colouring was different, to be sure. Her hair had by then faded to ginger with wings of silver, but our faces and figures were almost identical. She was dressed simply but elegantly in indigo silk, with a single large pearl set in gold and sapphires at her throat. I could feel tears welling up, and sensed that she struggled as well. Just then, the parlour-maid entered with a tea trolley. My mother dismissed her, saying she would serve the tea herself.

Alone again, we fell into a long tearful embrace, and tea was ignored as we sat knee-to-knee holding hands, our words falling over each other. She knew of my childhood from Nan's yearly reports, but it was for me to tell her of my father's last days and his sad end. She listened in silence, the tears falling unchecked, occasionally shaking her head as if to throw off her grief. There was no doubt she had loved my father truly and deeply, and that she loved him still.

She said she had sometimes thought to remove me to a better situation, but was reassured by the bond I'd formed with my grandfather. I learned that I had three half-brothers, the eldest, Alex, following in his father's footsteps, the second, Peter, a quiet and bookish schoolboy, and the third, Elliot, still too young to have revealed much of his nature. As much as she loved them, she saw little of herself in them, and this made my appearance all the more miraculous. We engaged from that first day in the free and open communication which we still share.

As we bade goodbye, she removed a little ruby ring from her finger and slipped it onto mine, saying my father had had a great fondness for rubies. We would meet the following morning at her dressmaker's establishment where a private salon was available. With my head in the clouds and my feet barely touching the ground I entered my mother's carriage and returned to Graham's, to discover that a room had been engaged for me. Nan insisted on warm milk and a long nap, so I gratefully retired to the comfort of my new bed.

Madame Felice was the name of my mother's dressmaker, but her true name was Fanny Gosling, a Londoner through and through. My mother said she had no need to look to Paris so long as she had Fanny, and it was clear that there was a strong affection between them. In appearance she was like a pouter pigeon, dressed in shades of grey, clucking and cooing, her imposing bosom preceding her everywhere. She had a small neat head with piercing dark eyes, which gave the impression of missing nothing. It was she who had created my mother's wedding dress, and as I later discovered, also my beloved russet velvet. She seemed to take an almost motherly interest in her ladies, and to my puzzlement said she was delighted to see me again.

The first order of business was to measure me. For the present I was to have three summer dresses, two for daytime wear and one for evening, with all the appropriate undergarments and accessories. Fanny said my mother's dress form would do nicely, and the two of them had a long and heated discussion regarding fabrics, colour, cut and trim. A shoemaker was brought in to create a last, and I was assured that I would have two new pairs of shoes within the week. There was a discussion about corsets and hairdressing, and some illustrated ladies' magazines were produced to inspire us. It was like a dream.

A basket was brought in from my mother's carriage for an elegant picnic; paper-thin slices of duck and ham, Stilton cheese and lovely soft bread with a buttery crust, and at the end a fruit compote spooned over cake and laced with some kind of cordial that made me quite giddy. It took two cups of tea to clear my head so that I could fully absorb my mother's story.

I will not repeat here my mother's version of her liaison with my father, for although it was a revelation to me at the time, it doesn't substantially differ from my father's account in these pages. What was paramount to me was her story of my own beginnings.

After their bitter parting she had left the Skeddings and Belfountain for her husband's, Commander Blackwood's, house in London, the very one where I had met her on the previous day. She was with child, friendless, and aside from her husband and two younger brothers, had no family or influence. In her despair she had turned to the only person in London who had shown her compassion, Fanny Gosling, the little dressmaker who had dried her tears on the eve of her wedding. Fanny became her saviour, wasting no time on recriminations, and telling her not to fret, for she would arrange everything. She had a discreet word with her neighbour, Eva Graham, about a room for my mother's lying-in, and found a midwife to attend her. My mother spent the last two weeks of her pregnancy as Mrs. Edson at Graham's Hotel.

It was an easy delivery, for though healthy, I was very small. The question of my future weighed heavily on her, and she was almost at her wits' end when an answer appeared in the person of Nancy Bell.

Nan had come in from the country at seventeen to help her aunt Eva as a maid of all work at Graham's Hotel. She had been easily taken advantage of by a young army officer who seduced her with declarations of love and the promise of marriage. When she told him she was carrying a child, he had denied it was his, calling her a schemer and a whore. Her uncle Bert had gone to the young man's superior officer to demand that things be put right, but the man responded rudely, saying Nan would be lucky to get twenty pounds for her trouble and he would not see the career of a promising young officer compromised by some scullery maid. This might have been the end of the affair, excepting the young man in question, embarrassed in the eyes of his superior, had lured Nan to a meeting with the promise of a reconciliation, and enlisted two of his fellow officers to give her a vicious beating. She was then in the seventh month of her pregnancy, and nearly lost her life. The child, a girl she named Angel, was later born cruelly deformed, and died within an hour of struggling for her first breath.

My mother became aware of Nan as a silent figure who slipped in and out of her room carrying out various housekeeping tasks, but had taken little notice of her until she found her weeping over me in my basket, the front of her blouse stained with the milk from her breasts. She sat her down, and had the whole dreadful story from her. In this moment she conceived what she believed to be an inspired solution to both their dilemmas.

She hired Nan as a wet nurse, and, having nearly recovered her strength, returned to Windward House to await her husband's imminent return.

She would approach the young man's commanding officer with what she called a bit of benevolent blackmail, saying that she, Lady

Blackwood, had a special interest in the welfare of a certain Miss Nancy Bell whom she knew to have been cruelly used by one of his men, and that restitution must be made. She stressed that the young man should consider himself lucky that she had not as yet publicly exposed his criminal behaviour in the matter of the beating, and she trusted disciplinary action would be taken. If two hundred pounds for the support of the mother and child were delivered to her at Windward House, she would pursue it no further.

This sum, promptly delivered, financed the journey of Nan and my infant self to Kingsfold, and paid Nan's salary and my upkeep until such time as my mother's inheritance was realized, and she could assume the full burden herself.

Of her subsequent life she said little save that she believed she had otherwise been an exemplary wife and mother. Commander Blackwood, now Admiral Blackwood, retired, spent most of his time at their country estate in Derbyshire writing his memoirs. The three boys were at school for the greater part of the year, spending the summers in the country where she would join them. She said that as much as she enjoyed the freedom of her life in London and her busy social calendar, she had for some time been finding little satisfaction or purpose in what she did, and that she had now found this purpose in me, her only daughter.

We then discussed what would become of me. She said she had hoped to elevate me socially, but that my strong country accent was a serious impediment. I'd become so easy with her that I'd unconsciously fallen into my accustomed manner of speech. I replied in her own light musical drawl that she needn't concern herself in that regard, as I had some talent for accommodation. She laughed that tinkling laugh my father has described.

"Well, well, my girl, I think you'll do very nicely. There is an old friend I should like you to meet. I think he'll find you both amusing and challenging."

There was still the problem of my parentage. She had thought to introduce me as the daughter of an old school friend, but clearly our resemblance suggested some family connection, and so I became Elizabeth Brightly, the orphaned daughter of a distant cousin, and she would be my aunt Tess.

Nan had settled in at Graham's, helping Eva in the kitchen and taking over the serving of meals. Eva was glad of the help, as she said that many of the young girls now had factory jobs, and turned up their noses at the wages and hours she offered. I enjoyed their gentle gossip after supper in the kitchen, but was happy to gain the solitude of my room to ponder the extraordinary change in my circumstances.

The next days were taken up with fittings for my dresses, and learning how to walk in my new shoes with their little raised heels. I received a note from Sarah Green saying she had news for me, so I made my way once more to Barker and Son in one of my new dresses, this time being ushered through with some deference on the part of the clerk. Over tea I regaled her with the astonishing events that had unfolded. She said she was pleased to augment my good fortune with the princely sum of seventy-two pounds over and above her advance, and despite my urging would take no recompense. She suggested that I leave some of the money with her so that she could invest it for me, saying it was risky to keep such an amount about my person, and I needed to look to the future. I wisely agreed, and this sum was the beginning of savings and investments that would later sustain me through a time of great need.

It was almost a week later that my mother and I kept an appointment at the Cleary Academy for Young Ladies. Anthony Cleary was the old friend she had mentioned, an elegant bachelor of about fifty, with impeccable social credentials and a prestigious address, but meagre means. He was, however, much in demand as a respectable companion for unescorted ladies who wished to attend the many dinners, balls and evenings at the theatre during the season, which was how my mother had met him. They shared a sardonic wit, a love for gossip and a contempt for intellectual and social poseurs, and so had become fast friends. The Cleary Academy for Young Ladies, which properly prepared the daughters of the newly rich for their entry into polite society, had been my mother's suggestion. She'd grown impatient with Tony's constant complaining about how damnably hard-up he was, and suggested that his one solid asset, his grand but neglected town house, could become an ongoing source of income if he would employ his considerable charm and connections to exploit the social aspirations of the new moneyed class. He embraced the idea, and the Cleary Academy was born.

The two greeted each other warmly. She introduced me as Miss Elizabeth Brightly, and we sat down to discuss my enrollment. It was my mother's little joke that she'd told him only that I was a poor rela- tion she was disposed to take pity on, and we had gigglingly agreed that I'd address him in my broadest country accent. I was dressed simply but most prettily in one of my new dresses, my unruly hair smoothly coiffed, and I sat silent and demure as they discussed my transformation to a lady.

When finally he turned to me to ask what I made of all this, I replied, "Well, sor, it all seems a bit hoigh and moighty fer moy tayste."

He flinched visibly, then, with a dark look at my mother, recovered himself to say that although I seemed a most charming young woman, I might be better suited to some other, more use- ful form of instruction. I replied with precisely his own inflection that given the opportunity we might reach some mutually agreeable understanding regarding my improvement.

Shock and anger built for a moment on his face, then he exploded with laughter.

"Tess, you devil, what have you brought me!"

She joined in and said, "Tony, I'd like you to meet my daughter, Beth. I think the two of you will come to like each other quite well."

She must have trusted him absolutely, for she revealed all my circumstances, and why we had come to him. He heard her out with a sort of half-smile which grew broader as the story unfolded, and he was openly grinning by the time she had finished.

"But this is too delicious," he said. "Tess, I had no idea of your checkered past, and your Beth is extraordinary. Are you sure you don't wish to be an actress or courtesan, my dear? With your attributes and accomplishments you could make a fortune!"

I assured him I had modest ambitions, and all I desired was to fit seamlessly into my new situation giving my mother no cause for embarrassment. He took this disappointment in good humour and told my mother it was time for her to depart, for he and I had much to discuss.

It was settled. The next phase of my "practical education" would start immediately. I was to listen carefully to my mother's manner of speech and become totally attuned to it, for from this point on I must use no other. I would suppress any signs of intelligence and erudition, as these would not be considered virtues. Tony himself would instruct me in such things as deportment and proper forms of address, and he assured me that by the time we parted company I would have acquired a polished veneer of social respectability, and considerable skill in the indispensable art of the social insult. My ability to sing and play the pianoforte would be useful, but although he personally found my repertoire most amusing, it would decidedly not do in my new situation. I was not to cheat at cards, indeed, I must learn to lose charmingly. My grooming would be supervised by my mother, and my penmanship, table etiquette and conversational French would be taught by Miss Passwait, a plain, large-boned woman who favoured me with a curt nod and a frosty smile. My natural abilities for music and dance would need discipline, and I was introduced to Monsieur Jean Baptiste, the music and dancing master.

Tony and I fell easily into the same sort of banter that he and my mother enjoyed. We would collapse into helpless laughter as I regaled him with my exploits as a thief and a card sharp, and he in turn would tell me of social disasters he had witnessed, and in some cases orchestrated, and through it all, I learned. He once declared that my life so far had been decidedly more Artful Dodger than Amy Dorrit.

I made no friends among my schoolmates with one exception, the person who was to become my dearest friend in all the world. Her name was Adela Buckthorne—Addie—daughter of a prominent diplomat. She and her brother had grown up in the capitals of Europe, and though younger than I, she had an air of sophistication that made me feel like a gawky child. She was fluent in French, Italian and Spanish, with a working knowledge of German and Russian. In appearance she was taller than I, and slim as a reed with an abundance of golden hair, and enormous blue eyes. I suspect we were initially drawn to each other because we were older than the other girls, but we quickly formed a strong bond, and she was the last person to whom I ever revealed my true past. I learned as much about survival in my new situation from Addie as I did from any of my lessons at the Cleary Academy.

She had been sent back to England from Paris in disgrace when her parents discovered she had a lover, and not just any lover, but a married French diplomat more than twice her age. They adored each other, and he had showered her with gifts. The gifts had betrayed her, for she could not account for them to her mother. She found herself exiled to the London house of an aged aunt, and to the Cleary Academy, where she was, as her mother put it, to regain her Englishness and find a suitable husband.

When I told her of my affair with Julian Bendick and my subsequent disappointment, Addie laughed and said, "Don't lose heart, dear girl, for romance is certainly to be had, and bodily pleasures well worth pursuing." She illustrated this by reading to me some steamy passages from the letters of her lover, Armand, which she still secretly received through her brother.

Sadly, Monsieur Baptiste, the handsome young music and dancing master, disliked me from the outset. I'd been looking forward to my dancing lessons, and did my best, but it seemed nothing would please him. I don't believe I'm being immodest when I say that I was quicker to learn, and more graceful than my classmates, but time and again he would patiently forgive their ineptitude while I would be asked to repeat figures that I had performed perfectly well at the outset. My piano instruction was punctuated by raps across the knuckles with his baton, and my playing suffered for it. I was at a loss to understand his hostility, and finally confided in tears to Addie. Having no pretensions to musical ability and being already well-practised in all the popular forms of dance, she had not witnessed his behaviour, but showed no surprise.

"Beth, you goose, it's jealousy pure and simple. It's obvious that you're a great pet of Mr. Cleary's, and Monsieur Jean and Mr. Cleary have a very close relationship indeed. I'm astonished you haven't noticed."

This was a revelation, for it had never occurred to me that men could have such feelings for each other, and jealousy was not an emotion I'd ever inspired in anyone. I expressed this confusion to Addie, and she said that in Paris it was an ill-kept secret that people had lovers of all kinds, and that she personally knew of a married lady within the diplomatic community who had had several female lovers.

I was determined to resolve the situation. I restricted more of my time with Tony to lessons, and put myself out to be helpful to Jean, offering to drill some of the more clumsy girls—which resulted in some softening of his attitude, though we were never to be friends.

This was only one of many undercurrents at the Academy. One morning I surprised a tearful Miss Passwait as I arrived for my French lesson. She made every effort to conceal her state, but I was moved to ask if she were unwell, and if there were anything I could do. My concern crumbled her reserve and opened the floodgates altogether. She wailed that there was nothing anyone could do, for her life was in ruins, and what would her dear papa have said.

Pansy Passwait was the daughter of a university professor, plain and well past marriageable age, with little money and no skills beyond a modest classical education. She too had been a victim of paternal tyranny, although in different form, for her father, a respected scholar and acknowledged authority on the ancient Egyptians, must have been the most helpless man alive. Upon her mother's death she had inherited the daunting task of managing every aspect of his life, from running the household, to maintaining his wardrobe, to organizing his finances and paying the bills, and in the end as his health and intellect deteriorated, she had even written his dissertations and marked his papers. She'd thought herself very fortunate indeed to find employment with the Cleary Academy, for although the salary was small, room and board were included, and it was an eminently respectable position. The problem, it transpired, was that Tony hadn't paid her at all for several months, and her small inheritance had dwindled to nothing.

When I asked if she had confronted Mr. Cleary, she turned beet red and said, "Oh no, I couldn't do that, for he might let me go, and then what would I do?"

This seemed a bit muddle-headed, but her anguish was so real that I pressed her further to see if I could make any sense of it. The fees Tony received were substantial, yet nothing of this was reflected in the house, which was sadly rundown, nor in the salary of poor Miss Passwait, nor anywhere else that I could see, save in Tony's wardrobe and lifestyle. It transpired that for all his wit, charm and elegance, Tony Cleary shared one disastrous flaw with my father. He had no concept of the conservation of money, for if he had it in hand, he would spend it, and if he didn't, he would lament it. He could be generous to a fault, but it was a fault indeed, for he was open to any hard-luck story if the teller caught him when he was flush, while others more reticent and more deserving could go begging.

It was not for nothing I'd spent all those hours with my grandfather. It was clear that accounts must be kept, fees must be held until obligations were met, and Tony must make do with the balance. The suspicion that my mother had rescued Tony on more than one occasion was confirmed by her grim response over dinner the following evening. I don't know what transpired between them, save that Tony's flamboyance was subdued for a time, and Miss Passwait in addition to her teaching responsibilities was elevated to the position of school administrator. When I next encountered her I was enveloped in an ample embrace.

Within four months I had advanced to the point where I was judged ready for my first introduction into polite society. The occasion was an informal evening of music and dance and a late supper hosted by my mother for a select group of young ladies and gentlemen of her acquaintance. I would wear my new evening dress, a confection of leaf-green watered silk with a froth of ivory lace at the neck and sleeves, my hair pulled back into a smooth chignon with loops of braiding. My slippers were embroidered satin of a dark green, and my mother had given me a little strand of pearls to complete the effect. I was enchanted.

I was clutching Addie's hand as we entered the house in Covington Square that evening. In the dining room a sumptuous buffet overflowed with tempting treats of all kinds, and I had a sudden vision of this silver-laden table through my father's eyes. We accepted a cup of punch, then moved to the sitting room where elegant little gold chairs had been assembled in rows. The entertainment was provided by a protege of Tony's, a young Austrian tenor who was, perhaps, more handsome than gifted, but he gave an enjoyable performance of three of Schubert's compositions with piano accompaniment by Jean Baptiste.

We returned to the dining room so that the sitting room could be cleared for dancing. I had another cup of the innocent-seeming punch and was feeling quite giddy. My dance card was full and the evening became a lovely blur of music and movement. The small orchestra leaned heavily toward waltzes with the occasional polka or mazurka, and I whirled the night away in the arms of at least a dozen young men whose faces ran together in my memory, with the exception of one. Embarrassingly, my most avid admirer was my own half-brother, Alexander.

He was exceptionally handsome in his naval dress uniform, his copper-coloured hair curling over his collar, and he most certainly knew it, for he was so dismissive of my attempts to discourage him as to suggest that he could not believe any woman might resist him. Since open rudeness was not an option, I tried to divert him with wit. Maddeningly, he saw this as flirtation. Addie and I fled the house at a much earlier hour than I would have wished, and the finale of my first social outing differed from that of the fabled Cinderella only in that both my slippers were accounted for.

The next morning, an enormous basket of flowers was delivered to me at Graham's, the accompanying note declaring how deeply he admired me. I would have put them out with the trash, but Nan said it would be sinfully wasteful and they would cheer up the guest parlour.

I was at a loss as to how to proceed, for every rebuff seemed to fire his ardour further. My mother treated it as a joke, saying it was puppy love and would soon pass. That is, until he boldly proposed to me two weeks later. Lady Blackwood sent an urgent message to Admiral Blackwood, and Alex was summoned to Derbyshire.

His addresses ceased as abruptly as they had begun, and I found myself oddly disappointed that he should have been discouraged so easily, but I subsequently learned he'd suddenly received his first commission and been ordered to report immediately to a ship which was to sail for the Suez within the week. I received a poignant note saying that most regrettably urgent duties had called him away. He declared his feelings for me were unchanged, but that in all conscience he could not hold me to any understanding we might have, for he would not be returning to England for some time. I felt a nagging sense of guilt that I might be responsible for sending him into danger, for the situation in that part of the world was extremely unsettled. My mother assured me that this was all part of a sailor's life, and it would probably be the making of him, but I knew she would worry.

Addie was a much greater success that season than I, for she was in her element in social situations, whereas I often felt as if I were suffocating. Her calm acceptance of her parental edict to marry confounded me, for I could not conceive of marrying a man I didn't love, but she said it was naive to think that marriage was anything more than a political and social arrangement, and she expected that once married, she and her husband would lead quite separate lives. I must, she said, learn to differentiate between love and marriage or I'd have a very miserable time of it. We agreed to disagree.

I finally confessed to my mother that although I was most grateful for the opportunities she had given me, I was unhappy in London and longed to live quietly in the country again. I knew she harboured hopes of an advantageous marriage, but having so long been a slave to my father's demands, I was reluctant to relinquish my newfound freedom for any man. She asked for time to consider my wishes, and a fortnight later summoned me to Windward House.

When my mother had come into her inheritance all those years ago she'd acquired several properties, and one of them had recently been vacated. It was, she said, a pretty cottage called Fallowfield close to the village of Edensgate in Derbyshire, some thirty miles distant from her husband's estate. Her intention was to deed the cottage to me, and to settle on me an annual income of two hundred pounds. She would visit me several times a year as my aunt, Lady Blackwood, thus ensuring my entree into the social life of the county, and once a year I would stay with her in London for a few weeks to refresh my wardrobe and regain my polish. I was speechless, and my eyes filled with tears of gratitude.

Nan, too, was tearful when I told her the news, for despite her loyalty to me and her affection for Eva and Bert Graham, living in London with all its unhappy associations had been a trial. She'd have had us packed and gone within the week, but my mother wanted time to have the house made habitable. The remainder of my stay in London was spent with a light heart, and enlivened by Addie's announcement that she was engaged to be married.

Addie had no personal fortune, but was a great beauty with impeccable social credentials as well as the potential of considerable influence through her father. She had no lack of suitors and had finally accepted Jacob Whitbread, a rising young solicitor and aspiring politician of respectable family. She confided to me that she found him handsome enough and intelligent enough to be tolerable. I found him a bit of a prig, but told Addie I had no doubt she'd soon cure him of that. Having assured myself this was what she wanted, I was genuinely happy for her. They would be married in the spring, and I was to be her maid of honour.

Meanwhile, my mother was in a fever to make sure that I would be properly attired for country life. Now that I was no longer on the hunt, I was free to enjoy the few entertainments available in London during the summer season. I spent much of the time with Addie as she assembled her trousseau, and with Tony and my mother saw several plays and concerts, most memorably an outdoor performance of the American compositions of John Philip Sousa which I found to be very masculine, loud and martial, setting the little boys to marching. The time passed quickly, but I grew increasingly impatient to see my new home.

I moved to Fallowfield Cottage in September of 1884, shortly before my twenty-third birthday. My mother would stay with me until Nan returned from Kingsfold with our belongings. I'd debated whether to make one last visit to my childhood home, but decided it was best to make a clean break from the past. I wrote a fond letter to Jos Cooper thanking him for his loyal friendship, and asking him one last favour, that being to deliver Nan and our goods to Edensgate with his trusty horse and cart. I also gave Nan a letter for Cousin Gracie saying that I was well and happy, and embarking on a new life as a companion to an elderly lady who was taking up residence in Tuscany for her health. I was now, truly, Elizabeth Brightly.

Fallowfield Cottage was much more substantial than the humble dwelling my imagination had created. It had once been the gatehouse of the Fallowfield estate, seat of the Fitzhelm family. I learned that the Hall at Fallowfield was inhabited by the baronet Sir Lyall Fitzhelm, his wife Lady Caroline and his two sons. My mother said the Fitzhelms had been selling off their holdings and living off the proceeds for some time, and that it was a great shame to see these old families decline.

I had little interest in such matters, for I was enchanted with my new home, the very picture of an English gentlewoman's dwelling in soft blue-grey stone, with diamond-paned windows, a slate roof and gables with green shutters. There were climbing roses 'round the door, and the walkway was bordered by a profusion of herbs and late summer flowers, which gave off glorious colour and perfume. The door opened to reveal the dark, polished floors of a whitewashed central hallway with doors on either side, and a generous staircase leading to the bedrooms above. To my left was a cherry-panelled study and library with a jewel-coloured Turkey carpet and a slight lingering scent of pipe smoke that reminded me of my grandfather. The next door revealed a lovely bright sitting room with French doors leading to the back garden, and to my delight, in one corner, a beautiful little pianoforte. To the right of the hallway was the dining room with a gleaming mahogany table accommodating ten, and I recall wondering if I would ever entertain such a number. Behind the dining room was the kitchen and pantry, and beyond that, a small apartment for a cook and housekeeper. On the floor above were four charming bedrooms with slanted ceilings, and a bathroom with, wonder of wonders, my very own painted porcelain bath, and a coal-fired boiler. My last words to my mother that night were that I could live happily here for the rest of my life.

Nan and Jos arrived in the afternoon three days later, my mother having departed that morning. They'd had a pleasant journey, staying with members of Jos's large and far-flung family on the way. He'd brought his oldest boy, Zeke, to keep him company on the way home. It was wonderful to see him, and to hear the proud news that he had a new baby, the last of his five children, named Gerald after my father. I dug through my belongings for my father's engraved pewter christening mug to give to the baby, and silently prayed for all concerned that the resemblance would end with the name. Jos wished me great happiness in my new life, and we bid a last affectionate farewell.

Nan toured the house with me, but could barely conceal her impatience to put the kitchen in order, saying the cook's quarters would do her very well. We then unpacked what we had salvaged from our former life. I wanted to burn my old clothes, but Nan said they would serve as dusters, and so I carefully wiped down all my grandfather's books, notebooks and the portfolio of musical manuscripts with one of my old petticoats, and lovingly placed them on the bookshelves in the study, giving Old Nick in his casket a place of honour on the mantelpiece. I removed this journal from its hidden drawer, placing it by my bed to read for the first time in its entirety. My collection of paperweights and the erstwhile miniatures of my parents graced a tabletop in the sitting room. The apostle spoons were displayed above the sideboard in the dining room. The little camphor-lined wooden chest Grandda had made for my treasures I placed at the foot of my bed. The old life and the new were now harmoniously blended.

After a simple supper in the kitchen, Nan and I sank gratefully into our beds.

Once established in my new home, I needed to find some purpose for a life that had never been idle or without responsibility. At first I read constantly, but found myself restless and dissatisfied. By the end of the first week no one had come to call, and I began to think that some rumour of my past must have followed me; however, Nan returned from the market in Edensgate to say that the local ladies were most curious, but shy of approaching someone of my apparent social standing for fear of being rebuffed. I visited the vicar of Saint Mark's, Abner Gentles and his wife, Cornelia, saying that I looked forward to attending Saint Mark's, and hoped they would call upon me if there were any community activities where my participation would be welcomed. This brought a flood of invitations, and I found myself busier than I wanted to be. I easily turned any overt curiosity to sympathy by playing the brave orphan, thus discouraging even the most determined inquisitor.

One morning in late November I was called upon by Cornelia Gentles. She was in the habit of visiting three mornings a week with a certain Miss Budge, an elderly lady, bedridden and almost blind, to read for her the newspapers, ladies' magazines and popular novels provided by her niece. Mrs. Gentles said she was presently so overcome with her other parish duties that it would be a great kindness to both of them if I could take her place. I agreed, and soon formed a very pleas-

ant acquaintance with Clarissa Budge, who although in her eighties
and sadly afflicted possessed a quick intellect and a lively interest in
the world outside her bedroom. She loved a good gossip, and was an
invaluable source of information about my new neighbours.

The light of her life was her grandnephew, Preston Collingford,
who was pursuing a career in the classics at Cambridge in the hopes
of an eventual professorship, much against the wishes of his father
who expected him to assume a position in the family china and pottery firm. He was a most serious young man, totally unmindful of
his unfashionable appearance, with a rather vague and gentle nature,
and truly devoted to his great-aunt, who wholeheartedly supported
him in his scholarly pursuits. There were those in the village who
spitefully suggested that his devotion was entirely driven by the fact
that she paid for his education, and he was her only heir, but I had no
doubt his affection was genuine.

One morning I appeared at the usual time to find Clarissa
with a most peculiar-looking man. He was securing her signature
on some papers, and seemed quite disconcerted by my arrival. He
hastily stuffed the documents into his breast pocket. I must remark
on how he appeared to me then, for it was as if every part of him
were exaggerated, his hair a little too long with a peak that came
quite far down on his forehead and brushed back with some strong-
smelling pomade, his face composed of curiously mismatched features, bushy eyebrows, small close-set eyes, a narrow beaky nose, and
full, red, almost girlish lips. The oddity extended to his dress as well,
for although it was his obvious intention to mirror the latest style, his
waist was too defined, the lapels of his coat too wide, and the bright
blue colour too jarring.

He introduced himself as Osbert Lynche, taking care that I
should know that Lynche was spelled with an *e*, and said he was Miss
Budge's man of business, come to consult with her on some minor
matters. To my embarrassment, he made a deep bow and kissed my

hand, leaving a wet spot, which I was hard-pressed not to wipe off with my handkerchief. Taking his leave, he said he would abandon us to those simple pursuits which amused gentle ladies like ourselves. I thought he was quite the most odious man I'd ever met, but did not say so to Clarissa, who thought him a most clever and capable fellow, and said he relieved her of a great deal of worry.

Nan and I spent a quiet Christmas together that year, and my mother joined us to celebrate the New Year. Nan outdid herself in the kitchen, and the three of us enjoyed our first dinner in the dining room, a magnificent meal of roast duck stuffed with apples and walnuts, escalloped potatoes, and carrots and parsnips with a brandy glaze, finishing with a flaming plum pudding. Breaking my usual rule, I had two generous glasses of wine, and we spent the eve of 1884 in that wonderful glow of easy camaraderie that only comes with shared experience.

It was to be an extraordinary year.

Clarissa Budge passed away in February. She had contracted pneumonia despite the well-tended fire in her room and the many shawls and blankets wrapped 'round her. I was very sad for I'd become quite fond of her. Then came the sensational news that her estate was depleted to the point of nonexistence, save for the house itself. All of poor Preston Collingford's academic dreams were dashed, for there was no money to support him further, and it appeared he was destined for employment in the china trade after all. He confided to me that he'd found no trace among his great-aunt's papers of what had happened to her former holdings, and that her accounts showed no unusual movement of funds, save that the rents had not been paid in for some time. I felt obliged to tell him in confidence what I had observed regarding Mr. Osbert Lynche, but upon being confronted, Mr. Lynche declared with some appearance of injury that Miss Budge had terminated their association with no explanation shortly after I'd seen him. He concluded that some unprincipled scoundrel must have wormed his way into her confidence, though none of us was aware of any such person. Preston was obliged to abandon any further inquiry for he possessed neither the proof nor the funds to pursue it.

In March I purchased a lively little grey spotted mare, named Jenny after my father's much-loved old horse, and rode each morning for an hour or so. I refused to ride sidesaddle and had flouted convention by having Fanny Gosling create a riding habit with a long divided skirt which looked like any other when I stood, but allowed me to straddle the horse when I rode. This caused considerable gossip, but my association with Lady Blackwood was not to be lightly dismissed, and my costume, like my independent and single state, was labelled an eccentricity.

It was on one of my morning rides that I first met my Rennie. Jenny was walking sore-footed, and I'd dismounted to see what the problem was. She'd picked up a stone in her right front shoe, and having no tool to remove it, I was searching for a pointed stick for the purpose. A shadow fell over me, and I looked up to see a tall figure on horseback enquiring if he could be of service. I explained my predicament, and he lightly jumped down, pulled out a pocket knife and deftly removed the offending stone. He introduced himself as Renforth Fitzhelm, and I recognized the name as being that of Sir Lyall's younger son. He politely offered to help me remount, and lifted me as easily as if I were a child, his large hands completely encircling my waist.

He complimented me on my riding costume, saying, "V-very sensible. D-dangerous damfool devices, sidesaddles. Always th-thought so."

I would later learn that Rennie only stuttered when he was nervous, and that young ladies made him very nervous indeed. He was tall and solidly built with a lock of fair hair that fell over his soft brown eyes, and a shy smile that caught at my heart every time I saw it. I fell in love with him from the moment I laid eyes on him, and miraculously he fell also.

Who'd have dreamed that Rennie, who couldn't tell a poem from a parsnip, would be the man who restored my faith in romantic love? He showed his regard for me in a hundred little ways, sometimes joining me for my morning ride, or suddenly appearing at my side when I accompanied Nan on market day. I might find a pretty nosegay of flowers on the doorstep, or he'd come to the kitchen door with a pheasant or duck from his shooting. He had a natural grace and loved to dance, my Rennie. From the very first time we danced together at a village fete, it was as if we shared one body.

As we grew to know each other his stutter all but disappeared, and we conversed on a broad range of subjects. His education had been sadly neglected, but he was hungry for knowledge, and loved to have me read to him. I soon realized I had only one rival for his affection, and that was Fallowfield, for he knew and loved every inch of it, and mourned the loss of any piece of it as if it were a part of his own body. He had what seemed to me very sound ideas as to how the estate could become profitably self-supporting, but said that neither his father nor his older brother would heed him.

That was a magical spring. The weather was glorious, and Rennie and I rode most mornings. Although we never lacked for conversation, we were just as happy to ride in silence. He'd often join Nan and me for supper at the cottage, and we'd play whist or checkers in the sitting room afterward. From subtle touches we moved to gentle embraces, and from those embraces to lingering kisses and beyond, nothing forced, nothing assumed. He was, in every way, the man of my girlhood imaginings.

Addie's wedding was to take place at the end of June. I was preparing to travel to London when Rennie appeared to ask if I would come to dinner at Fallowfield Hall the following evening. He'd seemed most reluctant for me to meet his family, and Nan thought this to be a slight on his part, but I sensed it was prompted by protectiveness toward me, and hadn't pursued the subject. I recalled from my gossips with Clarissa Budge that Rennie's older brother, Michael, was considered to be wild and a bit of a lad with the ladies. She had concluded that as the oldest son and as heir to the title he had been overindulged by his father, whom she characterized as rude and overbearing for all that he was a baronet. There was a daughter, Margaret, who had scandalously eloped with some sort of tradesman some years previous, and who had not been seen or spoken of since. Lady Fitzhelm was reported to be rather frail and sickly, and Rennie as a boy had been largely left to his own devices. I looked forward to the evening with some trepidation, for Rennie's demeanour had not been reassuring.

He came in a trap to fetch me, speaking in nervous bursts as we made our way up the long drive to Fallowfield Hall. It was the first time I'd been so close to the Hall. It was built in the Palladian style, but even my untrained eye could see that the symmetry had been spoiled by some later additions, and it showed evidence of neglect both in the grounds and in the facade. The imposing front door was opened by a surly looking man in an ill-pressed suit. Rennie introduced him as Savidge, the butler, and we were conducted down a gloomy, cavernous hallway to the drawing room, where I met Sir Lyall, a florid and portly man with a booming voice who first acknowledged then ignored me, and Rennie's brother Michael, who introduced himself with an over-elaborate bow, and a squeeze of my hand which was a little too lingering. I was told that Lady Fitzhelm was delayed at her toilette and would join us for dinner.

There was a strong physical resemblance between the two brothers, but they couldn't have been more different in manner, for Michael was a swaggering sort of fellow showing those early signs of dissipation around the eyes and mouth that I'd observed in some of the young habitués of my father's establishment. He treated me with an exaggerated and condescending gallantry, which I found most distasteful.

I don't know when I've experienced a more appalling evening. Rennie's stutter returned tenfold in the presence of his father and brother, and they spoke to him as if he were a half-wit. Lady Fitzhelm joined us at dinner with a narrow-featured lady in her thirties who was introduced as Savidge's wife, Edwina, housekeeper and compan-ion to Lady Fitzhelm, and this was to be the entirety of the dinner party seated at one end of a table intended for twenty or more. I observed a marked intimacy in the way Mrs. Savidge brushed against Sir Lyall's back as she took her seat.

Lady Fitzhelm seemed to be in a sort of trance, responding to my attempts at conversation with a rather confused smile. Her hair was in danger of escaping its pins, and her dress, though handsome, had a stain on the bodice, and was incorrectly buttoned down the back. Mrs. Savidge was most attentive, regularly filling her water goblet from a silver pitcher she kept by her, and encouraging her to eat, although I saw no food pass her lips. Sir Lyall and Michael spoke mainly to each other except to solicit agreement for something they'd said or to demand more wine, and as Rennie looked thoroughly wretched and seemed incapable of speech, I made some effort to address myself to Mrs. Savidge, who replied in monosyllables.

We were served by Savidge with the assistance of a terrified-looking young girl. I scarcely remember what we ate, and couldn't wait for this dismal affair to end.

At the conclusion of the meal, Mrs. Savidge said that Lady Caro-line wished to retire, though I'd yet to hear the lady herself utter a word. As I rose to bid her good-night I caught an unmistakable whiff of juniper, and realized the clear liquid in her water goblet had in fact been gin. Rennie excused himself to escort his mother to her room, Sir Lyall declared he was going to his study for a smoke, "by God," and I was left in the dining room with Michael. He'd had a great deal to drink, but it was no excuse for what followed, for he pressed me up against the sideboard with his hands roaming over me, saying he couldn't understand why a juicy jade like me would waste herself on his feeble brother, and he'd show me what a real man was like.

At that moment I blessed Sergeant Crake for his instructions on how to repel unwelcome advances. A swift knee to the crutch, and a hard butt with my forehead to the bridge of his nose as his head dropped forward immediately extricated me from his loathsome embrace, and, calling me a "bloody bitch," he limped from the room streaming blood from his nose just seconds before Rennie returned. I can say that from that moment forward on those few further occasions when we met, Michael treated me if not with respect, then at least with caution.

Rennie was miserably silent on the brief journey home, and I think he would have fled without a word had I not caught his arm and drawn him into the kitchen, saying that I wanted a cup of cocoa. Hope rose in his eyes; and we sat talking and holding hands with studied avoidance of any reference to what had transpired, when suddenly he dropped to his knees in front of me.

"My dearest Beth," he said in a great rush of words, "you've now seen the very worst of me and my family, and cannot help but know what a poor excuse for a man I am. I have very little income, and no expectations of more, but I love you with all my heart, and if you would become my wife I would be the happiest man on earth."

I think it has to have been the saddest proposal ever made by any man to a woman, and I didn't know whether to laugh or cry, but instead I said, "Rennie, my love, of course I will marry you."

His response was to burst into tears and bury his head in my lap.

When at last he left me, I ran to wake Nan and tell her the news. She hugged and kissed me, saying he seemed a good lad, and as I was a sensible girl we might very well make a go of it. I replied there was nothing sensible about it, for I was head over heels in love.

I was to leave for London in two days' time, and the next afternoon Rennie appeared to announce he would accompany me, for having informed his father of our engagement and receiving neither encouragement nor opposition, he desired to solicit the approval of my aunt, Lady Blackwood. Since I would have an escort, Nan elected to remain at home.

Rennie would stay with his sister Margaret and her husband Charles Grindle. It was ten years since Rennie had helped his sister to escape Fallowfield Hall when Sir Lyall, outraged by what he considered a most presumptuous proposal, locked her in her room and drove her suitor from the house with his riding crop. I learned that Charles Grindle, having begun his career as a humble glazier, had expanded his interests to include the manufacture of glass of every description, from the elaborate etched and stained glass windows in demand for elegant new houses, to crystal both for the table and for illumination, to the specialized tubes and containers used for scientific research. He now employed over a hundred men, and Margaret was the proud mother of three girls. Rennie looked forward to sharing his happy news with her. As he left me at Covington Square, we arranged that he would come for tea the following afternoon.

I spent the next morning with Addie, who was glowing in a way that suggested the relationship had progressed well past a mere arrangement. When I taxed her with this, she blushed and said she'd spouted a great deal of nonsense when she was younger, to which I replied gravely that indeed a whole year had passed. She was overjoyed at my own revelation. She gave me a thorough tour of their London apartment and accompanied me to Fanny Gosling's salon to collect my dress. Addie's satin and lace wedding gown, embroidered with pearls, was by Worth and had been brought by her mother from Paris. Mine was a copy of Worth in ecru silk created by Fanny and which I thought would do beautifully for my own wedding. I arrived at Windward House barely in time to meet Rennie for tea.

I'd already broken the news to my mother and we laughed over my description of the dreadful dinner. I declared it was Rennie I was marrying, not his family, but my mother replied dryly that unless we moved to some other locality I'd soon find I'd married his family as well.

When Rennie arrived, I left the two of them alone and went to the kitchen to supervise the tea. When I returned, my mother was embracing him, and his face was wreathed in smiles. The engagement was now official.

The following day was completely taken up with Addie's wedding, a modest affair of just over two hundred people. Addie's honey-coloured hair was swept up into a coronet of the same white roses that filled the church, and at her throat was a delicate choker of seed pearls and diamonds given her by Jacob's mother. The bride and groom were obviously besotted with each other. The happy couple departed by coach, and would stay for a few days at the family home in Brighton before departing for an extended honeymoon on the continent. They promised to return in time for my own wedding in September.

The celebration went on well into the small hours. Rennie had accompanied my mother during the ceremony. I rejoined them to find him surrounded by an admiring bevy of young girls with signs of rising panic in his eyes. I signalled to my mother, and we gently extricated him, escorting him around the room for introductions, and keeping up such a stream of chatter that Rennie scarcely needed to say a word beyond "How d'ye do?"

The following morning I visited Sarah Green to tell her my happy news, and to deliver thirty pounds to be added to my nest egg. Under her stewardship the capital had swelled to over two hundred pounds.

In the afternoon, Rennie and I had tea with his sister Margaret, a charming lady much taken up with her home and children. She declared I was the best thing that could have happened to her beloved brother. Rennie took the little girls out for a stroll, and Margaret and I engaged in some frank discussion regarding the Fitzhelm family. I told her of my experience at Fallowfield Hall, begging her for Rennie's sake not to tell him what happened between Michael and myself. She shook her head sadly. Michael, she said, had been a sweet but headstrong little boy, and once he understood the sun rose and set on him in his father's eyes, and there would be no checks to his behaviour, he had pushed it to the limits. Lady Fitzhelm's timid attempts to discipline him were met with harsh words about "smothering the boy's spirit," and she had finally surrendered, becoming a shadow of the mother Margaret had known and loved. Sir Lyall had never had much interest in his other children unless they displeased him, and after her elopement, Margaret had ceased to exist for him. Her one wish was to remove her mother from Fallowfield Hall forever. I promised to keep her informed of the situation insofar as I could, for I didn't expect to be spending much time at the Hall.

The next three months were spent in a cloud of bliss and anticipation, with the exception of a brief meeting I had with Sir Lyall. He'd ordered Rennie to bring me to see him. Rennie said he was quite prepared to tell his father to go to blazes, but I assured him I'd had considerable experience in dealing with intimidation.

The confrontation proved to be somewhat anticlimactic. Sir Lyall made it clear that he neither approved nor disapproved of the match, that he considered me acceptable as a daughter-in-law but otherwise inconsequential, and if I sought to elevate myself through marriage to his son and residence at Fallowfield Hall, I would be sadly disappointed. I calmly replied that I had a comfortable home and income of my own, and that living at the Hall was the last thing I envisioned. He countered that Rennie's income was insignificant and we needn't expect any support from him. I responded evenly that I certainly understood the Fitzhelm family was in no position to support us, and we would manage quite nicely on our own. He turned a most alarming colour, and was still sputtering as I took my leave. Although I felt I had acquitted myself rather well, and that Tony Cleary would have been proud of me, I feared Rennie would suffer the consequences. He later reported that his father had been oddly silent on the subject. He had, however, overheard him saying to Michael that I was "a hendsome enough gel and spirited with it, but over-small to be a good breeder." Michael had replied darkly that Rennie would have his hands full.

As there was no offer to celebrate our wedding at Fallowfield Hall, it took place on a beautiful fall afternoon at Saint Mark's on the twenty-third of September 1884, shortly after my twenty-fourth birthday. Mr. Gentles officiated, and Addie was my matron of honour. My mother was accompanied by Tony Cleary and Addie's husband, Jacob. Nan of course was everywhere at once. There'd been a death in Sarah Green's family, and she was unable to attend, but to my surprise and pleasure, a glowingly happy Pansy Passwait appeared with her fiancé, a rather weedy little man who had been a younger colleague of her father's, and who, it seemed, equalled and even surpassed him in helplessness. Otherwise, it was a small village affair. Sir Lyall and Lady Fitzhelm put in a brief appearance. Everyone said I looked radiant in Fanny Gosling's gown with blue cornflowers in my hair for true love and the pearl pendant which my mother had removed from her own neck to place on mine.

Rennie and I spent our honeymoon quietly at the cottage, and on that first night of our life together we sat in the garden like an old married couple, holding hands, drinking tea and watching a glorious sunset. I was already carrying our son Henry, but had waited until that moment to break the news to Rennie, for had he known he'd have trumpeted the news to the entire wedding party. Nan of course had guessed at once, and informed my mother.

Our first son, Henry Charles Fitzhelm, was born on April 3rd, 1885. He was followed three years later by his sister, named Jean Abigail after the grandmother I had never known, and our youngest son, George Francis, was born in the spring of 1895.

I will draw a veil over those years, for my own reading has informed me that there is nothing more yawn-inducing than some-one else's happiness, and I find that recalling that golden time only amplifies for me the sorrows that followed, but I will speak of our children, and of a few incidents that occurred.

Henry is so like his father in appearance it's almost as if Ren-nie were still alive in him. As a child he followed his father every-where, and couldn't wait until he was big enough to ride his own pony. Although he attended university he was a reluctant student and, sharing Rennie's attachment to Fallowfield, pined to be home again. In nature he is like a quiet lake, its surface unruffled by the wind with no hint of what lies beneath.

Jean, a darling girl with my father's blue-grey eyes but none of his nature, was married at eighteen to Frederick Stewart, a country curate, and they have as of this writing one daughter, Teresa Eliza-beth, my first grandchild. They're as poor as the proverbial church mice, and I help them whenever I can. Jean never gave me a moment of worry as a child, and we're very close. She is totally without arti-fice or hidden emotions, transparent as glass.

George was always a moody, restless little boy, but also quick and enquiring, loved music, and would sit entranced as I played the pianoforte and sang. When he was nearly four he discovered Old Nick in his casket on the mantelpiece in the study, and I found him asleep on the hearthrug cradling the fiddle in his arms. He was loath to surrender it, and I had to promise him that if he learned to play properly it would be his. I purchased a child-sized instrument for him which he disliked, for he said it had no face, and I arranged for him to take instruction from the organist at Saint Mark's. As with my father, music seems to be the one constant and calming influence in an otherwise turbulent life. He has the clever Joyner hands. I can only describe him as being for all the world like Stephen Leacock's horseman, riding off in all directions at once. I will admit only here that of all my children he is the closest to my heart.

We welcomed another child into our lives on New Year's Day, 1897. Rennie had gone to the stable in the morning to saddle his horse, for a visit to his mother. He heard a rustling in the hayloft above, and thought it must be some animal crept in to keep warm against the bitter weather. Instead he found a boy of about thirteen buried in the hay, gaunt and shivering in his ragged jacket and trousers. He tried to escape by the hay chute, but Rennie caught him by the waist of his trousers, and carried him into the warmth of the kitchen. At first he couldn't tell us his name for his teeth were chattering so, but after a hot drink and some scones he admitted that he was Jonathan Godskill, and begged that we wouldn't send him home, but would say no more. Rennie knew of the family, for they'd been tenants of one of the Fallowfield farms, evicted when the property was sold. He rode off to find the boy's parents, having learned that they lived in a hovel too wretched to be called a cottage some distance out of Edensgate.

When he arrived, the place had a deserted feel to it, with no smoke rising from the chimney. The door gaped open to reveal a scene of dreadful carnage. The twisted, frozen bodies of a woman and three small children lay in a welter of blood, and bloody footprints could be seen in the snow leading to the river. When Rennie returned with a police constable, they followed the tracks, but found no one. Three days later a man's body washed up downstream, dead from either exposure or drowning.

When Jonathan recovered enough to tell his story he said that his father had had no work for weeks, there was no food in the house, and the children were weak and fretful from hunger. He'd set out to see what he could beg from the neighbours, and was returning with some bread and cheese when he saw his father run from the house drenched in blood. Fearing for his mother and his little brother and sisters, he entered the house and found them as Rennie had described them. He had no memory of how he came to be in our hayloft. It was later judged that his father, Jonah God-skill, had gone mad, butchered his wife and children, then drowned himself from remorse.

I knew Rennie would feel responsible for this tragedy, since it was the clear result of eviction from a Fallowfield tenancy. Despite overseeing the day-to-day management of the estate he had no say in it, and constantly blamed himself for his inability to stand up to his father regarding the disposal of it. I deplored his feelings of guilt, but was happy to welcome Jonathan into our family. He worshipped Rennie, and he and Henry, being much of an age, shared a room and became fast friends.

We all grew older, Rennie more handsome, Nan rounder, and my mother more adventurous. Addie became very active in Jacob's political career, and I firmly believe has been largely responsible for his enlightened views on aid to the disadvantaged and the rights of women. They have three children, two girls a year apart, and four younger a boy. Our nest egg grew to over two thousand pounds.

As I didn't care for the Edensgate schoolmaster, I tutored the children myself. Once Henry had learned to read and write and do his sums, he had little interest in lessons, and preferred to be in his father's company with the horses and dogs. Jonathan was a hard worker but not at all inquisitive. Jean was a dedicated reader, but like myself at that age tended to fill her head with romantic non-sense. George, though still a baby, insisted on being included in the lessons, and proved himself to be a prodigy, for he was reading by the age of four, running to me several times a day to ask the meanings and pronunciations of words and phrases. He was fascinated by Grandda's journals, especially the one on locks and clocks and other devices, and by the time he was six, no lock was safe from him, and no clock intact.

Upon the death of his father in 1892, my half-brother, Alex, resigned his commission in the Royal Navy, and with his younger brother, Peter, a cartographer, embarked on a series of expeditions which were much lauded by the Royal Geographical Society. My mother realized her lifelong dream of travel to exotic places when she accompanied them to Australia, and later to India. Her humorous journals of their travels have since been published, and very well received. The brothers have gone on to make their fortunes in the mining industry since the youngest, Elliot, a geologist, joined them to form the firm of Blackwood Explorations. Alex, like his father, married quite late to a woman half his age. It seems a happy as well as a fruitful union, and with my own brood, my mother has quite a flock of grandchildren.

On one of my mother's visits she brought with her a young artist, Marie-Claude Guerin, who'd painted a portrait of my mother which pleased her very much. She commissioned Mademoiselle Guerin to do some sketches of Rennie and myself in our riding clothes preparatory to painting life-sized portraits. Although I found much of her work to be too influenced by the modern French school for my taste, she left us two of her watercolour sketches, which I had framed and hung over the fireplace in the sitting room. These sparse likenesses are quite startling in their honesty, and I like them tremendously. The final portraits were never executed.

In 1898 a letter arrived addressed to Elizabeth Brightly. It was from Jos Cooper, informing me that Grandda Gabe had died at the ripe old age of ninety-one, in the midst of his work as he would have wished. I was saddened by the news, and sent an anonymous donation to Saint Stephen requesting that Grandda Gabe and the

Joyner family be remembered in the prayers. Jos further reported that young Gerald had proved to be quite the gifted musician, and was now the proud possessor of Grandda's fiddle.

In October of 1899, our lives were brutally disrupted. Nan and Jean and I were sorting linens when Rennie rushed in, breathless and white-faced. Word had come that Michael had interrupted a robbery at his London lodgings and had received a mortal blow to the head. We later learned that his attacker was in fact the husband of a woman he'd been bedding, the couple having a long history of such actions. Nan observed that if you lay down with dogs, you rose up with fleas. I reminded her that Michael was not likely to rise up in any state before judgment day. As he was unmarried and had no issue, Rennie was now heir to Fallowfield.

His father's grief-stricken ranting about his unworthiness to take his brother's place, coupled with demands that he move back to Fallowfield Hall at once, threw Rennie into a state of near collapse. I did not delude myself that either of us felt much grief at Michael's death, but I knew my Rennie, and dreaded the moment when his shock gave way to guilt at having achieved his heart's desire at such a price. Our perfect happiness was at an end, and I could do nothing to retrieve it. It was with deep regret and mounting apprehension that I moved from my lovely cottage into the unwelcoming atmosphere of Fallowfield Hall.

I knew the house had been neglected, but I was unprepared for the state of dilapidation in which I found it. The number of servants living in had been reduced to five, two being the Savidges, one being Mrs. Vesey, the cook, and the others being two young village girls, sisters named Polly and Dora White, who were expected to clean, lay the fires, do laundry, help Mrs. Vesey with food preparation, and wait at table. Nan, bless her, pitched in wherever she could, though Sir Lyall made it clear no salary would be forthcoming from him. He also attempted to banish Jonathan to the stables, but Rennie dug in his heels and Jonathan shared a room with Henry on the nursery floor.

We occupied a gloomy first-floor bedroom known as the Ivory Room after two giant elephant tusks carved in the shape of ancient Japanese warriors that flanked the fireplace. No doubt they were masterfully carved, but I despised them, for they were the colour of corpses with leering faces. They terrified little George, and I had them removed to the attics along with the disintegrating oriental silk bed and window hangings. The room was certainly no testament to Edwina Savidge's housekeeping ability, and Nan and I spent two days cleaning the place, even removing a nest of mice from the lumpy feather bed, which could not have been turned in at least a decade, and eventually, with fresh draperies and bed linens and sunlight from the now-sparkling windows, it became quite habitable despite the faded wallpaper and crumbling plaster.

With the exceptions of Mr. and Mrs. Savidge, whose attitudes bordered on insolence, Nan and I got on well with the staff, and I was able to effect some changes which greatly enhanced the efficient running of the household, for this was one province where Sir Lyall seldom interfered. Nan and Mrs. Vesey became very friendly, freeing Polly and Dora to carry out their other duties. I began to spend time with Lady Caroline, and was able to write my sister-in-law that with my intervention there was some noticeable improvement. She enjoyed the presence of the children, and she and Jean grew quite close, though she tended to call her Margaret.

Sir Lyall was diminished by Michael's death—not in his nature, for he was as intractable as ever, but in his person. He'd suffered a fall shortly thereafter, and had lost some feeling and function in his left arm and leg causing him to cease most physical activity. His face too showed the effects, appearing pulled down on the left side, and his speech was slurred. Rennie offered to take on more responsibility, but his father roared that he wasn't dead yet, and threw an inkwell at him. Mrs. Savidge was constantly at his shoulder, whispering in his ear, and subverting any attempts I made to improve his diet or limit his consumption of alcohol.

I thus had little contact with Sir Lyall, who spent most of his time in his bedchamber or his study and took his meals alone, but on one notable occasion Mrs. Savidge came to me as I was dressing for my morning ride to tell me with her sly smirk that the master wished to see me. As I entered the study, Sir Lyall was seated at his desk, and I became aware of a man who stood with his back to me staring out the window. With no preamble or introduction, Sir Lyall said his estate manager had a tidy proposition for me, and that I should give it immediate consideration. The man turned toward me.

The hair lifted at the back of my neck, and my heart plummeted as I recognized Osbert Lynche. I managed to disguise my alarm with a polite smile and nod, carefully keeping enough furniture between us to avoid another kiss on the hand. He reminded me in his oily manner of our first meeting at the home of "dear Miss Budge," and said that his sister, Edwina, had told him of the fortuitous change in my circumstances. He then informed me that since I no longer had need of it, he had a buyer for my cottage, strongly advising me to seize the opportunity as the offer was fair and indeed generous considering the decline of property values in the district. He was little changed in his appearance or his manner. Indeed he was, if possible, more unattractive than when I'd first encountered him. I thanked him for his interest, and said that as I had no pressing need of the revenue, it was my intention to maintain the place so that my aunt, Lady Blackwood, could stay there when she came to visit. He replied with a bow that he only wished to be of service, and advised me to contact him if I had a change of heart. I said good day to him, and, feeling the need to dissipate my anger and alarm, went for a furious gallop on my poor Jenny, who having grown old and fat, huffed and puffed and complained bitterly at the exercise.

Clearly there was much more at stake than the fate of my cottage. Unbeknownst to me, the management and disposition of Fallowfield, the birthright of both my husband and our son Henry, had been, for some time, in the highly questionable hands of Osbert Lynche.

I informed Rennie of my misgivings. He mirrored my alarm and assured me that he'd try again to influence his father, but feared too much damage had already been done. He'd made a tour of some of the former Fallowfield properties, and to his bafflement found them deserted and overgrown. At one of them a rough-looking man had emerged from the house carrying a rifle, and asked why he was lurking about. When Rennie replied that he was merely curious, the man nastily accused him of trespassing and told him he'd best be off about his business as the Fitzhelms were no longer lords and masters there. Rennie couldn't imagine why anyone would purchase land only to leave it idle. Inquiries revealed only that the man's name was Orin Bender, that he appeared to be ex-army, and that despite having no obvious source of income he had recently acquired several local properties. Nothing else could be learned, for he kept himself to himself, and didn't drink at the village pub.

I resolved to keep a close eye on the Savidges and the comings and goings of Mr. Lynche. Nan had informed me there were certain objects recently missing, most notably a hideous but valuable pair of silver candelabra in the form of stags' heads that had formerly adorned the library. I confronted Mrs. Savidge, who said that one of the pair had fallen, a branch had broken off, and she had sent them out for repairs. As little else in the house seemed to merit such attention, I replied that an accident to one scarcely necessitated the removal of both, and I expected to see them returned immediately. The two red spots on her cheeks told me that despite her tight-lipped silence she was in a ferocious temper. As for Mr. Lynche, he continued to press me on the matter of my cottage, but I managed to maintain a veneer of civility, for I judged him to be a more formidable adversary than his sister.

Christmas that year was a subdued affair. Sir Lyall's health was deteriorating, though his temper was still healthy enough, and his complaints about the cost of the modest feast Nan and Mrs. Vesey had prepared took much of the joy out of it. Lady Fitzhelm, though still emotionally frail, was much improved physically and took genuine pleasure in the children's excitement.

My mother joined us in a quiet family celebration for the turn of the twentieth century. She actually flirted with Sir Lyall to the point where he became quite the genial host. I accompanied George on his violin in a spirited version of "God Rest Ye Merry Gentlemen," then the two younger children were sent off to bed. Henry and Jonathan, at fifteen and sixteen, were allowed to stay up and have a glass of champagne to toast the New Year and the new century. George, though barely five, was highly resentful, saying that his brother got to do everything. My mother was full of anticipation about her upcoming voyage to Australia. Her energy and enthusiasm were remarkable for a woman in her sixties, and she showed no sign of flagging. She would be gone for over two years, and I would miss her terribly.

Rennie and I were as much in love as ever. I've often regretted that I never revealed to him the truth of my origin, for I'm sure it would have made no difference, but some stubborn, fearful part of me would not let me confess, and finally it was too late.

In January of 1901, the country was reeling from the death of our Queen, Victoria, but our concerns lay closer to home. Sir Lyall's health was in steady decline, and by August of the following year he was confined to his bed. He could keep next to nothing on his stomach, and had become increasingly secretive and suspicious, allowing no one but Edwina to attend him. We were awakened one morning by Nan informing us that Polly had found him dead in his bed, and no sign of the Savidges. The doctor informed us he had not gone peacefully, but had suffocated from inhaling his own vomit.

The pair had not decamped empty-handed. Several valuable items had gone with them, including the infamous stags' heads candelabra. It was fortunate that Edwina's execrable taste had spared some of the finer, less ostentatious pieces. We made no attempt to trace them, for it was small enough price to pay, and more serious matters demanded our attention, for Rennie was now Sir Renforth Fitzhelm, and I, God help me, was Lady Fitzhelm.

Within a week of Sir Lyall's death, Rennie was confronted by a delegation of angry and worried tenants led by a man called Ephraim Best. The estate was so depleted that there were only five of them, and Osbert Lynche had informed them their tenancies would be terminated within the year. Rennie assured them that under his stewardship, no more Fallowfield properties would be sold, and their livings were secure. They departed much happier men, and Ephraim Best lingered to say that if anything needed doing about the Hall, he was our man.

Rennie spent several nights ransacking the estate room and his father's study and bedroom to find any record of transactions, but without success. His father had kept no accounts, his dealings had most certainly been in cash, and all that was immediately at hand was three hundred and twenty-seven pounds in crumpled notes and scattered coins discovered in a locked drawer in his desk, somehow overlooked by the Savidges. There was, however, a stack of unpaid bills and increasingly threatening letters from Michael's creditors in London.

Rennie's next visitor was Osbert Lynche, boldly declaring that he had in his hands signed commissions from Sir Lyall to sell off the remaining properties, and that as a courtesy he had come to inform Sir Renforth that he was going forward with these commissions. Rennie replied that in light of his father's obviously deteriorating physical and mental state, he considered any such agreements to be invalid, and he would meet again with Mr. Lynche when he'd taken the advice of a solicitor. He further demanded to see a record of all transactions regarding Fallowfield. He was vehemently outspoken in his condemnation of Lynche's character and practices, and threatened him with prosecution if he attempted to proceed. He later told me cheerfully that the bounder had left in a flaming temper. I cautioned him to be more tactful, for I had no doubt that Lynche was capable of being highly vindictive.

Within the week, Rennie had a confirmation from Addie's husband, Jacob Whitbread, that his position regarding Mr. Lynche was solid, and an investigation more than justified, especially as there was some question about Sir Lyall's competence during his final years. A note was dispatched to Lynche demanding that he present himself to Sir Renforth Fitzhelm at five o'clock the following afternoon.

Late the next morning of October 3rd, 1902, Rennie, Henry and Jonathan joined a party completed by Ephraim Best and two of the other tenants to track down a fox grown too old and too slow to hunt that was nightly raiding the henhouses. Rennie and I embraced, and I handed Jonathan a picnic lunch, for they were stalking on foot and I didn't expect them back before mid-afternoon. The remainder of that day was uneventful until, shortly after three o'clock, Osbert Lynche appeared unexpectedly saying some other business in the neighbourhood had been concluded more speedily than anticipated, and I was obliged to give him tea and entertain him while we awaited Rennie's return. I was finding it difficult to maintain polite conversation and was about to excuse myself when I heard the bang of a door and a loud cry. It was Jonathan who rushed in in a state of total disarray with tears streaming down his face.

"Oh, Mrs. Beth, it's Mr. Rennie. He's gone! They've killed him, shot him!"

I couldn't take it in. It was as if time were suspended in one of those classical tableaux from a parlour game, everyone arrested in mid-motion. Poor wretched Jonathan collapsed at my feet, his face buried in my skirts, the pale faces of Nan and Jean at the door; and then there was Osbert Lynche. As I sat in shock, a flash of expression I can only describe as triumph crossed his face, and in that instant I knew as surely as if Rennie had spoken in my ear that this man was responsible for his death. He quickly recovered himself, and moved toward me oozing solicitousness. The room darkened 'round the edges, and for the second time in my life I fell into unconsciousness.

I don't recall much of the next few days save that I lay alone in our darkened bedroom wanting to die. Nan's shadowy figure came and went. At one point Henry knelt beside the bed, holding my hand and weeping hopelessly. He'd stayed with his father's body until they brought him home, and had barely spoken since, but I could summon neither the strength nor the will to comfort him then. Sweet Jean slipped into my bed in the night to cradle me in her arms as if I were the child, not she.

Dear Margaret and her husband came at once to manage the funeral arrangements. They would take Lady Caroline with them when they departed, and offered to take the children as well, but the poor little souls wouldn't leave me. Addie, a true friend, had come also and she and Nan supported me between them as Rennie was placed in the family vault at Saint Mark's. My one conscious thought on that dreadful occasion was how he would have hated to be shut away in this cold, dark place. I vowed then that no other Fitzhelm would ever be shut in that awful tomb, and later had Rennie's body removed to a tree-shaded hillside overlooking Fallowfield in God's green earth and under the vault of heaven, as he would have wished.

As the first sharp edge of sorrow dulled, and I slowly returned to the world, I found two compelling reasons to live. The first was the children—for how would they survive without me?—and the second was a white-hot flame of hatred that burned in me and would not be extinguished until I had dealt with Osbert Lynche.

On the night I first appeared at dinner, Nan and Addie fussed over me, Henry hastened to pull out my chair, and Jean sat by me cutting up my food and urging me to eat. Poor little George was very sullen and angry for he could not understand where his father had gone, and why his world had been turned upside-down. He rejected any platitudes regarding Rennie being in heaven, and demanded he come home at once. I fled from the room in tears.

I grew a little stronger with each day, and found some solace in visiting the cottage to commune with Rennie's portrait. Though some might find it odd, even today it's my habit to share my thoughts with him in this way. I was there, sitting in the garden in the pale November sun, when I was approached by Ephraim Best, hat in hand, begging pardon for the intrusion, and saying there was something weighing heavily on his mind. He'd been turned back at the Hall by Nan, who said I was in no fit state to receive anyone, but had lingered in the vicinity until he saw me ride out.

His story was a riveting one. He swore to me that when Rennie fell, he had collected all the guns in the party and that none had been recently fired. He also stated it would have been impossible for any of them to have shot Rennie in such a way, for they had all fanned out in a line about a dozen feet apart to flush out the fox, and Rennie had been shot square in the chest. I flinched, and he apologized for his bluntness, but declared it must be said. He'd searched in the direction of the shot, and had found a depression in the tall grass the size of a man's body, and a single shell casing which he thought to be from an army issue Enfield. Whoever had shot my husband had laid in wait and killed him in cold blood. They'd refused to hear him at the inquest, claiming he was trying to ease his conscience and divert blame, but I accepted the truth of it absolutely. Asking him to speak of it to no one, I told him of my suspicions, saying I might have need to call on him further. He declared himself ready and willing.

The investigation into Rennie's death had concluded that it was a tragic accident. I hadn't protested, for with no proof I knew it would be considered the ravings of a grief-stricken widow, and besides, the Fitzhelm name no longer wielded its former power. I would bide my time. In hatred I'd found my strength, and in revenge my motivation.

Dear Addie had been with me for over a month, and was missing her husband and children. I thanked her in a most heartfelt way, and sent her home, for I had murder in my heart and didn't wish her goodness to be tainted by it. I longed for my mother's wise counsel, but my letter would not find her until she returned to London some months later. I was certain that Lynche would approach me, and fortified myself to bury my revulsion and hatred, and play the role of my life. The grief-stricken widow I certainly was, but I would also have to be bewildered, vulnerable and totally ignorant of Rennie's business dealings. I could only pray the man was arrogant enough and greedy enough to believe it.

It was in the last week of November that a note came from Lynche saying that although he did not wish to intrude on my grief, he had some urgent matters of business to discuss which would wait no longer. I put him off for a week, and wrote to Margaret accepting her invitation for the children. After much urging they agreed to go for a fortnight. Henry especially balked, but I convinced him I was depending on him to watch over his brother and sister, and they'd all be home for Christmas. Jonathan was courting Dora White and refused to leave, saying I'd need a man about the place. I was now free to set the scene for my revenge.

I invited Lynche to dine and further to discuss the future of the estate, as he had been so invaluable to my father-in-law. I begged him to be patient with my ignorance of business affairs, and hoped he'd be so generous as to advise me. He sent a most unctuous reply, calling me "dear lady," and saying that he stood ready to assist me.

I had to tell Nan something of my plan, for she was adamantly opposed to allowing "that mucky little worm" in the house. I assured her that I had my wits about me, and she needed to trust me that this meeting was essential to the future of Fallowfield and indeed of all of us, but I dared not tell her of my true intentions.

I needed a strong and trustworthy confederate, and took Ephraim Best into my confidence. He reported a peculiar circumstance to me, that being that Orin Bender, the rude man whom Rennie had encountered, had disappeared and his house stood empty. It seemed trivial at the time, but would soon make dreadful sense.

We would need another pair of hands to carry out my scheme, and Ephraim suggested Jonathan. I hesitated, but there was no one else. Jonathan eagerly agreed, for he'd loved Rennie dearly, and blamed Lynche for the destruction of his own family.

The evening came, and Lynche arrived, all ingratiating smiles and fulsome charm. Dinner at the enormous, dimly lit dining-room table would be a Spartan meal with no wine, as I wished to reinforce the impression that we were in highly straitened circumstances. It was a grim-faced Nan who served us, for I'd given Dora and Polly leave to visit their parents. When Nan left us, Lynche had the temerity to lecture me on being too soft and familiar with the servants, saying they would take advantage of me. I bit back a sharp retort regarding his sister being ample proof of that, but instead said mildly that, yes, he was probably right. I confined our remaining conversation to inconsequential matters, and noted with satisfaction his mounting impatience. Finally he could contain himself no longer.

"My dear Lady"—I was quite sick of his "dear lady"s by this time—"I think I may have a solution for your predicament. I have brought with me a simple agreement to relieve you of the burden of managing the affairs of Fallowfield, for I will not deceive you that Sir Lyall, and sadly Sir Renforth as well, have left things in a sorry state, and it will take some serious effort on my part to put things right."

I allowed a tear to run down my cheek, and thanked him profusely for his kindness, suggesting that we retire to the study where there still remained some of Sir Lyall's cigars and vintage port, for I knew that gentlemen appreciated such things. He was fairly purring by the time he had explained his document and laid it out on the desk for me to sign, and was sampling his second glass of port. I was pleased to note that he was beginning to slur his words, for following the instructions in Grandda's notes as to dosage and body weight, I'd laced the port with enough laudanum to render him unconscious for several hours. As he slumped in his chair, I called out to Ephraim and Jonathan, who secured him, and would remain with him while I carried out the rest of my plan, for the night had just begun. I felt a strange exhilaration rising in me, and joked with them not to sample the port.

It was quite like old times. I fairly flew to my bedroom, and dressed in Henry's outgrown riding breeches and coat and my own boots, covering my hair with a cap. In my pocket were Grandda's keys and tools. Jonathan had done his part, and in the stable I found both my Jenny and Lynche's horse, a big, raw-boned dun, saddled and ready to go. I mounted Jenny, pulling the dun behind me. It was a clear cold night, the moon so bright as to cast shadows on the frosted ground, so I had no difficulty in finding my way to Lynche's lodgings. I tied Jenny in a secluded spot, and led the dun to its stall, where I unsaddled it, threw a blanket over its back, filled the manger with hay, and broke the thin skin of ice on the water trough, for I reasoned that if anyone should see the animal they'd assume Lynche had returned, and think nothing of it.

It was then my confidence collapsed, for when faced with the reality of a locked door, my heart thumped so loudly and my hands shook so badly that memory failed me, and I couldn't summon up the skill to tackle it. I stood frozen for what seemed an eternity, when suddenly Grandda's voice came to me, instructing me to be still and breathe deeply. All at once the fearless child I had once been came to the rescue of the lost, frightened woman I now was, and it was as if small hands were guiding mine. The door clicked open, and I entered a hallway black as the hubs of Hell. Lighting my father's old lantern I climbed the narrow steps to Lynche's lodgings.

My search proved easy, for whatever resources Lynche possessed he did not spend on luxuries. His apartment consisted of two small airless rooms, one containing a desk, chair and cupboard, the other a washstand, a wardrobe and a sort of ship's bunk topped with a narrow pallet. The desk contained only stationery, writing implements, bills and a sheaf of letters, which I stuffed into the pocket of my jacket. The cupboard produced a much-marked map of the district, which I also took. As there were no pictures or other likely concealments for a safe, I prayed I'd find what I sought in the bedchamber, where the sickly smell of pomade and unwashed sheets nearly caused me to gag. In the wardrobe I found coat and trousers, two shirts, a pair of boots, and various collars, cuffs and smalls. The washstand held only a cracked chamber pot, and I began to despair of finding anything useful, but when I raised the pallet on the bunk, I could see the gleam of a metal-bound box through the bed slats. Forcing it open, I paused only to confirm that I had indeed found what I'd prayed for, then fled to where I'd hidden Jenny.

Having informed my accomplices of my return, I spent the rest of the night perusing the documents and the account book I'd found in Lynche's strongbox along with considerable coin and currency. The salient papers were a series of deeds and transfers that began to form a pattern. With Lynche as the agent, all the Fallowfield properties had been purchased by one Orin Bender at prices which even to my inexperienced eye seemed low. They had then been transferred to Osbert Lynche for the sum of ten pounds each. By my reckoning Lynche presently owned two-thirds of Fallowfield as well as several adjoining properties, all carefully outlined on the map. If I'd signed the agreement he'd set before me that night, he'd virtually have become the master of Fallowfield Hall and the remainder of its tenancies. Unless he had some mysterious master plan, he was a most peculiar sort of miser, for instead of gold he hoarded property, which once acquired, simply languished unsold and untenanted. The account book confirmed these transactions, for Lynche was a most meticulous villain and had recorded his commissions, amounts given to "O.B." for the purchases, and payments to "O.B." upon transfer, but the figure that stopped my heart was the amount of fifty pounds paid to "O.B." the day before my Rennie was murdered. This, I had no doubt, was the price of Rennie's life.

As the clock chimed seven that morning, I washed my face, smoothed my hair and dressed once more in my widow's black. I removed Rennie's pistol from the drawer of the bedside table, determined that it was loaded, and descended the stairs. I asked my cohorts to stand guard in the hallway, promising to summon them if I were in any difficulty.

Lynche was now awake and struggling, and as I removed the gag, became most angry and indignant, saying he'd have the law on the lot of us. I replied coldly that under the circumstances, his threats did not influence me. He demanded the reason for this outrage, but I cut him off, telling him that I held incontrovertible proof that not only had he plotted to ruin the Fitzhelm family but that most wickedly and cruelly he had hired an assassin to murder my dear husband. His eyes widened with alarm and a rivulet of sweat ran down his face even as he vehemently denied it. I assured him that his denials fell on deaf ears, and he should make his peace with God, for I intended to kill him. It was then that I produced the pistol.

This precipitated the loss of any pretense at cultured speech and a stream of the foulest invective, the mildest of which was calling me a jumped-up little get parading as a lady, and an interfering little slut. Once started, he could not seem to stop. Sir Lyall had been an old fool, besotted with his son, and bankrupting himself to provide that spoiled puppy with luxuries that he, Lynche, could only dream of. In the wake of the old man's grief for Michael it had been a simple matter for Edwina to fill his head with vile insinuations, and to lace his food with nux vomica. Sir Lyall had gone to his death believing that I was trying to poison him. Lynche was proud of his perfidy, his one regret being that he'd overplayed his hand, for if Sir Lyall had lived only a few weeks longer, he'd have had it all. When he started to slander Rennie, I gripped the pistol in both hands and placed the muzzle hard against his chest.

"I believe this is the entry point of the bullet that took my husband's life. It's only fitting that you should end the same way."

Something in my manner must have convinced him I was in dead earnest and that his life was indeed forfeit, for his diatribe stopped as suddenly as it had begun. He started to shake, and lost control of his bladder, then began to rock back and forth, straining against his bonds and keening like a wounded dog.

I could not do it. He deserved to die, and God knows I wanted him dead, but I couldn't kill him. Perhaps if he'd remained the vicious, snarling villain he'd first revealed, but this miserable, stinking, snivelling excuse for a man . . . I let out a great scream of frustration, and Ephraim and Jonathan rushed into the room to defend me.

Assuring them that I was unharmed and Lynche still safely secured, I said, "I must ask you to bear with me a little longer. I need you to guard this pile of offal while I think what to do with him."

I dropped the pistol, blindly climbed the stairs to my bedroom, retched up what little I had in my stomach, and flung myself across the bed, cursing my weakness with bitter tears.

It was thus that Nan found me, and gathered me up in her arms, as I poured out the whole dreadful story. She thanked God that He'd stayed my hand, and said He would show me the righteous path to a solution. As she bathed my face and stroked my hair a name surfaced in my memory, that of Preston Collingford.

Preston, thwarted in his academic ambitions by the death of Clarissa Budge and the subsequent revelations, had bowed to the inevitable and gone to work for his father. Surprisingly, he'd developed a keen eye for designs that would appeal to the newly prosperous, and had introduced several very popular china patterns most notable for their lavish use of gold. Upon his father's retirement, he had succeeded him as head of the firm. All this I knew because he'd spent considerable time and money refurbishing his aunt's old house, where he now lived with his wife and a veritable army of children. As a token of his gratitude for my kindness, he'd presented me with a lovely tea set, the teapot, milk jug and sugar bowl painted with a likeness of my cottage surrounded by all the flowers of an English garden, and the twelve cups and saucers each representing one of those flowers. When we met in the village, he would talk of those happy days, lamenting the sad end of his youthful ambitions. Surely he, of all people, would have some understanding and sympathy for my present situation, and might advise me as to my next step.

This being a Sunday and not yet ten o'clock, I donned my hat and coat to attend the morning service at Saint Mark's. As we emerged from the church, I sought Preston out, begging him to pardon my intrusion, and asking if he could spare a few minutes to discuss a matter of grave importance. He sent his wife and children ahead in the carriage, and as we walked I acquainted him with the horrendous events leading up to my confinement of Lynche. I could see from his rising indignation that he didn't question the truth of my allegations, and that this formidable man was a far cry from the mild, scholarly youth I remembered.

"Lady Fitzhelm, I am entirely at your service. Return to Fallow-field, and I shall join you there sometime this evening. Have no fear. Lynche will pay dearly for his transgressions. Aside from the outrage he has perpetrated upon you, his injustice to my aunt and myself has for all these years been like a festering wound in my heart, and it's time we were both purged of him."

Lynche had been allowed to bathe, wrap himself in a sheet and eat. I returned to Fallowfield to find that his keys had been discovered hanging from a leather cord about his neck. I sent Jonathan to his lodgings to collect his belongings. Sensing that his demise was no longer imminent, he regained some of his former arrogant nature and complained of rough treatment, but Ephraim shortly convinced him that he'd best remain silent.

As there was no action I could presently take, I retired to my bedroom and busied myself with tidying up. The jacket I'd worn on my wild ride had been flung to the floor, and as I picked it up, I discovered the letters I'd stuffed so hastily into the pocket. In reading them, I found one sad story after another—heartbreaking pleas from those he had dispossessed, begging for a little more time, to wait 'til the harvest was in, to pity their aged parents. It emerged that his habit was to loan money against property at exorbitant rates, and then to foreclose when the unfortunate borrowers were most extended. I began to think some good might come of this affair, and that if I did nothing else, I could at least redeem my weakness by redressing these wrongs in Rennie's name. I vowed also to restore Fallowfield to a prosperous state as the birthright of our son Henry.

Preston Collingford appeared that evening in the company of two sturdy men from his factory. His intention was to place Lynche on the first available ship sailing to some remote part of the Empire, with only the clothes on his back and sufficient money that he would not starve. Everything else would be stripped from him, and he would be warned that should he ever return to this locality we would bring the full weight of the law down on him. Based on the letters I'd found, we determined that Lynche must return those properties to their owners. The Fallowfield tenancies he was to sign back to me.

My last contact with Osbert Lynche was to dictate to him a letter to be delivered to his lodgings saying that urgent matters had called him permanently away, and that his landlord should take his horse as payment for any outstanding obligations. Preston Collingford and his two henchmen bundled Lynche into the carriage, and departed for Liverpool. To my knowledge, beyond the recipients of his perceived charity, no one in the village displayed any curiosity about his disappearance. It was as if he had never been. He never by so much as a word admitted guilt in Rennie's death, and continued enquiries have revealed no trace of Orin Bender.

I of course can never forget, but I was determined that life at Fallowfield should go on. Preston hired a solicitor to return the properties anonymously to their rightful owners, and I personally approached former Fallowfield tenants regarding their reinstatement. I gave to each a sum of money sufficient to carry them through to the first full harvest, assuring them that no rents would be due until then. Ephraim Best received free tenancy for his lifetime, and remains my valued friend.

When I asked Jonathan what he wanted most in his life, he unhesitatingly answered that it was to marry Dora White, and to farm Brookside, where he had lived so happily with his family. I agreed, and in return asked only that he never speak of these events, and that he always remain Henry's good friend and right-hand man.

The children returned just before Christmas, and to this day Henry and Jean know nothing of what took place. George, of course, will read this account, but I have sworn him to secrecy regarding anything he learns here.

I will once again move quickly through the years that followed.

Christmas that year was a quiet affair, but I felt something was needed to dispel the winter gloom, and reaching back to my childhood, had Abner Gentles place in the parish announcements an invitation to all to celebrate the feast of Saint Stephen at Fallowfield Hall. We opened up the old conservatory for the occasion. Jonathan fired up the boiler, declared it sound, and hot water coursed through pipes that had once provided a tropical atmosphere for exotic plants and trees. Broken panes were replaced, and the ladies of the parish mustered an army to scrub away the grime of years until the glass fairly sparkled.

On the day, trestle tables sagged with the weight of the feast brought together by all those good people for a celebration which would become a much anticipated annual event, everyone eating, drinking and dancing, snug against the winter cold, yet still under the stars. Jonathan announced his engagement to Dora White, and was toasted by all. Little George, then seven, was a great success on his fiddle as we resurrected some of the old dance tunes from Grandda's portfolio, and we closed the celebration with a sweet little waltz called "Columbine," so popular then, with everyone singing along. It still brings tears to my eyes. If only my Rennie had been there to dance with me once more.

> *We will walk again that dappled lane*
> *Where you promised to be mine,*
> *And so lovingly you'll cling to me*
> *My sweet little Columbine.*

My poor old Jenny foundered in her stall early that January, could not rise, and Jonathan had to put her down. I was tearful for days.

Henry began his short-lived university career. In his letters he complained bitterly that he was treated as an uncultured country bumpkin and begged to come home.

Only receiving my letter upon her return, my mother descended in April, clucking like a mother hen about my lack of colour and loss of weight. She was very brown and fit, having abandoned all concern for her complexion in the heat of the Australian sun. She told me she'd left her corset at an Aboriginal camp, and intended never to wear another. We had a good laugh guessing what the inhabitants would make of it. The laughter breached something in me, and I broke down.

At my mother's insistence, Jean and George and I accompanied her back to London, Henry still being at university. I had not comprehended the full weight of my ordeal until I was away from Fallowfield and the burden lifted. I was suddenly weak and helpless as a newborn, and given to unprovoked fits of weeping. My mother briskly delivered me to Fanny Gosling, saying there was nothing like a new wardrobe to fortify the spirits. We spent several evenings at the theatre with Tony Cleary, creaky and crotchety but still elegant and wickedly funny.

I started to read again. My mother recommended *Madame Bovary*, but it was a bad choice, for I could not stomach its dreary inevitability and did not finish it. In fact, the only joy I gained from literature was sharing the sublime silliness of Edward Lear and Lewis Carroll with the children. George was insatiably interested in my mother's travels and the artifacts she had acquired, and she seemed to have limitless patience for his questions. She won his heart forever with my half-brothers' old copies of *Treasure Island* and *Two Years Before the Mast*, but the books that most captured him were two volumes penned by the gentleman pirate and privateer William Dampier called *Voyages and Descriptions* and *A Voyage to New Holland*, which he'd discovered in the small library Admiral Blackwood kept at the house.

My mother had invested heavily in Blackwood Explorations and was unable to aid me financially, but my visit to Sarah Green was a heartening one. My savings had grown to over four thousand pounds. With careful management, I could finance some much-needed repairs and improvements to Fallowfield Hall, and see both Henry and George through university.

I told Sarah of my mother's notion that there might be some quite valuable pieces of furniture, pictures and other items stored in the attics at Fallowfield, and she visited me in the company of her husband, Asa Green, an appraiser and auctioneer for a London auction house. I thought to increase our capital by auctioning what I could, then closing off the attics and most of the old nursery floor, making the ground floor and first floor of the Hall both habitable and presentable. The enterprise was a great success. Taking my mother's advice, I replaced some of the heavier furniture from the ground floor with older, more elegant pieces from the attics. The remainder brought in a gratifying sum, including the dreadful ivory warriors, which fetched an astonishing amount. This afforded us at least the appearance of prosperity and would allow Henry to put a confident face on his role as Sir Henry Fitzhelm.

Jonathan and Dora were married that spring, a modest but joyous occasion, and the new couple settled into Brookside. We would miss Jonathan's constant, steady presence at the Hall, and with Dora gone, Polly suggested bringing their youngest sister Evie into service.

Having rejected university life, Henry returned home, and with my guidance threw himself wholeheartedly into the management of the estate. The responsibility sat easily on him, and it was clear that like his father his ambitions stretched no further than the boundaries of Fallowfield. I worried that other than Jonathan he had no firm friend-ships, but was impartially charming and friendly to everyone, male and female alike, showing no interest in any of the eligible local girls. I did wonder if some part of his emotions had frozen at the moment of his father's death, and that past that point no one was allowed into his heart.

Jean, who was fourteen by this time, had learned what I could teach her, and spent much of her time in the kitchen with Nan and

Mrs. Vesey. She loved to cook and bake, and had a magical hand with pastry.

I now had considerable time to devote to George's education. Although often moody and rebellious, he possessed an intelligence and curiosity that made him both a delight and a challenge to teach. One stormy afternoon as we passed the time playing a sort of two-handed whist, I thought to amuse him with a little sleight of hand. He was fascinated, giving me no peace until I'd shown him my entire repertoire. He then set about perfecting his own technique, and would not be satisfied until he could win consistently. Alas, I should have taught him how to lose as well. Mathematics, which had previously bored him, became irresistible when applied to the calculation of odds, and we developed a playing-card version of Kim's Game to increase his powers of retention. At the time, it was no more than an amusing way to engage his intellect, and I thought myself very clever, for with George, if a subject didn't interest him, it didn't exist.

He now played Old Nick, though he was forbidden to take him from the house, and I'd found him another instrument to take away to school when he started in September. Even then he had my father's touch, and it was a delight to hear him play.

By 1910 Fallowfield was modestly flourishing, Henry seemed genuinely content for the first time since Rennie's death, Jean was most happily married and expecting my first grandchild, and George was at Harrow.

I received a letter from Sarah Green saying that when I was next in London, there was someone she'd like me to meet. I thought she was matchmaking. My mother had made some fruitless attempts to introduce me to eligible men, but for me, there would only ever be Rennie. I answered Sarah lightly, telling her it would be no use, but she replied that indeed this was not her intention, and she would enlighten me when we met. As it transpired, the subject was indeed matrimony, but it was Henry who was the object. An acquaintance of hers, a widower, sought a husband for his only, much-loved daughter. I instantly recognized the name, Seth Goldring, of the Goldring stores.

As with Sarah's family, the Goldring fortunes began with a caravan that toured isolated villages loaded down with everything a housewife might need, from pots and pans to fabric and trims. Emmanuel Goldring had opened the first Goldring Store in Manchester in 1886, and over time established stores in several other provincial centres. When he died, his son, Seth, was already at the helm, having opened the now-famous London store. He'd subsequently formed Goldring Import Export, and according to Sarah, having acquired wealth and influence beyond anyone's imagination, was now in active pursuit of a knighthood. Part of his strategy was to marry Ruth, his daughter and only heir, to some eligible young man with a title. He found no lack of candidates, but Ruth, it seemed, would have none of them.

"Why Henry?" I asked.

"I have the feeling they might suit," was Sarah's reply. "There's no harm in them meeting. You'll like her. She's a charming girl."

My feelings about arranged marriage are already well documented here, but I saw no reason why the two shouldn't meet. In a brief encounter with Seth Goldring, I was very frank about the family circumstances and my reservations, and we agreed that neither of us would impose any expectations on such a meeting.

A team of horses could not drag Henry to London, and so I invited Ruth and Seth Goldring, my mother, and Sarah and Asa Green for an autumn weekend at Fallowfield. My mother came early to help with preparations. Much time was spent fussing over menus, and two first-floor bedrooms were opened and aired for the Goldrings. My mother and the Greens would dine at the Hall, but would stay at the cottage with young Evie to see to them.

The Greens and Goldrings arrived in Seth's automobile, causing quite a stir in the village. Seth informed me with all the pride of a five-year-old with a new toy that it was a Crossley, direct from the factory, having the power of twenty-two horses. When I replied mildly that I found one quite adequate for my needs, he shot me a pitying glance.

He was about my age (I was forty-nine), a short, broad-chested bull of a man, with bushy eyebrows, receding hair and bristling with energy. My mother called him a rough diamond, and Nan declared him common as mud, but though hardly a gentleman, he was very shrewd and intuitive and knew precisely when to pull in his horns. We understood each other very well.

Everyone loved Ruthie. She was tall and slim with a face that was classically beautiful rather than pretty, with thick, dark, curling hair and eyes so deep a blue as to be almost violet, and glowing with quiet intelligence and humour. She managed her father in so deft a manner I wondered if he were even aware of it.

Dinner that night was a lively, unpretentious affair. It was wonderful to hear laughter ring out in the dining room, which had always held the bleakest of memories for me. Henry behaved with his usual deference and charm, seeming no more nor less interested in Ruth than he was in anyone else. Ruth, however, could not take her eyes off Henry.

The next morning, Henry and Jonathan took Seth Goldring out for a bit of shooting. The three of them returned in the highest of humour with a brace of pheasants, and Seth clapped Henry on the shoulder, declaring him the best of hosts for allowing him to bag the lot. The rest of the weekend passed in a similarly pleasant manner, closing with an evening of cards and music. Ruthie was an accomplished pianist with a lovely voice. She and Henry danced together, and seemed to get on famously. Seth Goldring declared he would send me the best gramophone his stores offered, and a collection of recordings to go with it, saying I'd be amazed at the sound. Indeed I was, for when I wound it up, it sounded like nothing so much as a cat with its tail caught in the mangle.

Sarah was right. The girl was perfect. I need not have worried about any arrangement, for Ruthie adored Henry from the moment she saw him, and Henry, it appeared, was perfectly happy to be adored.

It was not a long courtship, indeed barely a courtship at all, for Ruth and Henry were immediately wrapped up in the restoration of Fallowfield Hall, discussing their plans as if they were already married. Seth had previously settled a staggering allowance on Ruth, and would settle a similar amount on Henry the day they were wed. He further offered pay for all work done to Fallowfield Hall as a wedding present. In keeping with newly established precedent, they would officially announce their engagement at the Saint Stephen's Day celebration, and it was agreed they'd marry twice, once in a private ceremony performed by a Jewish priest, and later in a public one at Saint Mark's with Abner Gentles presiding. I'll confess the one thought which sustained me through this period was that when it was over I could return to a simple life in my cottage with Nan and my memories of Rennie, leaving the burden of Fallowfield to others.

My granddaughter Teresa Elizabeth Stewart was born that November of 1910, a beautiful little girl with her father's fair hair, and her mother's sweet nature. Jean, like her namesake, was a natural wife and mother, and positively glowed with joy.

George came home for Christmas. Having been grudgingly accepted by the bloods at Harrow, he'd become quite the little public-school snob, making disparaging remarks about his brother marrying a Jewish shopkeeper's daughter. This disrespect for Seth Goldring created a war in him, however, for as much as he professed to dislike the man, he loved and coveted his automobile. It was quite comical to watch him attempt to be civil to Seth in order to have access to the vehicle. Seth chose to be amused rather than offended, and a sort of truce was reached when he offered to teach George to drive in return for cleaning and polishing the car. It was immaculate from that point on.

Ruth and Henry's formal wedding took place in April of 1911 at Saint Mark's, and was the grandest in recent memory. It was agreed they were a most extraordinarily handsome couple. I didn't know most of the people who attended. Arrangements were happily out of my hands, and I had friends and family to support me throughout the ordeal. The newlyweds had generously invited the village to the reception and ball that followed. As had Rennie and I, they'd elected not to travel, but rather to take up their life at Fallowfield, and I happily retreated to my cottage. Henry to this day has never been farther from his home than London, and that only under protest. Their first son, Alistair Renforth Fitzhelm, was born within the year. You'd be hard-pressed to find a prouder, more indulgent grandfather than Seth Goldring, who immediately set about securing places at the best schools for the infant Alistair.

Work began at once on Fallowfield Hall, and indeed goes on to this day despite the current lack of able-bodied men due to the war. Two of the more awkward additions were demolished at once, and the classic lines of the house began to emerge. Neatly groomed lawns and gardens replaced the tangled neglect of years.

It was during George's final weeks at Harrow that my hopes for him began to unravel. I received an urgent note from my mother saying there had been an unfortunate incident, that George was with her in London, and I'd best come at once. Seth Goldring kindly offered to drive me there in his automobile, and I arrived looking like I'd been through a hurricane.

I found George ensconced in a bedroom at Windward House sporting a blackened eye, a chipped tooth and three cracked ribs, and with a martyred air that put me instantly on my guard. He said he'd been the victim of a vicious and unprovoked attack by a gang of sports at a public house frequented by Harrow boys. The school having recently suffered adverse publicity with regard to reports of bullying, the headmaster was relieved rather than angry when George refused to name names. He allowed that if George finished his last few weeks with an approved tutor he could graduate with the rest of his classmates. It took me about twenty minutes to winkle the truth out of him, and even then I had to weed through a wilderness of excuses and justifications.

He complained that he'd been so hard up he couldn't even afford to have a few drinks with his friends. This was a rebuke for me, because I'd refused Seth's offer to subsidize him, and even more cruelly in his eyes, had turned down the offer of a motorized bicycle. As a result of my perceived repression, he'd been forced to supplement his allowance playing popular songs on the fiddle with a pianist at the pub on weekends. He became aware that some activity was taking place in an upstairs room, and discovered the attraction was cards. He inveigled his way into the game, and from that point profited quite nicely at the expense of the sports, for as he said, he could hardly cheat his blood chums, which nice distinction didn't impress me one whit. The young fool had won so consistently that although they never actually caught him cheating, the sports had meted out some adolescent justice, even smashing his fiddle. I thought it a blessing he hadn't been sent down, and feeling I should share some measure of blame, I was not so severe with him as I should have been. He would remain at Windward House. We'd engage a tutor, and he'd be off to Oxford as planned the following September.

It was the beginning of a long downward slope.

I thought he'd settled in quite well at Oxford, and began to breathe more easily as his first year proved to be free of incident, and indeed his progress in the sciences encouraged me to hope that he might have found a focus for his energies.

In November of his second year, I was in London to visit my

mother, who at seventy-five had finally ended her travels. She had ingested a parasite on an expedition to India and Nepal, and that, along with a violent reaction to the cure, had greatly weakened her constitution. I was spending as much time as possible at her side.

I was in a bookshop trying to find something that would capture her interest, when I came upon a new publication entitled *The Country Apothecary—An Illustrated Study of Rural Medicine in the Early 19th Century*, authored by a certain Dr. Packingham whom I knew to be one of George's professors. Although it purported to be the result of years of research, I had only to glance through it and come upon the drawing of a man-shaped root with a comic face that had delighted me as a child to recognize it as my grandfather's work.

I left at once for Oxford with the book in hand, and confronted George at his lodgings. I was so angry I actually struck him across the face. He swore he had innocently mentioned the old ledger to Dr. Packingham, who had asked if he might examine it. He claimed to be mortified at his teacher's deception. Things went from bad to worse, for when I threatened to expose his precious professor, he was forced to admit that he'd exchanged the ledger for favourable examination results. He pleaded that he'd learned a valuable lesson, and if the truth came out, he'd certainly be sent down and his teacher's reputation ruined. I didn't care tuppence for the man's reputation, but the family's reputation and George's future were another matter. I told him if he made any attempt to warn Dr. Packingham, I'd completely wash my hands of him. The deceiving doctor I would handle in my own way.

Wishing to allow myself a cooling-down period, I returned to Fallowfield to discover that not just the botanical notes, but also Grandda's notes on bone-setting and midwifery and the two Albinus volumes on anatomy were missing.

I wrote to Dr. Packingham requesting an appointment to discuss George's studies and was received with an elaborate tea in his rooms. I came straight to the point, informing him that if he did not immediately surrender the ledgers and the two volumes of Albinus I would publicly challenge his authorship of *The Country Apothecary*. He argued that it was impossible to completely comply with my wishes, as a second book, *The Country Midwife*, was already in the hands of his publisher, and the pair of Albinus' had been sold to a German collector with half the proceeds going to George. He would return the original ledgers, but the antique volumes were irretrievable, and the money gone. Bowing to circumstance, I took the two ledgers and returned to Fallowfield feeling every minute of my fifty-four years.

George stayed with me at the cottage that Christmas. I could barely bring myself to speak to him, and he spent most of his time sulking in his room playing Old Nick. His playing might have softened my heart, but I saw too clearly that a ghost from my past had returned to haunt me in the guise of my son. George had not inherited the crueller side of my father's nature, but his recklessness, fecklessness and total disregard for the consequences of his actions were all too familiar. Not only was he unlikely to reform, but he would inevitably do something so reprehensible that I would not have the power to conceal it.

I no longer had any hopes for his future at Oxford, and indeed, within the year he was expelled as the instigator of a scheme to sell copies of upcoming examinations. His knowledge of locks had allowed him to steal, copy, then replace the papers undetected. It was poor judgment in his choice of confederates that had been his downfall, and it was fortunate that college authorities decided they did not have enough proof to prosecute in the matter of theft. Unless I could secure him a commission, he would certainly be conscripted, and I feared that with his emotional volatility he would not survive the bloody conflict in France.

Knowing little of George's previous history, Seth Goldring was sympathetic when it came to his disgrace, putting it down to sowing his wild oats, and saying that since he didn't seem to lack enterprise, he'd find him a place at Goldring Import Export. This would secure him an exemption from military service, as many of Goldring's goods and services were deemed crucial to the war effort. George seemed almost enthusiastic, and I hoped against hope that he wouldn't squander this chance to redeem himself.

As yet another step in his pursuit of a knighthood, Seth had established the Goldring Institute, a free school that taught basic education, useful trades and business skills to promising young men from the London slums, thus affording them a better chance at life, and also providing Seth with an endless supply of grateful and loyal employees. It was inevitable that one of them should revert to type, and equally inevitable that he and George would find each other.

George's new best chum was Tom Wilbur, the youngest child of five parented by a seamstress and a merchant seaman. With an absent father and a mother who worked long hours, he'd taken to the streets at an early age and would have ended his life in prison had it not been for the intervention of a crusading priest named Father Timothy. The good Father was famous for his championing of hard cases, and counted the salvation of Tom Wilbur as one of his successes. Tom was a star student at the Goldring Institute, and had worked his way up to an assistant warehouse manager's position at Goldring Import Export by the time George arrived.

George delighted in his new situation, and his letters were full of descriptions of performances seen at the London music halls, and riotous evenings of music, dancing, girls and gambling with his new friend.

I met Tom Wilbur in March of 1916, when George brought him to Fallowfield for a family celebration, the christening of Ruth and Henry's baby daughter, Caroline Victoria. They arrived on twin motorcycles, and George was beside himself with pride. The machines looked very new, and I asked George how he'd managed it on a shipping clerk's salary. He breezily declared it was second-hand, having been in a smash-up, and that with a loan from Tom he'd gotten it for a song. I thought to warn Tom about lending my son money, but something about him put me off for all that he seemed an attractive, open-faced fellow, and I decided to hold my counsel until I had a better sense of him. Nan said butter wouldn't melt in his mouth.

The final blow fell three months later. Seth had been concerned for some time that the bold hijackers of some of his transports were aided by an informant within his company and had narrowed his suspicions to Tom Wilbur. I only learned of this when Seth came to me to tell me that Tom, when confronted with the facts, denied nothing, but said that he wouldn't "go down for it alone," and that George was "in it up to his ears." Seth, though livid with George, was sympathetic to me, and offered what I thought was a more than generous solution.

This brings me to the end of my story, and a decision no mother should have to face. I've made an agreement with Seth that in return for his promise not to prosecute, George will immigrate to Canada, and work for Goldring Import Export in the city of Halifax under the watchful eye of a manager who will be fully appraised of his previous history, and will dismiss him at the first sign of misbehaviour. He will also receive a modest allowance, which will cease if he attempts to set foot back in England.

George, uncharacteristically, has made no protest, but refuses to speak to me, and the reproach in his eyes is more than I can bear. As I pack his trunk, I will also place in the secret drawer of Old Nick's casket my father's musical composition "Joyner's Dream," the gold watch given to my father by my mother, the little ruby ring and the pearl pendant which my mother gave to me, and the copy of *Gulliver's Travels* which both George and I loved so as children. Last of all, I include this journal, which is the only true legacy I can offer him, for as much as Henry and Jean are Fitzhelms, George is a Joyner to the bone.

My dear boy, I love you more than I can say. I pray you will read this journal with an open heart, preserve its secrets as I have done, and in time add your voice to the others here.

God bless you and keep you safe, my darling. My heart is finally, irrevocably broken.

(I include here three letters found between the pages of the journal. L.A.F.)

September 23, 1921

My dear boy,

Such sad news. Within the space of a month I've lost two of the people I loved most in the world, my lovely Nan, and my own darling mother whom you children called Aunt Tess, and you and Addie are the only ones to whom I can confide the full depth of my grief, for I had two mothers and now I have none.

Nan had gotten quite fat and short of breath, and her knees could not easily bear her weight. Still, she insisted on preparing my breakfast although I had forbidden her to attempt the stairs, and she stubbornly persisted in tending her vegetable garden, wearing no hat to protect her from the sun. In the heat of August I was helping her clear out the remains of the bean patch, when she suddenly sat down quite hard in the midst of the cabbages, and I had considerable difficulty getting her up and into the shade of the kitchen. She was a most alarming colour, and I had to apply cold compresses to lower the heat of her body. She insisted she was fine, and just needed a bit of a lie-down. She was still sleeping at dinnertime, and I didn't rouse her, thinking the rest would do her good. When I didn't hear the kettle in the morning, I came down to see how she was, and found her dead in her bed, for all the world as if she were still sleeping. Her age, I believe, was eighty-one.

Mother's constitution had been seriously weakened by the

parasite she picked up all those years ago on her voyage to India. She was receiving large doses of morphine for abdominal pain. My half-brother, Alex, and I were spending as much time as possible with her, and came to like each other very well. His brothers Peter and Elliot are still on a Mongolian expedition, and will not hear of their loss until they return.

It's my belief she'd had enough of suffering, and took a massive dose of the drug, though the doctors deny it. Alex confessed to me that in those final days she'd revealed our true relationship. I thought he'd hate me for the years of deceit, but he declared that no, it was a relief, for it made everything clear, and we embraced as a brother and sister united in grief.

One small joy that has come from this is that I shall at last be able to give you some substantial aid. My mother left me her shares in Blackwood Explorations, and Alex and I have come to an equitable agreement regarding their sale to him. It amounts to some twelve thousand pounds, and as I am already well provided for and Henry has no need of it, I will divide it between you and your sister, Jean. I trust you will use it wisely.

I have two wishes concerning you. The first is that you marry and lead a more settled life, and the other that I will someday see you again, for I miss you more with each passing day.

Your loving Mama

June 12, 1944

Dear Georgie,

I hardly know how to begin, so I'll just blurt it out as I usually do. Our darling mama died in the early hours of this morning. Jonathan's daughter Nancy Godskill found her sitting up in her bed, the lamp still burning, and a book fallen from her hand as if she had just drifted off. Nancy telephoned Ruth and Henry, and Ruth called me. We're all devastated, as I know you will be, and I wish I could be with you to dry your tears as I did when you were little, but I'm sure your dear wife will comfort you. I enclose a letter Mama was writing to you. It's unfinished, but I knew you'd want to have it. My thoughts and prayers are with you.

Your loving sister, Jean

June 11, 1944

My darling boy,

I've suddenly realized it's been over two months since I last wrote to you, and you'll be wondering if I'm still alive. You must be so proud to have two boys at university, and little Georgina sounds like an absolute pet. I do wish you'd reconsider and bring the whole family to spend Christmas here. Ruthie and Henry put on a marvellous spread, and would be delighted to have you. There's plenty of room here at the cottage for you and Alma, and the children could stay with their cousins at the Hall. Do please come. I'm longing to see you, and it would be wonderful to play the old tunes as we used to.

Not much new to tell. I lead a very quiet existence these days. Jonathan and Dora's youngest girl, Nancy, is staying with me. They named her for Nan, you know, and it's nice to have another Nan in the house. She dreams of being a nurse and midwife, and I'm encouraging her by improving her reading and writing skills and giving her access to Grandda's notes. Her father has become a rather conservative old stick, and has very antiquated opinions about women working (as if we didn't all work like slaves anyway!). You'd think the war would have changed most everyone's views on that.

You'll remember Ruth and Henry's youngest, Nicholas,

now fifteen. Nicky is very good to his old grandmama, and we're great chums. He spends most weekends with me, and I'm teaching him how to play cards. He cheats outrageously, and with such an angelic countenance as would be a dead giveaway in any serious game. He's devilishly handsome, and I'm sure will cut a very wide swath with the ladies before he settles down.

Alistair has made a great success of Goldring since his grandfather died, and at thirty-two is quite the rising star in the world of finance. I must admit, I don't understand half of what he says, although it seems to me that a great deal of it is new terms for very old practices. Still, he's a nice boy, although I find his wife, Millicent, a bit of a snob. Who'd believe I'd be a great-grandmama twice over?

I've renewed an old acquaintance. You may recall Mademoiselle Guerin who did the watercolour sketches of your father and me. She's quite famous now, and Ruthie has commissioned her to paint two life-sized portraits to hang on the landing of the great staircase at the Hall based on her original sketches, so it seems I'll have a surrogate to keep a sharp eye on all the comings and goings at Fallowfield. She's agreed to do her preliminary work here at the cottage, as I cannot bear to be without your father's likeness even for a day.

Feeling envious of the freedom of young girls these days, I thought I'd follow mother's lead and give up my corset, but my poor back complained bitterly at the lack of support, and I'm forced to accept that when she did it she was twenty years younger than I am now. My health is otherwise good, although I need my father's old stick now to help me get about. I've been a bit tired lately, and take little naps to restore myself. I'm feeling the need of one now, and will finish this tomorrow . . .

Chapter 5

GEORGE FITZHELM (1895–1961)

My Life So Far
by George Francis Fitzhelm, Esq.
January 10, 1917

*H*aving read the dubious family history my mother has presented to me, it seems I run pretty true to form, and as I'll certainly have the time, I think I'll start a journal of my own.

So here we sit, Old Nick and I, two days out, in a cabin the size of a butler's pantry, contemplating our future in a country we know nothing about, and feeling heartily sorry for ourselves. My gramophone is regrettably packed away somewhere in the hold, and, having digested the aforementioned history, I'm ironically reduced to rereading the travels of Gulliver, the only book I have with me. No Brobdingnagians so far, but plenty of Lilliputians on board.

I suppose I should feel a great deal sorrier if I were Tom Wilbur, occupying a similar-sized prison cell for the next five years. No hard feelings there. He did what he had to. He'll be all right. He's salted away a nice *bit of lolly for when he gets out, and he's an enterprising fellow as I have reason to know. Must drop him a note when I get settled to let him know where I am.*

I do think it bloody unfair that I should be shipped off to God knows where for the sake of some glorified shopkeeper's lust for a knighthood and a great cursed heap of bricks and mortar that should have been levelled to the ground years ago. Not Henry's fault. He's a thoroughly good sort with a brain the size of a pea, and imagination and ambition to match. Mind you, Ruthie has brains enough for both of them, and the old man's money takes care of the rest. If Ma hadn't been so stiff-necked, I'd have had my share, and none of this need have happened.

Poor Ma. I'm sorry to have caused her grief, but after all, a chap has to have some decent clothes and money in his pocket if he's to keep up with the other young blades on a tenth of their income. The remittance is pretty beggarly, but I like the idea of making that pompous old windbag pay, and it will give me time to find my bearings.

AUGUST 1960

How strange to be confronted with one's twenty-two-year-old self. What an insufferable little prat I was, but it's an accurate portrayal, and I'll let it stand. Now that I approach the venerable age of seventy, I've decided to add my story to the family record, and pass it on to my daughter, Georgina. I'll accomplish this by copying selected entries from my old diaries, and adding current comments. The diaries are a bit spotty at times, and end abruptly in 1944, with my mother's death, so I'll have to rely on my highly fallible memory to provide the rest.

JANUARY 12

Things are pretty dismal on this deck. A dreadful woman with two painfully plain daughters has got wind of my family connections. They're related to the owners of the steamship line. Unless I'm shockingly rude, I'll have to spend most of the trip avoiding them. There's some hearty military brass off to recruit more colonial cannon fodder, and two chaps who are likely prospects for cards. I'll see what a casual hint in that direction leads to.

Everyone is desperately trying to look like they're having a jolly time dancing to the prehistoric dance band. I thought I might find a kindred spirit there, but they might as well be grocers' clerks for all the interest they show in music. Mind you, the thought of playing for this crowd of Philistines would certainly take the joy out of it for me.

There couldn't be a worse season for travel than this. My clothing is sadly inadequate. It's very rough and windy, and so bitterly cold I thought my ears would fall off, and of course we can't show any lights, or we'll be torpedoed out of existence. I'm told there are icebergs to consider as well. There's nobody aboard this rusting tub that doesn't absolutely have to be here.

I detect music drifting up the stairwell from the bowels of the ship, mainly ragtime and jazzy stuff. Jolly good. Someone down there is a smashing guitarist. Not a gramophone. Too many stops and starts. An investigation is in order.

JANUARY 14

Made a tidy profit at cards last night. If this keeps up, I'll be flush for the duration. Pretty simple really—win two, lose one in no particular order, take care to be obviously down and disappointed every so often. Learned my lesson there. One of my new best chums, Angus McSorrel, is somebody in Halifax, and promises to introduce me around when we make shore. Don't mind playing the aristo card when it serves me. One of the military types, a colonel, has been dropping nasty comments about why an able-bodied young fellow like myself isn't in the army. Pretty beastly.

Made the acquaintance of one of the engine crew, and got the tuppence tour of the engine room. Fascinating how powerful steam is. I have some ideas about that. I'll see if I can finagle a visit to the wireless room, although they're a bit shirty about it. Top secret, don't you know.

The mystery of the music is solved. A coloured orchestra, anticipating a German advance on Paris, got out while the getting was good. When their motor ran out of petrol, they encountered some of our boys, and thanks to a young officer who was a ragtime fanatic, the three of them ended up as orderlies on a hospital ship sailing back to England. They're now working their way back to Canada as stokers.

This was how I met Desmond Miller. He'd have been in his late twenties at the time. Light-skinned, short and skinny with enormous hands and feet, startling green eyes, and a face more humorous than handsome, orphaned at ten, raised by an aunt and uncle. He and his friends, Eli Turner and Kip Bundy, were from Truro, Nova Scotia, but had migrated to New York to join the ragtime revolution. They'd gone to Paris as part of a coloured musical revue, and stayed on, performing in a nightclub as the Nubian Knights with a singer and acrobatic dancer with the unlikely name of Tilly Teasel. Kip showed me a photo of them in turbans, vests and satin bloomers, like something out of a Christmas pantomime. Tilly had a wealthy lover and a swank apartment, and decided to wait things out, saying the Germans would be ready for some exotic entertainment if they reached Paris, and no bones broken if they didn't, but the boys didn't fancy their chances. When their motor died, they had to hoof it. Des sliced his foot on a piece of rusty metal, and was in pretty rough shape by the time they reached British lines.

Once in England, they needed transport home. Des's aunt Ida had written to him saying that a certain Reverend White was trying to form a battalion of coloured volunteers to fight with the Canadian troops. Eli and Kip planned to sign up as soon as they returned, and Des would join them as soon as his foot healed up. The steamship line hadn't been keen to hire them, as the rest of the crew would refuse to share quarters, but able-bodied men were hard to find, and they offered to do the work of six for the pay of three, bunking together in the stokers' quarters. Initially they regarded me with silent but palpable hostility, but I refused to be put off. I later learned they thought I was some sort of spy for the steamship line.

JANUARY 17

Des Miller is a marvel. It's fascinating to watch his long fingers on the strings, for at times they move like spiders, and at others they barely seem to move at all. Eli's bass viol and Kip's drums, being too bulky to carry, rest with Tilly in Paris, but they've improvised, Eli with a sort of washtub and broom-handle contraption strung with twine, and Kip with a series of wooden crates, metal containers and saucepan lids which he plays with wooden spoons and basting brushes he's pilfered from the kitchen. It's impossible to stand still when you hear them. They've gotten over their objections to my playing along with them, but I shall have to be careful how I manage it, or I could get them into hot water. Mind you, it would get the dowager and her daughters off my back. Consorting with coloured labourers, can you imagine?

Des was writing tunes even then. I suggested a title, "Slap and Tickle," for one of his pieces, as it was both percussive and melodic, and he liked the double entendre. It became quite a dance craze in the late twenties.

JANUARY 23

Finally met Angus's wife, Marguerite, whom he calls Maggs, a name she obviously despises. She'd supposedly been confined to their cabin with mal de mer, and he kept making apologies for her. I'll say she's a real corker for looks, but tends to regard her fellow passengers as if we were something stuck to the bottom of her shoe. She unbent considerably on learning that I was the brother of a baronet, and I'm so desperate I'm tempted to try my chances there, but Angus is a decent sort, and besides, he may be useful to me in my new situation. A pity they don't have chambermaids on this floating prison. I really don't fancy the steward.

The lads and I are getting on like a house afire fuelled by the gin I've liberated from the ship's stores. I'm really getting the hang of the music, learning to play around the notes, and answering some of the lines Des plays. Last night I ended one of Des's tunes, "Have Your Cake and Eat It," with a thrilling harmony line which left us all laughing. They're fascinated by Old Nick's head, and Kip is carving a woman's face into the head of Des's guitar, which he calls Elsie after the first woman he ever made love to. We dock in a few days, and I can't wait to have my feet on solid ground again.

JANUARY 24

Last night we were joined by one of the immigrants from steerage. He's a Russian Jew, a tall, skinny, oriental-looking fellow with a dazzling smile who's a real flash on the accordion. It emerges that his name is Giorgi, last name unpronounceable. He spent ten years on the Trans-Siberian Railway earning his passage to England with his accordion, living on the train and playing for food and whatever coin the passengers could spare. What a life! He has an uncle in Toronto. The ship's wireless operator keeps him posted on what the Bolsheviks are up to. It's funny having two Georges, but Des has taken to calling me Slick. He says it's because of the way my bow slides over the strings, but I can't help feeling he knows a damned sight more about me than I do about him. We dock in three days.

Giorgi and I still play chess once a week. He's over eighty now, and a great grandfather. He doesn't play any more because of arthritis in his hands, but in his youth he was a piano prodigy. When his parents were slaughtered in the pogroms of 1905, he fled into the countryside, and would have died of starvation and exposure if he hadn't found shelter with an old woman who had lost her son. He stayed with her until she died and he was thrown out of the house by her relatives. I think he must have been about seventeen when he boarded the Trans-Siberian Railway. For a man whose life has been one tragedy after another, he maintains a remarkably sunny outlook. When he was filling out his Canadian citizenship papers, they asked him to fill in the blank for his name, and he said, "Vat iss blank?" and that's what they wrote down. He's George Vatisblank to this day. He thinks it a great joke!

JANUARY 26

We reach Halifax in the early hours of tomorrow morning. It's very grey and cold, and they say we should expect fog; not, I hope, enough to prevent us from docking, but I don't expect to get much sense of my New Jerusalem on first viewing. I'm to be met by my employer, Edgar Sweeting, who presides over the Canadian arm of Goldring Import Export. I'll be a glorified shipping clerk once again, on probation of course. First order of business, a proper winter coat, muffler and galoshes.

Our little orchestra played together for the last time tonight, though we've sworn to keep in touch. Des has given me his aunt Ida's address in Truro, and Giorgi the location of the shop of his uncle Avram, a furrier, in Toronto. I begin to think I might enjoy this new life.

JANUARY 29

I'm presently occupying the highly feminine former bedroom of my employer's married daughter. He says I'm welcome to stay until I find some suitable rooms of my own. I don't mind it. At least I avoid the expense of a hotel. He seems a decent sort, although I'll have a better sense of that when I actually start working for him. His wife is a comfortable sort of woman, and they have an excellent cook.

Despite the weather, I've been able to get around a bit now that my motorbike has been off-loaded. Halifax seems very small and provincial after the fleshpots of London, and I expect I shall have to make my own entertainment here, though Des tells me there are booze cans and gambling dens if you know where to find them. It's a real harbour town with lots of ups and downs, and bloody great earthworks on the harbour-facing hillside. Smashing fun on the bike. I'm quite a sight in two fishermen's jerseys and a woolly hat. Angus has invited me to dine at his club, and says he'll put me up for membership. Pretty easy pickings there, I reckon.

FEBRUARY 12

The work is easy enough, but blindingly boring. I keep a record of all goods— amounts, costs, weights and dimensions. We ship to England every two or three months depending on how much we've accumulated. I've had errant thoughts of stowing away, but I'm afraid I'm too fond of my comforts, and too unsure of a prodigal's welcome.

Angus has sponsored me for the Liberty Club, and I'm to have full membership privileges while I await my formal invitation. I suspect he's gingered up my social status, for I'm greeted with excessive backslapping and hand-pumping whenever I put in an appearance. If I wished, I could dine out almost every night. Conveniently for me, they believe I've been sent here by Goldring to learn the business from the ground up. Can't imagine where they got that idea.

I sense I'm overstaying my welcome with the Sweetings, although I've been the epitome of a gentleman and nothing has actually been said. A pity, because decent lodgings could cost a packet, my salary is pretty paltry, and my stipend from home isn't due for two more months. A supplementary source of income is definitely in order. The Liberty Club it is.

FEBRUARY 19

Rode out to Truro yesterday to see Des, and met his aunt Ida and uncle Ray Jackson. They have a neat little one-storey cottage, but very crowded, as they have their daughter, her husband and new baby living at home. Des is like a son to them, and I'm warmly welcomed to dinner—or supper, as they call it. Aunt Ida's chicken and dumplings are ambrosial! Aunt Ida is Temperance, so Des and I headed out to the local to hoist a few and play with Kip and Eli. I don't think I'd chance it without Des. I got some pretty ugly looks. He's recommended that I stay away from the gambling in this part of town, as money and tempers are short, and knives and razors are common. Best to limit my gaming to the more civilized confines of the Liberty.

MARCH 3

Kip and Eli are finally shipping out with the 2nd Negro Construction Battalion, some six hundred men. Back to France after all this. At first the army refused to have them, but Ottawa has intervened. Des still limps a bit, but says he wouldn't go now even if he could, since the army doesn't consider coloured men good enough to die for their country. He's found a job in the railroad yard, shovelling coal once again. I bought him some heavy leather gloves to save his hands, but he insists on reimbursing me when he gets paid.

I've found new lodgings. My landlady is Mrs. Flora Chester, a young war widow of good family, but left with a large house and scant means of support. She's looking for a boarder of good character and respectable employment. Angus to the rescue once again with a glowing reference. I shall have a generous second-floor room at the front of the house, and breakfast provided. I have my eye on her departed husband's motor, which she's unable to drive. I rather have my eye on the handsome Flora as well.

I was tootling around the harbour on my motorbike last week when I heard the sound of fiddle music, and came upon the most extraordinary place, a quaint little public house called the Kettle of Fish, frequented by sailors and fishermen and the like. The atmosphere is a pungent mixture of tobacco smoke, perspiration, the sawdust on the floor, and the incredible aroma of an enormous cauldron of fish stew, which is ladled out to the patrons in pottery bowls with big chunks of fresh-baked bread. The music issued from a very old man who plays in a most unique way, for he sits up on a straight-backed chair, holds the fiddle to his chest, and as he plays his feet keep time with a sort of intricate jig. The melody seemed oddly familiar to me, and I suddenly realized that I knew it from one of Ma's manuscripts. The old boy's name is Jack Roy, a Newfoundlander. He calls the tune

"L'Oiseau Bleu." I'll write Ma to see what title she has. I'm guessing it's one of the tunes preserved from the repertoire of Blind France.

Kip is buried somewhere in France, the victim of a sniper. Eli was invalided home a wreck of a man, his lungs destroyed by mustard gas. He died three years later of emphysema. I thank God Des never signed up. Ditto for me. I'd have been a washout.

The Kettle of Fish was a popular gathering place for local musicians, and Old Nick and I became regulars. I'd appear with him under my arm and would be invited to jump on board, or I'd play one of my pieces and they'd join in, picking up any tune from one hearing. Friendly, unpretentious fellows, all of them, and I felt very much at home. "L'Oiseau Bleu" became the foundation for "Bluebird Blue," one of my most requested dance tunes.

March 10

The most extraordinary thing has happened. I dropped by the Kettle of Fish last night, and all thoughts of music fled when I spied a face I'd never thought to see again. It was that murdering bastard Osbert Lynche in the flesh, not dressed in his former pretentious style, but rather looking like a grizzled badger in a fisherman's jersey. I knew him instantly, but he didn't recognize me. I was, after all, a mere sprout when he'd seen me last. My first thought was to bash his head in, but I calmed down enough to decide I didn't want to hang for him. It appears he's some sort of travelling agent for an insurance firm. As Nan is so fond of saying, "a cat can't change his stripes." He's bound to be up to some mischief, and I shall certainly winkle it out.

Sweeting informs me he's sending a most favourable report back to Seth Goldring. He's very impressed with the improvements I've made in his billing and accounting system, although I only did it to save myself work. The files were an absolute dog's breakfast, and I got tired of searching through endless stacks of old paper just to confirm a supplier's history.

I've also created a more efficient way of weighing and measuring our goods which are often unwieldy and odd-shaped. I now spend more time in the warehouse than I do in the office, and have become a pretty fair judge of how much cargo space we'll need. I'm to replace the head clerk, who's retiring within the month. The rise in salary will be much appreciated.

I've been far too circumspect regarding Flora Chester, for it seems she's more than willing. I seldom come in at any hour now that she doesn't offer me a whisky and soda, and a cozy chat in her sitting room. I couldn't be happier. I'm randy as a goat after three months of abstinence. She's agreed to sell me the car, a Model T Ford in superb condition. It's hardly been driven, and the engine is clean as a whistle.

I have fond memories of Flora. It seemed that Captain Chester, although an exemplary soldier, had been a less than ideal husband, so any fears I might have had about Flora expecting me to make an honest woman of her were quickly dispelled. She swore if she ever ventured down that road again, he'd have to be very rich. She eventually married a banker.

As for Lynche, it didn't take long to discover that he was now plain Bert Lynch, and made his living selling life insurance to miners, loggers, fishermen and others in risky occupations who could ill afford the monthly premium. At first I wondered if the whole operation might be bent, but the company seemed legitimate enough. It took a neat bit of detective work on my part to find out just how low he'd sunk.

MARCH 23

Hallelujah! Money from home and a nice long letter from Ma. She's over the moon at my success here, and has high hopes that, if I keep it up, all will be forgiven and I can come home. Not bloody likely! Angus is going to introduce me to his tailor and shirtmaker now that I can afford to spruce up my wardrobe.

Jean has a new baby, another girl, called Mary Carolyn, and Ruthie has hatched again, their third, a boy called Rupert Gabriel. The further down the pecking order I am from that bleeding house and title, the better I like it.

I've inherited a rather lucrative legacy from my predecessor here at Goldring. It seems he was in the habit of accepting quite substantial considerations from some of the fellows that do business with us, and who am I to break with tradition? It's all very discreet; a nod and a wink and an envelope slipped into my pocket. Add that to my rise in pay and what I'll get for my bike, and I shall pay for that lovely motor in no time.

Des is getting itchy feet. He talks about going back to New York, or possibly to Montreal or Toronto. He misses Kip and Eli, and is desperate to play music full time again. If he goes, I shall have to give serious thought to joining him.

I'm looking forward to loosing the hounds on Bert Lynch. He'll do prison time if there's any justice. Ma will be pleased.

There's a gap of some weeks in the diary, which I'll attempt to fill from memory.

Bert Lynch proved true to form, though not on so grand a scale. I got my first clue when Cecil, one of my chums at the Kettle of Fish, told me what a fine fellow Bert was. Cecil's sister was the widow of a sealer who had perished when an ice floe had broken up. When she applied for her insurance, Lynch informed her that the premiums hadn't been kept up, rendering the policy invalid, and she had no receipts to prove otherwise. He claimed to be so moved by her plight that he offered to put things right if she could make up the missing amount along with a small consideration for his efforts, some twenty dollars in total. To her, a widow with four small children, it might as well have been a hundred. Cecil and his brothers contributed some, and her husband's parents managed to raise the rest.

A mild flirtation with a girl at the insurance office gained me a glance at the file. It showed regular payments recorded in different hands with different inks and pens right up to the date of the fatality. A letter from a concerned citizen to the manager of the company generated a thorough investigation, and several other incidents were uncovered. There was considerable public outrage, and the judge was pretty severe. I thought I'd be jubilant at seeing Lynch get his come-uppance, but the experience left me feeling decidedly flat. I knew that sensation intimately. It inevitably preceded one of my fugues. My mother always downplayed these episodes, claiming I was sulking or shamming in some way, but I know from this journal that she feared I'd inherited my grandfather's instability, which indeed I had, and have, although it's eased somewhat with age. Sadly it plagues my daughter as well. I can see that it also affected the entries in my diaries, for the gaps seem to occur when I was either in the depths or on top of the world. And all those years growing up I was told I was just bloody-minded!

Flora, bless her, put it about that I had influenza and was confined to my bed. She washed and fed me like a baby. I was absent from Goldring's for over a month.

MAY 17

I've emerged from my miasma to find glorious sunlight and flowers everywhere. The gardens here remind me of home.

Flora has been an absolute brick, much better than I deserve, but then I've always been lucky with women. In the midst of my confinement I was actually demented enough to propose to her, but she very prudently refused me.

Sweeting has been most accommodating. We'd just finished dispatching a shipment when I was struck down, so things were slack anyway. He feels if he makes a success of me, it will win him points with Seth Goldring. When Hell freezes over, I'm afraid. Oh well, at least it keeps me out of the trenches.

Des says he won't stay on much beyond Christmas. He intends to head west, Montreal first, and if that doesn't suit, Toronto. He has a cousin there.

We play a couple of times a week in what he calls a blind pig. It has no name, and is somewhat of a moveable feast, relocating when things get too hot for comfort.

Des has a chum in New York who can send him all the latest sheet music, not that he can decipher it, for although he can read and write, he's had no musical training. I'm teaching him what I know and he's very fast. Once we establish the melody, he has a much better grasp of the rhythm than I do, so I'm learning as well. It's impossible to find new recordings for my gramophone here, and the old ones are worn past playing. I've ordered the latest from Goldring, and given Des some cash to send to his New York chum.

My birthday tonight. Can you believe it? I'm twenty-three! Dinner with Angus at the club to celebrate. He's in the doghouse with Maggs again. A brisk round or two of poker should brighten him up and cheer me considerably in the process.

August 20

Hotter than Hades. I don't know what's worse in this bloody country, the summers or the winters. Too hot for lovemaking. Flora and I have retreated to our separate bedrooms, and I lie naked, panting like a dog, sweating like a pig. I've taken to driving the car around at night just to feel a breeze.

I met a girl back in July through Maggs McSorrel. Frances Bostwick. Her father owns several warehouse properties on the harbour. Definitely one of the old fraternity here. She's very young (seventeen), and quite silly. I normally couldn't be bothered with her, but she is very pretty, and then there's the money. Her mother encourages a match, and I'm considering it, although her father is a tougher proposition. I've talked it over with Flora, who says that although she'd miss me, she understands. Sometimes she's a damned sight too understanding.

September 9

Dinner with Frannie's parents last night. Herbert Bostwick now accepts me as a rather unpleasant fact of life and the feeling is mutual. Frannie's

*mother is pushing hard for a formal engagement, but I'm procrastinating
madly. I may have to bolt.*

*Got a birthday package off to Ma. I left it a bit late, so it won't reach
her in time, but as they say, it's the thought that counts. It's a beautiful little
ermine hat and muff, very stylish. Frannie picked it out. Haven't told Ma
about her yet. Hedging my bets.*

*Des and I wrote a great tune a few nights ago. He calls it "Hot Cocoa."
He's starting to write parts for other instruments. Damned exciting. I can
hear it all in my head and I'm itching to play it with a full ensemble.*

*Same old humdrum at work. One more shipment to go out this year,
the first week of December. Mainly pelts to cover the backs of the wealthy
predators who shop at Goldring's.*

OCTOBER 2

*The engagement is announced! Fortunately Frannie insists on being a June
bride, so I can enjoy my bachelor bliss a while longer. Angus has put me on to
a jeweller who'll allow me to pay for the ring in instalments. It's a small sap-
phire surrounded by diamond chips, and Frannie's plump little hand flashes
it at every opportunity. I was damned if I'd give her Ma's ruby. There are
plans afoot for me to work for her father. I'll put MY foot down about that!*

*Des wants to go to New York. I worry that if he goes, he'll go for good,
so I'm begging some time off to go with him. The Model T should get us
there and back in a breeze.*

*Flora is being courted by a brewer and has cut me off. His beer has a
decidedly skunky flavour in my opinion.*

OCTOBER 10

*Hooray! We're off tomorrow. I've got two spare tins of petrol in case of
short supply on the road. Sweeting has agreed to ten days, although he's not
pleased about it. I suspect his next report will not be quite so glowing. We
figure it will take us just over two days to make the trip. As the weather's
still fairly balmy, we can sleep in the car.*

I never wrote about our trek to New York, but I remember it vividly.

New York, at that time, was awash with patriotic fervour, the United States having finally entered the war. There were flags everywhere, and even the music reflected the gung-ho attitude. The Yanks were going to clean up the whole mess in short order.

Des and I stayed with his friend in Harlem where the patriotic spirit was significantly soured by racial reality. Coloured men were not welcome in the trenches. "No news there," said Des. I kept my head down and my mouth shut, for Harlem was a foreign country where I didn't know the language and my white face was like a red flag. If not for Des I'd have been thoroughly intimidated, but he could defuse things by simply saying, "He's just here for the music, brother. Let it rest."

What a revelation to be among people whose commitment was so absolute—musicians, dancers, actors, painters, playwrights and poets, who would starve and live in squalor, doing anything simply to be able to continue doing what they were driven to do. Even their clothing was a testament to unfettered creativity, the men in brightly hued suits and ties and the women like tropical flowers. It was as if magical ideas were floating in the air, and you had only to reach up and pluck them. Those few days and nights were full of exhilarating colour and movement and words and music, music, music. We drank and we played 'til we dropped, and when we revived we played again. If we hadn't run out of money, we might never have returned to Halifax, and when we did, both of us knew it was only a matter of time until we moved on. It was suddenly, stunningly obvious. Unless I committed myself to playing music I would never be anything more than a talented dilettante, and that was no longer enough.

For me, the paradox of my mother was how fearlessly, even ruthlessly, unconventional she could be in the pursuit of the crushingly conventional, and how determined she was to impose that order on all around her. God help me, I did try to please her, but couldn't sustain the effort. It was never that I *wouldn't*, but rather that I *couldn't* conform, for it simply wasn't in me. In Halifax I'd constructed the kind of comfortable cage she would have approved of, but the door was still open. I would fly with Des in January, and not look back.

OCTOBER 23

Trying my damnedest to hold things together until the New Year. Hard to have such a delicious secret, and no one to share it with, even Flora. She's given the brewer his marching orders. She declares he's "as tight as the bark on a tree." Women can be brutally practical.

Frannie is driving me mad. She affects an infantile manner of speech when we're together, and the stream of drivel is endless. Every time she asks me if "Georgie Porgie loves his little Frannie Wannie," my stomach starts to churn. I anxiously await the next bribe from Seth Goldring, certainly the last I'll see from him. I'm building up a little nest egg, keeping my fingers crossed that Sweeting doesn't discover what I've been up to with the books.

NOVEMBER 15

Jack Roy has died. The poor old boy passed quietly two nights ago in his room above the Kettle of Fish. He has no family, so we held a wake for him last night, and a whip 'round raised enough money to bury him. Musicians gathered from miles away, and the music and drinking went on well into the morning hours. It started off quite solemnly with sad slow airs, but the momentum built, and we finally sent him off with a riotous jig. His fiddle rests over the bar, and his empty chair sits in a place of honour. When I leave here, some small piece of me will remain with these good fellows.

Frannie is very put-out with me. We were to attend some social engagement last night, and I failed to appear. She claims to be mortified. When I attempted to explain where I'd been, she said she could not under-stand why I would associate with such ignorant, uncouth people. I replied that she was absolutely right, she failed to understand the least thing about me. It was our first real quarrel, but I'll wager it's not the last.

Haven't seen much of Des. He's working the night shift.

NOVEMBER 18

Enjoying the brief respite the quarrel has given me. Had a rather pitiful note, apologizing and begging me to forgive my silly little Frannie. I forgive her—I just find it impossible to tolerate her. Sometimes I think I shall explode.

NOVEMBER 30

Working like a slave at Goldring's, which allows me to avoid spending time with Frannie, who, although petulant, is obliged to accept it. The last shipment of the year sails on December 4th, and from that point all my efforts will be concentrated on escape!

DECEMBER 2

Had the mother of all quarrels with Frannie tonight. Just the excuse I'd been looking for. After she'd favoured me with yet another puerile endearment, I asked her to be good enough to speak to me in an adult manner, for if I'd wanted to marry a five-year-old I'd have found one that was a great deal more intelligent. She was first shocked, then tearful, then furious. She actually stamped her foot, then flung the ring at my head, saying she never wanted to see me again. I caught it neatly and tucked it in my vest pocket. As a parting volley I said that I pitied the poor fellow she did marry, and so I do, for he'll undoubtedly pay for all my shortcomings. I left her house whistling, feeling as if the weight of the world had been lifted from my shoulders. I'll go back to the jeweller tomorrow to see what he'll refund me on the ring.

Although not noted in my diary, the events that followed were so extraordinary as to be recorded in the history books.

Our final shipment for the year departed on schedule the morning of December fourth. It had a full escort, as there were troops and supplies on board as well. The docks were crowded with foreign sailors and the air filled with a cacophony of languages. Navigation was slow and hazardous, as both the inner and outer harbour were full of vessels of all kinds and nationalities, and we heaved a sigh of relief as the captain radioed back that they were safely in open water.

I was tucked up in bed with Flora the morning of the sixth of December when we were jolted from our sleep by a great shock. It was as if all the air had been sucked from the house, then a sound like thunder multiplied. We first thought it was an earthquake, then that we'd been bombed by the Germans. We felt cold air rushing through the house, and threw on our clothes to reconnoiter. The front windows of the house were shattered; shards of glass and broken crockery, overturned furniture and other debris everywhere. It was fortunate that only the stove in the kitchen and the fireplace in Flora's bedroom were lit, for it was apparent that some of our neighbours had not fared so well, and there was already a thick pall of smoke in the frigid air. I had a moment of panic for Old Nick, but found him safe and sound, though his casket had suffered a nasty dent. My next concern was the car, but other than a shower of dust and pigeon droppings, it too had survived. I fervently prayed that Des and his family were safe, and vowed to reach them at the first opportunity.

Our location in the southern section of the city had saved us. Most of the north end and Dartmouth had been levelled by a cataclysm of monstrous proportions. I refer, of course, to the Great Halifax Explosion when the Belgian relief ship, *Imo*, collided with French munitions ship, the *Mont Blanc*.

I returned to the house to find that Flora had taken in our neighbour, Mrs. Brent, who was suffering from hysterics. She administered hot tea laced with brandy to the poor lady, while I foraged with Mr. Brent for something to board up the broken windows.

We demolished Flora's woodshed, and the Brents' garden fence, and concentrated on Flora's house, as it was the least damaged and could thus shelter us all. In the midst of all this my mind was working furiously. It suddenly struck me that now would be the ideal opportunity to disappear. It was only a matter of time before Sweeting discovered irregularities to the tune of two hundred and some odd dollars, and I had no desire to be around to face the consequences.

I had a hurried conversation with Flora, telling her how I'd planned to leave in January but that it seemed fate had presented me with an opportunity I couldn't ignore. I begged her to tell anyone who enquired that I'd gone out in the car shortly before the explosion, and she'd heard nothing from me since. She reluctantly agreed. Giving me one last warm embrace and a lingering kiss, she ruffled my hair and wished me good luck and Godspeed. I gave her fifty dollars to cover the last of the payments on the car, and promised to write. Returning to the wreckage of my room, I gathered up my belongings and loaded them into the car.

Driving to Truro was a nightmare, for there was debris everywhere. Buildings were collapsed in on themselves like accordions, and God help anyone trapped inside. It was as close to a war zone as I ever want to know. The smoke made it hard to breathe and almost impossible to see. I could hear women sobbing and children wailing, and I kept being stopped by men desperate to get to their homes and families, some with bloody, makeshift bandages and blackened faces, who rode on the running boards, the fenders and even on the roof. When we came to an obstacle, they'd jump off and clear the way, then climb back on board. I picked up and dropped off as many as I could on my circuitous route, and finally arrived at the Jacksons' cottage just after six o'clock that evening, as the first flakes of snow began to fall.

They were all safe and sound. The house was in a low-lying area, removed and shielded from the blast, although they'd certainly felt it. Des, having finished the night shift, was home and had just gone to bed when it happened. We later learned that the railroad yard where he worked had been gutted. Aunt Ida and several other ladies were cooking copious amounts of food, collecting blankets and clothing, and organizing ways to get it all to the church to serve those fleeing the disaster. The car and myself as driver were commandeered, and Des and I made several trips to collect and deliver more necessities as the weather closed in and we found ourselves enveloped in a full blizzard.

I told Des it was time. He didn't ask what I meant, but simply nodded his head. We left a day later for Montreal.

DECEMBER 12

This is the first moment I've had to myself since we left Halifax. We arrived in Montreal two days ago after a hellish journey, driving almost non-stop despite sub-zero weather and terrible roads, stealing frozen blankets off a clothesline to keep warm and clipping dollar bills to the line as payment. We're living in a sort of rooming house over a cabaret called La Magie Noire that Des knew about. The rooms are pretty bleak; peeling wallpaper, sagging beds, questionable linens, and ice on the lavatory walls. Fortunately, each room has its own stove, and we have a good supply of coal.

The proprietor is an immensely fat fellow called Emil Ducharme, who cheerfully tells us he inherited the place from his mother, who ran it as a brothel. Most of the rooms are for his "girls." He has no problem with Des being coloured, for he says he's a mongrel himself, being French and red Indian on his father's side, and Negro and Chinese on his mother's. We'll start playing downstairs tonight with a piano and bass. No salary, just passing the hat and all we can eat and drink. Emil says he doesn't care what kind of music we play, so long as his boys and girls can dance to it.

I've written to my mother and Flora. I've asked Ma not to tip my hand just yet, as there may be repercussions arising from my hasty departure.

DECEMBER 21

We have an orchestra at last! The pianist is French, classically trained, name of Richard, known as Rick. His repertoire leans toward the floridly romantic, and he's not too receptive to the jazz Des and I play, but what Emil says goes, and he likes what we do. The bassist is a tall, gaunt fellow with a thatch of yellow hair that gives him the appearance of a broom set up on its end. His name is Fernand, and he doesn't talk much, but plays well enough. As of two nights ago, we also have a drummer. His name is Ulysses Leroy. He is the biggest, blackest man I have ever seen, and sports a flaming red scar down one side of his face. He speaks a bastard mixture of English, French and Spanish, and hails from someplace called Haiti. He's crazy about Des, but, judging from the way he glowers in my direction, he doesn't much care for me.

Received a letter from Flora saying that Sweeting came looking for me two days after the blast. He and the Missus survived it without a scratch although he suffered some hearing loss from the concussion, but the Goldring office was blown to blazes and all the records burned. My luck seems to be holding. Poor little Frannie and her parents were not so fortunate. They perished when their handsome house overlooking the Narrows was reduced to matchsticks. I'd had no desire to be a part of that family, but would never have wished such an appalling fate for them.

The Kettle of Fish is no more. I feel moisture running down my face, and realize I'm weeping.

I have a letter from my mother that I still treasure. Having said how relieved and happy she is that I've survived, she proceeds to berate me for frightening her so, then says, and I quote, "*I haven't the least desire to know what occasioned your hasty departure, but considering my own history, I can hardly fault you for wishing to start afresh. I cannot help but think, however, that blowing up Halifax Harbour in order to do so was excessive in the extreme.*" I laughed 'til my ribs ached, and it still brings a smile to my face after all these years.

Ulysses Leroy played with Des and me for years, and never soft-ened toward me. Lee, as we came to call him, had escaped from a Haitian prison in a small boat, and was the only survivor to make it across open ocean to the coast of Florida. He'd found his way to New Orleans and played with street musicians there, but left in a hurry after killing a man, travelling first by steamboat to St. Louis, and then to Chicago and Montreal by freight car. The scar that stretched from the corner of his left eye to his mouth had been inflicted by a machete when he was a plantation worker. He seldom drank, but constantly smoked foul-smelling hand-rolled cigarettes which I didn't recognize at the time as marijuana. Fortunately it had a calming effect on him, for the only time I ever saw him drunk he was terrifying. Lee ended up in hospital several years ago in the last stages of emphysema. I heard about it from Giorgi, and went to visit him. He was in a piteous state, shrunken almost beyond recognition. The cantankerous old bastard was actually glad to see me. We talked about the old days for a while, but he suffered a horrendous coughing fit and I had to fetch a nurse. His wife, Hattie, could only visit once a week, as she had arthritis in her hips and needed two canes to get around. I arranged a regular car for her and told her to call me if Lee needed anything. I did see him one more time before he died, but I find it difficult to be with the sick and dying. Perhaps it's my own mortality I feel.

DECEMBER 26

Emil treated us to a Christmas dinner of spaghetti and meatballs last night, then we played into the small hours. Rick has a pleasant tenor voice, although his approach to the lyrics is a little stiff. I want to play only our own tunes, but Des is adamant that we need to introduce the crowd to our music by mixing it with more popular songs like "Bill Bailey," "After You've Gone," and Emil's favourite, "Chinatown, My Chinatown." "Darktown Strutter's Ball" is certainly the most requested. Des says it's about an event in Chicago that the local swells put on for ladies in the "oldest profession."

More than a few of our "ladies" fall into that category, in fact my new girl-friend, Marie, has been plying her trade since she was fifteen. She's a great girl, and tolerates no nonsense from me.

I've become considerably less fastidious in my dress and my outlook since I've been here. No one judges you by your clothes or your manners, but I've had some rather cutting remarks on my "posh" accent don't you know. I fail to see why I should be singled out in a city that sports accents from every corner of the world.

Looking forward to New Year's Eve. Emil says the feast will be Chinese.

Ah, Marie! I hadn't thought about her in years. Her name was Marie Murphy, and she was the most extraordinary looking girl—elegant legs and delicious shoulders, with milk-white skin, rich auburn hair and startling green eyes. Despite her Irish name and colouring, she was as French as she could be. She wore vivid colours, giving her the appear-ance of some rare tropical bird. I can't say that I sought her out, but rather that she decided on me, and when I eventually asked her why, she declared that I had lovely manners, opened doors and pulled out chairs for her, and didn't knock her about. So much for my manly charms.

I should explain about Emil. He wasn't a pimp or procurer, but rather a sort of Papa to the girls. He rented them rooms at reason-able rates, and kept a watchful eye on them. They adored him, pam-pered him, fed him and bedded him. At night he presided over the Magie Noire like a great, fat, smiling Buddha, his head with its halo of silver hair bobbing to the music. He said the music brought in the girls, the girls brought in the boys, and the boys brought in the cash.

I drank too much, had more and better sex than I'd ever dreamed of, slept all day, and played all night.

JANUARY 18, 1918

God bless Ma! She's invented some whopper about me having regained con-sciousness in a Montreal hospital, suffering from amnesia, with absolutely no memory of how I got there. The upshot is that my allowance is still in effect, and an advance included in her latest letter. I celebrated by taking Marie to tea at a posh hotel. I wore my best suit, and Marie did me proud by appearing in a lilac satin turban and an immaculately cut lady's ensemble of royal purple velvet made for her by one of her favourite customers, Monsieur Maier, a master tailor with a ritzy clientele. She's very formal with all her gentlemen. She says it keeps things civilized.

The money didn't arrive a minute too soon. Our take from passing the hat increases with time, but divided between five or more of us, doesn't add up to much, and Emil is still disinclined to pay us. Des and I are constantly composing new tunes, and I'm now attempting lyrics. My latest effort is called "Ah Oui, Marie"—about guess who? She thinks it's brilliant, but Rick says the words are unpoetic, unsingable. I take his point. I'll put a little more work into them.

MARCH 2

A disturbing development. Perhaps it was inevitable that our success would attract some unwelcome attention. Des and I walked into the kitchen last night and interrupted a heated conversation between Emil and a big, red-faced man in a black overcoat and fedora accompanied by two tough-looking fellows in porkpie hats. We quickly excused ourselves, but not before hearing what Des with his time in Paris and I with my schoolboy French interpreted as a very nasty threat. When we asked Emil about it, he said with a philosophical shrug that wherever there's cake someone wants a slice of it. I naively suggested he contact the police, but he replied that they WERE the police and it's just a part of doing business. Marie knows the man, Paul Cochere, and says cochon *would be a better name for him. She says none of the girls will go with him since he never pays, and he nearly throttled one of them when she demanded her fee.*

As for the aforementioned success, we are currently the talk of Montreal, and starting to bring in some big spenders, which makes everyone happy. The music gets better and better. Des is introducing chords I'd never have dreamed of, divine dissonance, and the Latin feel of Lee's rhythm is almost hypnotic. I can't believe I waited so long to do what I was always meant to do.

MAY 17

Another birthday! Twenty-four. I can scarcely believe what's happened to me in the space of a year. We had cake and sparkling wine, and wore silly paper hats. I feel like part of a family. I don't know when I've ever been happier!

I'm amazed at how little time we actually spent in Montreal. Back then, it seemed to go on forever. Word about the band spread quickly. There was talk of recording. One of our big spenders had an in with the Berliner Gram-o-phone Company, and was ready to finance us. We believed our repertoire could outdo anything that was currently popular if we only had the chance. It was like living on a cloud. A hot-air balloon is more like it, for one bullet brought it all down in flames.

Cochere and his two henchmen had become fixtures at the place. Emil said they were just making sure everything stayed peaceful, although we'd never had any serious problems, and the fat man was not his usual jolly self.

It all fell apart when Cochere demanded that Emil make him a partner, an outrageous demand, but he made it clear there was no option. Agree, or Cochere and his thugs, with the full authority of their badges, would shut him down. It was the first and only time I ever saw Emil angry, virtually sputtering. He vowed to fight, but it was never a contest.

It was in the first week of June. We'd had a particularly good night, another new tune enthusiastically received, the place filled to capacity, everyone happy. Marie and I were getting ready for bed, when she decided to go downstairs for a brandy. No more than five minutes later, she burst into the room saying we must leave at once.

She'd seen too much. They'd kill her if they found her. She wasn't one to lose her head over nothing, so I roused Des, telling him all hell was breaking loose and we had to get out. I grabbed Old Nick in his casket, my recordings and gramophone, and Des packed Elsie in her case, bundled up his manuscripts and sheet music. Then we scooped up as much as we could of our clothes, throwing them into the back seat of the car which was parked in a shed behind the place. At this point Lee poked his head out of one of the girls' rooms to find out what all the commotion was. When he saw we were leaving he insisted on coming with us.

We could hear the sounds of a noisy search going on upstairs, the girls cursing and screaming as their doors were shouldered open. Lee was securing his drums to the roof of the car when Cochere's two henchmen appeared. Fortunately, they had no guns, only billy clubs, and Lee, in an amazing feat of strength, grabbed both of them by the throat, lifted them off their feet and banged their heads together, leaving them slumped on the floor, an astonishing performance!

I was just getting the Ford up to speed when Cochere appeared in the alley behind us and fired several shots. At least two bullets hit the car, fortunately missing the gasoline can I'd stored in the boot. I later found that the bullet that shattered the back window had hit the front seat a scant inch from my back.

Marie finally calmed down enough to tell us what had happened. She'd been behind the bar getting the brandy when she heard raised voices and a crashing sound from the kitchen. When she crept to the door and peeked in, she saw Cochere and his two men standing over a bloody and unconscious Emil, tied to a chair, which had tipped over. Cochere was cursing, waving his pistol and saying, "The fat fool will never agree." He put the gun to Emil's head and pulled the trigger. Marie said she must have screamed, for Cochere turned and saw her. She ran up the stairs as if the very devil were after her.

Dazed though we were at this disastrous turn of events, it was obvious our time in Montreal was over. We headed west once again, Des, Marie and me in the front seat with Lee sprawled like a pasha on top of our belongings in the back, an endless, bone-jarring journey. We didn't talk a lot, partly because with the back window missing it was impossible to hear anything over the noise, but also because each of us was lost in thought. It was a tired, dishevelled and disheartened little crew that finally pulled into Toronto.

AUGUST 21

I've been in a black mood, not fit for anything, but the incomparable Marie has found us cheap accommodation, the entire attic of a once-handsome dwelling fallen on hard times and now a rooming house.

Our landlords are vaudeville performers, a fiftyish husband and wife, Hope and Sid Vandervent. Their particular turn apparently consists of Sid, in full evening dress with a little cockscomb hat on his head, making various bird calls, while Hope, in sequined corset, mesh tights and ostrich feathers, responds with coquettish chirps. It ends with a whistled duet of "She's Only a Bird in a Gilded Cage." The thought of Hope in tights makes me shudder, for she's built like a barrel on stilts, and Sid looks like a monkey with a bad toupée. I don't wonder they're out of work, or "resting," as they call it. The house actually belongs to Hope's aged father, who wisely keeps to his room back of the kitchen.

Hope and Sid have the master bedroom on the second floor. Another bedroom is occupied by two amiable lads from Newfoundland who work in an abattoir, and the last by an ordinary-looking but decidedly odd fellow called Maurice who doesn't seem to work at all, not that I can fault him on that account. The former dining room is home to another couple, Mel and Ginger Merchant. Ginger's a burlesque artist, a singer and dancer with a small rat-like dog she carries everywhere. Mel calls himself a comedian, although I have yet to witness any trace of humour in him. They seem to be "resting" also. Fortunately the only time we see our fellow inmates is when we collide in the kitchen. The builders of the house had the foresight to put in plumbing for the servants, so we are spared the ordeal of sharing a lavatory.

It's only in the last day or so I've ventured out, to find that the streets are as stiflingly hot and airless as our attic. Marie wants to lie low, as she's afraid that even here Cochere may have eyes. We're known to our landlady as Mr. and Mrs. Joyner. We have less than a hundred dollars between us, but with reasonable economy we should be able to survive for several more weeks.

Marie's been in touch with one of her girlfriends in Montreal, who says Cochere and his men set fire to the kitchen of Magie Noire to cover up Emil's murder, and the flames spread to the upper floors, driving everyone out onto the street. Cochere's been asking everywhere for us. I'm beginning to think I'm some sort of jinx, as disaster of one sort or another seems to dog me, but Marie says I'm being an "enfant," and not everything has to do with me.

Des and Lee are living over a yard goods store on Spadina with Des's cousin and his wife, as most rooming houses won't take Negroes. His cousin is a streetcar conductor, and is trying to find jobs for them as well. We desperately need a place to play.

AUGUST 30
We've found Giorgi! He lives with his uncle, the furrier, not far from Des and Lee. He's learning to be a cutter but says, jokingly, that he's not "cut out" for the job. His English has improved since we saw him last. He was playing piano part time for a lady preacher called Mrs. Aimee Semple Mac-Pherson who had a popular mission here, but she's moved on, and he hasn't had access to a piano since. It's wonderful to see him again, and I start to feel hopeful, for he says we can practise at night in the workroom of his uncle's shop. All we lack now is a bass.

SEPTEMBER 6
Our landlady is a drunk. When we come in at night she's slumped in a chair in the front parlour with the phonograph scratching away at the end

of some unfortunate recording. Her preferred tipple is cheap sherry. God knows where she gets it in this uncivilized country. The Holy Joes and politicians have made it nearly impossible to find anything worth drinking. Marie says Sid and Mel are on drugs of some sort. I hadn't noticed, but she has a sharp eye for such things.

The other night over fish and chips in the kitchen, Ginger treated us to her "routine." She appeared dressed as a prepubescent girl, clutching the wretched dog, his mouth and nose smeared with butter. As she sang a highly suggestive song about Daddy's little girl, bumping and grinding and exposing her frilly undies, the dog licked his lips in a most lascivious way. We dutifully applauded, then beat a hasty retreat up the back staircase to our attic. Marie thought it hilarious, but I was appalled. I'm determined not to succumb to my evil mood.

SEPTEMBER 20

Sid and Mel are definitely bent. Whenever I come down the back stairs to the kitchen I hear a mad scramble, and find the two of them smoking at the bare table with a highly exaggerated nonchalance. Mel tries to sell me gents' apparel at greatly reduced prices. Says he knows someone in wholesale. Considering his taste in neckwear, I think I'll pass.

Marie is homesick and desperately wants to go back despite the danger. She says Toronto has no heart, and she can't even find a decent bottle of wine. I don't say she's wrong, but now that we're playing again I have no intention of going anywhere, so we're at an impasse.

OCTOBER 2

It's all over with Marie. I suppose it was bound to happen, but I can't say I handled it well. She asked me if I thought we should get married. I hesitated, finally saying, "Well, perhaps some day . . ." She then informed me she'd received a letter of proposal from Monsieur Maier, he of the purple velvet ensemble. He's offered to endow her with all his worldly goods, for better or for worse, in front of a priest if she wishes. I lost my temper and

accused her of selling herself to an old man. She turned quite icy and said,
"That's what I do, cheri."

> *I've given her what money I have, and put her on the train. I can't*
> *even afford to get drunk.*

When I left her at the station, Marie turned to me one last time and
said, "Georgie, that is a bad house. You should move."

I wish to hell I'd listened to her.

OCTOBER 7
Sid and Mel have a proposition.

> *A couple of nights ago, I arrived at my lodgings to find Sid in a real*
> *pickle. Having lost his key, he was trying to rouse Hope from her stupor*
> *by hammering on the door. Being a bit tipsy I decided to show off and*
> *stupidly whipped out my handy, dandy pocket knife instead of my key to*
> *jimmy the lock. He was excessively grateful, declaring I was some sort of*
> *magician. I jokingly said it was just one of my many talents, and retired*
> *to my attic.*

> *The next morning there was a pounding at my door and Sid pushed*
> *his way in, saying, "I'm tellin' you, Mel, you've got to see this. The guy is*
> *a genius!"*

> *He then insisted I go through the house opening one lock after another,*
> *doors, drawers, a wardrobe trunk, a rusty old padlock. They finally left me*
> *in peace, and I went back to sleep.*

> *Then last night in the kitchen we sat down with a quart of gin and*
> *they told me what they've been up to. They're burglars, targeting shops and*
> *warehouses, strictly a smash-and-grab operation, a crowbar applied to the*
> *back door and a quick getaway with as much as they can carry. Very primi-*
> *tive and noisy. Mel said that with my talent and my car I'd opened a whole*
> *new set of possibilities, and was I game? Being absolutely skint, I haven't*
> *totally dismissed it.*

I'm ashamed to admit I went for it. My involvement was straight-forward. Sid and Mel chose the targets. I drove the car and gained entry. It was all penny-ante—merchandise rather than cash. They'd flog the goods and give me a cut, which covered my rent, food and booze. I was drinking heavily by then, but at least hadn't suc-cumbed to cocaine, which was the drug of choice for the two of them. Oh yes, I tried it, but the resultant euphoria and sense of invincibility were a little too familiar, and I didn't care to precipi-tate the crushing depression that would certainly follow. Alcohol was more predictable, cheap and still easily come by if you knew where to get it.

Then the unthinkable happened.

OCTOBER 10
Old Nick is gone. Stolen. I feel like my hands have been cut off.

This was my lowest period. Much of it I don't remember.

Hope had evicted Maurice, the oddball second floor tenant. She confiscated his key and said he could have his belongings when he paid up. The two young Newfoundlanders thought it unfair so they lent him a key. He waited until everyone was out, then took not only his own things, but went through the house taking anything of value he found. Old Nick's casket was too bulky to carry, but my beloved fiddle was gone.

No one could have been sorrier than those two boys, and they'd paid dearly for their kindness. All the money they'd saved to send home to their families was gone. Sid and Mel ranted and raved, say-ing they'd "find the bastard and do for him," but it was all hot air. An hour later they were passed out at the kitchen table as usual.

The open casket sat like a gaping wound. The bastard had stolen my life. I threw myself fully clothed on my bed, and lay there unbelieving, catatonic.

It was in this state that Mel found me the following day. He shook me roughly and told me to snap out of it, declaring he'd had a brilliant idea. The plan, such as it was, was to rob a bank. He said we'd need at least two more men to help carry off the loot he envisioned—and did I know anyone? I must have been out of my mind. I said I knew a couple of fellows who might agree. I went to see Des and Lee, who by then had their own rooms at Spadina and Adelaide. Des was working as a handyman, and Lee had a job as a dishwasher at a hotel.

They'd just finished breakfast when I knocked on their door. Des was sitting on a packing box, playing Elsie. Lee threw one dark look at me and went out, slamming the door behind him.

Des said, "You're looking rough. What's on your mind, Slick?"

I quickly outlined the scheme, justifying it with talk of how it would put us all back on our feet. I could buy a new fiddle. We could smarten ourselves up and find a decent place to play. It would solve everything.

Des sat very still, shoulders hunched, head averted, his face a blank. When I finally ran out of words, he shook his head resignedly and spoke to me as if I were a backward child.

"Now you listen and listen good, Slick, because I'm not saying it but once. I know losing your fiddle has hit you like a death in the family, but this is crazy. Those low-life hopheads will chew you up and spit you out without a second thought, and here you are trying to pull us into this mess with you.

"Do you think we'd ever have hooked up if it wasn't for the music? The only way we're alike is we have the gift, and that's a precious thing, but look at you, a spoiled little mama's boy who's always got some ace in the hole. If we was to get caught those two would sell us out in a heartbeat. Next thing you'd go crying to your mama and get some smart lawyer who'd tell the judge how this poor white boy got led astray by two no-account Negroes. There'd be a smack on the backside for you, and Lee and I would end up in a prison cell for the best part of our lives.

"Get out of my sight 'til I simmer down, and if you ever dream up anything like this again, I'll pour a quart of booze down Lee's throat and turn him loose on you. Believe you me, he's just waiting for the chance."

There is one isolated entry in my diary at this time.

OCTOBER 13
I've lost Old Nick, Des, Marie, everything. I want to die.

I told Sid and Mel to forget it, but they wouldn't let up, and I'd lost the will and the reason to argue. I think I tried to commit suicide by robbery.

It was about two in the morning when we left the house. Sid drove. I'd finally sold him the Ford, although he could only give me thirty dollars down. The two of them were so awash with cocaine and booze and adrenaline it's a wonder we didn't have a smash-up, but I was totally detached, as if I were watching it all from a distance.

Mel's brilliant plan was to have me crack open the front door of the bank in full view of the street while they waited in the car. Although security measures weren't as sophisticated in those days, there would certainly be an alarm. I had enough remaining presence of mind to convince Sid to pull the car into the alley at the back of the building so I could stand on the roof to force a lavatory window.

Once inside, the pair of them were so high they blundered about like a couple of bull elephants, laughing and roughhousing. I yelled at them to shut up—that I couldn't hear the tumblers. When I finally cracked the combination, they rushed into the vault like kids turned loose in a toy store, smashing open deposit boxes, stuffing jewellery into their pockets, throwing papers around, while I stood with the electric torch, viewing the frantic scene like a movie. In a flash of sanity, I dropped the torch, slammed and locked the vault door, tripped the alarm, and beat a retreat out the lavatory window, bouncing off the car roof and tearing down the alley like a scalded cat.

I couldn't go back to the house. The place would be overrun with police in no time, and Mel and Sid would certainly implicate me. Thank God I hadn't given the Vandervents my real name. I had only the clothes on my back, but at least I was free.

It was a mild night, and I walked for what seemed an endless time with no idea of where I was. There was a river with mist rising off it, not a building in sight. It was almost dawn when I spied a bonfire under a bridge, silhouetting the seated figures of three men. I approached them with caution, but they gestured in a friendly way that I should join them.

They were immigrants, Italian brothers, working as labourers but unable to afford lodgings. They did, however, have food and a jug of wine, which they generously shared. I devoured the fresh bread soaked in olive oil, ripe tomatoes and spicy sausage roasted on sticks over the fire, washed down with the rough red wine. They spoke little English, and I spoke no Italian, but we communicated with a few words and gestures. They were the Capellis, Carlo, Franco and Felix. Felix, the youngest, pulled out a wooden flute and played a poignant melody. His brothers sang along, their ragged voices making up in feeling what they lacked in finesse, something about angels or a girl called Angelina. My eyes closed, and I slept like the dead.

I awoke mid-morning to find the ashes cold and the Capellis gone, but tucked into the front of my coat was some bread and sausage wrapped in butcher's paper, and in the crook of my elbow the remains of the jug of wine.

I wandered the rest of the day and most of the night, finally falling asleep against a pile of rubbish in an alley. By noon the next day I had to accept that my entire resources consisted of one dollar and twenty-two cents, for a repeated search of my pockets would yield nothing more. It was enough for the pint of medicinal alcohol I bought from a drugstore. My state was beyond anything I'd previously experienced, and from that point I survived on instinct alone.

Being a vagrant is like being invisible. People refuse to see you. At first I was angry and frustrated, but I came to accept it, and even depend on it. I used my scruffy appearance to intimidate, becoming a shameless panhandler, never straying far from the source of the cheapest booze. When hunger drove me to eat, I stole from street stalls, or rummaged through waste bins, but mainly I drank anything I could get my hands on. It's a wonder I didn't go blind.

A few events are clear. Once a policeman roughly evicted me from the doorway where I'd been sleeping, and as I walked aimlessly I heard the familiar sound of a brass band. It took me back to my days in London, and the band that played on a street corner near the Goldring warehouse. What had Tom Wilbur called them? The Sally Anns. I followed the strains of "The Lights Along the Shore," and came upon a strange sight. It was indeed a Salvation Army band, but made up entirely of children, the youngest about nine or ten, the oldest about fifteen, their hats much too big for their earnest faces, and their spindly legs like sticks in their puttees. The tuba and bass drum nearly overwhelmed their players, and although they performed passably well, there was something desperate and joyless about it. As I stood transfixed, someone spoke, and I turned to face a formidable-looking woman in a severe uniform and Victorian bonnet.

She said, "Brother, I think you are in need of a hot meal and a place to sleep."

If I'd detected the least hint of pity or condescension in her steady grey eyes, I'd have cursed her and moved on, but I saw only honest concern, and followed her to a men's shelter where I was fed a generous bowl of hot soup with fresh bread, and a mug of strong tea with milk and sugar, the first real food I'd had in days. I can taste it even now. I was provided with a rough blanket, an old but clean shirt and trousers, a threadbare towel, a bar of soap, a comb, and a razor, and was shown to a shower. The feeling of warm water coursing over my body was so luxurious I almost groaned, and was loath to end it. By the time I'd shaved, I felt a little like my old self again. I stayed at the shelter for three nights, sleeping in a crowded dormitory on a narrow cot, surrounded by the sounds and smells of twenty other lost souls, until claustrophobia and the desperate desire for a drink drove me onto the street again.

I received one last gift from the shelter, an army greatcoat, smelling of gasoline from the cleaning of it, with dark patches where the former insignia had been. That coat became my refuge. I relied on its warmth and weight, its deep pockets and the borrowed regard and generosity bestowed upon me as a veteran down on his luck.

I was attacked and beaten, once by another vagrant who tried to steal my coat, and once by a gang of street toughs just for the hell of it. As a result, my left eyebrow is dissected by a scar and I have a bump on the bridge of my nose where it was broken. It does add some character to an otherwise ordinary face.

There is one final episode that stands out. Christmas, the New Year and the end of the war had come and gone with little notice from me other than a vague memory of a Christmas dinner in some church hall and being roused out of my stupor by bells and horns and cheering in the streets. By February, I was suffering from malnutrition and fever, with a racking cough. At dawn one morning I found a gap in the railyard fence and went looking for an open boxcar to sleep in, for the wind off the lake was particularly bitter. I had just settled in and was nursing the last of my pint when a loud voice startled me, causing me to spill the remaining few drops.

"Ere, ere, wot's this then?"

I stifled a curse and sat up smartly, for it was a sound I hadn't heard since I'd left England, an East End London accent.

"George Francis Fitzhelm at your service, sir."

"Blimey! An Englishman, and a gent and veteran too, I'll be bound. Mervyn Dickie, that's me, sir," and he shook my hand, filthy as it was.

In appearance he was as close to a bulldog as a man could be—about fifty with a thick body, bowed legs and a pugnacious demeanour that proved to be completely at odds with his nature. He was the first person in weeks to treat me with any civility, and I found myself oddly unwilling to deceive him.

"You find me in difficult circumstances," I said. "An Englishman I certainly am, and a gentleman I once was, but a soldier I've never been." Then my cough overtook me.

"You'd best come with me, young George," he replied. "A mug of tea, a bacon sandwich and a good fire will set you right."

He led me to the gatehouse where there was a coal-fired stove, and brewed some tea which he topped up with whisky.

"Don't mind if I 'ave a drop meself," he said. "My old woman belongs to this here Temperance Union, and don't allow it in the 'ouse."

He was as good as his word about the food as well, and we were soon engaged in reminiscences of London. He'd been gone some twenty years, and we had no memories in common, but it pleased him just to talk about "the ruddy Old Smoke" as he called it.

Throughout the day my fever worsened, and I'd nod off, jerking awake as he returned from his rounds. I recall certain parts of our conversation as if my brain had somehow recorded them; how he and his wife and five children had immigrated and how hard things had been at first. His two oldest boys now worked at the stockyard, one daughter worked for the telephone exchange, another as a housemaid, and his youngest boy, just thirteen, worked as a newsboy and shoeshine boy in the carnival atmosphere of Yonge and Temperance.

I told him the story of my life, and in one extraordinary moment of coincidence we discovered a connection. When I mentioned Tom Wilbur, his attention sharpened, and he asked me if I knew the name of Tom's mother. I said her name was Florence.

He exclaimed, "Well, I'll be bound! That has to be our Flossie, my oldest brother's girl! She that married that no-good Ken Wilbur, him that was never home except to put another baby in her belly, and her half-blind from doing fancywork on ladies' dresses. Wouldn't hear a harsh word about him neither, even raising all those nippers on her own, and now you tell me her Tom is in prison. What a stunner!

"Now you see, that's what 'appens when there's no man about to keep things in order. Women are too soft by half. Look at you and Tom. If your da had been alive when you first stepped out of line, he'd have sorted you out in a hurry, and you'd have thought twice before you put your foot in it again, and if Tom's old man had been where he ought to have been, Tom wouldn't be where he is now. You take my youngest, Alfred, a real little man, helpin' out his mum and me, holdin' his own with the street toughs, the dregs of society swarmin' 'round him. Now I'm not a hard father, but he knows he'll feel the back of me 'and if he don't keep to the straight and narrow, and that's as 'ow it should be."

I drifted off again thinking that it wouldn't be such a bad thing to have Mervyn Dickie as a father, and remember nothing more until I opened my eyes to find myself lying on a pallet in the corner of a small plain room in my own nightclothes, with Old Nick's casket by my side and the greatcoat folded under my head. I thought I must be dreaming or in some sort of purgatory, but reasoned that if that were true, Old Nick would be safe in his accustomed place. I struggled to sit up, but found I was very weak, with a blinding headache. With the last of my strength I lifted the lid. The bow still in place, but Old Nick gone. Not a dream. I slid back into darkness.

It was Giorgi's room. His soft snoring comforted me when I woke in the night. I have fleeting memories of cabbage soup spooned into my mouth and whispered conversations in Russian mixed with my dreams.

It took me a while to piece it together, but the facts are that Mervyn Dickie, having finished his shift, and recognizing that I was dangerously ill, had convinced the driver of a delivery van to transport us to a hospital charity ward. He told the sisters I was George Francis Fitzhelm of no fixed address and left me in their care. I remained there either unconscious or raving for several days, hanging between life and death and clutching my coat as if my life depended on it. (I later had it carefully cleaned, and it hung in my closet for years.)

The newspapers had been full of the sensational arrest of two would-be bank robbers found mysteriously locked in the vault of a downtown bank when the police responded to the alarm, but no mention of George Joyner. I suspect the police held back the information hoping I'd think it safe to return to my lodgings, for they certainly grilled Giorgi when he innocently dropped by to visit me a few days later. Fortunately, he'd encountered Hope Vandervent depositing my worldly goods at the curb. She jumped at his offer of six dollars for the casket, and threw in my clothes to the bargain. It was all the money he had at the time. He and Des followed accident and death reports, and made weekly rounds of shelters and charity wards, asking to be notified immediately if anyone answering to the name of Joyner or Fitzhelm turned up. Thanks to the kindness of Mervyn Dickie, almost four months later I did.

When I next opened my eyes, it was Des's face I saw.

"Hey, Slick," he said, "you gave us quite a scare. Nice to see those baby blues again."

"Sounds like a song if ever I heard one," I croaked, and we laughed, although it hurt to do so for my lungs were still affected.

It took the better part of a year to totally regain my health.

Strangely, I'd all but lost the desire to drink, and to this day I'm a moderate drinker. It was also the end of my criminal career, for it seemed that much of the wild side of my nature had departed with Old Nick. The length and depth of my fall seemed to have given me a temporary reprieve from depression, and it was more than four years before I experienced another episode. Fortunately, along with this journal and a few other treasures, my diary had remained undiscovered in the bottom of the casket and I continued to make brief and sporadic entries.

FEBRUARY 16, 1919

Now that I'm back in the land of the living, I've been taking stock of myself, and have found the cupboard pretty bare. Bless Giorgi for saving what he did. My phonograph and recordings are gone, likewise my gold cufflinks bearing the Fitzhelm crest. I still have my seal ring. The only thing that kept me from selling it was that, short of cutting off my finger, I couldn't remove it. It's nothing short of a miracle that I have Old Nick's casket intact. If only I had Old Nick. Must get to the post office for my mail. Ma will be frantic that I haven't written in so long.

FEBRUARY 20

Two letters from Ma. The first, thank God, has my allowance, and bears the news that Seth Goldring has his knighthood at last. I suppose I could return, and all would be forgiven, but I firmly believe that whatever future I have is here. At least now I'll be able to repay Giorgi. The second letter displays some alarm at my silence, and I've written to reassure her that I am alive and well, which is all she needs to know. Can't bear to tell her about Old Nick. All my enquiries have been fruitless. Not a whisper.

Giorgi claims to have found a violin for me. It's in the possession of a lady named Madame Stein, who he thinks might be convinced to part with it. Having resigned myself to my loss, I know I must move on. Lord knows how I'll pay for it.

FEBRUARY 22

I am overcome with excitement, for I'm now the proud possessor of a violin. It has none of the wild bright sweetness of Old Nick, but has a lovely dark rich voice of its own.

My benefactress is Madame Berthe Stein, an elderly Austrian lady, very aristocratic in appearance but sadly reduced in circumstances. The violin is a German instrument of a warm red-brown colour, and although it's unlabelled, she declares it to be an excellent late eighteenth-century copy of a Stainer. At first I thought it a lost cause, for when I asked her the price she drew herself up and replied that she could not bring herself to sell it under any circumstances. I'm afraid my disappointment was ill-disguised. I apologized and rose to leave, but she surprised me by asking if I'd play something for her.

I don't know what possessed me—it certainly wasn't calculated to display any virtuosity I might have—but I chose to play "Columbine," the pretty little waltz that Ma and I had always performed to close the Saint Stephen's Day celebration at Fallowfield. It was an emotional rendition, for it brought back an overwhelming flood of memory. When I looked up, Madame Stein's eyes too were full of tears. She asked me to play it again, and accompanied me on piano. She says I remind her of her husband, and the violin is mine if I'll come and play with her once a week. I'm quite undone by her extraordinary generosity, for I know the instrument is very dear to her, and I suspect it's very valuable indeed.

Berthe and her husband had lived over the little shop where he built and repaired violins and other stringed instruments. After his death, she'd sold it to purchase the small cottage she now shared with her husband's widowed sister, Esther Weingarten. Some months before I met her, she'd come into Giorgi's uncle's shop to enquire if her beautiful old sable coat, a wedding gift from her father, could be altered, for she said that at eighty-two she had shrunk to the point where it would cover two of her. Giorgi struck up a conversation with the elegant old lady, and discovered that she'd been a classical piano accompanist for many years, and now supported herself by giving lessons. Having no access to a piano, Giorgi offered to keep her instrument in tune if she'd allow him to play it for a few hours a week. She'd been delighted with his offer, and they'd become fast friends.

The violin was that of her late husband, Isaac. They'd been popular café performers before immigrating to Canada over forty years earlier. Their repertoire was largely romantic music with a preference for Strauss, and it was this music we played together in her tiny, crowded parlour, her handsome quarter-grand piano taking up fully a third of the room. I looked forward to these occasions, though they made me quite homesick. She welcomed me every Wednesday with pastries and coffee, her silver hair piled up on her head. Often Giorgi and one or more of her students would join us, and so it became a sort of salon. I cannot begin to express the sheer joy I felt in playing again.

MARCH 18

I have a job, or should I say a position, with a gentleman's haberdasher, Viceroy Tailors. My employer is Irving Klemitz, a rotund, cheerful little man and superb tailor, who believes my English accent and manners lend a nice tone to the shop. The salary is minimal, but I'm impeccably dressed, as he feels I'm an excellent advertisement. We agree that the current trend toward extra-wide pant legs is an abomination.

Des has found a bass player, a young American named Rob Pitcher, originally from Chicago. As with us at the Magie Noire, he witnessed something he shouldn't have, and found it healthier to leave the country. He's an experienced jazzman and knows all the popular tunes. We've added "After You've Gone" and "Ja Da" to our repertoire. We played two nights ago at the Occidental Hall, and were well received. The coloured crowd likes our music, and is more tolerant of us than any white crowd would be so long as we stick close to the bandstand and stay away from the girls. There are a couple more of these halls we can play, but otherwise, we're limited to house parties and fraternities.

We have a name! The papers have been full of stories about Woodrow Wilson and the League of Nations, and I thought, considering our diversity, the Hot League would be apropos. The boys seem to like it.

The Occidental Hall is now a popular tavern.

Things were very different back then. Being a mixed-race group was a serious drawback. We couldn't perform at any of the hotels, or whites-only dance halls. If we'd been all coloured or all white, there wouldn't have been a problem, but none of us was interested in playing with anyone else. We were confident that what we did was unique and exciting and just what people would want to hear if they got the chance. We made our money from passing the hat, and we all had daytime jobs, so we got by.

In the spring of 1920 I was going out with a girl who was a salesclerk for the T. Eaton Company. Gladys, her name was. We'd planned, one night, to go to the amusement park at Hanlon's Point, but she wanted a spaghetti dinner, so we went to a little place on College Street called Bellissimo which I knew because of the speakeasy in the backroom. There was a quartet playing—accordion, clarinet, bass and drums—mostly Italian melodies but some popular tunes. The clarinet player seemed familiar, and it finally dawned on me that it was Felix Capelli, the youngest of the three brothers who had been so kind to me. He was a first-rate clarinetist and played flute and saxophone as well.

I approached him and reintroduced myself. He embraced me like a long-lost friend, and we spent the rest of the evening talking about everything that had happened to us, and about music of course. Felix was a real jazz fanatic and had an extensive collection of recordings. Gladys was disgusted with me, and finally went home. Felix became the newest member of the Hot League.

His brothers, Carlo and Franco, were now contractors, organizing immigrant crews for construction companies. At first they'd worked out of the basement of a Catholic church, but had recently rented a storefront. (The family still owns a big construction firm, as well as a popular restaurant.)

MAY 17, 1920

Another birthday! Twenty-six! A long letter from Ma with the latest news. Poor Jean has had a miscarriage. I must write to her. Finally had a letter from Tom Wilbur. He heard through his mother that I'd fallen on hard times, and was pleased to know I was now back on my feet. They're releasing him from prison in a year and a bit. Still the same old Tom, full of money-making schemes, most of them pretty shady. I'd written to him suggesting he follow Grandfather Gerry's lead and open a private gambling club. Ma says there are plenty of fellows who've made big money during the war and are looking for places to spend it. I suggested these chaps would love to belong to just the sort of club that would never have them as members, top-hole, very smart, with every appearance of being exclusive. Precisely what I'd do here if I had the money.

Berthe Stein becomes more and more frail. Esther is hard-pressed to take care of her, as she's nearly as old herself. Giorgi and I drop by regularly to deliver groceries and do chores. It creates a bit of a dilemma, however, for Berthe, a gentlewoman to the last, insists on being fully dressed and coiffed when we come, and the effort is very hard on both of them. It breaks my heart.

JULY 24

Berthe's funeral was yesterday. Giorgi and I attended with Esther, her son Samuel and his wife. I was pleased and surprised at the number of people who came on such short notice. Many of them were former students of Berthe's, one of them now an acclaimed concert pianist. I shall miss her dreadfully, as will Giorgi. Even in death she continues to touch the lives of those who knew and loved her. I of course have her wonderful violin, and

Esther is to inherit everything else except her piano, which, bless her, she has left to Giorgi.

I've been going through my old photographs. I bought a box camera around that time, and was an enthusiastic amateur photographer. There are some candid shots of the boys in the band, and a lovely one of Berthe and Esther in their garden, but most of them are of pretty girls, Gladys, Ethel, Connie, Barb, Gloria—I barely remembered them until I saw their pictures again. There's a classic photo of Des holding Elsie, a rare grin on his face. I must remember to give it to his grandson. As evidenced by a shot of me in a straw boater, striped blazer and white flannels, I continued to cut a dashing figure, sporting some of the finest tailoring in Toronto.

There are few diary entries after Berthe Stein's passing in July of 1920—most to do with places we played, new tunes and arrangements and a succession of players, none of whom stayed with us for long—'til my mother's astonishing letter of October 1921. That letter changed everything.

NOVEMBER 10, 1921
Unbelievable news from Ma! Six thousand pounds! I feel like a millionaire.

I'm broken-hearted about Nan. Ma will miss her terribly. I was also very fond of Aunt Tess, although I still find it hard to think of her as my grandmother. I have much to thank her for. In her lifetime she encouraged in me a sense of adventure and endless possibility. In dying, she will turn a pipe dream into a reality.

Next week I meet with the Capelli brothers to form a partnership to purchase the Regal Hotel. I spotted the "For Sale" notice some months back, but never dreamed I'd be in a position to buy it. It will be a private hotel, members only, with a new gaming and club room on the top floor, retaining the small but elegant bar on the first floor, and last but certainly not least a smart supper club where the main dining room is now. Finally, a perma-

nent home for the Hot League. We've built up quite a following among the flash fellows who made their fortunes during the war and smart young whips from the university. I'm sure they'll jump at the chance to belong. It will be a male bastion, except for the supper club, where ladies will be welcome if escorted by a member. I am over the moon!

The Regal was a small hotel in mock-Tudor style, built to serve passengers arriving at Canadian Northern Railway's Yorkville station. The line had been acquired by Canadian National a couple of years previously, and with the planned diversion of all tracks to the lakeshore, construction of the new Union Station well underway, and plans for the large company-owned hotel which would be known as the Royal York across from it, the owners of the Regal had seen the handwriting on the wall and decided to sell up. My windfall couldn't have come at a better time. I would put up my cash, and Carlo and Franco would provide the labour and building supplies. They insisted it be called Fitzhelm's, and I didn't object.

It took over six months to complete the work, and there were times when I thought it would never be done. The new supper club would be completed as quickly as possible so we'd have money coming in while the upper floors were being redecorated. Our members thought it a bit of a lark to pick their way through the construction chaos in the lobby to reach the art deco splendour of our new hundred-and-sixty–seat supper club. I moved into the fifth-floor suite that would be my home, office and workshop until I married Alma. The other two suites on that floor were joined to become the member's lounge and games room with its large roof garden and famous view of downtown. I limited myself to two or three friendly games of poker a week.

With the installation of Giorgi's piano on the bandstand early in December, it became a reality. We celebrated that night with pre-war champagne, and played until daylight, departing only when the plasterers and painters showed up for work. By the time we officially opened on New Year's Eve, 1922, we had forty-six paid-up members. We finally put a hold on new memberships at three hundred.

JANUARY 1, 1922

What a beginning to a new year! Fitzhelm's is a fact, and I sit like a mogul atop my little kingdom with a view of Yonge and Bay streets running south to the lake, and Bloor Street to the east.

Last night was an unqualified success. The Hot League has never sounded better. We have new saxophone and trumpet players, Felix on clarinet, me on the fiddle, and Lee on drums. Giorgi was always brilliant on the accordion, but on the piano he's a genius. Des plays like a man possessed. I'm nominally the bandleader and a decent player, but he's truly the heart and soul of the group, and his clever compositions and arrangements shine like diamonds on a debutante. To think it all started so humbly in the stokers' quarters of a passenger ship only five years ago. I am almost afraid to sit back and enjoy it for fear the other shoe will drop.

Members range from the sons of the wealthy and influential to the cream of the new entrepreneurs—definitely not your father's club. Their girls, like butterflies, fill the dance floor with bright colours and floating draperies, doing the Charleston, the shimmy and the lindy hop.

Friends and family members were all present, Des's cousin Calvin and his wife, Edie; Giorgi's uncle Avram and aunt Katya and his fiancée, Lina; Esther Weingarten, her eyes sparkling and her cheeks quite pink from all the attention; and my guests of honour, Mervyn Dickie and his wife, Judy, who managed to overcome her prejudice against alcohol for the grand occasion. The Capellis were in full force as well—Franco with his new wife, Sofia, Carlo with a heavily made-up girl called Betty, and Felix's girl, Gabriella. They brought with them an imposing silver-haired man named Silvio Pesci, who'll be supplying our liquor. As a hotel we can buy our spirits from the distilleries, but Carlo says we'll get better prices, variety and quality from Silvio. Beer comes straight from the brewery.

I've spoken with Mervyn Dickie about hiring his youngest boy, Alfred, now fifteen. We'll start him off as a boot boy and bellboy, but if he's as smart and as keen as Mervyn says he is, he'll have every opportunity to work his way up. It's the least I can do.

Things will be tight for a while, for there's still a mortgage to pay. None of us has given up our steady employment, but I'm confident that we're on our way.

I still have the original show card from the easel in the lobby. The Hot League had a portrait taken in full evening kit provided by Irving Klemitz at cost. We all have that somewhat frozen look common to posed photographs of the time, but still appear very suave and sophisticated, with the exception of Lee who always looked as if he would burst out of his clothing at any moment. The caption says, "Dance the night away to the mellow melodies of the Hot League." There are two more photos, one of myself as bandleader, my hair slicked down like patent leather, and the other of Des and Elsie with the caption "Featuring the dazzling arrangements and guitar stylings of Desmond Miller." Des has had his hair straightened and brilliantined for the occasion, and sports a ruffled shirt with his new tux.

The Capellis managed the day-to-day running of the place. Much of the staff was Italian, although some of the kitchen staff were Chinese, and we managed to lure away an experienced French chef from another hotel. The menu was simple, but the food was excellent and moderately priced. Most of our profits came from the sale of booze, and believe me, our crowd could drink! We maintained a compatible relationship with the police by hiring off-duty constables to keep an eye on things.

Alfred Dickie is now the chief executive officer of a large hotel chain.

MARCH 2

Des is in love! Her name is Winsome Joseph, and she's twenty-two to Des's thirty-two, but there is no question she's as smitten with him as he is with her. He brought her to rehearsal a couple of days ago, and insisted she sing a number with us. I'll admit we all rolled our eyes a bit, but we should have trusted Des, for she has a lovely contralto, very smooth, perfectly in tune, with a uniquely conversational approach to the lyrics. She's attractive but unusual in appearance, slim and aristocratic, very like the pictures I've seen of the Egyptian queen Nefertiti, with her hair pulled up in a sort of coronet of braids. We'll definitely feature her as a vocalist. Des has had lady friends from time to time, but this is the real thing. To be honest, I could fall for her myself. Our crowd is going to eat her up.

Win was the daughter of Jamaican immigrants, her father a Baptist minister and her mother a schoolteacher. They clearly had higher ambitions for their only daughter than a lowly jazz musician, but once Win made her decision she wouldn't be swayed, and she and Des were married within the year. It's a source of sadness to me that their son, Purcell, has never shown the least interest in music, although he looks so like Des that it stops my heart to see him. In fact, he's a draftsman working for the City of Toronto in public works, but Win tells me her ten-year-old grandson, Desmond, is very musical, and loves his grandfather's recordings. She's promised him Des's guitar once he's learned to play.

SEPTEMBER 2

I've become friendly with one of our members, a permanent resident at Fitzhelm's called Jimmy Swift. Jimmy's a real entrepreneur, always on the go. Got his start manufacturing communications equipment for the Canadian armed forces, and subsequently landed several lucrative military contracts, but with the war over and the contracts terminated, he's looking for other ways to keep his factory up and running.

We got to talking because I want to install a loudspeaker system in the club to amplify voices, and to play recorded music when the band isn't performing, and I knew he had experience in electronics. He said he could come up with something dandy, and started drawing diagrams on the tablecloth. We bounce ideas around like tennis balls. It's my theory that the cabinet for a speaker should throw the sound forward and amplify it just as the body of a guitar does, so I'm experimenting with various kinds, shapes and thicknesses of wood. The finished product should be both decorative and functional.

I've finally bought a new car, a Ford. Partly a sentimental choice, but also because the old Model T never gave me a minute of aggravation. It's a custom model with a natural maple and mahogany body, removable top and the new balloon tires, very sporty, and rides like a dream although the surface on the streets is a nightmare.

Jimmy and I became business partners. We called our new venture the Swift Sound Reproduction Company, quite a mouthful by today's standards. We later shortened it to S.S.R. I've always had good ideas, but lack the technical know-how and resources to carry them out. Jimmy has the kind of mind that doesn't rest until it figures out how to make things work. The patents we developed, along with my musical copyrights, will be my legacy to my daughter, Georgina, since my sons control their grandfather's company.

DECEMBER 3

A nasty situation has arisen involving Esther Weingarten. A man called Elmo Tonks, who recently rented the cottage next to Esther's, has been calling her names and harassing her on the street until she's afraid to go out of the house. He's escalated his behaviour further by throwing refuse over the fence into her front garden, then calling the authorities to complain that she's a Jew and a foreigner who lives like an animal. He even left the stiffened body of a neighbour's beloved cat on her doorstep, although it's not provable that he was responsible. Her son, Sam, wants her to move in with him and his wife, but she refuses, saying she won't be driven out of her home by such a creature. He called to see if I could reason with her.

Tonks is one of those rabble-rousers who make speeches on packing boxes down on Temperance whenever there are enough gullible souls gathered around to listen. Win says her father has confronted him more than once. His particular rant has to do with preserving the purity of the white Christian race by putting a stop to immigration. He's hardly an advertisement for superiority, being ill-spoken, and greasy-haired with bad teeth and an eruptive complexion, those being his more attractive qualities. Esther is shaky but defiant, saying she saw enough of his ilk in Austria when she was a girl and won't be intimidated by the likes of him. Giorgi will stay with her for a few nights until I see what can be done.

I'd encountered plenty of racial prejudice working with Des and Lee and this episode shouldn't have surprised me, but I was shocked by the blatancy of the attacks. I called on Tonks to see if he could be reasoned with, but immediately found myself accused of being a traitor to my race, and threatened with dire, if unspecified, consequences. A visit from two strapping police constables persuaded him that his activities as a public orator could be cut short by public nuisance charges and a hefty fine, with incarceration as a possibility if he persisted. Their arguments must have been pretty forceful, for he disappeared shortly after that, and his pitch on Temperance was taken over by an anarchist.

JANUARY 3, 1923
The Hot League hosted a riotous New Year's Eve at Fitzhelm's. We introduced two new numbers, "Can't Get Enough of That Jazzy Stuff," and "Brandy in My Coffee," along with a smashing arrangement of "Ain't We Got Fun." Win Loves Ruth Etting, and performed two of her songs. The crowd adored it.

I've met a great girl, Alma Daviston. She's the cousin of one of our regulars. He brought her to our New Year's celebration. She's a refreshing change from the bottled blondes with bodies like boys that seem to be the thing these days. We danced every dance when I wasn't on the bandstand, and she's agreed to accompany me to see Little Lord Fauntleroy *at the Majestic next week. I'm told that I, especially, should get a good laugh out of it.*

This was my first meeting with Alma. She wasn't a beauty by the standards of that time, quite voluptuous in a long dress of emerald satin, her dark blonde hair in a coil at the nape of her neck rather than fashionably bobbed, but when she smiled, her whole face lit up with humour and intelligence. Not love at first sight, but certainly a strong mutual attraction. She was twenty, attending university, full of challenging ideas and ambitious plans, and a voracious reader. Finally a girl I could talk to.

She was also very rich, the only child of Palmer Daviston, heir to the Daviston mining empire, though I hadn't a clue when I first met her, for she was less than forthcoming, not that I was particularly straightforward myself. A good joke on both of us. We immediately became a couple. How ironic I should follow Henry's example and marry an heiress.

FEBRUARY 20

Lee has a girlfriend! I'd been concerned about him because he seemed so lost since Des hooked up with Win, but I needn't have worried. Her name is Hattie Wicks, and she has a little girl named Reba whose father is not in evidence. Hattie's about as big as a minute, but bosses Lee around like a drill sergeant. Despite our differences, I'm truly happy for him.

Des and Win are to be married in May. I'll be twenty-nine. High time I thought about getting married myself. Wouldn't that be the answer to Ma's prayers!

APRIL 3

I've popped the question to Alma—not very romantic I'm afraid. I'd written to Ma to tell her I'd been thinking about it, and she pounced, demanding dates and details, so I thought I'd better follow through. Alma's agreeable, but nervous about breaking it to her parents. It's suddenly all so serious.

On another front, Jimmy Swift and I have been tossing around ideas for recording the band. I thought we'd have to go to Montreal or even New York, but Jimmy's more ambitious. He wants to set up a recording enterprise of our own. I'm dubious, because the companies that make the equipment seem determined to keep it to themselves and control what's recorded, but Jimmy says he has some wartime chums at Bell Laboratories and Western Electric, and that if he can finagle a tour of their premises he can probably figure out what they're doing. He also intends to visit the U.S. Patent Office to see what they have on record. He doesn't lack for enterprise—or nerve. I must admit the thought intrigues me, that and the possibility of live radio broadcasts. The cowboy singers are way ahead of us there.

MAY 12

Des and Win were married yesterday afternoon in her father's church, a truly joyous occasion. Win was regal in white satin, and Des couldn't stop grinning and pulling at his bow tie. If Alma and I are one-half as happy, we'll be very fortunate indeed. I've loaned them the Ford, and they're driving to Chicago for their honeymoon. They should hear a lot of great music while they're there. Rob Pitcher's mother is very ill so he'll be travelling with them, and staying on. Guess we need a new bass player.

Alma and I have been reading to each other, and are currently enjoying Sinclair Lewis's Main Street. *We plan to tackle* Ulysses *next to see what all the fuss is about. She's going to speak to her parents about our engagement tomorrow night. As their only child, she's under pressure to marry someone in their crowd. I've given her some ammunition by finally 'fessing up about my family, and she thinks her mother's enough of a snob to go for it. I'm presentable enough. Not a bad catch on the surface, but I'll admit Alma's a little out of my league. We'll see.*

MAY 18
Des and Win have been arrested! Nothing they did, but rather that they were a Negro couple driving an expensive car, which they didn't own. They spent the night in a Michigan jail because they couldn't reach me. Fortunately I was able to set things straight this morning, but it's a sorry end to their honeymoon.

MAY 30
What an ordeal! Alma and I had dinner with her parents last night to see if I passed muster. Her mother, Pamela, was a great beauty in her day, but she goes a little overboard now and looks rather like a painted doll. Still, she made every effort to be pleasant. Palmer Daviston divides his time among golf, tennis and sailing, with his business interests a distant fourth, leaving us damned little to talk about, but we gamely retired to his study for brandy and cigars after dinner. He's not a bad old bird, but when I tried to explain what I did for a living, I might as well have been speaking Swahili. At least I didn't trail my shirt cuffs in the Béarnaise.

In retrospect, I realize that the Davistons considered me a passing fancy as far as Alma was concerned, just one in the eye for the stuffy parents, but she and I suited each other down to the ground, pairing physical compatibility with stubbornly independent natures. By the time they figured out we were serious, Alma was pregnant.

AUGUST 11
We've broken the news to the Davistons. They want to put a respectable face on it by throwing a lavish wedding with half the city invited, but we're balking. I'm for a quick ceremony at city hall, and a celebration at Fitzhelm's afterward. Alma agrees.

AUGUST 15

The deed is done! We're married in the eyes of the law, if not in the eyes of God and the Davistons. Our witnesses were Des and Win, Giorgi and Lina, Felix and Gabriella, and, despite his grumbling, Lee and Hattie. She must have read him the riot act. It was short and sweet, then we headed for the club and got very silly on champagne.

Alma's parents have bowed to our fait accompli, *and we've unbent to the degree that we're attending a fancy reception for family, friends and acquaintances after the fact. According to Alma, her mother is telling everyone who'll listen how wonderfully impetuous young people are these days, and weren't we clever to avoid all the upset of a big wedding. I'm not looking forward to Ma's response. She'll be livid with me.*

SEPTEMBER 2

I've quite settled into being an old married man. Alma has added some nice touches to the suite, but it's pretty crowded. I'll probably keep it for an office, and we'll start looking for a house. Alma's starting to show a bit, and is the picture of health. Win says it'll be a boy. Palmer Daviston will be making school arrangements for the poor little beggar if it's true.

Ma's letter is about what I expected. How could I? My selfishness knows no bounds. She'll never forgive me. When are Alma and I coming to Fallowfield?

One of the benefits of marrying well was that suddenly the Hot League was in demand for society functions. There were some initial reservations about the makeup of the band, but after I convinced one of Pamela Daviston's chums to treat us, myself included, as hired help and feed us in the kitchen, things smoothed out nicely. The fees were excellent, and we could count on at least a dozen of these engagements a year.

In January of 1924 I suffered a brief but severe breakdown coupled with pneumonia. I should have expected it, what with all the changes in my life, but I'd avoided it so long I guess I'd thought myself cured. Poor Alma carried the brunt of it. I hadn't really warned her about my little problem other than telling her before we married that I could be a moody brute at times. Still, she took it in her stride, closed the shades and had another bed installed in the suite, saying that with the size of her belly she was more comfortable sleeping on her own at this point. My only memories of this time are listening to King Oliver over and over on the phonograph, and Alma's soothing voice reading me verses from *The Rubaiyat*. I was pretty much *non compos mentis* for about eight weeks.

NOVEMBER 16

Tonight we introduce the new amplification system Jimmy and I have been working on, although it's mostly Jimmy's efforts that have carried it forward since I've been out of the picture. I finally feel like playing again. The boys have been limping along pretty well without me, but are glad to have me back. We rehearsed this afternoon, mostly familiar pieces, but Win is introducing Bessie Smith's song "Ain't Nobody's Business," which is great fun to play. With the new microphone, she won't have to push her voice so hard. I'm exhausted but happy.

Alma gets bigger every day, but is cheerful with it, and looks quite beautiful. The Davistons insist on buying us a house and have one all picked out. I haven't seen it, but Alma says it's perfect. The one fly in the ointment is that it's only a block from the Davistons in Rosedale. I'll let Alma run interference there. I must say her trust fund was a godsend while I was out of commission, but surprisingly I find I'm old-fashioned enough to want to pay my own way from here on. Let it all go to young Algernon, or whatever the hell we decide to call him.

I still live in the same house, a nice old Victorian. It has seven bedrooms and four baths, so I can rattle around endlessly. It's situated on a ravine, with an enormous coach house in the back where I converted most of the ground floor into a workshop with a sort of club room on top where I could gather with old chums without upsetting the household arrangements. When Fitzhelm's finally closed its doors and was slated for demolition, I had the old mahogany bar dismantled and installed here. It's where I now spend most of my time, and indeed where I'm writing these very words.

DECEMBER 18

The Davistons want Alma and me to celebrate Christmas at their house in the Bahamas. It would be nice to escape the winter, but I'm concerned about Alma travelling in her condition, and besides I'd have to be back here in time for New Year's as it's one of our biggest nights. Can't let the boys down. Alma says she'll fly down on her own and stay until February, getting back in plenty of time to have the baby. Junior isn't due until sometime in April, but it still worries me. This baby business is uncharted territory.

I don't like the sound of this Hitler fellow in Germany. Jail seems like the best place for him. There are a few yahoos here who think he's the great white hope, and Ma tells me he has admirers in Britain as well. He seems to be very good at getting people worked up, but then some people will believe anything.

I'm definitely taking a pass on Nassau.

JANUARY 1, 1924

Another year gone! Great doings at the club last night. Must admit I went over my limit, and have a bit of a head this morning, or should I say this afternoon. Really missing Alma.

FEBRUARY 20

Alma's due back in two days. Can't wait to see her. She says she's as big as a house.

I've been reading in the newspapers about Gershwin's new composition, "Rhapsody in Blue." He's top-notch, so it's bound to be good. They'll have a recording out soon, so we'll actually get to hear it. Giorgi's excited by the concept of classically arranged jazz. He and Des have started work-ing along the same lines, although Giorgi admires Dvořák and Des's taste runs more to W.C. Handy. I'm skeptical about the appeal of longer jazz-influenced compositions in our context. Sounds more like concert fare to me.

MAY 10

We are the proud parents of a seven-pound twelve-ounce baby boy as of 11:22 last night.

Alma thinks Douglas Fairbanks is "the bee's knees," so we'd gone to see The Thief of Baghdad. *I guess the excitement was too much, for her water broke, and I rushed her to the hospital. He's a wrinkled, red-faced little fellow with a healthy set of lungs, but Alma says he'll improve. She's worn out, but otherwise in good form. Ma fell to pieces when I broke the news by transatlantic telephone. You'd think she'd be used to having grand-children by now. He's to be christened Augustus Renforth Fitzhelm. Quite a moniker for the size of him. Our birthdays are only a week apart. Seems impossible I'll be thirty next year.*

Alma and Gus and I moved into the new house with a wet nurse, cook and housekeeper. The entries in my diary thin out consider-ably at this time, and mainly deal with ordinary family matters and with patents and copyrights that are well documented elsewhere, so I'll follow Ma's lead here and gloss over a few years, adding the odd entry where pertinent.

Alma miscarried, a girl, in the summer of 1926. She was devas-tated, but determined to try again, and on November 3rd, 1927, our second son Charles Palmer Fitzhelm was born with no complica-tions. We agreed we wouldn't have any more, and Alma went back to school to finish her history degree. She had a sharp intellect, and it was a pity her father never considered involving her in the business.

I regret that Alma and I were less than exemplary parents. I was preoccupied with the band, the club, and S.S.R. Limited, and Alma was absorbed in her studies. We had a succession of extremely competent nannies. Alma saw this as normal, for it was how she'd been raised, and I meekly acquiesced. Perhaps it was my own lack of a father that left me unprepared for the role, perhaps it was pure self-ishness. We saw the boys, immaculate, at breakfast and at bedtime, like two peas in a pod. I did attempt to read to them when they were older, but their tastes ran more to *The Boys' Own Annual* than any of the childhood classics. One book that truly drew them in was the jungle adventures of Carveth Wells, but I definitely lost favour when I refused to buy Gus a machete, and anticipating his next move, warned his grandfather off the purchase as well. Being totally unath-letic, I was useless as far as their sports activities were concerned. Alma could at least swim and skate and ski with them. They went to their grandparents most weekends and holidays. Unlike myself at that age, they were extraordinarily polite and well behaved, at least on the surface. They still are. Just how little I really knew about them was brought home to me recently, when I discovered a rusty old tin box buried in the garden. In it was a piece of parchment, carefully burnt around the edges, and written in what could only have been child's blood, "The Charter of the Bloody Pirates Club—brothers together forever against bullies, braggarts, cheats and dirty liars," and signed "Gus and Charlie."

FEBRUARY 13, 1928

Des and Win have a son, Purcell Joseph Miller. Win was in labour for several hours, and finally had a Caesarean section. The baby at almost nine pounds is healthy enough, but poor Win! They say she shouldn't have any more, which is a real blow.

Des was in such a state of worry and frustration at his own helplessness that Win ordered him to go to work so she could get on with it, and he got the call at the club shortly after midnight. He's certainly the proud papa, but concern about Win is uppermost. He couldn't play worth a damn last night, and it'll be the same tonight if he shows up at all.

The Hot League expanded, contracted and expanded again. We welcomed Rob Pitcher back from Chicago. By 1930 we had a full horn section, and were using the club to record for the first time for our own Swift label. I'll never forget the thrill of hearing our recordings of "Bluebird Blue" and "Slap and Tickle" played on the radio for the first time. Win quit performing after Purcell was born, and we hired a new singer, a real heartthrob and a total pain in the posterior called Alvin Barton, who thought he was Rudy Vallee.

It was a great time for music. Casa Loma had Billy Angel and the Spirits of Rhythm and the Palais Royale had various orchestras, the Royal York and the other railroad hotels across the country featured their own bands. Some orchestras, like Mart Kenny and the Lombardo Brothers, travelled constantly, but we had little reason or inclination to tour. We had Fitzhelm's.

Des and Giorgi completed their jazz opus, a thirty-minute composition which they called "Night Train to Harlem," and we performed a limited ensemble version of it to mixed reaction one night at the club. I think it's quite a remarkable piece, but a little too long and highbrow for our crowd—you couldn't dance to it. Des's dream of performing it as written was never realized. Our recording budget wouldn't stretch to a symphony orchestra.

There was a growing demand for S.S.R. loudspeakers and microphones, mainly for public address systems, but also for the nightclubs and dance halls that had sprung up when prohibition was repealed in '26. Fitzhelm's wasn't affected by the ready availability of alcohol, as we had a loyal membership, and our designation as a private club allowed us to avoid many of the restrictions that plagued other licensed premises.

Jimmy Swift's attention was diverted from mere sound reproduction by a recent invention they were calling television. That and
the development of medical equipment based on sound waves totally
captured his imagination, while I concentrated my efforts on the
amplification of instruments, and my ill-fated invention of an electric lawn mower. I nearly electrocuted myself when I ran over the
cord. A gasoline motor makes much more sense.

DECEMBER 27, 1929

*I'm in heaven. Alma has given me the complete Okeh Records collection of
Joe Venuti for Christmas, and I only gave her diamond earrings. What a
fiddle player! The Blue Four (Five and Six) are a brilliant group, and the
boys and I have been listening to them non-stop. One can't help but think
what might have happened if we'd gone to the States, but I can't complain.
I'm a lucky, lucky man.*

Those recordings revitalized the Hot League. We'd been cruising
along with little effort, so secure and complacent that we'd stopped
taking even musical chances. Des had never stopped writing, but I
hadn't written anything new in three or four years. The tune "Lucky,
Lucky Man" was the beginning of the most creative period of my
life. We made seven recordings in the next three years, and our
exposure on radio assured steady sales. A newspaper article at the
time declared us to be Toronto's hottest dance band. Win handled
the mail-order business of Swift Records from home.

In 1931, Alma replaced her father as chair of the Daviston Charitable Foundation. Both the boys were in school by then, and having
completed her master's degree, she'd been looking for something
to keep her busy. Palmer was delighted to abdicate and devote even
more time to his leisure pursuits. The foundation had always supported modest scholarships and conservative charities, and Alma's
progressive ideas were quite unsettling to the board of old boys who

were used to meeting twice a year to rubber-stamp the recipients. Her first project was to be a home for unwed mothers, which would not only see the girls through pregnancy but support them in keeping their babies, and train them for respectable employment thereafter. It was her firm belief that society did not benefit from making pariahs of these girls, and that the institutional upbringing of their children, rather than turning them into useful citizens, only served to fill our prisons. When the shock waves reached Palmer Daviston, he put his foot down and ordered her to confine herself to less sensational proposals. She backed down temporarily but became more devious, concealing the true nature of some applications until after funds were approved, and so, slowly, the foundation advanced into the twentieth century.

As time went on, Alma's charitable interests took her further and further afield, and though I was proud of her, I couldn't help wishing she'd spend more time at home.

OCTOBER 10, 1931
A letter from Ma. She's pressing hard for us to visit. I claim work as an excuse, but the truth is I can't see myself ever returning to Fallowfield. She says the English newspapers are full of reports on the London riots protesting the cuts in unemployment benefits, and that although the authorities claim Communist agitation, it seems highly unlikely that all five thousand protesters have a political agenda. Even here there's talk of Communist speakers being arrested. Alma and I agree that, Communist or not, there's a valid point to much of the rhetoric.

DECEMBER 27
The house is eerily silent. After Christmas Eve here, Alma and the boys left for the Bahamas and won't be back until the second week of January. The cook is off as well, so I'm bach-ing it at the club. I've protested against the boys missing so much school, but Alma has hired one of the Daviston

foundation's scholarship boys to tutor them. Palmer insists on giving them sailing lessons, which scares the hell out of me. After all, Charlie's only five. Grandpa dotes on the pair of them, and they adore him as well.

Gearing up for another New Year's at Fitzhelm's. It will be quieter this year.

Despite the dampening effect of the stock-market crash in '29, we didn't really begin to feel the effects of the Great Depression for another two years. I remember Mervyn Dickie telling me his job was becoming more difficult every day with desperate men using desperate means to ride the trains. He said it broke his heart to see so many honest, decent fellows driven to such reckless and lawless behaviour and it went against the grain to have to be so harsh with them.

Recalling what it was like to be on my uppers, I hired a young fellow called Neil McKay when he came to the door looking for yardwork. At sixteen, his child allowance had ended, and he didn't want to be a burden to his family. The government's northern work camps only paid twenty cents a day, so he'd hitchhiked to Toronto, but found that whatever job he applied for there'd be four or five girls still living with their families willing to do it for less. He worked for me for fifteen years, and eventually married Georgie's nanny.

As for Fitzhelm's, we certainly lost some stalwarts to the crash, but their places were readily filled by ambitious young entrepreneurs. Always some who make money out of hard times, and for others an evening of drinking and dancing was the perfect way to lose one's blues. The tone of the place changed, of course, and I missed the earlier, more gentlemanly days, but we survived.

Alma held a charity dance marathon at the club to raise money for soup kitchens. It brought in over two thousand dollars, and she matched it with money from the foundation. Even those dinosaurs couldn't take issue with starvation.

It was in the spring of '32 that Alma made the first of her foreign treks. She'd had reports that Daviston funds for a milk program for African children were being misspent, and was determined to see for herself. I didn't want her to go, and when I ventured to ask if African children actually drank milk, we had a huge row over it. She went. When she returned three months later we had quite a passionate reunion, which, to our surprise, resulted in her third and final pregnancy. Our daughter, Georgina Elizabeth Fitzhelm, was born in May of 1935.

Georgina was a tiny, angelic, pink and white child with a curly abundance of pale strawberry blonde hair. As Alma was taken up with her causes, and the grandparents were besotted with the boys, Georgie and I became great chums right from the start. She'd sleep in her cot as I pottered around in my shop, and I'd sometimes take her to the club with me for rehearsals. She never fretted, and could sleep through anything. For whatever reason, I found myself able to be more of a father to her than I'd been to the boys.

At first they treated her rather like a family pet. She was after all a girl, and there was a considerable age difference, but as she got older, she began to interfere in their games, resorting to more and more disruptive behaviour if they tried to ignore her. She grew to be such a nuisance that they became quite cruel to her, and froze her out of their activities altogether. As Alma was often away by then, I was pretty much on my own dealing with a very unhappy five-year-old.

She was unfailingly sweet and affectionate with me, so it was a shock to discover she'd become a little tyrant with the domestic staff. She would only have been six when Neil McKay came to me, very white-faced, saying that I mustn't believe what Miss Georgina accused him of; that it wasn't in him to behave so. She'd threatened to accuse him of touching her under her dress if he told me he'd caught her sneaking out of the house after dark. God knows how she'd conceived such a notion. When I confronted her with it, she was all wide-eyed innocence, declaring that she couldn't imagine why Neil would say such a dreadful thing.

I was disturbed enough by the incident to question the house-keeper, Mrs. Kelly, and Laura, the nanny. At first they tried to excuse Georgie, saying she was very excitable and impulsive, and too young to understand the consequences of what she said and did, but the subsequent litany of tantrums and sulks, cruel pranks, unjust accusations of theft and threats of dismissal left me shaken. It was as if my angelic little girl had become some sort of Jekyll and Hyde, and it wasn't lost on me that these were disturbing echoes of my own youthful behaviour. I feared that before long I wouldn't be able to control Georgina's actions any more than my mother had mine.

Fortunately she'd started school by then, and I endeavoured to occupy the balance of her time with lessons of various kinds, piano, dance, voice, drama, hoping this would afford her some of the attention she craved and keep her out of mischief. If I'm honest, I'd have to say that she never had the makings of a truly inspired per-former, but if genius could be acquired through sheer enthusiasm she'd have been brilliant. Like my mother, she was a wicked mimic and loved to perform. She was such an exquisitely beautiful child it was hard to take your eyes off her, and it allowed one to overlook her shortcomings.

When I finally got to talk it over with Alma, she insisted on sending Georgie to a psychiatrist. She was in analysis right into her teens, but in my opinion she was dancing circles around him by the time she was eight.

JANUARY 20, 1939
Alma and the children are just back from the Bahamas, looking very brown and healthy. Georgie hates it there, poor mite. Gus and Charlie always off on their own or on the boat with their grandfather, Alma busy reorganizing

the foundation's school program down there, and when the kid finally finds someone her own age to play with, Grandma Pamela lectures her on the inappropriateness of a friendship with the cook's granddaughter. I was livid. Alma claims she was unaware of the incident and will tackle Pamela about it, but the damage is done.

Despite the freezing weather, Georgie spends much of her free time with a neighbour boy, Teddy Crewe, in the tree house I built for her down in the ravine. God knows what they talk about, but they laugh a lot. He's a nice enough kid, but a bit shy and delicate, and Georgie's very protective of him. Alma and I attempted to socialize with the parents, but it's a lost cause. Eustace Crewe somehow manages to be a bully and a bore as well as a Babbitt, and I feel heartily sorry for that nice little wife of his.

Ma says young Alistair is preparing to step into his grandfather's shoes at Goldring's. The old man's health is failing, and Ali's been groomed from birth, may he have joy of it.

Ma says everyone over there is pretty worked up over the Mosley controversy, big pro- and anti-Nazi rallies, and the newspapers report similar activity in the States, so we'll undoubtedly see it here as well. Ruthie's heavily involved in relief for fleeing Jewish refugees.

Jimmy's re-establishing all his old military contacts. He says there's no way in hell Hitler will stay out of Poland, and if the Brits are in it we're up to our necks in it too. I hope he's wrong, but he's much more savvy about these things than I am.

A funny story about Eustace Crewe. Although he was successful and had married money, he was very tight-fisted, but he couldn't stand to be outdone. If someone in the neighbourhood bought a new car, you could wager that within weeks Crewe would have a more deluxe model. I swear he had a different suit for every day of the week. On the other hand, his wife, Marjorie, had to practise extreme household economy, her mother having tied up all her money in trust so that Eustace couldn't get his hands on it. The odd times we socialized, I was struck by the pristine condition of the house, and Georgie told me that except for on social occasions everything was covered with dust sheets with runners over the carpets. She reported that most of the actual living was confined to what had been the cook's sitting room next to the kitchen.

Teddy and his sister were allowed few of the indulgences of an affluent childhood. In fact it wasn't until Georgie rode over to show off her new bicycle that Teddy got a much more expensive one. She obviously thought long and hard over this, then enlisted me as a co-conspirator, and from then on, if Teddy needed, say, a camera for a school project, Georgie had only to show up at the Crewe household bragging about her new Brownie for Eustace Crewe to buy Teddy a Rolleiflex. Perhaps it was petty of me, but it gave me a great deal of private amusement.

Jimmy Swift reorganized and retooled the factory for military contracts. I had little to do with it, as it came under Swift Communications rather than S.S.R., although I did benefit from a couple of the patents. It was mostly girls hired for the assembly line, as Jimmy said there was no use in training boys only to have them sign up.

I was too old for military service, of course. We all were, but the Hot League did their bit, holding free servicemen's nights at the club on Mondays. We also hired a bus once a month to play dances near the base at Trenton. Alma organized volunteers from her old school to come along as hostesses to dance with the boys. Despite the chaperones, more than one romance developed, much to the dismay of the girls' parents.

I took Georgie to see *The Wizard of Oz*. She adored any kind of fantasy, and was enchanted. I'd always read to her, *Peter Pan*, *Alice in Wonderland*, and the most dog-eared of all her favourites, T.H. White's *Mistress Masham's Repose* with its delightful references to Gulliver and the Lilliputians. The actual *Travels* were a bit over Georgie's head then and I never quite got around to it later. I've passed it on to her son, Eddie. In fact, I've given him all her books, which otherwise would have sat here in her bedroom like a collection of forgotten friends.

Georgie's fantasies these days are more theatrical than literary. Gina Jardin she calls herself. I've been to see most of her performances, but there's too much sexual innuendo and leering double entendre for my taste, and, what's more, being delivered by my daughter. Perhaps I come from a more subtle age. She says I'm just an old prude.

Although the war affected all of us, here we had no concept of what it was like to be under constant threat of attack. Even the relative peace of Fallowfield was shattered. A quote from one of Ma's letters around this time . . .

> "*I am spared the worst aspects of rationing because, despite the regulations, Jonathan sees to it that I have an egg for my breakfast, butter for my toast, and honey instead of sugar for my tea. I do suffer pangs of conscience whenever he brings me a nice little piece of beefsteak for my dinner. So many people with children going without.*
>
> "*Ruthie has organized another scrap-metal drive, but I can't spare even one more pot from my kitchen. I'm down to bare bones already. I think it's sad that so many beautiful and useful things must be broken up and melted down, but needs must, as Nan would have said.*
>
> "*Ruthie's turned the nursery floor and attics into a sort of infirmary for convalescent officers, and has installed a lift for the purpose. I see them about the grounds, poor devils. They have to be in pretty bad shape by the time they come here, shell shock and nerves as well as physical damage. I've started having some of them to tea. It probably bores them silly, but perhaps it will help spur their recovery, and I need to feel I'm doing something.*

*Addie's taking in children from London. Their parents are
frantic to get them away from the bombing, and the sea air at
Brighton will be good for them, but it must be a horrible wrench
for all concerned.*

*"You'll remember Ephraim Best. He lost over twenty ewes
and lambs when a German bomber dropped the last of its deadly
cargo on his north pasture. Fortunately his prize ram was spared.
I thought it a cruel and vindictive act, but Henry informs me
that the pilot was simply lightening his load to save fuel for the
return journey. I still think he should burn in hell, or at the very
least suffer the effects of one of his own bombs."*

As much as I've enjoyed revisiting the past, I can no longer
avoid dealing with events I have not allowed myself to contemplate
for years. Here is the last entry in my diaries.

MAY 17, 1944

*A quiet birthday dinner last night with Alma and Georgie. Gus, our college
football hero, had a game, and wherever Gus is, there's Charlie. My God,
I'm forty-nine! More than half my life over. Where did the time go?*

*Had a celebratory lunch with the band at the club. "The old man" was
in for some serious ribbing, but I gave as good as I got. Felix at forty is the
youngster in the group, and he and Gabriella are expecting their sixth pup.
He says he intends to raise an entire soccer team. Wonder how Gabriella
feels about that. Our mood was pretty buoyant what with news of the latest
bombing raids over Germany. Predictions are that it will all be over by this
time next year.*

*Carlo's had an offer for the club. They want to demolish it and put up
an office building. We've talked it over and agree that the offer's not nearly
high enough, but it's a good indication that we're sitting on a prime piece of
real estate.*

I must have broken some fatal mirror, for in the seven years between 1944 and 1951 I suffered one blow after another. I'll attempt to reconstruct these events, but my actual memory of them is patchy.

The first blow was my mother's death in June of 1944. The news didn't reach me immediately. The family tried to call me at the house, but I wasn't there, and Alma was in Ottawa lobbying for war refugees. Ruthie sent a telegram, which I found when I returned home the next day. Three days later a letter from Jean containing my mother's last words arrived by transatlantic clipper.

I reveal here for the first and only time that when my mother died I was in a Niagara Falls hotel suite with Eustace Crewe's wife Marjorie. I have no excuse. To suggest I felt sorry for her would be self-serving, to say the least. She was a sweet, pretty little woman, desperately unhappy, and Alma's good works were keeping her away from home for longer and longer periods of time. I was lonely, and took advantage of Marjorie's unhappiness. The affair ended almost before it began. The hell of it was that Alma had finally convinced me to swallow my pride and visit Fallowfield with her and the children when the war ended, and I'd just sent off a letter to that effect. It could not have reached my mother in time. The final bitter irony was that she left me Fallowfield Cottage in her will.

Alma returned from Ottawa to find me in a pitiful state, unwashed, unshaven and raving. Her parents pressured her to have me committed to a mental institution, but she refused absolutely. It became obvious that she couldn't cope alone this time, and out of desperation she finally settled for what she believed to be the only possible alternative.

The Daviston foundation had put considerable money into hospitals and medical research facilities. One aspect of that research was electroshock therapy, and after consultation with the specialists involved, it was concluded that I might benefit from the procedure. I underwent a series of treatments—half a dozen, I think. It was declared a great success, and in a way I suppose it was, for I was no longer depressed, and the gaps in my childhood memories meant that my antipathy for spiders was gone. In fact, for a time I didn't feel much of anything. The resultant damage to my spine eventually put me in a painful back brace, which I still wear, but the most devastating side effect was that I lost my ability to improvise and compose music. I could still read and play the notes, but the connection with the music was gone. I can't recall which American writer said that he feared if he lost his devils, he'd lose his angels as well. The worst of it was the pity I saw in Des's eyes when I attempted to play.

Alma hired a secretary for me called Karl Kovitch. What all of us knew but never discussed was that he was a sort of minder for me in case I went off the rails again. He's an intelligent and useful fellow with the sinewy physique of an Olympic wrestler, and he started me on a calisthenics routine, which he said would improve both my body and my spirits. Perhaps it did, as by the end of the year I'd regained some semblance of normalcy.

Alma and Georgina celebrated New Year's with me at the club. Georgie, every inch a girl at twelve, was very proud of her first long dress, a pink lace confection. The boys were in the Bahamas. I could almost pretend that it was like old times with the band, except that I was reading the charts as if seeing them for the first time, and declining the solos. I was more puzzled and frustrated than sad or angry about it, as if this were something I should easily be able to do, but my hands and my brain wouldn't cooperate.

Franco and Carlo came to me with another, much higher offer for Fitzhelm's, but I couldn't bear to think of selling it, as the club and the band were the last remaining vestiges of my former life. It was becoming less feasible to operate the place privately, and when the last of the memberships expired, we opened it to the public as a hotel and nightclub.

In the early hours of November 12th, 1946, Des Miller was struck down and killed by a hit-and-run driver. We'd been rehearsing for the upcoming weekend. I'd painstakingly memorized my solos from our recordings, and was starting to feel more confident. Des and Giorgi had decided to walk home. They'd just said goodnight and parted company when the car, moving erratically and at a high speed, hit Des, throwing him over the hood where he hung until the driver made a sharp turn, landing him on the street. The car never slowed. Giorgi saw the whole thing and swears the driver deliberately swerved to hit Des. He ran to help him, but Des was gone by the time he reached him. Strangely, Elsie was intact in her leather case. Des's final instinct had been to protect the guitar by turning away as the vehicle struck him.

Giorgi first called me, then the police, and I remained with Des while Giorgi went to break the tragic news to Win. I was determined that my dear friend be treated with the respect he deserved, and this thought alone held me together through the whole dreadful ordeal. The driver and the car, a late-model, dark-coloured Chevrolet, were never identified. Earlier that day, Remembrance Day, the three of us had placed a wreath on the cenotaph for Kip and Eli, then retired to a local bar to reminisce. It was something we did every year, and something Giorgi and I still do, although now it's as much for Des as it is for the others.

My one enduring memory of the funeral is of Win collapsed on her mother's breast at the graveside next to eighteen-year-old Purcell, the image of his father, standing bravely at attention with his grandfather's hand on his shoulder.

I went home, put on my pyjamas, opened a quart of Scotch, and disappeared for three days. It was Karl who found me, curled up in the tree house, wrapped in my old army greatcoat.

Alma was on a tour of Chinese orphanages and couldn't be reached, so it was up to my father-in-law to decide my fate. Palmer was well into his seventies by then and totally out of his depth. He immediately fired Karl, and scheduled me for another series of shock treatments. I endured two sessions before Alma got home and put a stop to it. She'd always blamed herself for the damage inflicted by the first treatments. Her relationship with her father had never been an easy one, and she rarely spoke to him after that. Karl was re-hired, and is still with me.

After Des died, neither Lee nor I ever played music again. Giorgi said that when he broke the news, poor Lee roared like a wounded bear, and punched the wall with such force that he broke his right hand and had to be taken to the emergency ward. After the funeral I didn't see him again until all those years later in hospital, but I learned from Giorgi that he had taken a job as a night watchman.

I lost touch with Win as well, not by choice but because her family closed ranks, discouraging any connection with her old life, and I, of course, had my own demons. Felix, Giorgi and Rob kept the band going, but modelled it more after Benny Goodman's orchestra. I'd sometimes go to hear them for old times' sake. We sold Fitzhelm's in the spring of '49.

At seventeen, Georgie was an extremely beautiful young woman, and a determined and indiscriminate flirt—boy crazy they call it these days. Although very bright, she seemed unwilling or unable to take anything seriously, so I was pleasantly surprised when she and Teddy volunteered as campaign workers for a promising young politician called Ernest Dwyer Daid. Those in the know predicted that he might climb as high as the Prime Minister's Office, and the first rung on the ladder was to win the seat of a retiring local MP. Alma pitched in with some aggressive canvassing to bring out women voters. The campaign was a resounding success, and Daid went to Ottawa, quickly earning a reputation as a real firebrand. There was a great deal of speculation when, some years later, he suddenly withdrew from the political arena altogether, citing family responsibilities. A shame, really. I thought him a very capable fellow. There was talk of Georgie continuing to work for him when he went to Ottawa, but that ended with the news that she was pregnant. She refused to divulge the name of the father, saying only that they had an arrangement. Although I had my suspicions, she already had a reputation for being wild, and frankly it could have been any one of a dozen young fellows buzzing around her at the time.

Then she announced that she and Teddy were getting married. Everyone but me seemed to think this a marvellous solution. I've always liked Teddy, but you'd have to be blind not to know what his sexual persuasion is, and it seemed to me the whole idea was a recipe for misery, though in retrospect I have to say Teddy has been much more loyal and forgiving than any conventional husband.

The wedding was an elaborate social spectacle with all the trappings that Alma and I had spurned. Georgie insisted on retaining the family name, and three months later, on December 3rd, 1950, my first grandchild, Edward Francis Fitzhelm, was born. When I visited Georgie in hospital, I asked what she was going to call him, and she said "Eddie." I asked if she meant Edward or Edgar, and she replied with a sly smile that it didn't matter, I could please myself.

I offered to help her and Teddy buy a house, but she said it was already taken care of. They found a little Victorian on McCaul Street. I wasn't wild about the neighbourhood, but she said it was close to all their friends at the university, and would suit them perfectly.

The final blow was Alma's death in the summer of 1953, after which I sank into the deep, abiding melancholy which inhabits me today. Alma had continued her relief work with Chinese orphans. The conditions were appalling, she was very hands-on, and she contracted cholera. They flew her to the British hospital in Hong Kong, but nothing could be done. Her funeral was the last occasion on which the whole family was together. I still miss her terribly.

One of the things I've always found maddening is that when one is sitting quietly having a good think, there is always someone who'll say, "Here, you're not doing anything, come and do this." I believe these "do nothing" times have always been my most productive, and I highly resent the intrusion. About ten years ago I finally found the solution for this in fishing. I can spend the whole day in my waders or out in a rowboat with a line in the water, and no one would think of interrupting me. I make no pretense of being a sportsman, and couldn't care less about catching anything. Since Palmer died, I've made good use of the Daviston family cottage on Georgian Bay. He left it equally to the children, but Georgie has no interest in it and the boys and their families are only there the odd weekend or for summer vacations. Since my time is my own, I'm there most weekdays during the good weather.

I've made a conscious effort to spend time with my grandson, Eddie. As parents, Georgie and Teddy "don't have a clue," as she herself is so fond of saying of me. Teddy at least is concerned. When he told me that Eddie was having a hard time reading in class, my first thought was that he might need glasses, which turned out to be precisely the case. Typical obliviousness on Georgie's part. At seven, Eddie is a solemn little fellow, always with his nose in a book now that he has his glasses. Although he seems to enjoy the childhood classics I read to him, his taste runs more to practical how-to texts. In fact, the Meccano set I bought him last Christmas has been so popular, I'll certainly get him a supplementary set. We have great fun inventing things in my workshop. I took him fishing for the first time last year. By the next time, he'd read up on the subject, and was so full of information I thought our quiet time was over, but he's not a naturally chatty child, and we soon settled back into companionable silence.

We had a wonderful week together this past July, out on the water early in the morning, eating the lunch Karl made us and washing it down with iced tea, throwing our lines in the water once again, cleaning our catch at the dock, wrapping it in leaves as Eddie tells me the Indians did, and taking it back to the cottage for supper, very happy in each other's company. I feel a special kinship with him, as we've both suffered from that unique childhood anxiety of knowing that adults are keeping important secrets from us. For me it was the truth of how my father died, which I only learned when I read this journal. As for Eddie, Georgina doesn't allow him the comfortable fiction that Teddy is his father, but denies him the name of the man who is. I know it troubles him, for he finally plucked up the courage to ask me, not that I could enlighten him. He may never know, but I suspect he'll survive it as we all do.

Much of my time now is spent putting things in order. I've left Fallowfield Cottage to Eddie and arranged with Henry and Alistair for its maintenance. I like to think he'll eventually spend time there. Along with *Gulliver's Travels* and Georgina's books, I've already given him the Hot League's recordings along with the rest of my record collection, our arrangements, and my violin. I don't feel the urge to pick it up any more, especially since Giorgi can no longer play. The boy doesn't seem to be in the least musical, but I trust him to respect and treasure these things.

Giorgi dropped by while I was packing them up, and we listened to the records one last time, two old men shedding tears over past glory. The original S.S.R. speakers still sound wonderful, and when I closed my eyes, I could almost imagine we were all together again. Although it's no longer given to me to be able to play like that, I know from the recordings that I was an innovative, and often inspired, player. I still occasionally dream of playing Old Nick.

I'm not sorry to have passed the recordings on. They made me too unhappy, and one thing I've learned about my emotional failings is that it doesn't do to upset myself. Giorgi informs me that Fitzhelm's is now a huge hole in the ground. I haven't had the heart to go and look.

Georgie's pretty well fixed. She'll have my patents and copyrights, her trust fund and her shares in the Daviston Corporation, although Gus as chairman has contrived to set it up so that he and Charlie and the other directors get nice fat salaries, with most of the remaining profits reinvested in the business. The other shareholders, including Georgie, get pretty short shrift. I confronted Gus about it, and he said that if Georgie had more money she would only spend it. His logic escapes me. I've advised her to take her rightful place on the board, and disrupt their games like she used to, but she says she can't be bothered.

One of the reasons I've waited this long to complete my account is that although Georgina is the logical recipient of this journal, I always feared she might find in it some justification for her more bizarre behaviour. Unfortunately she suffers from the Joyner malady as well. I hope she finds, as I did, that its grip loosens somewhat with age. I've asked her to add her own voice when it's time, and to pass it on to Eddie. Georgie, I do apologize that there is now only one page left in the journal, and I hope you will rise to the challenge.

With the camouflage of my rod and reel, I've had ample time to ponder the imponderables. Regarding God and heaven, I have to declare myself undecided. I'd like to believe that there's a place where I could be with my mother and father, Des and Alma again, and that Des and I, Elsie and Old Nick could play together once more in some celestial band, but I refuse to see the hand of God in my fortunes and misfortunes. Those events were decidedly orchestrated by human hands, my own in particular.

I feel I'm in my second exile. The first began all those years ago when I left home, family, friends, and all that was familiar and dear to me to come to this country. Now, all those things have left me. I'm glad to be finishing this. My back has been giving me merry hell lately, and the painkillers make it hard to concentrate. It'll be an invalid chair next.

It's time to put out the lights and head up to the house, where Karl will be waiting with my bedtime cognac and codeine. He'll deliver this journal and Old Nick's casket to Georgina tomorrow.

— GEORGE FRANCIS FITZHELM, NOVEMBER 11, 1960

Chapter 6

GEORGINA MARGARET FITZHELM (1935–1985)

SEPTEMBER 1981

*I*t's me, Gina, finally rising to the challenge. Wasn't it just like Pappy to leave one blank page and tell me to get on with it? As for reading the foregoing, wild horses couldn't have stopped me, and what a hoot to discover that I'm not just a chip off the old block, but also a genuine nut off the old family tree. He passed this on to me back in 1960, just before I went to California, and he was pretty gaga toward the end so I never got to talk to him about it. An escalating series of strokes, they said. I blame the damned shock treatments.

I have to say he was less than candid on certain subjects, and for all his carry-on about my behaviour, I suspect he secretly enjoyed it. Come to think of it, there are some things I learned at Daddy's knee that owe much more to family tradition than proper parental guidance. Pappy's words to live by—"People can rattle on all they like about playing the hand you're dealt, my dear, but I can assure you it's a damned sight better to be the dealer." I'd have made it his epitaph if my brothers had let me.

I'm really doing this for you, Eddie. I've made a proper balls-up of everything else in your life, and I want to get this right, so I'm writing a sort of appendix in the form of a letter. Memory is notoriously unreliable, and I'll have to fight my natural inclination to enhance the facts to make a better story. I've always worked best to a packed house, always been better at comedy than drama, so I think it profoundly unfair to be delivering the dramatic role of my life to an unsympathetic audience of one, but here goes . . .

(I've included here Georgina's letter to my father found with the journal. L.A.F.)

November 1981

My darling,

Yes, I know you hate it when I call you that, because it's what I call everyone, but you truly are my darling, my only child, and you'll be relieved to know that's as maudlin as I intend to get. I've sent Teddy with this letter and a family heirloom, a casket made by our many-times-great-grandfather, Frank Joyner. The fiddle is long gone, but if you press the carved rosettes at the bottom on either side, it will release a clever hidden drawer containing some family mementoes, and a journal. I strongly urge you to read the journal before you continue with this letter, as it will make more sense in context.

This isn't a plea for forgiveness. We're way past that. It's more a desire to carry out Pappy's wishes and a hope that you'll at least understand me—so I won't pull any punches.

I'm dying. Teddy's been after me for ages to cut out smoking and drinking, but I don't see much point in that now. The lungs are shot, the liver is shot. The hell of it is my heart's still sound as a dollar, and will undoubtedly go on ticking long after the rest of me is ready to pack it in. I've had to cut back on smoking anyway because of the oxygen at night, and being pre-diabetic I've cut back on the booze as well, so all my bad habits are deserting me anyway. They've got me on some extraordinary drug now (yes, it's legal, my dear, they call it pain management), so if I drift off-subject from time to time you'll have to bear with me.

I called my parents Mammy and Pappy like the Li'l Abner comic strip. They thought it was funny, and it was a way of thumbing my nose at the little princes, my buttoned-up brothers, who always called them Mother and Father. I loved them both dearly, but Pappy was pretty closed down even before he went off to the nuthouse (as Grandpa Daviston so charmingly referred to it. Do adults think children are deaf?), and as for Mammy, well, it was always clear that tubercular Eskimos, African lepers and starving children in India and China had much more legitimate claims on her time than I did, privileged little brat that I was.

Pappy covered my childhood well enough, but there are a few errors, omissions and incidents worthy of further comment. I do regret the Neil McKay episode. He was innocent of course, a nice, decent man, but at that age I had no concept of the fallout. I knew a hand up the dress was wrong because one of Grandpa's friends had tried it, and when I protested, he gave me a silver dollar to say nothing about it. At least now when I encounter a stunt like that, I know what I'm doing, and I'm much more expensive. On the bright side, it got Pappy's attention in a big way and started me on the road to my brilliant career.

I used to love going to Fitzhelm's. I can still hear that music in my head, and the guys in the band were so sweet to me. They'd let me sing with them, and I got to know all the old tunes. Des was a lovely dancer. He'd waltz me around the floor just like a grown-up lady. Pappy was so done in by Des's death he never noticed I was grieving too, not just for Des, but for him, and for the end of all that. I think that's why I've always been great pals with the pit musicians for my shows. I just feel comfortable with them.

Teddy's been my best friend in the world ever since I can remember. I'd have been about five and Teddy six when we discovered a newly hatched cicada down in the ravine. We were examining it with the clinical detachment of the very young, and I was saying, "There's his leg, and there's his eye, and there's his wing. Where's his heart?"

"It's in his mouth," said Teddy.

We both fell down laughing, and we've been laughing ever since. The tree house Pappy built me was our hideout, Teddy from his father, me from my brothers, right into our teens, and it was there we cut our palms, mingled our blood and swore we'd be friends forever. Sounds corny, but we were dead serious. It was a shocker to find out Pappy had a fling with Marjorie Crewe. I tell Teddy everything, but I've never told him that.

Contrary to popular opinion, I do have a brain, but I've always found it better not to advertise it. It's astonishing what people will let slip if they think you're too dim to understand, and when you look like I do, that's a given.

At first I did really well in school, but it fell apart when my name came up for head girl. I thought I had a decent chance. I was popular, pretty, an A student, all the right family credentials. My rival was Dorothy Ecks. I'd always liked the name Dorothy—Judy Garland and all that—but this Dorothy was a wicked witch, if ever a witch there was. She told everyone that her father had it on good authority that Pappy was crazy, a certifiable mental case, and like father, like daughter. She then spread it around that I was a tramp based on a snogging session I'd had under the bleachers with her brother, that traitor. I retaliated by cornering her in the school lavatory, saying I'd show her what crazy was. I wrestled her out of her underpants, flushed them down the toilet, and promised that next time I'd strangle her with them. I was quite proud of myself, considering I was only five-foot-three and she seriously outweighed me, but nobody else saw it that way. The toilet backed up and it was a mess however you looked at it, as it gave her all the ammunition she needed to put an abrupt end to my budding political career. I was suspended for two weeks, and school was plain hell after that. She's in real estate now, and it gave me great satisfaction to read in the paper recently that she and her husband are up to their ears in the current city planning scandal. People don't change, and I've discovered if you wait long enough, they usually get what's coming to them. I call it Gina's curse. Effortless revenge.

Teddy had pretty much burned his bridges at U.T.S. as well. He'd been less than discreet about his crush on the school's star athlete, which earned him a bloody nose and a cracked rib when the aforementioned star and two of his buddies cornered him in the locker room, and that was just the beginning. The bullying got so bad he was afraid to go to the lavatory.

Since we had no reputations left to protect, we decided to give them all something to talk about. We became terpsichorean terrors at school dances, Astaire and Rogers for the Noxema set. "Acting out," my shrink called it. I recall "Shoo-Fly Pie" and "Zip-a-Dee-Doo-Dah" were big back then (they don't write lyrics like that any more. Pappy and I had gone to see *Song of the South*, and I'd just adored it). Those were the days when a teacher would move through the crowd with a ruler making sure that bodies were at least six inches apart. Now, six feet is more like it. Where's the romance in that? During breaks I'd amuse myself by flirting with the other girls' boyfriends. My measurements were pretty impressive even then, so it wasn't hard to get attention. It never ceases to amaze me how predictable men are.

For all my flirting, I never took any of those boys seriously, because by then I was already "doing it" with Mickey Schuyler.

Mickey would have been in his late twenties then and I was almost sixteen. He was an ex-jockey turned trainer and riding instructor, and I took riding lessons from him twice a week, no pun intended. We "did it" whenever the opportunity presented itself, usually on a blanket in one of the horse trailers. I wasn't so concerned with comfort in those days. It was all very hush-hush, of course. I didn't care, but Mickey said they'd throw him straight in the clink if they caught us. It was Mickey who introduced me to pot and hash. He used to smuggle the stuff across the border in the horses' hay bags. It was everywhere in the horsey world back then, but the school crowd hadn't discovered it yet. I still like an occasional puff to settle my nerves. Just so you know, we don't keep it in the house since the bust. Teddy stashes it in an empty paint can in the garden shed.

Funny how an old song can set you off. Every time Christmas rolls 'round and they play "Let It Snow" on the radio, I think of Mickey and me freezing our asses off in that damned horse trailer, high as kites and giggling like fools. I did warn you I might wander. It's tough trying to squeeze your life into a few pages. Poor old me! Time out.

Now about the wedding. I totally understood Pappy's objections, but I was up the spout and too far along to do anything about it. Not that I didn't want you, my darling, I did, and Mammy and Pappy were at least philosophical about it, but the grandparents and my brothers reacted as if I'd purposely set out to expose them to public ridicule. I wish I'd known then what I know now about your uncle Gus's begetting. That would have shut him up.

The marriage not only placated everyone (certain rumours having reached the ears of Teddy's father), but freed us to live our own lives, and as a bonus, launched the career of Teddy's boyfriend, Sergio, who was acting as best man, *acting* being the operative word. He'd designed a clever wedding dress to disguise my obvious bump, and it caught the eyes of several wealthy ladies of a certain age who were quick to see the advantages of strategic drapery for the less-than-perfect figure. He does cut like an angel.

The wedding reception was like a lovely costume ball—the cake divine, the champagne endless, wonderful dance band, and I was the star of the show. The newlyweds then retired, happily intoxicated, to separate bedrooms in their little castle on McCaul Street, a modern Jiggs and Maggie. It's still the perfect house. It'll be yours when I'm gone.

I kept the family name and put *father unknown* on the birth certificate, so you were christened Edward Francis Fitzhelm. You were the best baby, so good-natured. At first I wasn't going to breastfeed you for fear it would ruin my figure, but then I read somewhere that it actually helped tighten the stomach muscles. It certainly expanded my bustline, and I found I actually enjoyed it. How Oedipal is that?

Teddy was still at U of T then, English Lit and Fine Arts. We were eager to get to work on the first of his musical revues, a real stinker (sorry, Teddy) called *Lilies for Milady*. I guess I'd thought having a baby was something like having a tooth out, but it left me exhausted and seriously down in the dumps. Everybody talks about postpartum depression these days, but back then they just told you to pull yourself together, that you weren't the first woman ever to have a baby. It certainly messed up my body chemistry. Even Teddy didn't get it. My weeping fits drove him to distraction. We finally put everything on hold for a few weeks after I fainted in rehearsal. I brought you to all the run-throughs, and you slept in a drawer in the dressing room every night during the performance.

Then I was hit with the news that Mammy had died. The only thing that kept me from feeling sorry for myself was the worry that Pappy might have another breakdown, and your uncles would try to put him away. I spent as much time as possible with him, but we really got on each other's nerves. He finally told me to go home, that Karl would look after him.

It used to make me sad to see so little of myself in you. You have Pappy's brains and clever hands, but you have your father's eyes. God, I adored that man. Sorry, dearest, I can't say any more on that subject. After all, a deal is a deal, and I'm a real gent when it comes to promises, which is why I don't make many.

I don't know what happened to my sweet laughing little baby. Almost from the moment you could string a full sentence together it was as if you'd become someone else's child, a changeling, so solemn and disapproving. Every time I'd try to hug you, a bone would get in the way, an elbow, a shoulder. Do you even remember how we used to dance when you were little, my darling? We'd come home after a show, you dead to the world, me still wound up, a bit drunk if the truth be known. I always needed a couple of martinis to unwind. I'd wake you up and sing to you as I spun you 'round the room, and you'd scream with laughter. Do you remember that song?

> The music, the moonlight, the stars in our eyes.
> Too old to be innocent, too young to be wise.
> Strangers, then lovers in a world torn apart,
> We knew in our hearts we were leaves in the storm.

Not exactly a lullaby. A little too Kurt Weill, but you didn't seem to mind. It was the title song from *Leaves in the Storm*, Teddy's first professional effort, a dark musical for the post-war generation. Unfortunately, despite the gorgeous music and my stellar performance, it was a little too dark and sank like a stone, but I've always loved that song. Anton Polichek wrote the music. A dear man, but very intense. Hungarian or Czech, I forget which, just off the boat then with barely any English, a prodigy in his own country before the war blew everything to hell and the Russians moved in. Glorious melodies, heartbreaking arrangements. We had a brief thing, but I called it off. He was just too depressing. He's a famous conductor now.

That would have been in '55, because Teddy threw a combination wrap party and twentieth birthday bash for me when we closed. We were all pretty gloomy and needed cheering up. Sergio whipped up the most outrageous dress for me.

The theatre was a converted union hall, and the owner was Greek. Chris something. His fractured English was peppered with all these words and phrases he'd picked up from the cast. There'd been some controversy about my costumes, as Sergio had been quite naughty. To be honest, it probably brought in what little audience we had. One of the reviewers called me a blonde Betty Boop, the bastard, and I'd been going for Dietrich.

Sergio was with me when Chris burst into the dressing room waving a newspaper and saying, "Gina, Gina, Gina, you must not be making such big spectacles of yourself! They will be shutting me up, and then what will my poor wife and children do?"

It was all Sergio needed. At the party we unveiled his creation, a plain black cocktail dress with giant gold sequined spectacles framing my breasts, the earpieces hooked over my shoulders. It certainly lightened things up. Sergio always called me GinaGinaGina after that.

It was Teddy who came up with my name. We'd discussed the pros and cons of Georgina Fitzhelm, thinking the family connections might bring in some investors, but I knew the first thing any potential money would do is talk to my brothers, and we'd be sunk for sure. I was already Gina, and Teddy said we needed a second name that was a little exotic, French perhaps. There was an English actress Teddy liked called Elvira Garden, so it wasn't much of a leap. Gina Jardin it was.

Our crowd was like a big dysfunctional family. Half of them I never knew their last names, and I suspect even the first names were largely fictitious. It was a suspension of judgment that allowed us all to be whatever we wanted to be, or at least imagined we were, Gina the beautiful and brilliant variety artist, Teddy the successful playwright, producer and entrepreneur, Sergio the queen of haute couture—dancers, musicians, painters and poets, Gypsies all of us. Our little house, being the most permanent domicile, was where everyone gathered. It wasn't unusual to find someone passed out in the bathtub or draped over the toilet in the morning, and you, my angel, slept through it all.

I was seeing Darcy Tenderfield then. He was something big on Bay Street with scads of money and an eye for young girls. I was in my twenties, but still looked like an innocent, albeit generously endowed, schoolgirl, a stroke of luck with the gene pool that has served me well into my forties, and I can still turn heads when I make the effort. I'd spotted Darcy as a likely bet for investment, and he paid off in spades. The first show he backed was called *Lucky, Lucky Man*, featuring two of Pappy's tunes. Pappy tried not to show it, but he was tickled pink.

It wasn't a complicated plot, a sort of *Life of Riley*, working-class family in which the father has a gambling problem. This escalates to the point where everything they have is at risk. Finally, the mother, who has never gambled in her life, buys a lottery ticket, wins a fortune, and they live happily ever after with her holding the purse strings. I was the wayward sexpot daughter who finally meets the man to put her on the straight and narrow (that was Kevin Collery, devastatingly handsome and great in bed, but thick as a brick). My big number was "Heavenly Body," one of Pappy's tunes. The grandmother was a bingo addict, and the number that closed the first half, a hilarious geriatric conga line kicking up their heels to the Latin beat of "Bingo! Bingo! BIN-go!," always brought down the house.

It was that rare animal, a Canadian hit, so we extended the run, then toured for six more weeks. I didn't want to drag you around the country, so I hired our next-door neighbour, Mrs. Corso, as nanny and housekeeper. It seemed endless, six nights a week and a matinee on Saturdays. I was on stage, singing and dancing, for most of the two-hour show, and managed to pace myself right up to the end, but the day after it closed I was a basket case.

I've since learned to roll with my emotional ups and downs, but back then, other than the postpartum thing, I'd never experienced anything more extreme than sporadic fits of the blues. Everything ached. I cried at the drop of a hat, could barely force myself to get out of bed to pee, and every little noise was like an explosion in my ears, and poor Teddy, I'd alternately beg him to help me then accuse him of deliberately trying to drive me crazy. In desperation he phoned Pappy, who recommended a doctor. The doc prescribed something to relax me, and ordered absolute rest and quiet. I became quite attached to those lovely little pills.

Thank God Pappy took you under his wing. He was such a solitary soul after Mammy died, and I think you were very good for each other. I was certainly in no fit state to take care of you, in fact I could barely stand the sight of you, so it was up to Teddy and Pappy and Mrs. Corso. I did try to make it up to you once I was back on my feet, but you didn't want me. I'll never forget the day you came to me and said in a very businesslike manner that you'd prefer I didn't go to your school or talk to your teachers and could Teddy please do it instead. I was very hurt. I'd been perfectly charming to those people.

Once I was feeling fit again, Teddy offered me the lead in *Good Night, Juliet*, his modern musical version of *Romeo and Juliet*, and we went to work. He certainly got scooped on that one. It died in rehearsal when the reviews broke for *West Side Story*. To top it off, Darcy ditched me for Gillian Newby, the conniving bitch.

I gave her her start, you know. We needed someone to play the tomboy kid-sister in *Lucky, Lucky Man*, and I wasn't about to have another blonde or a redhead in the show, so when this mousy girl showed up to audition, I told Teddy to give her the part. The press loved her, and she started getting some very good offers, including a highly lucrative one, fancy apartment, expense account, etc. from Darcy Tenderfield. She'd made a dead set at him of course. He eventually dropped her to marry some nobody who I've been told looks a lot like me. Gina's curse strikes again.

Around this time I got a call from your uncle Gus inviting me to lunch. He was being civil, which set my antennae humming. I'd seen him only two weeks before at your uncle Charlie's wedding and he'd been very rude. Pappy had asked me not to be too conspicuous, so Sergio whipped up what I thought was a demure little A-line dress of raw silk in a delicious shade of fuchsia, very Schiaparelli. Perhaps it was the picture hat with pink cabbage roses that set Gus off, God only knows. I was just grateful not to be a bridesmaid. The designer of those dresses should have been shot! Empire waistline, a bilious shade of green with yellow rosebuds and trailing pink ribbons—spring garden theme my eye!

So there was Gus, inviting me to lunch as if he'd never referred to me as an inconsiderate, disruptive little tart. My curiosity got the better of me and I agreed. He'd reserved at one of those stuffy businessmen's restaurants downtown that stink of cigars and money, and you'd think I was a Martian from the way they all stared at me.

Making small talk was pretty heavy going for both of us, so I told him to cut to the chase. It transpired that Charlie had gone off on his European honeymoon without leaving Gus a proxy (how's that for inconsiderate!), and there was this very tight vote coming up for the Daviston board. Years back, Grandpa had brought in investors when he wanted cash for expansion, and although he kept the majority of the stock in the family, the old martinet was suddenly answerable to other people. He'd retired by this time, but Gus couldn't assume the chairmanship until he was forty, and the interim chair was dead set against some deal he'd cooked up. Having no interest in the business, I'd always ignored the notices, and the board treated this as an automatic abstention, but now dear brother Gus needed my vote.

I automatically said no, I'd give my proxy to the chairman. Gus's face turned an alarming shade of red, which darkened to puce when I told him he ought to watch his blood pressure. He said I had no idea what I was playing around with, and at the very least I should do it for the family. I replied that if by the family he meant himself and Charlie, he was barking up entirely the wrong tree, and I hadn't forgotten about the closet. At first he pretended not to know what I was talking about, then got very defensive and accused me of being childish, that it was ancient history, this wasn't personal, it was business. I shouted that it was ALL personal to ME! and swept out with a movie-star wave and dazzling smile for all the heads turned in our direction. Other than a few stilted words at Pappy's funeral, we didn't speak again until I blackmailed him into paying for Teddy's legal defence in '76.

My reaction *was* childish, but that child had a long-standing legitimate beef. You may have wondered why you barely know your uncles or their families. Normally I'd avoid the subject like poison, because, like Pappy, I've learned not to upset myself unnecessarily, but I feel I owe you some explanation.

I was only five, and it would have been a weekend, because the boys were home from school. They'd cooked up some sort of exclusive club between them, passwords, handshakes, secret charter, the whole bit, and God knows why but I was desperate to join. I pestered them to the point where they finally said yes, but I'd have to be initiated. This consisted of tying me up, gagging me, then locking me in a third-floor closet. I went quite willingly, thinking, I suppose, that it wouldn't be for long. They promptly forgot all about me, and just buggered off. I was there for almost six hours! At first I just lay there in the dark, and I must have drifted off for a bit, because when I woke up, I didn't know where I was and panicked.

Mammy was away and Pappy had gone out without telling anyone where he'd be. My nanny was called Laura, one of Mammy's sad cases, a big plain girl of about seventeen whose mother couldn't keep her but wouldn't give her up for adoption, so she'd been stuck in an institution until she came to work for us. She worshipped Mammy, and spoiled me rotten. Laura had been helping our housekeeper, Mrs. Kelly, with the ironing, and suddenly realized it was past lunchtime, and she hadn't seen me since breakfast. She told Mrs. Kelly and ran to fetch Neil McKay. They searched the house and grounds, but couldn't find me anywhere. By the time Pappy got home, they were frantic. He was just at the point of phoning the police when the boys showed up, and, having little choice, confessed. Poor Pappy, to be confronted with the hysterical, smelly little creature he liberated from that closet. My face was blotchy and covered with tears and snot and dust, and when I could no longer hold it, I'd peed myself. I grabbed Pappy 'round the neck and wouldn't let go. He was so angry I could feel him shaking, and I was sure it was my fault. He finally managed to loosen my hold, and passed me to a tearful Laura. He told her to clean me up, feed me, then bring me to his study.

Mammy firmly believed that children were rational beings who should be reasoned with, not physically punished. Pappy and she had agreed they'd never spank us, so when we'd been really bad, we faced loss of privileges and the dreaded "talking-to." I'd have preferred the spanking. I was expecting the worst for causing all the trouble, but when Laura delivered me to the study in my nightgown, there were Gus and Charlie looking like thunder. Pappy ordered them to apologize. Charlie mumbled something, and Gus could barely force himself to spit out the words. Pappy asked if the apology was acceptable, and I said yes. I later learned they'd both been grounded for a month, which meant Gus would miss the big track meet he'd been training for. As we left the room he glowered at me as if I were the lowest form of life on earth. Charlie hissed that if I hadn't been a sucky baby, Pappy wouldn't have made such a big deal of it, and I'd ruined Gus's run at the championship. From then on, it didn't matter what I did, there'd be some withering remark from one or both of them. They stopped short of physical abuse beyond the occasional pinch or shove, and were careful around Pappy and Mammy, but the little cruelties were constant, and I, not wanting to be a baby, never told.

You might think I'm making too big a deal of this, but I can't describe how terrifying that experience was. With my mouth gagged and my nose stuffed up from crying, I thought I would suffocate, nobody would ever find me, and I'd die alone in the dark. It was after that the nightmares started, and I couldn't sleep unless the light was on and the door open. I'm still like that. My shrink said that incident was at the root of my antisocial behaviour. What a genius!

I need to rest now, my darling. I'll continue this tomorrow.

From '58 to '61 I enjoyed a brief movie career. In the summer of '58, one of Teddy's university acquaintances, Cyrus Huffman, decided to be a film director, and since he claimed not to have a sous to his name, it became a sort of community effort. Huffman was the type who consistently wore mismatched socks, dirty dungarees and a moth-eaten sweater with no undershirt, but I'd always thought his teeth were too good and his attitude too condescending for the working-class rebel he claimed to be. We later discovered that his father owned a dry-cleaning empire, and several sizable chunks of downtown Toronto.

I put in a little money, and the actors, including me, donated their services with the understanding that in the unlikely eventuality of box office revenue, we'd share, and so the whole thing lurched forward. We were expected to improvise our parts and the sketchy storyline all but disappeared as shooting progressed. The concept was a sort of Hitchcock/noir/horror production, very vérité, all gloomy shadows and odd angles. There was certainly a lot of gore. I was drenched in chocolate syrup for most of one day, which would have been nasty enough, but with the temperature in the nineties and hordes of insects descending on our ravine location, it was a nightmare, and the look of horror on my face absolutely real. I got really testy when Huffman started picking small, sticky corpses out of my décolleté for the close-ups.

When he reached the point of putting a title to it I suggested *The Sundae Massacre* with a poster featuring the two scoops of my chocolate-covered boobs. Huffman got quite huffy about it and accused me of not taking him seriously. The result, *The Rosedale Ripper*, was highly and unintentionally hilarious, becoming an immediate art-house hit, and boosting his already inflated opinion of himself. We never saw a penny out of it, of course. I have a print of it somewhere.

He now directs and produces television dramas for his sins. A couple of months ago I had a call from a terribly earnest young man asking me if I'd present an award to him. Seems he's being honoured as a pioneer in Canadian film. I told him they must be scraping the bottom of the barrel if they were honouring Cy Huffman, and asked him what it was worth to have me put in an appearance. He laughed nervously and said he'd get back to me. He hasn't.

That film somehow reached the eyes of a man called (I swear) Howard Fagin, who introduced himself on the phone as a Hollywood producer. After naming several of his films, none of which rang a bell, he started rattling on about my huge potential, but finally got down to brass knockers, saying I could be the new Mamie Van Doren. I told him I thought the old Mamie had quite a few miles left in her (rather prophetic, as it turned out), and why didn't we concentrate on little old me. What he was really looking for was the new Marilyn Monroe—who wasn't?—but I figured what the hell, nothing ventured, and a trip to Hollywood would be good for a giggle at the very least. I agreed to fly to Los Angeles for a screen test.

I thought it would be fun if you and Teddy came with me, but Teddy was committed to produce and direct a play by some new writer he was excited about and you said you'd rather stay home with Teddy and Pappy and your friends, so Mrs. Corso moved in for the duration. I ended up flying all on my lonesome.

Sergio's smart matching coat and dress were suddenly drab and conservative compared to the bright colours and casually sexy clothing I saw on California women. Howard Fagin's assistant, a harried-looking middle-aged woman called Charlotte Raines picked me up at the airport. She'd reserved a suite for me at the Chateau Marmont. I loved the romantic, if somewhat faded, Spanish elegance of the lobby. The suite had seen better days, but it was clean and comfortable, and more importantly had a kitchen which Charlotte, bless her, had stocked with food and booze. She'd send a car for me the following evening to take me to dinner with Howard Fagin and his wife, Denise. I unpacked, had a stiff G-and-T and sank into a long, dreamless sleep.

The palm trees around the pool at the Chateau were pretty shopworn, and there was an aura of dog piss as I ventured down in my swimsuit early the next morning. Two of the whitest young men I'd ever seen sat under a big umbrella in baggy bathing trunks and took turns pecking away at an enormous typewriter. They introduced themselves as Harvey and Bernie, recently transplanted from New York, very smart, sweet boys, up-to-the-minute on Hollywood gossip, and happy to have any excuse to stop working. They'd had an off-Broadway success with a play they'd written, and were now writing the screenplay. We became instant pals. Harvey was married, and trying to save up enough money to bring his wife to California. Bernie, who looked a little like Sal Mineo, developed a bit of a crush on me, but I'd tagged him as one of those rare birds who mate for life, which can be really tiresome, so I never followed through. But they turned out to be an invaluable source of information, and great company.

Fagin, they said, was a fellow New Yorker, Brooklyn actually, who'd gotten his start in the late '40s producing one of those Saturday-matinee, hard-boiled detective serials. He'd moved to Hollywood in '51 to produce another serial called *The Ghost Rider*, followed by *The Ghost Rider Returns*, which featured a sort of supernatural cowboy hero and his juvenile sidekick. Teddy, the film buff, tells me there were lots of jokes in the gay fraternity about that relationship. Howard then started his own production company, Fagin Films, and churned out three or four B movies a year. Harvey and Bernie agreed the films were more like D or E, but at least they weren't X. I might have drawn the line at that.

He had a reputation for bedding his leading ladies. Denise, his wife, had starred in a couple of his early films, but had sidestepped the fate of Howard's other conquests by getting pregnant. Apparently the marriage hadn't altered his mating habits, so I was forewarned.

Dinner that night was at the Fagins' home in Beverly Hills, cocktails and alfresco Mexican dinner by the pool. Denise had introduced herself over the phone that morning, telling me to be ready by seven, and to dress casually. The boys clued me in that this was code for tailored slacks, a silk shirt and loads of gold jewellery. A quick shopping trip with Bernie on his moped took care of the clothes, but my budget didn't stretch to gold, so I opted for understatement and wore my mother's diamond earrings.

Howard would have been about fifty, built like a tank, square face, thick neck, and a thatch of silver hair, but curiously dainty hands and feet. He was a hard-headed businessman, determined to eliminate any element of chance in a very chancy business, thus having a great distrust of imagination and absolutely no sense of humour. It was actually what I liked about him. Since he had no intellectual or creative pretensions, you always knew where you stood.

Denise was a tough, smart cookie with a successful real-estate business, a real plus for Howard as she could also scout locations. The dinner was obviously her opportunity to give me the once-over. We both recognized that becoming friends was an excellent way to keep Howard on his toes. I made an early night of it, and limited myself to two margaritas as I wanted to look fresh for the screen test the next morning at six.

I'd imagined a screen test would be a sort of audition, so I showed up at Fagin Films' warehouse studio in rehearsal clothes and full war paint with a recording of "Heavenly Body" from *Lucky, Lucky Man*, expecting to dazzle everyone with my routine. Charlotte Raines looked momentarily nonplussed at my getup, then hustled me off to Makeup.

The people who worked for Howard generally fell into two categories, young would-be's and old has-been's. What we had in common was that we all worked for peanuts, as Howard had a standing reputation as the biggest tightwad in Hollywood. The would-be's were generally the production team and the younger actors. They seldom lasted more than one or two productions before fleeing to greener pastures. You'd be surprised how many of the who's who of Hollywood worked for Howard at one point or another. The has-been's were more permanent, having burned a few bridges or lost their currency elsewhere. When I was there it was Arne Hoechstra the makeup artist, Kenny the hairdresser, Penny the wardrobe mistress, and Charlotte Raines. Everyone, including the actors, did double duty, as Charlotte assigned whoever was handy to any odd job that came up, so we learned to make ourselves scarce. A third category was the crew. They'd been with Howard since year one, liked the steady work, and, being union, couldn't be intimidated or chiselled.

Penny measured me from top to bottom, then disappeared into the costume racks. Kenny rewashed and set my hair, then turned me over to Arne Hoechstra. Arne was a rather bitchy old queen who'd worked with everyone who was anyone at some point or another. We got off to a rocky start, as he had to remove my own makeup job before he could begin, but he warmed up as we got to know each other, gave me some useful tips and told me some delicious Hollywood gossip which I've been dining out on ever since. He was a genius. I couldn't understand why he was working for Howard, until he confided to me that he tended to get "a touch depressed," that it made him "a little unreliable," and that "movies are a very unforgiving business, my dumpling." He gave me strict orders to stay out of the sun, and to cut back on cigarettes, desserts and hard liquor, as he wasn't a magician.

The test took all day. Shots of me from every angle with different lighting, costumes and looks. The cameraman, a real sweetie, assured me that I didn't have a bad side, had beautiful skin, and that shooting me would be a breeze. The "look" that was ultimately decided on was ultra-glamour, lots of mascara and false lashes, an exaggerated crimson mouth, and my red-blonde hair bleached to glow-in-the-dark albino and teased into candy floss. That whole process took over three hours. Everyone except me loved it, but since I'd evidently passed with flying colours, I batted my inch-long lashes and kept my big crimson mouth shut. Howard escorted me upstairs to his office at the end of the day, and presented me with a contract as if he were handing me gold. He'd have had me sign it right then and there and seal it with a quick roll in the hay, but I said I'd read it over and sleep on it, solo, thank you.

Even I could tell that contract was tantamount to slavery—endless options with no raise in salary, no script approval, in fact no say whatsoever as to whether I'd do a film or not, and I could be fired at any time. To survive in Howard Fagin's Hollywood I'd need two things, an expensive lawyer and a cheap car.

Bernie and his moped to the rescue once again. We rode out the next morning to a famous Hollywood used-car dealership. If you had a television, you couldn't escape the ads. The salesman had just the car for me, a real steal. A year-old canary yellow Chevrolet convertible had just come on to the lot in perfect condition except for a little staining on the white leather upholstery. He seemed oddly anxious to get rid of it, considering it was such a little beauty. I paid five hundred dollars down and drove off, feeling every inch a star.

As for the lawyer, I got lucky there as well. Harvey had a fraternity brother who'd recently passed the California bar and was starting out on the bottom rung of an established movie-business law firm. He was anxious to start building his own clientele, and Harvey said he'd go easy on me regarding the fee. We arranged a meeting for late that afternoon.

The contract, in the words of my new lawyer, Al Sachs, was "dreck." By the time he'd deleted the unacceptable bits, there wasn't much left, so he drafted a new agreement for a first movie with options for two more, and a modest pay raise for each. I'd have one right of refusal for each option, and some limited script approval, a far-from-perfect deal but one that Howard might be persuaded to swallow. I was advised to make myself unavailable, so I had the revised contract delivered to Howard the next morning along with Al Sachs's business card, and Bernie and I drove down to Tijuana in my new car. When we got back to the Chateau late that night, the desk clerk handed me a stack of messages saying it was not his job to take abuse from callers, and would I please tell Mr. Fagin to modify his language in the future, or his calls would not be accepted. The last message said to show up the next morning to sign the contract minus the right of refusal, pick up the script and begin my fittings. We'd start shooting within the week. Al Sachs was a treasure!

The title, *The Sunset Vampire*, says it all. I was the vampire, with the emphasis on *vamp*. It was Howard's first attempt at colour, and Penny whipped up a dress of ruched panne velvet in vivid scarlet, provocative in ways that even Sergio hadn't thought of. Combined with my new look and long blood-red fingernails, it was arresting to say the least, and to complete the transformation I affected a Zsa Zsa Gabor accent. When they viewed the first day's footage, the dress flashed and blurred like crazy and my hair was phosphorescent, but Howard shrugged this off as special effects, saying it gave me a nice spooky appearance.

The plot was minimal. Handsome young men start disappearing from ritzy Hollywood cocktail bars, never to be seen again. I would first lure, then seduce, and at the optimum moment bare my fangs and exsanguinate my conquest in an enormous canopy bed with black satin sheets. Tacky in the extreme. Other than Arne's artful dribble at the corner of my mouth, there was no visible blood, the bulk of it supposedly having disappeared down my gullet. The strategically placed stake-through-the-cleavage scene at the end is one of my finer comedic moments. It almost got us an R rating. The director was one of the would-be's, Terry Conley-Browne, very English, very suave, very available. He actively encouraged me to camp it up. Who wouldn't play a villain, given the opportunity?

The best thing about the script was the changes Bernie and Harvey and I made. We spent several evenings around the kitchen table or in a booth at Barney's Beanery replacing my lines with outrageous vampire one-liners. We shamelessly stole some old chestnuts—"I don't drink . . . wine"—as well as some originals—"I'd like to continue our evening in a different vein . . ." I'd never had so much fun. I offered to ask Howard for a screen credit for the boys, but they weren't keen to be associated with one of his films. Funny how things change. They're both very successful now, and I read a recent interview with Harvey where he bragged about working on that dialogue.

Sunset Vampire spawned a very creepy stalker, a man who'd made me the focus of his erotic fantasies. I couldn't go anywhere without seeing his leering face. I even considered buying a gun when the police told me they couldn't do much unless he actually attacked me, but the problem solved itself when he broke into the studio and attempted to steal the scarlet dress I'd worn in the movie. I guess you could say he was caught red-handed. I was pretty shaken up, but it got a lot of publicity when Howard leaked the details to the tabloids, that and the fact that the cops had seized my car as the scene of the crime in the grisly rape and murder of a teenage girl by her mother's boyfriend. It seemed that the upholstery stains were, wait for it, blood. Howard was ecstatic. He was buying Denise a new car, and with the settlement Al Sachs got me from the car dealership (emotional hardship and career damage) I bought her classic T-Bird. Red, of course.

By then we were already at work on *The Vixen Bride*, loosely based on some Chinese legend about women that turned into foxes at the full moon. Howard had jumped on it as a nice twist on the werewolf theme. I died in that one as well, a heart-wrenching scene of the foxy me being hunted then savaged by a pack of dogs, and as I expire I transform back into my miraculously intact and artfully exposed human form. Bernie and Harvey contributed to that one as well, and Terry directed.

Around this time I got a letter from Teddy saying that things were ticking along okay on the home front. He included a note from you. Would you believe I still have it? I think it's the only thing you ever wrote to me.

(I found the letter in Gina's safety deposit box, and have included it here. L.A.F.)

Dear Gina,

How are you? I'm doing fine. I got an A+ in math, an A in art and a B in social studies. Miss Koenig says if I'd get my mind off outer space and back on Earth I'd do better. Grandpa took Cam and Ken and me to see Forbidden Planet *for my birthday. Leslie Nielsen is my favourite actor. Teddy gave me twenty dollars to take us all out for treats after. It was a lot of fun, so don't worry about a present for me.*

Goodbye for now, your son,
Eddie

I felt so guilty for missing your birthday, I moved heaven and earth to find a *Forbidden Planet* poster and stood in line for two hours with all the other plebs to get it signed for you.

I'd assumed Terry would direct my next film, *Curse of the Black Widow*, as well, but he had other plans. The new director was Pieter Wilhelm Gunter, recently arrived from Germany—P.W. as he magnanimously invited me to address him. We immediately butted heads because he was not just an arrogant bastard, but also a real fascist when it came to following the script, and he constantly addressed me as if I were a two-year-old.

"Now, Gina, there is a reason ve have a script, my dear, and ve must respect its integrity. I know you vill get it right if you chust concentrate. Vun more time please, as vritten."

That kind of bullying condescension brings out the absolute worst in me. "Now, Vil-helm," I'd say in precisely his own pompous tone, "this is not Shakespeare, my dear, this is not 'Var and Peace.' Gott himself could not alter the integrity of this script!"

I managed to slip in a few changes simply because Howard wouldn't allow another take, but the infighting really wore me down, and there was another complication adding to the already poisonous atmosphere.

Howard's wife, Denise, had gone back east for a family funeral, and Howard took this as his cue to make a definitive move on me.

His office was up an exposed flight of steps and had a large interior window that allowed him to see what was happening on the set. He was notorious for inviting aspiring actresses up to the office and screwing them on top of his desk so he could survey his little empire during the act. He'd then "surprise" his conquest with a piece of jewellery, which he'd produce from his desk drawer. Did I mention his lack of imagination? I wasn't about to join that club.

It was the summer of '61, and *Curse of the Black Widow* was complete except for dubbing in the dialogue. Howard summoned me to his office, supposedly to talk about renewing my contract, and made a grab for me. I fought him off, spike heels being useful in a clinch, and told him in highly unflattering terms what I thought of him and his movies, then marched out past the sound crew with as much dignity as I could muster considering my shirt had lost its buttons.

I was living in a nice little furnished bungalow in Culver City by then, and as I walked in the door, the phone rang. It was Teddy. Pappy had suffered a stroke, then a second one in hospital. He was temporarily stable, but all bets were off as to how long it would be before another, likely fatal, one. It was time to go home.

I called Howard to tell him I'd come in the next day to finish the recording, then fly to Toronto that night. When I arrived at Fagin Films the next morning he was already in the midst of a screen test with a grotesquely endowed redhead he'd obviously had waiting in the wings. He informed me he no longer required my services, and that my severance cheque was on his desk. I was furious. I stomped up the steps, slamming the office door behind me. He'd deducted a ridiculous amount for the unfinished recording, and written on it, *termination of employment*. I considered trashing the office, but a rather delicious little revenge occurred to me. Employing one of Pappy's parlour tricks, I slipped the lock on his desk drawer with my nail file, removing a velvet box containing a gold bangle. I wish

I could have been there when Howard went to reveal his "surprise" to the redhead.

Back at the bungalow, I called Al Sachs and told him everything. I wanted to sue, but he advised me to cut my losses. He didn't believe Howard would be so stupid as to report the theft. I had no agent, and didn't delude myself that I had any future in movies. When Al offered me a fair price for the T-Bird and said he'd take care of any loose ends, I agreed. I took care of one loose end myself, putting the gold bangle into an envelope addressed to Denise Fagin along with a note explaining how I came by it. Al drove me to the airport that night in the T-Bird. I wouldn't miss Hollywood, but I was really going to miss that car.

It was over two years later when I saw *Curse of the Black Widow*. Teddy discovered it was playing in some grubby little West End movie house. I'd expected it to be bad, but it was worse than I could have imagined. That vindictive bastard had dubbed my dialogue with the flat Midwestern voice of Charlotte Raines, with little effort to synchronize it. I exploded, calling Howard Fagin every name in the book, and when I finally sputtered to a stop, an annoyed adolescent voice piped up from the row behind us.

"Jeezus, lady, it ain't that bad. She should get an Oscar for those tits!"

As I pushed Teddy into the aisle I muttered, "If you laugh, you're a dead man!"

He simply couldn't contain himself, and by the time we hit the street we were both in stitches. Teddy has categories for films. *Sunset Vampire* and *Vixen Bride* are in the "so bad they're good" category, but *Black Widow* isn't even on the radar. Fortunately it sank with barely a trace, although I recently had to sit through it at a Fagin Films retrospective organized by some overzealous B-movie fan. God knows where he got that print. I made a little speech which, I'm proud to say, had them rolling in the aisles.

It hit me very hard when I lost Pappy. When Mammy died, her remains were shipped from Hong Kong in no fit state to be viewed, and the closed coffin allowed one to pretend that she wasn't dead but simply off on some new crusade, and of course I still had Pappy. With him gone I was as desolate as any orphan. I'd spent several days with him at the hospital, but he was barely able to speak, and it was hard to connect the zombie in that bed with the father I adored. I know you wanted to visit him, my darling, but there was no point. He wasn't really there, and I couldn't bear for you to see him like that. The thing that truly broke my heart was that his hands were constantly moving as if he were playing his fiddle.

I invited all the old gang to the funeral. We were pretty stone-faced at the graveside, except for poor Giorgi who cried like a baby. My brothers and their wives, having barely acknowledged our presence, left immediately, and Teddy took you home. The rest of us retired to the Capelli brothers' restaurant for a sort of wake. We ate, drank wine, reminisced and played all the old records. Lee was gone by then, but Giorgi, despite the arthritis in his hands, managed to play the piano and I sang "Bluebird Blue" and "Heavenly Body" with Felix on clarinet and Rob on bass. We all wept buckets. It was a fitting send-off.

Jimmy Swift took me aside and said that when I was feeling up to it we should talk about Pappy's patents and shares in S.S.R. When I met with him a few weeks later, he explained that most patents had a lifespan, and over time most of those Pappy had left me would become obsolete. He offered to buy them at a price based on projected revenue, and convert the proceeds into Swift Communications stock. This combined with the song copyrights, and my shares in Mammy's trust and the Daviston Corporation, would give me a tidy income. I didn't take in everything he said, but Pappy had trusted him and I didn't hesitate to do the same.

Jimmy's long gone now, but Swift Communications continued

to prosper. Five years ago it was bought out by Grandtech Industries, and they paid me off to the tune of half a million. Except for the interest, I haven't touched a penny, and it will be yours when I'm gone.

I didn't feel much like performing after that. Teddy had projects that were already in the works and didn't include me, and I didn't really need the money. I half-heartedly worked on a show called *An Evening with Irving Berlin* with an old piano-playing pal, but Berlin's publishing company wouldn't give us the rights to perform it, so it died on the vine.

My thirtieth birthday passed quietly, largely because I'd threatened to murder anyone who mentioned it.

In '64, I finally met someone from Pappy's side of the family. You'd have been about thirteen or fourteen by then, and would remember him among the other "uncles" as Uncle Nicky, but he was actually my cousin, Nicholas Fitzhelm, the last great love of my life. Judging from Grandma Beth's last letter to Pappy, she'd had a soft spot for him too, and no wonder. He was a charming, handsome, incorrigible rogue with a more-than-passing resemblance to Cary Grant, which he exploited shamelessly. Flirting was as natural to him as breathing, and just as unconscious. He could enslave a coat-check girl by telling her she had the face of a Raphael Madonna, but if you brought it up five minutes later, he'd have forgotten all about it. He played the piano, sang as well as any crooner and danced beautifully, so he fitted right in with our crowd. I fell hard, and I believe he did too.

He'd gotten into some financial mess in England, more to do with negligence than intent, and had been exiled by big brother Alistair to Goldring's Canadian subsidiary until things cooled down. Another family tradition, apparently. Married of course, to someone he always referred to as "a good egg," so I eased my conscience with the assumption that it wasn't a love match. It was pretty torrid while it lasted. We talked about marriage, but it was a non-starter. Aside from being already married and cousins, and all the upset that would cause, we were too much alike. There have been very few men that I've felt I could be absolutely myself with. Teddy, of course, is one, and Nicky was another.

Goldring kept Nicky on a pretty tight leash, so he supplemented his salary with gambling and was very, very good. Over half his income came from high-stakes poker and blackjack, and he wasn't stingy with it. We wined and dined lavishly at the best and the worst places, and I had to watch what I admired in a shop window, or it would be delivered to my door the next day. We were inseparable for just over a year, and when inevitably he went home to the good egg and the kids it nearly killed me. His parting gift was the lovely heart-shaped diamond pendant I still wear every day along with Mammy's earrings. I'd thought of giving it to your wife when she brought little Leslie to visit me, but, considering how that turned out, I'm glad I squelched the impulse. Still, as much as I cherish it, I'm not so selfish as to have it buried with me. It will be in my safety deposit box along with Pappy's signet ring and a few other trinkets.

The rest of the '60s was rather a blur for me. I like to think I was a bit of a female pioneer in that era of do-your-own-thing and free love, both male inventions, of course. Free love, what a silly concept that was. You always pay one way or another. Once again the house was a twenty-four-hour magnet for all kinds of offbeat types, painters, poets, draft dodgers and musicians. I was missing Nicky terribly, and had too much time on my hands. Teddy was either working or with Sergio, and you were seldom home except to sleep.

I can't tell you how sorry I was when the drummer for the Wholly Rollers got into your room and smashed your dinosaur models. He was out of his mind on acid, of course. Believed they were going to attack him. When I think of the hours you put into building them . . . If it's any consolation, they dropped him shortly after that. I admit I overreacted when you put that ugly metal gate and padlock on your bedroom. Well, it was a bit of overkill. A dead bolt would have done the trick. Within the year you'd moved out and rented that poky little apartment with your friend Junior, but I never got around to removing that gate. When the police raided the house in '76 I had a hell of a time trying to explain that it was meant to keep people out, not in, and that you, the supposed inmate, were long gone—but I'm getting ahead of myself again.

You'll recall my boyfriend at the time was that Cuban song-writer and political activist, Federico. Unfortunately he wore the regulation Che Guevara kerchief and beret, but he had the most beautiful brown eyes. His songs were in Spanish so I didn't have a clue what they were about, but I loved the sound of his voice— almost as much as he did. We hung out at a coffee house called Java. Perhaps if I'd been younger I'd have appreciated it more, but the endless musical meanderings and youthful poetic angst punctuated by the gargle of the espresso machine drove me up the wall, and I'd have killed for a stiff drink. It didn't last long because Federico was deported as a draft dodger and political agitator. Turned out he hadn't fled from Cuba, but from his wealthy right-wing family in Miami, and I wouldn't even mention it except there's no doubt in my mind that's when I first became "a person of interest" to the police. It was a crazy time. Too much booze, too many drugs, and I did it all. Looking back I can't believe how incredibly naive I was, how stupid to think it wouldn't come back to haunt me.

By '67, except for an occasional nightclub performance of stan-dards I could sing in my sleep, I'd been out of circulation for almost six years. The inactivity and indulgence had taken their toll, and I was starting to look my age. It was time to clean up my act. I told Teddy I needed to get back to work. He was producing and directing a sort of folk opera called *The White Oaks Trilogy*, and said if I'd put the chorus through their paces it would free up the musical director to work with the principals. They were a good, hardworking bunch of kids and we had a lot of fun together. This gained me some reputation as a vocal coach, and I started giving lessons. It kept me busy, but I was really missing the spotlight.

The news that you'd gotten married totally bowled me over, and I had to read it in the newspaper. You weren't even twenty and, as I later discovered, your wife, Victoria, was at least three years older. What were you thinking? You'd made it abundantly clear you didn't want to go to university, and were determined to make your own way without any support from me, but it was a real blow to discover how completely you'd shut me out of your life. Even if you didn't want a big wedding, you could at least have invited Teddy and me. We wouldn't have let you down. And then to learn a year after the fact that I was a grandmother, and you hadn't bothered to tell me. I realize I've been no bargain as a mother, but that gutted me. Not even so much as a photo. I have to stop here. Medication time.

Right around the time your little Leslie was born in 1970, Teddy had enough interest from a group of regional theatres to put together a touring company of Noel Coward's comedy *Blithe Spirit*. I couldn't wait to get my teeth into the part of Elvira, the ghostly wife. My hair was quite long at that point. I went platinum again, and wore it in a Hedy Lamarr sweep. Sergio weighted my ethereal grey draperies with lead shot so they appeared to float in slow motion. Until I got the hang of manoeuvring in this creation I was constantly tangled up, my ankles and thighs were black and blue, and the other cast members learned to steer clear of me.

Teddy in a stroke of genius had cast Neville Mars, a wonderful old English character actor, in the part of Madame Arcati. He was totally over the top, and the audience adored him, in fact they loved the whole show. The six-city, four-week tour was a great success, and we revived it the following year for another three weeks on the road, then two more weeks in Toronto. The Toronto write-ups were glowing except for one reviewer in the *Globe and Mail* who said that at times my performance bordered on burlesque. He's dead now.

On tour the cast is your family. You develop a sort of exclusive language, a shorthand made up of the punchlines of jokes and all the indiscreet or funny things everyone's said or done during the run. When it's over, everyone scatters back to their so-called normal lives as if that closeness never existed. You were gone and Teddy wasn't around much, so I returned to an empty house, opened a bottle of gin, and climbed inside.

One by one most of the old regulars drifted back, bringing with them a few new hangers-on. The first to appear was our pot-and-hash connection, a thoroughly slimy individual named Harry who seemed to have some sort of radar that told him when his services were welcome. I kicked him out when he insisted on pushing cocaine and heroin at me as well. I was in total agreement with Pappy's reservations about cocaine, and the idea of sticking a needle in my arm was revolting. I love a toke from time to time, and my pills are a necessity of life, but I've always been a martini girl at heart. I'd give my soul for one right now, but these days I get the hangover before I get the buzz.

You must believe me when I say I had nothing to do with Victoria and those two old harpies bringing little Leslie to visit. What'shername, Rachel, called me out of the blue one afternoon, saying they were in Toronto buying school clothes, and thought it was time we met. I was in bed with Niles Gunsell, the guitarist for a rather arty English band called Chiaroscuro. I didn't care for the music, but he was adorable. I immediately called Teddy, who said he'd come at once, then I flew into panic mode, checking for stragglers, spraying Chanel around and frantically trying to hide anything iffy. I couldn't rouse Niles, so I assumed he'd be out of it for the duration. I barely had time to slip into one of Sergio's tie-dyed silk caftans, slap on some makeup and run a brush through my hair before the doorbell rang.

I don't know what I expected, but to say Stantons and Fitzhelms lived on different planets would be a gross understatement. Victoria was extremely pretty and seemed very sweet but barely said a word, and the aunts were so permed and girdled, so grim and charmless, Eddie. I don't know how you could stand it. After giving me a critical once-over and wrinkling her nose at the perfume, the first thing that captured Rachel's attention was Hans Poelman's nude portrait of me over the fireplace. She couldn't keep her eyes off it. I suddenly realized I hadn't removed the hookah from the coffee table. It had been there so long it was like part of the decor, and it was hardly something I could bury under a cushion. Fortunately Teddy arrived and distracted them long enough for me to stick it behind the door. They seemed to find Teddy respectable enough, and I thought things were looking up when they accepted a cup of tea. Leslie climbed up on the couch beside me, and opened his mouth like a baby bird as I fed him treats. What a darling, and so like you at that age. It was almost like having my own little boy back again.

Those two gave me a grilling that would put the Gestapo to shame, and though I thought I acquitted myself rather well, I was feeling the strain, dying for a drink and a smoke, and wondering if they'd ever leave. Just then, Niles wandered in wearing nothing but a vague smile. He removed a bottle of twelve-year-old Scotch from the liquor cabinet, and wandered out again, saying, "Hair of the dog, love." He did have expensive tastes, that boy.

Rachel shot out of her chair, snatched little Leslie away from me as if I had the plague, and they were all out the door before I could manufacture an explanation. Poor you. I can only imagine what you had to deal with when you got home, and if that was the beginning of trouble in paradise I'm truly sorry, my dear, but it wasn't my fault.

Oh hell! I can't put this off any longer. Less than a year after that, everything went pear-shaped, and it was all so damned idiotic!

Teddy and Sergio belonged to this private club for gay men. Teddy wasn't that keen, but Sergio was a real social butterfly. The location was one of those European steambaths you used to see over in the Bathurst area. The problem was that whoever had organized the club side of things had neglected to change the designation of the building, and it was still listed as a public bathhouse. This meant the police were perfectly within their rights to raid the place. Feelings were running high over the violent homosexual rape and murder of that poor little shoeshine boy, Emanuel Jaques, so they threw every charge they could think of into the warrant, declaring it a gathering place for known sexual deviants and suspected drug dealers. There was something about it being a speakeasy and a common bawdy house as well, because I remember Teddy saying that bawdy it might be, but he resented the hell out of being called common.

All they found were a few men lounging around in robes and bath towels drinking illegally, so everyone was released after a night in a holding cell; however, the police used the little they did find to obtain search warrants for everyone's homes, and the address on Teddy's driver's licence was here.

I was in one of my fugues and recovering from bronchitis. I'd taken a sedative, unplugged the phone, and was drifting off when I heard a pounding at the front door. By the time I got downstairs to open it, they were trying to break it down. Three enormous police officers shouldered their way past me with no explanation. I was told to sit in the kitchen and to "shut up and stay put" as they proceeded to systematically tear the place apart. By the time Teddy arrived, my teeth were chattering like castanets. He tried to get me out of there but they wouldn't let him. Finally a senior officer showed up, and seeing I was genuinely ill, allowed me to go next door to Mrs. Corso, who poured brandy down my throat and put me to bed.

We'd been living in a dream world. Operate outside the rules long enough and you tend to forget the rest of the world doesn't approve. We'd deluded ourselves that times had changed. Trudeau was in Ottawa, Carter had just moved into the White House. Things like this weren't supposed to happen. In brief, they found about half an ounce of pot, traces of hash and accompanying drug paraphernalia, and my collection of pills, some prescription but most not. Very disappointing for them, I'm sure, but it didn't stop them from slapping a trafficking charge on the pair of us. Teddy insisted that everything was his and I'd known nothing about it, but the police weren't buying it. My name was on the house, and the cache of pills was clearly mine. I was already on file because of Federico. That I was knowingly married to a homosexual undoubtedly clinched it.

We called the only criminal lawyer we knew, Junior's father, Lester Fairplay. You'll recall he was quite notorious back then for his bombastic defences of drug offenders and political protesters. Neither of us was keen to turn this into a crusade for gay rights or the legalization of marijuana, so after the bail hearing I decided to bite the bullet and approach my brother, Gus. It wasn't the money. I could easily have paid, but the police were looking to make an example, and Gus's law firm, Fitzhelm, Fitzhelm and Morgan, and his position as chair of the Daviston Corporation gave him just the kind of political clout it would take to make them back off.

Gus knew all about the bust, and assumed I was coming to him for money. I could tell by his sanctimonious expression that he was looking forward to turning me down and pontificating in the process, so I jumped in with both feet.

"Here's the deal," I said. "Get us a top defence lawyer and call in some favours or I'll be forced to confess the juicier parts of my life story to the press. I can promise you a bravura performance, and they'll have a field day. If you play ball, I'll not only keep my mouth shut, but you'll get my permanent proxy, and a signed agreement stating that if and when I sell my Daviston shares, it will be to you."

I could almost hear the gears shifting as he digested the terms of my bribe. He tried to rearrange his features into the reasonable and businesslike Gus.

"Georgina, my dear," he said. "Consider the family. Think of our poor father's name and reputation."

It dawned on me that digging into my past would expose Pappy's mental history as well and might raise some questions about my brother's competence, to say nothing of the effect on Daviston stock, and this had him more worried than any of my shenanigans.

"Pappy's dead. It's my and Teddy's survival that concerns me, and I don't intend that either of us should spend a day in prison over such trumped-up bullshit. You've heard my terms. What's it going to be?"

"I have to talk this over with Charlie. I'll let you know in a couple of days."

It was a smokescreen. I knew I had him.

Our lawyer was a fraternity brother of Gus's called Jeremy Porteous Flynt who looked like Margaret Thatcher in a pinstriped suit. I'll admit he was good at his job. No pretense at friendliness. He separated our cases, and the charges against me were dropped. He then negotiated to have Teddy's offences reduced to consensual homosexual activity, public indecency and possession of less than an ounce of marijuana. Teddy wanted to plead guilty and be done with it, but Flynt convinced him that if he pleaded not-guilty and won, he'd have no criminal record, and if he lost he'd be no worse off.

The trial lasted two days. Flynt advised me not to attend, and since the more sensational stuff was off the table, the press got bored with it. Teddy got off with a fine and six months' probation, and we both heaved a great sigh of relief. Teddy said he saw Rachel and Sarah in the courtroom both days looking like they were the judge and jury. I'm so sorry, Eddy. It floored me when I heard they'd hired Flynt to draw up a separation agreement. If only you'd told us. That tricky bastard used privileged information from his conversations with us, and at the very least he should have faced ethics charges. Teddy says there are rumours he might be disbarred for his role in the Horning Galleries fraud. I hope I live long enough to see it.

Since he was forbidden to fraternize with Sergio, Teddy stuck pretty close to home during his probation. It was like old times. We saw a lot of movies and plays, and caught up on our reading. We went to see *One Flew Over the Cuckoo's Nest*, and I got all tearful thinking about Pappy.

Teddy made use of the time to block his production of *The Real Mrs. Hardwicke*, my final theatrical triumph. It was loosely based on a sensational murder trial from the late '50s, where a woman was charged with shooting her wealthy husband, then mutilating him with kitchen shears. The husband's sister (that was me) is to all appearances a rather silly and shallow woman, but becomes an avenging angel, demanding justice for her poor sainted brother. The climax comes when my sanity begins to disintegrate under questioning, very schizophrenic and Ophelia-like, and it's revealed that the murdered man was a sadistic, twisted son-of-a-bitch, that both the wife and I were his victims, myself from the time I was a child, and that I, not the wife, was the murderer. Not surprisingly, the prosecuting attorney bore a less-than-flattering resemblance to Jeremy Porteous Flynt. It was a great critical success, praised as "an absorbing and suspenseful courtroom drama," and I was singled out for my "chilling transformation" on the witness stand. I was thrilled for Teddy when it was optioned for a film. Unfortunately his conviction barred him from working in the States.

About halfway through all this, Teddy's probation ended, and he was finally able to move in with Sergio. It was what he'd always wanted, and I was happy for him, but I wasn't prepared for how deeply it affected me. We'd been living separate lives together for so long, and though we were still the best of friends it was hard to accept that I'd no longer have him to talk to at three in the morning when the dark closed in.

My role in *Mrs. Hardwicke* was very demanding and I was in bad shape. I barely completed the Maritime tour that followed the Toronto run, and my old enemy, depression, was waiting for me when it ended. Mrs. Corso was in her seventies by then, and it was obvious I'd have to hire someone to care for me full time. This was how Enid Gaunt came into my life.

I interviewed half a dozen candidates, but they were too touchy-feely and chatty for my taste. I wanted someone who'd take charge and not come running to me every five minutes, and by God that's what I got. Enid was no beauty, thin and sharp featured, with lifeless hair, frumpily dressed, so I figured there wouldn't be any boyfriends. Her former employers, she said, were an elderly couple who'd retired to Arizona for their health. Her reference stated that she was efficient and hard-working. I now recognize it was pretty brief and impersonal, and I guess that should have been a red flag, but I was sick to death of interviews, and hired her.

She was a decent if uninspired cook, and it was a luxury to have my breakfast in bed and other meals at predictable times. Despite her obvious disapproval of my drinking and smoking habits, she didn't belabour the subject, and I must say that the house was, for the first time, immaculate. She also acted as a sort of secretary. I got quite used to her answering the phone with "Jardin residence. Whom may I say is calling?" Eventually I was trusting her to answer correspond-ence, handle the banking and pay bills as well. I barely had to go out the door.

It was when the depression lifted and my health rallied that I began to chafe at having everything done for me. Quite frankly, I was bored stiff. I couldn't understand why I hadn't heard from any of my old pals, and when I called them they were rather chilly with me. Mrs. Corso's visits were fewer and farther between, and when even Teddy stopped coming by, I began to smell a rat.

It came to a head one night when I was awakened by angry voices carrying up the stairwell. Normally I'd have been out like a light, but I was pleasantly sleepy and hadn't taken my sedative. One voice was Enid's, and I recognized the other as Teddy's. He'd apparently tried to let himself in, but found the lock had been changed. By the time I got downstairs Enid was threatening to call the police. When I ordered her to let him in, he was in a dreadful state, smelling of booze and sweat, his suit wrinkled, and his hair sticking out in all directions, not the calm, collected Teddy I'd always known. He said he'd been trying to reach me for days, and what the hell was going on? Suddenly everything clicked. I ordered Enid to her room, saying I'd deal with her later.

It was obvious that something had gone horribly wrong. I poured us each a stiff drink, and it all came out. He and Sergio after only a year of living together had had the most horrendous argument. Unforgivable things had been said. The only other time I'd ever seen Teddy like this was at his mother's funeral.

"He says it's me he loves and the others don't mean anything. He's always been like this, you know, but it's out of control now that he's older. I still love him, but I've finally come to my senses, and I'm damned if I'm going to share him with half the gay population in Toronto. Apart from my feelings, it's so bloody dangerous, and he just won't listen."

Teddy had stormed out of their apartment, and immediately phoned to let me know he was coming home, only to have Enid inform him in no uncertain terms that he wasn't welcome, and I wasn't seeing anyone. Not knowing what else to do, he'd checked into a hotel, but had become increasingly alarmed at not being able to reach me.

I finally managed to talk him down and he fell asleep on the sofa. I was totally drained, but the night wasn't over. I still had to deal with Enid, and the realization that I'd allowed myself to become a prisoner in my own house. All those times when she'd answered the phone, telling me it was nothing, a salesman or a tradesman, and that she'd take care of it. God knows what she'd said to people. She was in Teddy's old room. I opened the door to find her sitting stiffly on the edge of the bed as if she'd been like that, waiting, the whole time.

"Enid," I said, "I want you to pack your bag and leave in the morning. I'll give you a month's salary and a reference, and I'll pay for a room for a month to allow you to find another position. I think that's more than generous. Mr. Crewe is my husband and this is his home. You had no right to act the way you did, and I strongly suspect it's not the first time."

She protested that she was terribly sorry, she'd never meant to overstep, and it wouldn't happen again. I'd been so ill, and she'd only wanted to protect me. She even managed to squeeze out a few tears, but she was a rank amateur in the acting department, and I could see signs she'd already started to clear out. It was well after three by the time I got back to bed.

The next morning I saw Enid off to her rooming house by taxi. I gave her a reference that said she was efficient and hard-working, which was true enough, then went upstairs to help Teddy remove every trace of "that bloody woman" from his room. We opened the windows to air out the last of her violet scent, stripped the bed and turned the mattress. It was when we moved the bed back to its original position that we found a little coil-bound notebook behind a loose baseboard. Most of the jottings were indecipherable, but what was glaringly obvious was two pages of attempts to copy my signature. I hadn't been totally out to lunch. The only bank account she'd had access to was the household one. A thorough going-over

of my finances assured me that she hadn't gotten beyond petty pilfering, but it did add up to almost two thousand dollars in the eleven
months she'd been with me.

My inclination was to let it go. Good riddance to bad rubbish,
as Pappy used to say, but Teddy said I had to report it or she'd do the
same thing to somebody else. I reluctantly agreed, but was secretly
relieved when the police checked at her rooming house to find she'd
stayed only one night, demanded a refund and vanished.

I didn't care. Teddy was home.

After Enid's departure, things got very quiet. I read a few scripts, but
couldn't work up any enthusiasm. I helped Teddy out with revisions
and blocking on a couple of plays, and even attempted to write one
of my own, but even I could see it wasn't any good. To all intents and
purposes I was retired, and content to be so.

The shattering news of your arrest changed that. It was some
comfort that you and Teddy had kept in touch and he told me what
happened. Even if I'd only read the newspapers I'd have known you
were innocent. You simply aren't capable of such a thing. I wish
you'd let me help. I know Junior's your friend, and a decent lawyer,
but criminal law is not his forte, and I can easily afford a first-rate
lawyer. I can only wait and hope you'll change your mind.

That's about it. Gus and his wife now live in Grandpa Daviston's house in Rosedale. I'm sure it's been a great cross for him to
bear having only daughters, but he's compensated by raising them
to dutifully marry men just like himself. Charlie and his wife could
have had Pappy's house, but apparently she only likes new things,
so it was sold right after Pappy died. I hear they've built some kind
of pseudo-Italian villa in the Bridle Path area, all marble floors
and statuary and potted palms. A couple of years back I finally
sold them my shares in the corporation, so we have no further
reason to communicate. I'm still waiting for Gina's curse to catch

up with them, but perhaps just being who and what they are is punishment enough.

Now for the grand *mea culpa*.

I've been a total flop at relationships. I just don't seem to have the right wiring. Teddy says one of my more amusing contradictions is that I'm a cynical romantic. I see his point. I love fairy tales but don't for a moment believe in them. I've always found Prince Charming to be highly entertaining but terribly unreliable, and the illusion of romance far more thrilling than the reality. You might be surprised at some of the men I could have married, but nine times out of ten they were looking for someone they could feel superior to. Inevitably they'd suggest that perhaps I could be a little less flamboyant, less opinionated, and that would be my exit cue. It's probably no coincidence that the two men I might have made an exception for, your father and Nicky, I simply couldn't have—and then of course there's you.

You have every right to feel the way you do, but whatever my maternal shortcomings, I'm proud to say that at least I'll leave you and your little Leslie fairly well-fixed, and I've made sure that those Stantons won't be able to get their hands on it. I've given Teddy a lifetime tenancy in the house. I'm sure if you asked him to leave, he'd do so, but I don't need to remind you he's not only been a constant and faithful friend to me, but a far better parent to you than I could ever be. The one legacy I don't leave you, thank God, is the Joyner curse.

Don't worry yourself over my final disposal. Arrangements have been made to plant me next to Mammy and Pappy. These days I feel more and more like that poem Pappy used to read to me about "The Wonderful One-Hoss Shay," where every part collapses at once, leaving a pile of dust on the ground, and I'd considered cremation, but somehow the thought of being preserved long past my use-by date appeals to me. If the sweet hereafter is not some divine hoax, perhaps I'll see you there—but enough of this weepy stuff.

In a recent flash of self-pity I asked Teddy why he stayed with me.

"Well, old girl, I guess we're just used to each other," he said. "No illusions, no expectations, no recriminations, not such a bad life."

Not such a bad exit line either, my darling.

—Your impossible mother, Gina

Chapter 7

EDWARD FITZHELM (1951–1991)

(What follows I've edited from the taped conversations with my father. I've created a chronological order where possible, with occasional jumps for different tapes, different days, and I've omitted some things that have meaning only to myself and him. L.A.F.)

I've never been driven by ambition. Just as well, considering where I've ended up, but all I ever really wanted for myself and then for you, Twig, was a peaceful, happy life. I've given some thought as to why this hasn't been possible. In earlier times a monastery was the option, but I suspect that now, even in the cloister the world would intrude. Oddly enough, the closest I've come to achieving that ideal is here. Television and newspapers have ceased to have much relevance. My illness insulates me from the uglier side of prison life, Junior keeps me supplied with books, and now that I have this marvellous little machine of yours I can listen to music and read with only the routine interruptions of meals, maintenance and medication.

I don't know why you'd want to hear about your boring old father, but since you insist, you could say I was born in a trunk, that old showbiz cliché. Do you remember meeting your grandmother? You'd have been very young, but she'd certainly qualify as a memorable character. When I was little, she'd park me in her dressing room or hire out-of-work actors or dancers to babysit me. As a result I developed a pretty interesting infant vocabulary, was expert at making peanut butter and jelly sandwiches by the time I was four, and at six could beat just about anybody at poker except Gina, who was a ruthless player and a blatant cheat. No pretense at letting the kid win. I learned very early on never to play games with my mother.

She insisted I call her Gina. She said the word *Mummy* belonged in ancient Egypt. Beautiful, funny, charming, stunningly self-centred, she was the eye of the cyclone with the rest of us spinning around her. Those parts of my childhood when she was either physically or emotionally absent stand out as lulls in that storm, and my memories of her are split between the lovely, laughing, shining creature who could never stay still long enough to focus on me, and the dark, miserable shadow that couldn't stand the sight or the sound of me. It took me years to realize it wasn't my fault, that it had nothing to do with me. I suspect she died believing I hated her. I didn't, I don't, but I'd learned by hard experience to duck whenever the high beam of her attention swerved in my direction.

I was strangely disaster-prone as a kid. A snowplow buried me alive when I was six. At nine, a man in a car tried to snatch me on my way to school, dragging me by the hood of my parka for three blocks. That same year a loose pipe flew off a turning truck and broke my arm. I was like a magnet for any crazy person on the street, sprinklers started up at my approach, and if a flowerpot fell off a windowsill, you could bet it would land on me. Every time something positive happened, something negative would cancel it out. I guess I was lucky most of the damage was to my dignity. Gina once told me I reminded her of a character in her favourite comic strip when she was a child, a little guy named Joe with an unpronounceable last name and a permanent rain cloud over his head. The hard-luck kid, she called me. She thought it was funny, but it didn't do much for my self-esteem.

The people I knew I could depend on were Teddy, my grandfather, Mrs. Corso, and my friends Junior, Cam and Ken.

Gina and Teddy's relationship remains a mystery to me. It was clear he wasn't my father, that in fact he wasn't likely to be anybody's father. He was just Teddy, an island of sanity in the endless stream of Gina's friends, boyfriends and hangers-on. Not especially affectionate or easy to talk to, but I trusted him, and he always managed to find time for those things that slipped my mother's mind or were too trivial for her to bother with, permission and money for a school trip, coming to view my contribution to the science fair, meetings with my teachers. Not that I wanted my mother involved. When she did make the effort it was always a disaster, like the time she showed up to an open house at my school, breathless in spike-heeled boots and a mink coat which fell open to reveal a purple leotard and tights, gushing that she'd rushed straight from rehearsal because she wouldn't for the world miss something so important to her darling Eddie. Classic Gina. I was mortified.

Mrs. Corso saw to it that I had clean clothes, regular meals and got off to school on time. She'd take me shopping at Kensington Market, or her favourite Italian grocery on College Street, and I even went to mass with her. It was still in Latin back then, and I enjoyed the rhythm and ritual even if I didn't understand it. "*Ite, missa est.*" She gave me this Saint Christopher medal to protect me from my constant mishaps. She even taught me to cook, and I can still taste her homemade pasta with tomato basil sauce, warm fresh-baked bread dipped in garlic-flavoured olive oil, and as a special treat, chocolate raspberry tartufo. I loved tartufo.

It was my grandfather who rescued me from the gloom of my mother's depression and filled the vacuum of her time in Los Angeles. He introduced me to golden mornings fishing on Georgian Bay, the mist rising off the water, and only the songs of the birds, the lapping of the water against the hull and the breeze rustling in the reeds to break the silence. He always listened to me as an equal, and although he seemed sad, we seldom talked about sad things. He told me of his boyhood in England, Fallowfield where he grew up, and his mother who he said was the strongest, bravest woman he'd ever known. He spoke of my grandmother Alma, how beautiful and smart she was, and how proud he'd been of her world travels and good works. The only time he seemed truly happy was when he talked about his music and his band. Nights at the Bay by the light of a coal-oil lantern, he read to me the books of my mother's childhood, Baum's stories of Oz, *The Once and Future King*, *Tom Sawyer* and *Huckleberry Finn*, Robert Louis Stevenson, and Swift's *Gulliver*, the same ones I read to you. He encouraged me to draw and even framed and hung a sketch I made of him in his fishing gear. He taught me how to organize my ideas, trust my hands to carry them out, and improvise when conventional tools and materials weren't handy. We were always taking things apart and putting them back together, and I've kept all the funny little gizmos we dreamed up. Any virtues I've had as a father, I learned from him in the few years we had together.

I was eleven when he had his stroke. I was desperate to see him, but Gina said it would only upset me. I think she was jealous, and uncharitable as it sounds, she was playing the grief-stricken, devoted daughter to the hilt. I tried to go to the hospital on my own, but I was only a kid and had no proof I was family, so they turned me away. Thanks to Teddy I had one afternoon with him. I don't even know whether he could hear me, but I got to tell him how much I loved him, then sat with him until dark sharing the silence one last time. He died two days later.

When I lost him, I lost the Bay as well. Gina had a share in the family cottage, but because of her long-standing feud with my uncles and her aversion to roughing it, we never went. At Grandpa's funeral I overheard Uncle Charlie refer to me as "the little bastard," so I figured there'd be no invitations from that side of the family. I never saw the place again.

My father's identity was supposed to be a deep, dark secret, but you didn't have to be a genius to figure it out. It was Teddy who, in all ignorance, let the cat out of the bag when I was about fourteen. He'd mentioned that when she'd gotten pregnant with me, Gina, who had no patience for politics of any stripe, was an enthusiastic volunteer on the campaign team for a rising star in the Liberal Party called Ernest Dwyer Daid—E.D.D. "Eddie" was just the sort of nickname she'd come up with. I've looked up old newspaper articles where he's described as handsome and charismatic, and photographs of him show some likeness. I never felt the urge to seek him out, but I needed to know. He was married, of course. Most of her boyfriends were, and they usually went back to their wives. Even her cousin Nicky, the only one of them I ever liked, went back to his family in England and that was the last I heard of him.

Gina swore no child of hers would ever go to a private school, and it was one decision I never regretted, because in public school I found my lifelong brothers, Junior, Cam and Ken. I hope you have good friends, Twig. I don't know what I'd have done without mine. It's hard to say exactly what draws people together, but one thing that united the four of us was having larger-than-life parents.

Junior's dad, Lester Fairplay Senior, was a flamboyant defence lawyer famous for presenting his clients as underdogs persecuted by an antiquated and biased legal system. The press had turned him into an almost mythical figure. Judges and prosecutors despised him. Junior shared his father's principles and followed him into law, but totally lacked his showmanship and love of confrontation. We met on our first day of school. As both our names started with *F*, we shared a desk in the overcrowded classroom, and we've been best friends ever since. Junior was always the fat kid, so most people never saw past that to the smart, kind, loyal person he is. We met Cam in grade four, when Lester Senior defended Cam's dad, Big Jim Mitchell, in a slander suit filed by a city official of whom Big Jim had said, "I won't call him a liar, but he has a long-standing history of aversion to the unvarnished truth."

Big Jim was a legendary union organizer and negotiator who steamrolled any opposition with his broad Scottish accent, rapid-fire delivery and pugnacious stance. Cam's mother was Maggie Cameron, active in the Women's Teachers' Union, and a fierce advocate for women's rights. His sister, Nellie, was named for Nellie McClung. Cam's dream was to be a landscape gardener, an occupation his father dismissed as "an indulgence of the idle rich, and an insult to honest farmers." We shared a love for drawing and painting, and often went to Allan Gardens to sketch exotic plants and flowers. He lives in southern California now, and writes me funny letters full of the eccentricities and scandalous goings-on of his rich, famous and wannabe famous clients.

I overheard Kenneth Chin playing Scot Joplin in the school auditorium one afternoon and invited him over to listen to Grandpa's records with the other guys. He was the youngest and the only son of six children of an immigrant Chinese family. His father had risen from his first job as a waiter to become owner of the restaurant, and from there had built up a successful produce business, which, as Ken was constantly reminded, he would someday inherit. He constantly walked that schizophrenic line between being a Canadian and remaining a dutiful Chinese son. He'd studied classical piano from the age of five, but by the time I met him he was hooked on ragtime.

Being A students, we'd all skipped grades, so we were younger than most of our classmates. We might have been the backbone of the school chess and debating teams, but we were a washout for sports, me with my weak lungs and poor eyesight, Junior because of his weight, and Ken for fear of damaging his hands. Cam was a natural athlete, but hated competition. This plus our distinctly oddball interests branded us as eggheads, wimps and weirdos, but we didn't care because we had each other.

Teenage rebellion seemed pointless to me because nothing I could ever do or say would shock or embarrass my mother, so while the rest of my high-school classmates were torturing their parents with long hair, love beads, pot, and acid rock, the four of us were out on our bicycles scouring pawnshops, second-hand stores and garage sales for old 78s. We discovered Louis Armstrong, Louis Jordan and Spike Jones. We even dressed the part, sporting vintage wide-lapelled suit jackets and gaudy neckties with our blue jeans. Cam's tie had pink and purple orchids on it, and Junior's had a hula dancer with a palm tree. Ken's prize was an emerald green tie with a Dali-esque sweep of piano keys and scattered musical notes, which he had to keep in his locker so his dad wouldn't see it. Mine had tilted martini glasses with olives.

We had a passion for science fiction, and our expeditions expanded to old pulp magazines, *Amazing Stories*, *Weird Tales* and *Other Worlds*. I drew fantastic ballpoint tattoos up and down my arms, and my schoolbooks were filled with doodles of robots, alien monsters, muscle-bound spacemen, and impossibly endowed damsels in distress.

When Grandpa died I inherited his fiddle and started taking violin lessons, but the sight of Gina's expectant smile in the front row at my first performance froze me on the spot, and I never picked it up again. I did take up the guitar later, and by grade eleven the four of us had formed a combo called the Krazy Kats, with Ken on piano, Cam on bass and Junior playing drums. We weren't very good except for Ken, but we made up in enthusiasm what we lacked in talent. The high point of our musical career was performing at our fourth-year Ladies' Choice dance, which had a Roaring Twenties theme. None of the ladies chose us, although we thought we looked pretty sharp in matching white tuxedo jackets and ruffled shirts with red satin bow ties and cummerbunds we'd bought from a wedding rental place that was going out of business. Our big number was "Hold That Tiger," Spike Jones style, with kazoo and slide whistle, but I was quite proud of our version of the Hot League's "Slap and Tickle," a real tour de force for Ken, with nonsense lyrics contributed by me.

We all finished high school in the top ten and celebrated with a marathon meal at the Chin family restaurant, a treat from Ken's dad. I had a whole carp cooked with ginger and garlic, and I even tried octopus.

Ken would major in history and political science, Junior was going for his law degree and Cam had reached a compromise with his father, working for a landscaping outfit during the summer, then studying architecture and city planning. I didn't have a clue what I wanted to do other than get out of my mother's house as quickly as possible, so university wasn't an option.

Life at home was impossible. When Gina was in one of her frantic moods she couldn't stand to be alone, so she filled the house with phony intellectual and creative types and partied non-stop. If it wasn't some fake Cuban revolutionary or pacifist draft dodger, it was an acid-fried rock band passed out on the living room floor, and when one of them staggered up to the third floor and trashed my room, it was the last straw. I'll admit I'm a pack rat, and hold on to things long past the point of interest or usefulness, but that bastard smashed an old school project of dinosaur skeletons it had taken me ages to build. Gina said he was hallucinating, as if that were some sort of excuse. I freaked out, shouting I'd had it with her and her loser friends, and as soon as I could find a job I'd be out of there. I ran upstairs, slammed the door and fell on my bed amidst the wreckage blubbing like a baby, knowing I had nowhere else to go.

With Christmas and birthday money and allowance I'd managed to save up almost three hundred dollars, so the next day I went out and bought one of those big metal accordion gates and installed it at the top of the steps with the heaviest padlock I could find. I spent the rest of it on a suit, lied about my age and landed a part-time job as an office boy with a company called Hayden and Grange. That was at the end of July '66. I'd start in September.

The gang of four wanted to have a last fling before we scattered, so in August we went camping for a week at Algonquin Park. I hadn't been fishing since Grandpa died and I couldn't wait. Junior's graduation present was a car, a second-hand Chevy. Teddy gave me fifty dollars for gas and food, Cam borrowed his older brother's driver's licence to buy beer and Ken brought groceries and a battery-operated radio. We were flying as we piled into the car that morning.

We arrived late in the afternoon, chose a campsite, pitched our army surplus tent, and rented a canoe. We got a fire going and made a meal of hot dogs roasted on sticks and cold baked beans out of the can, washing them down with beer.

None of us were experienced drinkers, so it didn't take much to knock us out. Junior and Ken were still in their sleeping bags when Cam and I launched the canoe, and were just waking up when we returned with a dozen pickerel for breakfast. I cleaned our catch, dredged it with flour, and plopped a pound of shortening in the big black frying pan and put it on the grill just like Grandpa's man Karl had taught me. Then I made a foaming batter of beer and pancake mix, dipped the fish in it, and dropped it into the bubbling shortening. I can still taste that fish, absolutely fresh, and the crust crisp and golden brown. We ate so much fish that week we started making jokes about growing gills. Junior, swimming every day and cut off from his diet of hamburgers, fries and pizza, must have lost seven or eight pounds, and it looked really good on him. It wasn't long after that he met Grady, and they've been married for almost twenty years.

We solved all the world's problems that week—endless talk to a background of the Beatles and the Beach Boys. I remember the last night in particular. The Watts riots were still in the news, and James Meredith, the civil rights worker, had been shot down in Mississippi a couple of months earlier. I'd pompously said I was proud to live in a country which had welcomed escaped slaves, but Cam's mother had told him the history books were wrong about a lot of stuff, that there'd been slavery here too, and it was economics not morality that ended it. Ken told us how his mother's grandfather had come to Canada to work on the railroad, sending his wages back to his family. At seventy he'd gone home to his village in China to find his wife dead, and his children and grandchildren strangers. Ken's mother remembered being terrified by this crazy-looking old man in foreign clothes.

That night we pledged to make the trip an annual event. Junior and I planned to get an apartment together once he got settled at university and I had a few paycheques under my belt. It gave me something to look forward to.

I reported for my first day of work the following week. Hayden and Grange was an established, conservative firm, specializing in estate management and retirement funds. At almost sixteen I was by far the youngest employee. The salary didn't amount to much and I was basically an errand boy, but I was so anxious to show how keen I was I must have driven everyone crazy. I taught myself how to type and file, and was the first to volunteer if there was any extra work to be done. Evan Grange, the senior partner, seemed to find all this amusing, and would sometimes stop and talk to me. He suggested I look into some night courses in business administration and accounting. I was pretty happy with the changes in my life and counting the days until Junior and I got our own place.

On the first of December, four days before my sixteenth birthday, I received a letter from a man called Paul Overdall saying he'd been my grandfather's solicitor, and we needed to meet to discuss my trust. This was mind-blowing. I knew nothing about any trust. The only lawyer I'd ever met was Junior's dad, who favoured rolled-up shirtsleeves, suspenders and a crooked bow tie, and whose office looked like a bomb had hit it, so I was a bit intimidated by Paul Overdall with his elegant suit and conspicuously neat mahogany desk.

"In three days time, on your sixteenth birthday, you are to receive a substantial sum of money for such a young man."

"How much, sir?" I said, holding my breath.

"With accrued interest, after taxes it should be somewhere in the neighbourhood of sixty thousand dollars."

I was stunned. "I don't understand."

"Quite simple," he replied. "When you were born in '51, your grandparents placed the sum of fifty thousand dollars in trust for you. The terms being that you should receive the total on your sixteenth birthday. Your grandfather said he suspected you'd be wanting to make your own way by then. He was quite adamant that I should succeed him as trustee, not your uncle Gus."

I almost cried. It was as if my grandfather had risen from the grave to rescue me once again.

"I'm surprised your mother didn't mention it. She certainly knew about it."

That was Gina. When I was six or seven, Mrs. Corso, worried that I was receiving no religious or moral instruction in our godless household, taught me about sin—mortal and venal sin, sins of omission and commission. If she was a little fuzzy on some of the details, she was very firm on the concept. Being an analytical kid, I concluded that my own sins were of the mildly venal variety, and my mother's sins, aside from the obvious ones, were invariably those of omission.

She prided herself on her honesty, routinely telling me stuff that nobody my age should have been burdened with, but her honesty was selective, so while she never actually lied to me, she never really told me the truth either, not about my father, not about her rocky relationship with her family, and not about the trust. Would she ever have told me? Possibly, eventually, if it ever crossed her mind.

My birthday fell on a Saturday that year, and the gang decided to celebrate in Buffalo where the bars wouldn't enquire too closely about our ages. We jumped into Junior's car, arriving in Buffalo around six, had pizza and Chianti, then headed off to a strip joint where we ogled the dancers and drank endless pitchers of beer. The boys joked about getting me laid, but I was too drunk to stand, and on the trip home Junior had to stop several times so I could throw up. I still hadn't mentioned my miraculous windfall. I think I was afraid it might disappear in a puff of smoke if I did.

By the time I finally 'fessed up, I'd already made some decisions. At Paul Overdall's suggestion I put two-thirds of the money into a term deposit and the rest into my bank account. Junior and I scoured the want ads and proudly signed the lease on a two-bedroom apartment in an old building on Jarvis. I was free of my mother's house at last!

It was a typical bachelor pad, mattresses on the floor, a rickety card table and chairs, with a beat-up living-room suite and carpet donated by Junior's mother. We got sheets, towels and kitchen stuff from Honest Ed's, and built bookshelves out of cement blocks and boards. I splurged on a TV set and a new turntable, tuner and speakers, and it was home, sweet home.

I'd seen an ad for a five-year-old Volvo, and had been trying to figure out how I could afford it. Paying for it in full was one of the best moments of my life. Junior had already taught me to drive, so I'd aced my driver's test and was ready to roll. I drove that car 'til it literally fell apart, then bought another one just like it.

No one at the office knew about my change in fortune. I was now a full-time employee, liked my job and had no intention of leaving. Within the year I'd become assistant to the office manager. Her name was Karen, an attractive divorcee of about thirty. To say she took me under her wing would be an understatement. I suppose I should be embarrassed talking to you about this, but it was long before I met your mother, and I have to keep reminding myself you're not a kid any more. Besides, embarrassment is hardly an option when one's every bodily function is monitored by relative strangers on a daily basis. To put it baldly, we had an affair. I thought I'd died and gone to heaven, and of course I thought it was love. She, however, made it bracingly clear that it wasn't the first time she'd had this kind of relationship, and it certainly wouldn't be the last. I learned a lot from her, and have no regrets except that it made me a target for Evan Grange's nephew, Ronnie Kemper.

Ronnie was the son of Evan Grange's younger sister, and as Evan was a widower with no children it was a given that Ronnie, as the only boy in the family, would be his eventual heir, something which nobody at the firm was looking forward to. He'd have been in his late twenties then, a pompous jerk who constantly referred to his degree in economics. He was always sending me out to get coffee and doughnuts or to return things he'd bought and decided he didn't like, even to get his car washed. He had the hots for Karen, and when he discovered he'd been beaten out by a seventeen-year-old he got really nasty, calling me a high-school dropout, a brown-noser and an opportunistic little shit to anyone who'd listen. Fortunately he wasn't in a position to fire me. It didn't help matters when I nicknamed him Reggie VanDough after the snotty cousin in the Richie Rich comics. Everyone started calling him Reggie and it drove him nuts. I wasn't surprised when Evan asked me to come to his office one night after work, but instead of firing me he asked me to sit down.

"Edward, my boy, it's time we had a little talk. As regards you and Karen, I'm not a prude. You're both free agents, and damned good at your jobs, so there won't be any flack from me. Now I'm aware Ronnie's been giving you a rough time, and I want you to know where I stand. He's my baby sister's boy, and he'll always have a place here, but that doesn't mean I have to like him. He makes no secret of the fact that he considers me a dinosaur. He's got some dingbat ideas about investment, and when I put the brakes on him he complains you can't teach an old dog new tricks. What he doesn't understand is that this old dog can teach a new dog some pretty useful old tricks, and you, Edward, are that new dog." It seemed I was to become his personal assistant, a sort of protege. He brushed aside my gratitude, saying that at least I seemed to have a brain in my head, and some sense of what Hayden and Grange was all about. He went on to say, "What we are is salesmen, and what we sell is security. Now my nephew seems to think a client's money is his to play with, to gamble on his harebrained theories about the market. Most of the stuff he's pushing is up and down like a toilet seat, and if I let him do what he wants, the first dip in dividends would produce screams of agony that would deafen the dead. Our clients are either retired or planning to be. What they want, what they expect of us, is a steady income, and it's our job, Edward, to see they damned well get it."

I liked and admired Evan and desperately wanted that promotion, but wasn't looking forward to Ronnie's reaction. Evan was way ahead of me—Ronnie was to front a new division called The H&G Entrepreneur Fund, aimed at bringing in new, younger clients willing to take a flyer on some of his more risky recommendations with the possibility of making big bucks fast. Ego and new title aside, however, Ronnie wasn't stupid, and his dislike for me hardened into active loathing. It was mutual.

I spent the next months learning everything there was to know about Hayden and Grange, and on Evan's advice started tapping my little nest egg to make some modest investments of my own. When he made me a junior partner a couple of years later, Ronnie went ballistic.

We've never talked about how your mother and I met. I want to tell you everything, because it's important that you know we really loved each other.

I'd been with the company for over three years. Evan was almost seventy and though he had no intention of retiring then, he didn't want to work so many hours. I'd drive him to appointments with some of the older clients who liked home visits and personal attention, and generally only needed reassuring that everything was ticking along nicely. Evan would introduce me, and if things went smoothly I'd take over the day-to-day management of their port- folios with the understanding that he'd be keeping an eye on things. One of these was the Stanton estate.

After my crazy upbringing, the permanence and stability of Stanton and the family's place in it was a revelation. Miss Rachel and Miss Sarah Stanton were surprisingly receptive to the change in representation, and on my next visit seemed most interested in hearing about my life and my family. I dodged any discussion about Gina and Teddy, saying only that my parents were involved in the theatre. I talked instead about my grandparents, and the two of them were flatteringly attentive as I babbled on about the Fitzhelms and the Davistons. They invited me to tea the following Sunday, and that was when I met your mother.

I wish you could have known her then. She was a little older than I was, but so shy and pretty, and so ignorant of anything outside of Stanton that I felt like quite a man of the world. After tea Rachel and Sarah excused themselves, coyly saying they had things to do and that they'd leave us two youngsters to entertain ourselves. I was a little tongue-tied at first, but managed to tell her a bit about my work and my friends. She said she enjoyed reading and would welcome any recommendations for books she might like. When I got up to leave I said I very much looked forward to seeing her again. As we walked to my car she impulsively kissed me on the cheek, then blushed furiously and fled back into the house. I was hooked.

I became a regular at Sunday dinner, even attending church with them. As things progressed I was never precisely asked what my intentions were, but was given the distinct impression that a proposal would be welcomed. I bought an engagement ring, and asked your mother to marry me in February of '69. She accepted, and her aunts declared themselves delighted. They'd engineered the whole thing, of course. They were hell-bent on having an heir, and that was you, kid.

I brought a few personal things with me, my books, the Hot League recordings, Grandpa's fiddle, but it was clear from the start there'd be little room for anything of mine at Stanton House, so I stored most of it in the attic. Junior and Grady were keeping the apartment, so we agreed I could leave a few things in my old room, and stay over if I was working late.

The wedding was set for the first week of April, and we were suddenly swept up in a frenzy of planning. That is, I sat stunned as the frenzy went on around me. When it finally occurred to anyone to ask me if I had guests, I took the coward's way out and said that my parents would be out of the country, but I had three friends who would attend. I asked Junior to be my best man. He'd bring Grady, and Cam his sister Nellie. Ken was going out with a Jewish girl then called Sharon. Both their families were in an uproar about it, which I guess was the point. The aunts were a bit funny about Ken being Chinese, and I suppose they thought they were being tactful in suggesting he might be uncomfortable, but when I told them he'd be happy to play "The Wedding March" and some other suitable music on the wheezy old church organ, they were pleased enough. The regular organist would have cost them fifty bucks.

Vickie looked like an immaculate bride doll in her long white dress and veil, her face carefully painted, and her hair teased and sprayed into an elaborate pile of sausage curls. She had beautiful hair then, long and thick and dark and curly, and I hated seeing it like that, feeling like steel wool, but she was quite proud of her wedding coiffure, and we were two days into our honeymoon before I could convince her to wash it out. I was really angry when Rachel later bullied her into cutting her hair, saying it wasn't appropriate for a married woman.

Rachel and Sarah presided in pastel suits and flowered hats. Except for the guys and their dates, I didn't know any of the hundred or so guests. Margarethe Jensen supervised the buffet supper of jellied salads, cold meats and an endless variety of dessert squares surrounding the towering wedding cake. There was no alcohol, only lemonade and iced tea, so the boys and I slipped away for a quick one from time to time. I don't know if I could have survived the whole ordeal otherwise.

About five in the afternoon Vickie and I finally took off in the Volvo to catch an evening flight for our Florida honeymoon.

It was wonderful. Just the two of us with no responsibilities, no timetable, no aunts. The weather was perfect. The pink and white art deco hotel looked like our wedding cake. We spent mornings on the beach, and in the afternoon did all the tourist things, snorkelling, shelling, a trip to the Keys, even deep-sea fishing, although Vickie didn't care for it much. Somewhere in the boxes is a favourite picture I took of her standing on the beach in her bathing suit, sunburnt, laughing, with her eyes closed and her long hair blowing in the ocean breeze. Neither of us wanted to come back.

I should have put my foot down right from the beginning, but you have to remember I was only twenty. I never intended for us to live in Stanton. I thought we'd stay for six months or so until we found a nice apartment in Toronto near the office, but every time the subject came up, Rachel and Sarah had any number of reasons why not. The house belonged to Vickie after all, left to her by her father, their dear brother, and they were only the caretakers. Whyever would we want the expense of living anywhere else, and in Toronto of all places? The issue of her health had never arisen when we were courting, but became a primary argument when we talked of leaving. Didn't I realize that Vickie was far too fragile to manage a house without help? If I suggested we might like to be on our own, they made me feel like a bastard, saying they didn't want to be a nuisance and though it had always been their home they'd try to find someplace in the village. Once you were on the way, the refrain was that I'd be working all day, and who better to take care of Vickie and the baby than her two old aunties who'd raised her from the time she was a baby herself? It was an ongoing, elaborate game, and I didn't know any of the rules, the endless, meaningless corset of rules that controlled every aspect of our lives from the time we got up in the morning until we went to bed at night, and if you asked why, the reply would inevitably start with "We've always . . ." or "We've never . . .," as if that were reason enough.

"We've always had meat loaf on Mondays."

"We've never put garlic in the pot roast. Spicy foods overheat the blood."

"We've always said that alcohol is Satan's snare for the weak-minded."

"We've never drunk coffee after two in the afternoon."

"We've always retired by ten."

"We've never seen the need of a television."

I actually won that round. I retrieved my TV from the apartment, and mounted an antenna on the roof. Vickie and I would watch it in our bedroom after supper, with coffee, even exceeding the ten o'clock curfew despite bitter complaints about the racket. I kept a bottle of Scotch in my toolbox.

Even with my support Vickie could never stand up to them for long. It was your mother's house, but those two "ruled" it with an iron grip. You were born into it, so maybe it was normal to you, Twig, but for me, raised with no restrictions to speak of, it was really frustrating. I never knew when or how I'd be putting my foot in it.

It was the sugar spoon incident that gave me the first real taste of what I was in for.

Your mother and I had been back from our honeymoon about three months. We'd settled into married life, and had just gotten the happy news that you were on the way.

You remember fishing with me at the old quarry at Herry's Farm? Clear, deep, moving, spring-fed water, perfect for bass fishing, and I had my eye on one fish in particular, a magnificent five- or six-pounder that favoured a spot at the base of some slabs of granite. He'd ignored all my lures, and I'd been racking my brain to think of something that would tempt him. The answer came to me as I was eating my breakfast at the kitchen table one Saturday morning. The spoon in the sugar bowl was part of the old Stanton silver service, one of a pair, the other being reserved for the dining room. Generations of use had worn it down to almost paper thinness, and it suddenly occurred to me that the shape, lightness and brightness of it, combined with the delicate scalloping, would make it a perfect lure. I carried my prize down to the basement workbench, cut off the stem, filed down the raw edge, and drilled a couple of holes in it. With a swivel at one end and a hook at the other I had my lure, light enough to cast, heavy enough to sink down to the right depth, and the scalloping to give it an attractive flutter.

I remember every detail of that morning. It started out as a perfect day. My little aluminum boat was brand new then. There'd been some grumbling over the cost of the boat and trailer, but I was paying for it and for once your mother had backed me up. There was a smell of rain in the air, and a thin layer of moving cloud with the sun behind it reflected in the glassy water. If you gazed into it long enough, you felt a sort of seductive vertigo, as if you could fall down into the sky. I gently manoeuvred the boat into position, made a few trial casts with my new lure to get the feel of it, then went after my quarry. He struck on the third cast and headed for the bottom, but I knew I had him. He was a real bulldog, strong and stubborn, but I finally reeled him in. The lure was a winner. I caught half a dozen more bass that morning but they were pretty small stuff after that first giant, and I happily headed home around noon with my catch, to find Margarethe Jensen sorting through the garbage in the kitchen. Having followed strict instructions to report anything missing or broken, she'd dutifully mentioned the sugar spoon to Aunt Rachel.

She was close to tears as she told me, "She's got herself into a real tizzy over it. I don't know where else to look. She's as good as accused me of stealing it. Can you tell me why I'd steal some old worn-out spoon, then tell her about it? I've half a mind to quit. Let her put that in her pipe and smoke it!"

I apologized to Margarethe, helped her clean up the mess, then went to Rachel and confessed that I was the culprit, although I lost my nerve when it came to admitting what I'd done with it. I said I'd stuck it in my pocket to eat some canned fruit I'd taken as a snack, and it had fallen overboard. She was livid. Didn't I know that spoon was part of the silver service Archibald Stanton had bought for his dear Amelia when they were married in 1895, and that it was now the only missing piece? How could I have been so criminally careless? Was this an example of how the Fitzhelms were brought up? Sarah chimed in that I should be made to pay for it, but they couldn't agree on a value, and half my salary was turned over to them anyway. That lure is still in the bottom of my tackle box. I never had the heart to use it again.

The giant bass was like ashes in my mouth at dinner. When

Vickie and I went to bed that night I tried to tell her how silly I thought the whole thing was, but all she would say was that I should really try not to upset them.

It was my first real run-in with this obsession for everything Stanton, and only one of countless black marks saved and savoured by those two old bats to be used against me later on. There was an inventory once a year on Boxing Day, with every plate, every fork, every knick-knack accounted for, as well as every nick and scratch on the furniture. When Margarethe found a little pile of sawdust on the front porch it was discovered that carpenter ants had eaten into one of the supports, and an army of exterminators invaded every corner of the house, stinking the place up for weeks, irritating my already touchy lungs and sending your mother wheezing to her bed. Those bugs had no idea who they were dealing with.

I certainly did my bit to keep the old mausoleum going. With one bathroom in the place, I had to get up an hour early to accommodate Rachel's and Sarah's morning routines, despite the fact I was the one who had to get to work and neither of them was going anywhere. So I was greatly relieved, if you'll pardon the pun, when I got permission to expand the basement water closet to include a shower and sink for my own use. When the ancient toilet finally gave up the ghost, you'd have thought that venerable throne was another Stanton heirloom. Ole Jensen and I replaced it one weekend, and I jokingly offered to build a plinth for it in the garden with a brass plaque reading, "Flushed with success for a hundred years." That went over like a fart in church, I can tell you.

In retrospect, I'd have to say laughter was one of the things I missed most about my old life. Any display of emotion was regarded as being in questionable taste, and I counted it a real victory when I coaxed a smile out of your mother. Gina, for all her faults, had a great sense of humour, and I can still remember all of us, Mrs. Corso included, collapsing in helpless fits of laughter over some silly thing or other. Fortunately I still had my friends to laugh with when things got too grim, and then I had you.

The night you were born was the proudest moment of my life. Your mother came through it like a champ. I'd always thought those elaborate paintings of mother and child were corny and sentimental until the moment I saw the two of you in that hospital bed, glowing as if you were generating your own light. Your mother never looked more beautiful, and you, red, wrinkled and screaming, were beautiful too. I named you Leslie after my favourite actor.

We got home from the hospital to find that Rachel and Sarah had moved all my things out of our bedroom and into one of the spare rooms. They argued that with your mother's delicate constitution she needed time to recuperate, and since you'd be with her, all the ups and downs during the night would disturb my sleep. I put up with it for a couple of weeks, then moved everything back. You slept in the old Stanton cradle in our room. When you outgrew it, I built you a crib and we made a nursery out of our dressing room so you'd be close by.

It drove me crazy that whenever I showed Vickie any kind of affection in your aunts' presence, those two old biddies would get this expression on their faces as if they'd bitten down on something sour. You remember that look, Twig—lips pursed, eyes cast up toward heaven. I called them the Lemon Sisters after that group on *The Lawrence Welk Show* (God, I'd forgotten how much your mother loved that show). Whenever I'd hug you or kiss you I'd get some comment about coddling you. Ten times worse than any mother-in-law times two! Your mother had loosened up a bit, thanks to me, but she had a deeply conservative streak and unless we were alone she'd get embarrassed if I stroked her hair or patted her behind saying, "Not in front of the baby," or "What will people think?" I'd try to jolly her out of it by saying, "They'll probably suspect we're married," but it got worse as time went on.

I won't embarrass you with your first steps, your first tooth, or your first word. It wasn't *Mama* or *Papa*, by the way, it was *banana*. A real comedian.

Do you remember that little book I made for you about Wally the Walleye? It was our private joke that my drawings of Wally had Rachel's long face and grim mouth, and the eyes looked just like hers when the light hit her glasses. Fortunately she had too little imagination to see the resemblance.

And when I took you to the zoo? You were fascinated by the tropical birds, especially the toucans. I put together that other little book with poems I'd made up for you, sort of like the Edward Lear poems Grandpa used to read to me, but all about toucans. "How many cans can a toucan can if a toucan can can cans?" Total nonsense, of course, but you loved the sound of it, and, oh yes, "The Toucan in Love." Do you remember that one?

> The toucan in love declares his desire
> In an inky crescendo of feathers
> The lady toucan returns his regard
> Her colourful beak all aquiver
> Not to be confused with Colourful Bill
> Who is somebody else all together
> Inspired, he composes a toucan toccata
> And fugue for his ebon amour
> They dance the tango and the Spanish fandango
> To a flaming flamingo guitar
> Not to be confused with Flamingo Flambé
> A lesser performer by far

Your favourite drawing was of the two of them dancing the tango. Mine was Flamingo Flambé, a fan-dancing pink flamingo with decidedly female legs. I took those books with me when I left for fear they'd be eliminated along with all other traces of me. They said I was filling your head with nonsense, and I was, too. We did have fun, didn't we?

I don't know how I missed Grandpa Fitzhelm's old fiddle when I cleared my things out of the attic, but I was happy to know you'd not only found it, but actually played it. I was in the back of the balcony at your first school concert, but had to leave when I spotted your mother and Rachel. I was so proud of you.

I dreamed last night I went back to Stanton House. God, it sounds like the opening line of some dreary gothic novel, but I often dream about it. I was looking for you, but the place was deserted. I wandered from room to room pulling back the curtains, throwing open the windows, filling those dark, stuffy rooms with light and fresh air. It's a handsome house, but so buried in heavy furniture and draperies, busy wallpaper and useless bric-a-brac, crocheted doilies and runners everywhere, like a lovely woman in a dowdy old dress, but whenever I suggested some change . . . Well, enough said.

I thought I'd successfully eliminated Gina from my life until Rachel decided that you should meet your grandparents, so she and Sarah and Vickie took you on an impromptu visit. My fault, I guess, for making such a mystery of things. They were deeply shocked by what they called my mother's decadent lifestyle. It wasn't until years later that I learned what really happened that day, and by then it no longer mattered. At the time your mother absolutely refused to discuss it with me. I simply couldn't get through to her any more. She started complaining of migraines, and I was regularly banished to the spare room. More and more, the Toronto apartment became a sort of refuge.

When I left for good . . . well, it probably won't make much sense to you, it certainly didn't to me. My only defence is that I had no choice.

Junior phoned my office at H&G one day with the news that Gina and Teddy had been arrested, and had hired his dad, Lester Senior, to represent them at a bail hearing. Those were different times, Twig. It was a witch hunt. They were really after Teddy for being gay, and even worse, my mother was accused of being his accomplice in some sort of sex and drug ring! I have to confess my first thought wasn't for them, but rather how it would affect me. When the news hit Stanton House, all hell would break loose.

I went home that night as usual, saying nothing. I guess I'd learned a thing or two about omission from Gina. Everything seemed normal, no hint of anything wrong that night or the following nights, and I started to breathe a little easier. Teddy and Gina dropped Lester Senior and hired some big gun to represent them. My mother got off scot-free as usual. It was poor old Teddy who'd go on trial. We didn't get the Toronto papers at Stanton House. Jimmy Carter's victory in the U.S. election and a rehash of the whole Watergate scandal were hogging the attention of the press, so the story never hit the front pages. The Fitzhelm name was only mentioned in passing. I began to believe I'd gotten away with it.

You were going off to a kids' camp in Alberta that summer. I thought the aunts would veto the idea, but they surprised me by being all for it. I took you to the airport, and had to talk you into wearing the ID pouch around your neck with your ticket in it. You thought it made you look like a baby. Only eight, and very proud of yourself to be travelling on your own. As you joined the other campers, you were so excited you barely remembered to wave to me.

Life went on as usual, except I was missing you a lot. Evan had finally decided to retire, and I had my hands full at work, so I wasn't paying much attention to Teddy's case.

The guys and I made our annual pilgrimage to Algonquin. It turned out to be the last. Junior and Grady were getting married in September. Cam was moving to Vancouver to live with Jeanette, the girl he eventually married, and Ken's new girlfriend was a beautiful East Indian girl called Mina. It was a bittersweet occasion. Definitely the end of an era.

I returned to work. With Evan gone the atmosphere was pretty oppressive. There were rumours that Ronnie Kemper was negotiating to buy out Bill Hayden, and if that happened my junior partnership and small equity wouldn't be worth squat.

The only unusual thing at home was that Ole Jensen drove the aunts into Toronto two days running. Shopping, they said. They had such a suppressed air of excitement I thought they must be planning some surprise for your return. Big-time, as it turned out. They were attending the trial, of course, right in there with all the rest of the vulgar crowd, exactly the kind of public spectacle they claimed to despise.

I got home from work on a Friday night, and had just showered and changed for dinner when I was summoned to the parlour by Sarah and introduced to a man called Flynt.

In a truly diabolical move they'd hired Teddy's defence lawyer to draw up a separation agreement. Who better to know all the juicy details of Gina and Teddy's lives, and to blacken me through association? It was like a tribunal. The three women sat on the loveseat with Vickie in the middle. Loveseat, my God—I've just realized how ironic that is! Flynt stood next to them and I faced them all on a chair pulled in from the dining room.

He then informed me, "It is Mrs. Fitzhelm's wish to terminate your relationship. She claims irreconcilable differences, more specifically that you've been dishonest with her from the outset of your marriage, that you concealed from her certain aspects of your background which would certainly have deterred her from entering into any union with you, and that she has serious concerns about your continued influence on her son." *Her son!* "It is her wish that you leave the house immediately, and not attempt to make any further contact except through myself.

"If you contest," he continued, "I shall take it to court and reveal a family history of instability and details of the unsavoury nature of your upbringing that will certainly result in victory for Mrs. Fitzhelm. You will make no claim on Stanton property and she will make no claim on you with the exception of a monthly support cheque. There will be no divorce."

"We've never had a divorce in the Stanton family." That was from Sarah.

It was only later I discovered that you wouldn't even carry my name.

I told Vickie I loved her, that I couldn't believe this was her idea. I begged her to remember all the good things we'd shared, to break free and start over somewhere else with just the three of us. I asked her to consider how much this would hurt you. I don't think I've ever been so passionate or so eloquent. At one point I thought she might come to me, but my poor sweet Victoria simply wasn't strong enough to go against them. She sat there white-faced, saying nothing, her head down, her shoulders hunched and her hands clenched in her lap, while those two women smiled their tight, triumphant smiles. The thing that really killed me, Twig, was how calculated, how cold-blooded the whole thing was. You see, there was no real malice involved. They didn't hate me, they simply had no further use for me. I swear I'm not a vindictive man or a religious one, but I pray to God those two old biddies roast in an exceptionally hot spot in hell. From the moment you were born, they started driving a wedge between your mother and me, then devoted most of their waking hours to widening the rift. We never stood a chance. I still refuse to believe your mother was in on it. I couldn't have been so wrong about that.

They gave me two hours to clear out, not that I had much to clear. I managed to slip a note under your pillow, but now you tell me you never found it. Not knowing what else to do, I called Junior, and he and Grady took me in.

Junior was ready for a fight, calling Flynt an unprincipled bastard who should be disbarred for his flagrant use of privileged information. I'd refused to sign the agreement, thinking that if I could delay long enough your mother might change her mind. A couple of weeks later I made an attempt to go back with the hope that I might find her alone and talk some sense into her. Just outside Stanton, a police car pulled me over. The cop, a decent guy who'd been fishing with me a few times, got out of the car.

As I rolled down the window he said, "I'm sorry, Eddie. I've got nothing against you, and I hope this can all be straightened out, but I've got my orders, and if you come here again I'm going to have to arrest you."

They'd actually gotten a restraining order. When I discovered they'd enrolled you in that private school I thought I might be able to see you there, but one of your teachers, an old classmate of mine, told me the school had been warned to keep a sharp lookout for me and to inform the police immediately if I was spotted because I might try to kidnap you.

Going to court seemed to be the only answer. Junior and I fought for visitation rights, but the judge ruled completely in your mother's favour. The restraining order was a major factor, despite Junior's argument that there'd never been the least justification for it. If I tried to talk to you, if I was seen anywhere near you or your mother, they'd throw me in jail. The only concession we got was the letters I was allowed to write to you. When you didn't answer, I thought they'd turned you against me, that you'd washed your hands of me. I never dreamed they'd keep them from you altogether. I tried to convince myself you'd be okay, you'd get over it. You still had your mother, and the loss was all on my side. Hell, I don't know what I was thinking. The whole thing was beyond belief, and just when I thought things couldn't get any worse, they did.

It's always been one of my greatest fears that I'd inherit my mother's paralyzing depression. I even talked to Teddy about it once, but he said she'd suffered with it from childhood and assured me that if I hadn't experienced it yet I probably wasn't a candidate. Yes, I was depressed, devastated, a zombie, but I still managed to put one foot in front of the other, and throw myself into my work.

In late September of that year, Junior and Grady got married and moved into their new house. I was very happy for them, but I was a bit of a wet blanket at the wedding, and relieved to have the Jarvis apartment to myself.

News of the breakup had filtered into the office. Most of the staff were sympathetic, but Ronnie Kemper never missed a chance to get his digs in. One morning I found a note on my desk from Bill Hayden, asking me to drop by his office. Ronnie was already there when I knocked on the door. I ignored him and asked Bill what he wanted to talk to me about.

"Ronnie has brought it to my attention that we've had complaints about your handling of some of the accounts."

I bristled. "Which accounts? How many?" I said.

"Enough to cause grave concern. It's been suggested that you've been at best incompetent, and at worst that you've exploited client gullibility."

"I'll be more than happy to hear these complaints, and respond to them."

"That won't be necessary," said Bill. "We've lost one client and another is satisfied to let me deal with it internally and in the strictest confidence. I don't have to tell you how disastrous it would be for the firm if something like this became public. Your family's notoriety has already caused enough talk."

"So, as it stands, I'm subject to the vaguest sort of accusations, and I'm not allowed to know what they are or who's made them. How do you expect me to deal with this?"

"Just be aware that I'll be reviewing your accounts, and monitoring all your dealings until I'm satisfied there's no impropriety."

This was intolerable. It was all I could do not to explode and wipe the ugly smirk off Ronnie's face. I marched stiffly out of the room and went looking for the one person I knew would be straight with me.

Karen and I had remained friends. She knew everything that went on in that office, and had steered me through more than one tricky situation. When I told her what had happened, she laughed.

"Sorry, Eddie, it's just so ridiculous. There were two letters. One was from the Stantons complaining about your handling of the sale of Stanton Construction back in '69, and the other was from Mrs. Dolley's son-in-law claiming you unduly influenced her to his detriment."

It all came clear. Mrs. Dolley was one of my favourite clients, an elegant and autocratic old dame in her eighties who, though a little forgetful at times, had a wicked wit and was sharp as a razor where money was concerned. When her husband died she'd sold their enormous house to spend her remaining years in a lavish retirement complex, living off her considerable income and leaving the principal to be inherited by her only daughter. You can imagine the reaction when her son-in-law tried to have her declared incompetent and assume control of her finances. Apparently she'd turned him down earlier when he'd suffered some business reverses and needed cash.

"If he'd explained his situation and asked for the money in a civil manner I'd probably have loaned it to him," she later told me, "but he demanded it as if he had a right to it. Hannah's such a dish-rag it's hard to believe she's a daughter of mine. He bullies her, you know, and I was damned if I'd let him bully me."

The idea of anyone bullying Mrs. Dolley was ludicrous. Her lawyer had asked me for a statement as to her competence, and I wrote a letter confirming that she had an excellent grasp of her financial affairs. She subsequently added a codicil to her will saying that if anyone in her family attempted to pull anything like that again, she'd leave everything to Christian missions in Africa. I loved that woman. The son-in-law's accusation was sheer vindictiveness.

As for Rachel and Sarah, it was just one more example of the Stanton obsession. Stanton Builders had been a going concern in their father's day, and had continued to prosper as Stanton Construction under their brother, Vickie's father. After he died, the combination of absentee ownership and incompetent management took their toll. The work had pretty much evaporated, and the assets consisted of a sizable chunk of property with rundown buildings and an overgrown yard full of rusting, obsolete equipment and deteriorating supplies. There'd been a fire and the insurance rates had gone sky-high. The business was bleeding money.

One of the former employees, a man called Willets, had made a fair offer and been turned down flat. "Trying to rise above himself" was what Sarah had called it. I put together a simple chart showing how much money had already been lost and projecting future losses. Rachel and Sarah clearly understood, but they just couldn't let go, and although the property actually belonged to Vickie, she wouldn't oppose them. What finally clinched the sale was that Willets upped his offer and agreed to keep the name Stanton Construction for eight years, paying a thousand dollars a year for the privilege. What had prompted the letter was that the eight years were up and Willets had decided the name no longer had any value. It was now T.J. Willets Construction. No Stanton name, no thousand dollars, and it was all my fault.

I suppose I could have fought, but I had no fight left in me. If this didn't drive me out, Ronnie would only find something else. Feeling I owed him an explanation, I called Evan to tell him I was leaving. He said he wasn't surprised and asked me to wait a week before making a move. When he got back to me a few days later he'd spoken to all my clients and advised them to stick with me. Most of them did, including the indomitable Mrs. Dolley. I couldn't believe it. I'd never have presumed to approach them on my own. It only remained for me to negotiate a payoff for my equity and hand in my resignation.

Ronnie Kemper's parting words were, "I guess I should thank you for clearing out all the deadwood, you dumb bastard."

Hayden and Grange is now history. As rumoured, Bill Hayden sold out to Ronnie, and within a year, Ronnie had changed the name to K.C.C., Kemper Creative Capital, an oxymoron if ever I heard one. He almost went belly-up at one point, but managed to salvage it through heavy investment in new technology; however, I read recently that this year's dive in dot-com stocks has sunk it for good. I'm just glad Evan wasn't alive to see it.

At first I worked out of the apartment, but when Junior told me his father was retiring and his office would be empty I jumped at the chance, and Fitzhelm Financial Services was added to the titles on the door. We shared a receptionist and I hired a temp to do typing and filing.

There isn't much to tell you about the years that followed. Basically I worked from eight in the morning 'til seven at night, went home, ate dinner, had a double shot of Scotch, and fell into bed. I was the king of takeout. All the local fast-food places knew me by name and preference.

"Mr. Fitzhelm? Moo shu pork, fried rice, no peppers?"

It was routine that kept me going. Dinner on Wednesdays with Junior and Grady, Friday-night poker at the apartment. On the week-ends if the weather was good I went fishing. I saw a lot of movies. The Russian roulette scene in *The Deer Hunter* gave me nightmares.

I kept writing to you, but my only news came through my old school friend, your math and science teacher. He'd probably have passed on a message if I'd asked, but I didn't know if you'd be able to keep it from your mother, and if the aunts had gotten wind of it, it would have cost him his job and landed me in jail. He said he'd call if you needed anything, and sent me copies of your report cards and school photographs. I did venture out to the odd school function where I knew there'd be a crowd, but only long enough to catch a glimpse of you.

One bright spot was that Ken and I became weekend regulars at a great jazz club called George's Spaghetti House. His new girl-friend, a Brazilian girl called Sapphyre, sang with one of the bands. The musicians got used to us hanging around, and would stop to talk. When they heard my name was Fitzhelm, they asked if I was any relation to the George Fitzhelm who'd played with the Hot League back in the '30s and '40s. When I said he was my grandfather, it was as if we were suddenly part of the fraternity.

I was introduced to a man called Desmond Miller, who said his grandfather had played with mine. I knew the name from hearing Grandpa and his friend Giorgi talk about the old days, and of course I'd heard Des Miller's brilliant guitar playing on the old 78s. I hope you get to meet Desmond. He's a wonderful man and an accomplished musician, composer, arranger and teacher. He invited me over to his house one afternoon, to show me his guitar collection. His favourite is still his grandfather's guitar, Elsie. He was disappointed that I didn't play, but I assured him I was an avid listener with an extensive collec-tion of classic jazz recordings. When I told him I had all the old Hot League records and arrangements, he got quite excited, and asked if I had the score for something his grandfather had written called "Night Train to Harlem." I found it and gave it to him. He hopes to perform it with full symphony orchestra someday.

By '84 I realized that Ronnie Kemper was right about one thing. My client base was a classic example of the law of diminishing returns. They were dying off one by one, and their heirs were far more inter-ested in paying off mortgages, buying new cars and putting their kids through college than in long-term investment planning and estate management. I'd never had to solicit new clients, and had no idea how to go about it until Junior's wife, Grady, introduced me to a friend of hers, a terrific woman called Marion Gerston. She'd worked for a public relations firm, and had a lot of experience with ads, mailers and phone solicitation, but had quit when she realized there'd be no advancement. I said I'd show her the ropes and, if things went well, let her develop her own client list. She was a natural, smart as a whip and ambitious, with an instinctive grasp of investment. For a brief time we were more than business associates, but it didn't last. In my mind I was still married to your mother. We managed to remain friends, and when my life fell apart for good, it was Marion who held the business together.

Your mother's death knocked the wind right out of me. I broke down and cried when I read it in the newspaper, but suddenly realized this could be my one chance to get you back. I should have talked it over with Junior first, but instead I drove to Stanton for the funeral, thinking I could at least talk to you to ask you how you felt. I never even saw you. I was arrested outside the church and spent the night in jail for violating the terms of the restraining order. Junior got me released on grounds of extreme circumstances.

It's high time I told you about what brought me to this sorry situation.

Every year 'round January or February my lungs would act up. If I was lucky it would be mild bronchitis, but if I wasn't careful it would develop into full-blown pneumonia, and in '86, still grieving over your mother, I was really rundown and suffered a bout which put me in hospital for a week. When I got out I was weak and not up to much. Marion had everything under control, so I decided to stay in bed a few more days, but eventually ran out of food and woke up at midnight one night with my stomach growling and nothing in the fridge. The weather was freezing and the cold air was like a knife in my chest, but hunger drove me to bundle up and venture out to an all-night coffee shop called the Sunshine. I guess you could say it was my local, known for its generous all-day breakfasts.

I was sitting at the counter having pancakes and sausage when I heard a deep barking cough that rivalled my own, and turned to see a small hunched-up figure in a corner booth nursing a coffee cup and a cigarette. The cough shook his whole body, what there was of it, and through several layers of sweatshirts and a hood I could see that he was a pale, pinch-faced boy of about thirteen or fourteen. I asked the waitress what the story was. She said his name was Troy, and that he showed up two or three nights a week. She said he only ever ordered a cup of coffee, then loaded it up with milk and sugar and crumbled soda crackers, sitting there for three, four hours sometimes, but he was just a kid, and unless the place was busy she didn't have the heart to kick him out, especially on a night like this. I told her to get him what I'd had, then paid the bill and started to put my coat on. As I was leaving, he called after me.

"Hey, mister, what's your angle?"

"No angle. Eat up," I said, and left, thinking nothing more about it.

After that I'd see him around the neighbourhood, usually on his own, sometimes with another boy. He'd dip his head or raise his hand when he recognized me on the street, and if I saw him in the Sunshine I'd buy him a hamburger or a couple of doughnuts.

Eventually we started talking, and he told me he lived with his mother, that she worked when she could but that she'd been "sort of sick" for a long time. He couldn't remember his father. When I asked how they managed, he said welfare, but his mother had boyfriends who helped out. He laughed when I asked him about school, said it was a waste of time.

"Ma needs lookin' after," he said. "She ain't got a lot of sense when it comes to men. She tells me to get lost when she brings one of 'em home, but I stick around long enough to make sure there ain't any rough stuff, then I come here to wait it out."

He told me all this in a matter-of-fact way, no bid for sympathy. I was appalled. I couldn't help thinking, what if it were you?

Eventually he trusted me enough to drop by the apartment for something to eat, and to sleep on the couch for a couple of hours. I'd been using the spare bedroom as an office, and I stuck a cot in there for him. He was always gone by morning. In the few months I knew him I never met his mother or knew exactly where he lived, although I did meet his friend Kevin, who lived in the same Regent Park tenement as he did. Kevin's dad was a biker, in jail for drug trafficking, and it worried me that the boys looked up to him as some kind of hero.

One Friday poker night Troy showed up around eleven. He looked like he might bolt, but I told him it was okay, and to help himself to leftover pizza before he went to sleep. Junior raised his eyebrows at me, and asked what I knew about him. I told him what I'd learned, and he shook his head, saying he hoped I knew what I was doing.

Later that week he came into my office. "We need to talk. I've done a little checking on your young friend Troy. He and his buddy Kevin are well known to the police for petty pilfering and shoplifting, chocolate bars, chips and gum mainly, but the last time it was two cartons of cigarettes and uttering threats to a convenience store owner, and the cops figure it will escalate. His mother's a waitress when she works at all, but the bad news is she's a part-time prostitute and full-time junkie. One of her boyfriends is with Vice. He claims she's an informant, but there's little doubt the information flows both ways. Whenever Children's Aid puts Troy in care, she finds him and a phone call brings him running. I know your intentions are good, Eddie, but you need to be careful or you could get sucked into something really ugly. Leslie is just about old enough to choose for himself if he wants to see you, and you don't want to screw that up."

I saw his point, I truly did, but I couldn't just abandon the kid. I told Junior I'd keep my eyes open, and he, not being one to belabour a point, didn't bring it up again.

Marion had doubled our client list, and I made her a partner. Her efforts combined with my own investments had put me in a solid financial position. Where I lived on Jarvis was pretty seedy and the landlord wouldn't put any money into repairs, so I decided it was time to find someplace else to live. I was looking at one of the new lakefront developments, when my building suddenly came up for sale. I had an inspector in, and he said that despite neglect the place was perfectly sound. There were twelve apartments, the location was central and there were signs the neighbourhood was on the verge of an upswing, so I thought it would be worth buying, upgrading, and raising the rents. Besides, the place had been home to me for a lot of years, and I was comfortable there. I put in an offer, and it was accepted.

I called T.J. Willets to recommend a contractor. He said he'd organize it himself, and didn't mind driving downtown to oversee the job. He said with all the new suburbs under construction he had several crews going full time, that buying out the Stantons was the best day's work he'd ever done and he owed me one. He told me about a run-in he'd had with Rachel and Sarah. They'd confronted him about the name change.

"They started chewing on me about respecting history and how the Stanton name meant something in these parts. I told them all the Stanton name meant to me was the difference of a thousand dollars a year going into my pocket instead of theirs. They were mad as two wet hens. Said they'd sue me. I told them to go head-on, I could handle any 'sueage' they wanted to throw at me, and to get off my property. I fired up the backhoe, aimed it in their direction, and had the great pleasure of watching them run for it."

We had a good laugh over that.

He brought in a crew to replace outdated plumbing and wiring and said he figured the roof would hold for another few years. Some tenants complained about the inconvenience, but when I said I'd be more than happy if they'd vacate, most of them backed down, and I started to renovate the empty apartments. I did a lot of plastering and painting and some of the carpentry myself on weekends. It helped to fill the time, and I enjoyed it. I paid Troy and Kevin to fetch coffee and snacks for the workmen, and when one of the tenants, an old boy in his nineties, died leaving no heirs, they helped me clear the place out.

The old man had been even more of a pack rat than I was. The walls were lined with stacks of old newspapers and magazines to the point where there was only a narrow corridor through the rooms, as if he'd been living in a cave. The furniture was junk, but the collector in me wondered if there might be something worth keeping. I had the boys list and sequence the old magazines so they could check with dealers. They ended up making about two hundred dollars.

Around this time Willets reported to me that some tools had gone missing off the job, a tape measure here and a level there, and finally an electric sander. I asked Troy if he'd seen anyone hanging around the place, and he said he'd keep his eyes open. Two days later he came back with everything, saying that Kevin had taken the stuff to sell, and he'd straightened him out. I didn't see much of Kevin after that.

I hate talking about it, but you need to know what happened.

I was up to my ears in renovations, and one night I fell into bed exhausted around eleven. At first it was like a dream. I thought I was with your mother. I gradually came awake to realize it couldn't be her. It was Troy. My reaction was violent. I literally kicked him out of the bed, and when he got up I slapped him hard enough to knock him down again. The minute I did it I felt terrible, but it was too late. I don't even know if he heard my apology as he grabbed his clothes and ran from the apartment. When I calmed down, I tried to think of why he'd do such a thing. I felt as if I hadn't let just him down but also myself and you and anyone else I'd ever cared for, and as usual I hadn't seen it coming. Out of the past, the hard-luck kid rides again.

I didn't see him for about a week after that. I apologized again, saying he'd startled me and I hadn't meant to hit him. He said it wasn't the first time he'd been knocked around and he'd get over it. That made me feel even worse. He started showing up like before, but it wasn't the same. He was spending a lot more time with his friend Kevin, and that worried me.

It was around the time they'd indicted all the heads of the New York crime families, and both boys were fascinated by the mafia. They'd seen *The Godfather*, one and two, several times and really wanted to see *Prizzi's Honor*. It wouldn't have been my choice, but it was Troy's birthday and I'd promised to treat them. I was to pick them up at a nearby convenience store around six-thirty for a seven o'clock show.

As I pulled up, both boys came barrelling out of the store and jumped into the car. I was about to suggest we get some snacks for the movie when I realized Kevin was holding a gun, and as he shouted at me to "go, go, go," he thrust it into Troy's hands. It still hadn't dawned on me what was happening, but I instinctively grabbed the gun from Troy, threw it out the window and stepped on the gas. We didn't get far. We were suddenly surrounded by police cars, and armed officers with their weapons pointed at us. I got out of the car very carefully, and put my hands up. I've never been so terrified.

It was all over in a minute. They handcuffed us, and it began to sink in just how bad it looked for me. I don't know what happened to the boys after that. They took me to the station, booked me, and around midnight I got to make my one phone call to Junior.

Bless Junior. He didn't waste any time with "I told you so's," but immediately got down to the business of finding out what the charges would be. I spent the rest of the night trying to be invisible in a holding cell full of drunks and addicts and others I didn't even want to speculate about. I'll never forget the noise and the stench and the menace.

Junior was there the next morning for my bail hearing. I was charged with armed robbery with violence, employing minors for the commission of a crime, and fleeing the scene. As serious as the accusations were, I had no previous record, and because I was a respected businessman and property owner, the judge decided flight wasn't likely. Bail was set at a hundred thousand dollars. I knew I could lay my hands on fifty and Junior and Ken came up with the other fifty.

I now know that Kevin had stolen the gun from someone in his building. Troy claimed he hadn't known what Kevin planned to do until they were in the store. The store owner had stepped on the alarm when Kevin pointed the gun at him and ordered him to empty the cash register. The man tried to tell him he'd just made a deposit and there was no money, but Kevin blew up, called him a liar, and smashed him hard on the side of the head with the butt of the gun. When the man regained consciousness he said he hadn't seen me in the store, but the fact remained that I had driven away from the scene with the boys and my fingerprints were on the weapon.

I was arraigned, pleaded not guilty, and bail was allowed to stand. Gina sent Teddy to say she'd pay for a lawyer, and more surprisingly, Uncle Gus sent someone from his firm offering to represent me. I suppose he felt he was protecting the family name. I turned them both down, and put my faith in Junior.

The prosecution seemed very sure of their case, and pushed for a speedy trial, which was fine with me. I just wanted it to be over. The boys were to be tried separately as juveniles, and Junior believed the prosecution would try to lay it all on me. He said the prosecutor had got wind of the restraining order and Rachel and Sarah had been interviewed, but were thought to be too obviously vindictive and therefore not credible to a jury—thank God for that.

Teddy and Gina were there every day, and I asked Teddy if he'd move my personal stuff to my old room in Gina's house if I was convicted. I couldn't talk to Gina. I had enough to worry about without enduring her performance of how upset and concerned she was. I did notice that despite skilful makeup she looked ill, and Teddy confirmed this.

I was worried sick that you'd find out, but Rachel certainly wasn't going to tell you and at school you were known as Leslie Stanton. The front pages were full of reports on the hijacking of the cruise ship *Achille Lauro*, and the subsequent murder of an American tourist. I was barely a footnote in the annals of crime.

The prosecutor kept hammering on my driving the getaway car, my fingerprints on the weapon and the age of the boys. He also made a big thing of my not testifying on my own behalf, hinting that I had good reason to be afraid of what might come out in cross-examination. I was worried he'd find some way to introduce the terms of the separation agreement, the restraining order and the arrest at the funeral. He did attempt to put my relationship with Troy on trial. I saw Troy's mother for the first time when she testified. A thirty-something, emaciated, bleached blonde who said she suspected I was up to something, and I must be some kind of pervert, why else would I be interested in a boy his age? Junior objected and the judge asked that it be stricken, but the jury had heard it.

Junior asked to call Troy as a witness. The judge said he'd allow it, but because of his age and upcoming trial the courtroom would have to be cleared of all spectators. They'd gotten him a haircut and put him in a shirt and tie. He looked very small and defenceless in the witness box. Junior asked him point-blank if I'd ever made advances to him or threatened him in any way.

Looking me straight in the eye he said, "Nah, he never laid a hand on me. He's okay."

He swore I'd known nothing about the robbery until I pulled up in the car. Despite Kevin's statement to the contrary and the prosecution's attempts to claim intimidation, Troy wouldn't budge. It didn't get me off, but it probably got me a lighter sentence.

The jury, after two days of deliberation, convicted me on the evidence at hand, but recommended leniency. I was sentenced to ten years, six or seven with good behaviour I was told—but it looks like fate has arranged for an earlier release.

The boys were convicted as juveniles. I have no idea what happened to Troy. Junior said it would be better for me if I didn't ask. My appeal was denied.

Gina died within a year of my conviction. I should have tried to patch things up, but I was pretty angry and sorry for myself, and by the time I pulled out of it, it was too late. She somehow managed to die peacefully in her bed. Junior got me a day-pass to attend the funeral, and my escort was kind enough to remove the cuffs. I thought I'd feel sadness, anger, relief. I wanted to feel something. Even now I find it hard to believe she's really gone, all that restless, random energy burnt out and buried. The worst of it is, the whole time she was killing herself she was killing me too, with that permanent haze of cigarette smoke from the time I was in the womb.

I had a letter from Cam just the other day. He's retiring and his daughter is taking over the business. He says he and his wife Jeanette can't wait to move back here, that he's homesick for the change of seasons and misses the subtle and transitional nature of northern gardens. I hope he doesn't wait too long.

Ken wears his piano tie when he comes to see me. It always makes me smile. Lucky Produce is now a major supermarket supplier. His father is well up in his nineties, but still comes into the office every day and bosses him around. He was in his thirties when he finally settled down, with a girl from Hong Kong, more or less an arranged marriage, but they seem happy. They have three kids and one more on the way. He tells me proudly that his eight-year-old daughter is a natural talent and will be competing in the Kiwanis Music Festival for the first time this year.

Junior's been my rock and my lifeline. I couldn't believe it when he told me he'd contacted you, and I can't tell you how much it means to me that you aren't angry or bitter.

God, I'd give my soul for a Scotch right now. I really enjoyed those miniatures you smuggled in for me the last time. I'd like to take you up on your offer to make cassettes of the old Hot League 78s for me. It would be so great to drift off with that music in my ears. So many memories . . .

(On April 24th, 1991, my father died from a self-administered overdose of barbiturates. The following words are from my last recorded conversation with him. L.A.F.)

"Oh Twig, I had such a wonderful dream just before you came! . . . We were up at the Bay, just the three of us, my grandfather, myself and you . . . It was early morning and we were out in the boat with our fishing gear . . . There was a low-lying mist, and it was as if we were floating on the mist, not the water . . . The sun had just risen and was breaking through the clouds in shafts of coloured light, rose and gold, rose and gold, so beautiful . . . We could hear a loon some-where off in the distance, and I was saying, 'If only we could stay like this forever.'

"So beautiful, so beautiful . . ."

Epilogue

Stanton House, 2006

Yes, it's true. I live at Stanton House with my wife Persy and our twelve-year-old twins, Teri and Gerry. I'd intended to sell the old mausoleum, but Persy fell in love with it, declaring it a perfect place to raise the kids. After a thorough purge of late-Victorian furniture and decor and some much-needed upgrades it's a very different place. It's been nine years and we're very happy here—but let me go back to 1991 and the events following my father's death.

The attic room in my grandmother's house was filled with my father's childhood and I felt so close to him there that I curled up on his bed and opened the journal. It was like stepping out of my grey world into one of colour, not the bright, primary Technicolor of Oz, but the subtle jewel tones of a previous age in another country. At some point Teddy left a sandwich and a thermos of coffee, but the sandwich curled and the coffee went cold.

By the time I finished, I had the solution to everything. I could put five thousand miles and two hundred years between me and Rachel's persecution. I'd be another Chatwin, a modern Gulliver. I'd seek out the voices and the music that spoke to me from every page. I had a quest—to find a family and a fiddle.

I suspect it was this preoccupation that kept me from breaking down at my father's funeral, a simple service in a small chapel and, at my request, no flowers. There were eleven of us, myself, Teddy, Junior and Grady, Ken and Kim, and Marion Gerston. Cameron Mitchell and his wife had flown in from California, and at the last minute I'd called the Jensens. I was pretty shaky when I took the podium to speak and experienced some of that disembodied feeling that usually signalled a bout of depression, but I managed to struggle through it. Teddy had organized coffee and cakes back at McCaul Street so I got to speak with everyone.

As the Jensens were leaving, Margarethe took me aside and said, "I have more sad news, Leslie. Your aunt Sarah passed away about three weeks back. They found her floating in the mill race. She'd got so much worse after you left, but Miss Rachel refused to see it. Insisted it was all vicious gossip. They're saying the poor soul must have wandered out of the house at night and slipped and fallen in the dark. How she got outside without leaving a door unlatched I'll never understand. The place was locked up tight as a drum when I came to work.

"And I think Miss Rachel's been wandering herself. I was tidying her room, and there were her new slippers all caked with mud and stuck way in the back of the closet. She got so angry when I asked her what to do with them. Told me to mind my own business. You know how small she can make you feel sometimes. I'd have quit on the spot, but with Harry in college we really need the money.

"I was taking up her morning tea last week and heard raised voices in her room, some kind of argument. I couldn't imagine who she was talking to, then I heard her say clear as day, 'Don't be a fool, Sarah.' Scared the daylights out of me. I know it wasn't my place, but I called the doctor. She was herself again by the time he arrived, told him I was imagining things. Got another tongue-lashing for that. I'm sorry to add to your burdens, but I'm that worried and I don't know how much longer I can stand it."

I didn't want to hear it. I told her she should do whatever she thought best.

I'd gained considerable insight into my emotional ups and downs from the journal and Gina's letter. That the condition was hereditary was oddly comforting. After a long talk with Teddy, he recommended I see Gina's doctor, who prescribed lithium, but I found myself reluctant to take it as it muffled my senses, as if I were experiencing the world through gauze.

I was the sole beneficiary of my father's will. There was also Gina's estate which my father had never touched, and more astonishingly, Fallowfield Cottage. It made my head swim. I left it all in Marion Gerston's capable hands.

The journal became my map, my focus, my obsession. I grew expert at deciphering Frank Joyner's neat script, Gerry's angular scrawl, Beth's slightly back-slanted and rounded hand, George's precise, almost printed writing, and Gina's careless looping phrases. They were more present to me than poor Teddy, who hovered in the background like a mother hen trying to tempt me to eat. He must have felt as if Gina at her most manic had returned to haunt him.

I picked up my violin for the first time in months and memorized the three melodies of "Joyner's Dream." I started an Internet search for Old Nick. If he was still in Canada I might have a shot at finding him.

Between my Mac and the reference library I was able to piece together information on the village of Kingsfold (off the beaten track, charming and untouched), Saint Stephen by the Falls (a fifteenth-century Gothic gem), and Fallowfield Hall (historic seat of the Fitzhelm baronets, not open to the public). Barker and Son, Fine Silver still existed. Of Graham's Hotel, Madame Felice, The Cleary Academy for Young Ladies, and Lady Teresa Blackwood's London residence I found no trace, though there were still Blackwoods in Derbyshire.

The present baronet at Fallowfield was Sir Henry Fitzhelm, forty-seven, president and CEO of the Goldring Corporation. I wrote to introduce myself as Leslie Archibald Fitzhelm, great-grandson of George Francis Fitzhelm. I informed him of my father's death, acknowledging that I was a complete stranger while reminding him of the arrangement between my great-grandfather and the first Sir Henry regarding Fallowfield Cottage, and saying I wished to stay there for part of my journey. Ten days later I had a phone call from Sir Henry himself saying he was aware of the Canadian connection and that although he'd need some bona fides from me, he was inclined to accept me at face value. The family would look forward to welcoming me at Fallowfield. He generously offered the use of Goldring's guest suite while I was in London.

I applied for a passport and a credit card, bought a camera and luggage, and learned to drive. Part of my inheritance had been the last of my father's old Volvos. Teddy white-knuckled it with me through my learner's permit and had champagne on ice when I passed my driver's test. I spent a quiet Christmas with Junior and Grady.

An organized approach was best. I would begin at the beginning.

With a transcript of the journal and Gina's letter in my backpack, and my violin case under my arm, I boarded the plane for England in March of '92, to be welcomed at Heathrow by the absolute worst of English weather, a cold, grey, steady drizzle. I rented a car, consulted a road map and cautiously ventured out on the left-hand side of the road through a maze of roadways and roundabouts that eventually took me south. I've never been a confident driver and that trip scared me witless. Persy says I'll never die in a car accident, but rather at the hands of some enraged fellow motorist. She usually drives when we're together.

Several hours and several wrong turns later I pulled into the courtyard of the Kingsfold Inn, and was shown through an equally confusing maze of hallways and steps up and down to a narrow but oddly high-ceilinged room overlooking the River Bliss. It was, they said, the only accommodation they had with attached lavatory. In fact the bathroom was bigger than the bedroom, which, I deduced from the one tall window and the elaborate mouldings that crowned three of the walls, was a slice of something much larger. I had a dismal dinner of greasy mutton stew and some sort of sponge cake with jam on it, washed it down with warm beer, and retired for the night, thankful for the down-filled comforter on the bed and the ski underwear Teddy had recommended, warning me that some parts of England were still strangers to central heating—not a propitious beginning to Fitzhelm's great adventure.

Morning was more promising with some watery sunlight breaking through the clouds. At breakfast, cold sausage and rubbery eggs, cold toast and margarine, but with tea strong enough and hot enough to blister the roof of my mouth, the waitress informed me, as near as I could understand, that the inn was a patchwork of several buildings incorporating the original coaching inn, the old grain exchange and what was formerly a private house.

The motherly desk clerk who gave me directions to Saint Stephen by the Falls warned me I'd need "proper footwear, love." The High Street revealed a mishmash of storefronts at ground level, but above I caught glimpses of the original half-timbered facades. At a sort of general store and post office I bought a heavy pullover, thick woollen socks and wellingtons, then headed up the slippery cobblestoned path along the River Bliss following the noise of the falls, and there, illuminated by a single shaft of sunlight and swathed in mist, was Saint Stephen.

The dark stone of the church and old grave markers was mottled with bright green moss and the slates on the roof still glistened from the rain. The turf was spongy underfoot and, although I could see my breath, the air hinted of spring to come. The massive oak door swung silently open to reveal a cold, cavernous and gloomy interior, barely penetrated by glimmers of amethyst light from the narrow side windows, and the jewelled glow of a lovely old rose window through which the pale sun illuminated a simple stone altar with brass cross and candlesticks. There was a pervasive odour of mildew, snuffed candles and oil soap.

As my eyes adjusted I became aware of a shadowy figure to my right in an alcove formed by the stone supports for the ancient roof beams. My heart leapt. Surely this was John Joyner's carving of Saint Stephen the Martyr, his hand raised in blessing. Mindful of the polished stone floor, I slipped off my muddy boots, steadying myself by holding on to a knob at the end of the last pew, and sensed the knob itself had features. My hand was in fact resting on the head of Saint Nicholas himself! I had the most peculiar feeling, as if time had shifted and if I walked out the door and back down to the village it would all be as it had been over a hundred and fifty years ago. I was startled by a voice that seemed to come from Saint Stephen himself.

"All contributions gratefully received by the Saint Stephen organ fund."

A small, gaunt figure emerged from the shadows and revealed itself to be an old man dressed from head to toe in dusty black who peered up at me and identified himself as Sam Treadwell, the verger. I couldn't believe my luck.

"Just the man I want to see," I said, and introduced myself, saying I was seeking information on the Joyner family.

"And why would you be enquiring after Joyners?" he asked.

"My great-great-grandmother was a Joyner and I'm curious about the family," I replied.

"Well now, let me think. If I recollect properly, there's been no Joyners here since 1880 or thereabouts. I can show you the stones if you like. The last Treadwell buried here was my great-uncle Roland who died in 1942 at a hundred and one. Us Treadwells have cared for the church ever since I can remember. Don't know who'll do it when I'm gone. Most of the family lives over to Fenton-on-Bliss now. My good wife and I will be the last to live at the farm. None of the children seems to want that life, and I'm too old to work it properly. They're impatient to sell the place out from under us, but I intend to see they have a good long wait for it, God willing. My son Walter and his boys are in the building trade, you see, fancying up old ruins that was abandoned years ago and selling them to city folk who seem fools enough to buy anything. Treadwell Traditional Restorations they call it, but a pig dressed in silk is still a pig in my view."

He examined me out of the corner of his eye as he led me into the churchyard, past the D'Ursey family tomb to a group of stones half buried in brambles. There, surrounded by Treadwells, were the Joyners. One stone each for John Joyner and his wife, Molly, a broader stone with its poignant quote from Milton for Frank Joyner, his wife, Jean, and their infant daughter, a simple slab which read "Gerald Joyner, b. 1834, d. 1882—May he finally rest," and last of all "Clare Joyner, spinster of this parish, b. 1820, d. 1896." As we stood there in respectful silence I could almost feel their presence.

We sat down on a stone bench to talk and I asked about the Cooper family.

"Ah, that bunch. Breed like rabbits they do. They're everywhere. Old Timothy's still stablemaster up at the Willows and his oldest boy is head trainer now. Don't know why Squire Bliss puts so much stock in 'em. They're a wild lot, but clever with their hands I'll grant you. That young Joseph over to the garage has kept my tractor running long past the time when it should have expired. Wish there was a doctor could do as much for me. If it's Coopers you want, drop in to the pub at the inn tonight. Being a Saturday there'll be twenty or more of them drunk as lords and playing that heathen music."

We parted cordially with his invitation to early supper the following afternoon before evensong. It seemed I was now part of the family.

I stopped at a little tea shop on the High Street for a late lunch. They were a bit rattled by the unexpected customer and most of the dishes on the menu were "off, love," but I had some delicious potato and leek soup and crusty bread with local cheese. Persy says I'm much more human when I've eaten well. I returned to my room to write down the events of the morning while they were still fresh in my mind. I really missed my computer.

The tea shop was closed for dinner, so I was at the mercy of the cook at the inn: grey shepherd's pie, limp greens and lumpy custard with jam, washed down with hard cider. The wine was listed only as red or white and my courage didn't extend to sampling it.

At eight o'clock I walked through the private lounge and into the public bar to be met by a wall of voices and cigarette smoke. The voices dropped as every head turned toward me, then resumed as they turned back. In one corner the floor had been cleared to accommodate an old man tuning a guitar and a pretty, apple-cheeked girl of about fifteen with a mass of dark curls holding a fiddle. They were joined by a rough-looking man with a concertina, a pock-faced boy with an electric bass, a long-haired drummer, and a handsome woman of about forty who sat down at a battered upright piano. I found a space at the bar and ordered another cider.

The music was wonderful, traditional, with a pumping beat that made you want to get up and dance. They played non-stop for about two hours with various members of the crowd getting up and joining them to sing or take over one of the instruments, all except the fiddle, which remained in the hands of this remarkable young girl. She was so concentrated, alternately playing like a devil or an angel, that I couldn't take my eyes off her. When they finally took a break I made my way over to her and told her how amazing I thought she was. I said that I played as well and asked about her fiddle.

"It's called the grandfather fiddle on account of it was handed down from my great-grandfather, Gerry Cooper, the finest fiddler that ever was in this locality. 'Twas my grandda taught me to play, and when he passed by rights it should have gone to my da, but Aunt Betty said he didn't have the music in him like I did, so it come to me. It's an English fiddle, this is, and I'll stack it up against any fiddle made anywhere," she said proudly.

I couldn't contain my excitement. It had to be Frank Joyner's fiddle. I longed to hold it, but my eagerness must have been too obvious, for when I reached out, she stiffened, saying no one handled it but her. I apologized and went outside to clear my head and find some relief from the smoke. I wasn't alone. Three formidable-looking men had followed me, effectively blocking any retreat.

One of them said quietly, "And what would you be wanting with our Tina?"

Better to be taken for a harmless idiot than a potential predator. I pasted a big grin on my face, vigorously pumped each of their hands, and went into conversational overdrive, saying I was Leslie Fitzhelm, and what a pleasure it was to meet the famous Cooper family, and that fiddle, what a marvellous instrument, and that music, I'd never heard anything like it. I went on to say I was a Canadian visitor researching my family history here in Kingsfold, and did they have any knowledge of my ancestors, the Joyners? The two younger ones looked mystified, but the third, older one gave me a hard look and said I'd best speak to Old Betty. It transpired he was Tina's father, Silas Cooper, and the other two were her brothers.

They closely escorted me back inside, steered me to a bench by the coal fire and presented me to what looked like a bundle of different coloured shawls. It turned to reveal a fierce old female face surrounded by wisps of white hair, with one tobacco-stained claw clutching a hand-rolled cigarette and the other a pint mug. She was clearly unimpressed.

"Don't stand there gawking, you young lout. Sit down and state your business."

This, I discovered, was Tina's great-aunt, Old Betty. I introduced myself and explained that I believed Tina's fiddle was built by my several-times-great-grandfather, Frank Joyner.

"That fiddle has been played by us Coopers for well over a hundred year. I have the proof," she said.

I assured her I didn't question the ownership, but only wanted to confirm its history.

"As to whether you handle it, that's up to Tina, but if you care to come by and see me on Monday I might have something for you. I'll send someone to fetch you. You'd never find it on your own. Heard you'd been over to Saint Stephen talking to that sanctimonious old goat Sam Treadwell about Joyners. Suspected you'd get 'round to me sooner or later." She stubbed her cigarette, lifted her pint and turned her face back to the fire. My audience was at an end.

The music resumed. I bought a round and had quite a few new chums by the time the evening ended. Having grown up in a dry household I've learned to enjoy a drink but don't have much head for it, and the cider was both deceiving and deadly. I vaguely remember being supported up to my room by Silas Cooper and one of his sons and dumped unceremoniously on the bed, where I passed out. I woke about four in the morning, still fully dressed, with parched throat, a blinding headache and an urgent need to piss. Even in my addled state I could see the room had had a thorough going-over, but nothing seemed to be missing. I fell back into bed and didn't open my eyes again 'til almost eleven.

The good news was I'd missed breakfast. The bad news was that it being Sunday and the cook's day off, there were cold sausage rolls for lunch, which sat on my stomach like lead, a perfect addition to my massive hangover. I spent the early part of the afternoon writing down what I could remember of the previous night, then set off on the two-mile trek to Sam Treadwell's farm, figuring the walk would do me good.

The place was little changed from John Joyner's description, a rectangular two-storey stone house and outbuildings around a stone paved yard. I was greeted at the door by Sam's wife, Iris, plump as he was thin. The aroma emanating from the old cast-iron stove was tantalizing.

"I hope you don't mind," she said, wiping her hands on her apron, "It's just game pie and lemon curd tart. We eat lightly on a Sunday now with the children all grown and gone." She offered me a glass of homemade ginger beer, saying, "We've nothing stronger in the house. The doctor's forbidden Sam to smoke or drink spirits."

At this point Sam himself appeared, waved me into the parlour and shut the door behind us. He showed me to a chair by the fire, then, with an exaggerated wink, poured three inches of a pale amber liquid from an earthenware bottle into two thick glass tumblers and lit up a blackened old pipe.

"Iris worries about me, you understand, but a little nip just between us men and kinsmen at that won't go amiss."

We solemnly raised our glasses and I nearly choked. It must have been over a hundred proof. You didn't really get to swallow it. It sort of exploded in the mouth leaving an essence of apple on the palate with a slightly flowery aftertaste, but I felt it right down to my toes. I was more economical with the next sip, but finally drained the glass, and resolved to find more of it before I left Kingsfold. We chatted further about the Treadwell family and his work at Saint Stephen, then he stood up and squeezed my shoulder.

"Come along, lad. I've got something to show you," he said with another wink.

My knees were a bit wobbly as I followed him back through the kitchen to a little door at the end of the house which opened onto a long, low room with a workbench down one side and a store of various kinds of woods lining the other. In one corner was a stone sharpening wheel with a treadle, and neatly hung over the scarred workbench was a row of well-worn, handmade tools. The smell of wood shavings was like perfume.

"When I'm not carrying out my duties at Saint Stephen I spend most of my time here. Iris says it keeps me out from underfoot, but it keeps her out from under mine as well. Makes for an 'armonious union all 'round. Come have a look at this."

Lying on the workbench was a simple but beautiful cross about two feet long and a foot and a half wide, which, he informed me, was made of beechwood. Its hand-rubbed surface was inlaid with ivy leaves in pale green and at the bottom a scroll with the old English letters *IHS*.

"That's for the vestry," he said. "The old silver one was nicked by vandals. Nothing sacred any more."

He then took down a rectangular bundle from a shelf above the workbench and peeled back the brown-paper wrapping to reveal some old ledgers. When he opened the first I saw the words *Frank Joyner—his work—1829*. The handwriting was unmistakable, the strokes as sharp as if Frank had just lifted the pen.

"My great-uncle Roland followed these books right up to the time he died, and it was he who instructed me as a boy. I'm the last in the family to know how to do this kind of work. The young ones today don't have the patience nor the inclination."

I was awestruck, speechless as I reverently turned the pages filled with Frank Joyner's meticulous drawings, measurements, records of materials used, each ending with the date of completion and payment received. Just then we heard the sharp clang of a bell.

"That'd be Iris. Supper's on the table." He returned the ledgers to their place on the shelf.

Supper lived up to its promise. The game pie was indescribably delicious with a light, flaky crust and the lemon tart not too sweet, just perfect, although the ginger beer seemed flat and tasteless after Sam's ambrosia. Iris, I learned, had been the cook for the Bliss family at the Willows for almost fifty years, but was now retired. I complimented her and she beamed as I told Sam what a lucky man he was, then we left for Saint Stephen and the evensong service.

The atmosphere in the church could not have been more different. There was a golden glow from the old hanging lamps and the lace-covered altar was bathed in candlelight. The brass cross had been replaced with a fine old silver and garnet one. There were about a dozen souls in attendance, mostly elderly women.

I sat at the back in the Treadwell pew with Saint Nicholas at my shoulder as the vicar intoned, "The Lord is in his holy temple: let all the earth keep silence before him."

It was as familiar and enveloping as a warm bath. I half expected to hear the wobbly sopranos of the aunts singing the responses. The words came automatically, even the verses of "Abide with Me." When Sam approached with the collection plate I was generous. The organ was in serious need. At the conclusion I spoke with the vicar. He informed me that he was compiling a scholarly work on pagan survivals in rural communities. He was pleasantly surprised to discover that I knew of the Old Horse and the Saint Stephen's Day celebration, saying that Father Basil's detailed observations in the parish records had been most valuable to his research. Sam and I agreed to meet again before I left Kingsfold. As he departed his raspy tenor floated back to me through the darkness singing "A Mighty Fortress Is Our God."

I was jolted awake the next morning by a pounding at my door, one of the Cooper boys come to escort me to Old Betty. I splashed cold water on my face, ran a brush through my hair and threw on my clothes. He declared me pretty enough, and we set off in a bone-rattling old truck with my empty stomach lurching in protest.

Betty lived not in some rustic cottage, but in a relatively modern row house in a sort of suburb between Kingsfold and Fenton-on-Bliss. It was just as well I wasn't on my own as all the houses looked depressingly alike and few doors had numbers. Once inside the kitchen, however, similarity ended. It was oppressively warm and there was a pungent odour. A small black-and-white TV flickered silently in one corner, but the walls were lined with wooden shelves crowded with glass jars of various sizes and contents, whole leaves and teas, roots and twigs, powders and murky liquids, and even the skull of a small animal and some odd-shaped things I didn't care to conjecture about. If the vicar was looking for pagan survivals he didn't have far to go.

Betty appeared in a faded housedress and shapeless sweater, and my escort departed.

"Good morning, Mrs. Cooper. Thank you for agreeing to see me."

"It's *Miss* Cooper, but Betty does me. Come sit. I'm a martyr to my feet."

I pulled up a chair as she poured me a steaming mug of some sort of tea with scum on the top and a bittersweet aroma. I took a cautious sip and found it quite pleasant.

"That should settle your stomach and take care of that head of yours. Not used to drink, I expect. You were pretty legless the other night and I'm sure you had a tot or two with Sam Treadwell, the old soak. I've just had a chat with a friend of yours. He's been waiting on you."

At this point the whole visit went sideways.

"Friend?" I said. "I don't believe I have any friends here."

"Nothing to do with me. Says you called 'im up in the churchyard, a big handsome devil wants to know where the hell is Old Nick."

Despite the evidence of my eyes the room suddenly seemed very crowded.

"Um, could you tell him . . . Tell him . . ."

"Tell him yourself. He's dead, not deaf."

I was in serious trouble. Somehow this was all starting to seem reasonable to me.

"Uh, where is he?"

"There by the aga, large as life."

I turned toward the aga, and feeling idiotic addressed myself to thin air.

"If I'm speaking to Gerry Joyner, Old Nick was stolen from Beth's son George in Canada back in 1918. I'm trying to find him."

I had a brief impression of agitation, then nothing.

"He's gone off in a right old temper. Says he'll see about that. You need to be more careful what you wish for, young Leslie. Now about this fiddle business. Have a gander at this."

She held out a sheet of yellowed paper and I recognized Beth's handwriting. I copied it for my notes.

16th day of March, 1882

Dear Uncle Jos,

I wish to commit to your particular care the fiddle built by my grandfather, in memory of the great affection you held for my father and he for you, and also for the many kindnesses you have shown to myself and my family. I know that it could not be in better hands and pray that it will bring you much pleasure.

Yours in eternal friendship,
Elizabeth Joyner

"There's your proof," said Betty, and I hastened to assure her I'd never doubted it. "Now give us your hand."

Thinking the visit was over I put out my hand to shake hers, but she spread it, palm up, on the table between us.

"You've recently lost someone dear to you, a parent I should think, and you've come into some money and property. See, there's a diamond in your hand. Don't worry, I shan't ask you to cross my palm with silver," she cackled. She traced the lines with a nicotine-stained fingernail. "Humph . . . a lot of pain and anger and grief unfaced, and a long life of ups and downs still ahead of you, Leslie. You'll need something to keep you from mischief, lead you to your true love, all that twaddle."

She pressed into my hand a smooth black pebble about the size of a pigeon's egg with a white ring around it and a leather thong threaded through a hole in it, and watched as I hung it around my neck with my father's Saint Christopher.

"Now tell me what you think of our Tina."

I told her I thought Tina was a wonder and her inspired playing combined with her youth and prettiness might make a star of her.

"That's what I'm afraid of," she said. "It's a wicked world out there and I won't be around to watch out for her if she leaves here. Her ma died when she was but nine and she don't see eye to eye with her new stepma, so she come to me. I've been teaching her the old ways. She has the healing gift, but the music has the stronger pull. 'Twas my little brother, her grandda, taught her and he made me promise the fiddle would go to her when he died. Her stepma has pretty grasping ways with a lot of things that don't belong to her so I had a scrap on my hands, but her da backed me up and said she should have it." Old Betty suddenly looked very old indeed and said, "I'm knackered. The dear departed always wear me out. Good day and good luck to you, Leslie. You'll find your own way back."

The sound of the TV rose as I left.

I wandered around aimlessly for an hour or more until some good Samaritan gave me a lift back to the Kingsfold Inn. The world as I knew it had cracked down the middle with God knows what spilling out, but I didn't care. I felt fantastic. I filled the old high-backed iron bath with hot, rusty water and sank into it in a trancelike state. As the events of the last three days floated through my mind, I found myself fantasizing about living in Kingsfold, buying the Treadwell farm, playing in the pub on Saturday nights. It all seemed so plausible.

I woke shivering a couple of hours later with a clear head, a growling stomach and the conviction that I'd better get out of there before I went totally 'round the bend. I recorded the extraordinary events of the morning and went in search of food.

I endured another dreary dinner and was contemplating a solitary evening when an unexpected visitor stepped into the guest lounge.

"Hey, Mr. Fitzhelm." It was Tina Cooper, and under her arm was a plain wooden box fastened with a leather belt. "Aunt Betty says it's okay to let you see the fiddle."

"Please call me Leslie. You heard about my visit then."

"Oh yeah. She told me all about it when I got home from school. Heard she gave you some of her brew. She says that'll fetch the truth out of anyone."

"What the hell *is* that stuff?"

"Nobody knows. She's pretty close-mouthed about it, but I think it's some kind of fungus with a bit of chamomile thrown in to take away the taste. The boys have been after her to let them sell it, say they could make us all a fortune, but she won't give it up. She'll pass it on to me eventually."

This was not your average fifteen-year-old.

"Did your aunt Betty tell you everything that happened?"

"Oh, you mean the visitor. Yeah, she said you had a natter with some old geezer."

"Do you see them too?"

"Ever since I was a kid. They'd gather 'round my bed at night and stare at me. Didn't bother me. Just thought they were part of the family. Didn't learn 'til later that nobody else could see 'em. They don't talk much. Guess they figure no one can hear 'em anyway. We had quite a crowd at the pub the other night. The music pulls 'em in."

Tina opened the box to reveal Frank Joyner's fiddle wrapped in flannel. Not much to look at, dull brown with a long, narrow body. She lifted it out of its wrapping and offered it to me. I asked her to wait a minute, and raced to my room to get my penlight and grab my own violin. When I returned she handed me the fiddle and I shone the light into one of the "f" holes. There, neatly burned into the wood, were the initials *J.F.J.* and the date *1822*. Knowing its history and that it was modelled on Old Nick, I was desperate to hold it and play it. I looked at Tina and she nodded.

Fitting it under my jaw, I picked up the bow and played a little piece of Bach. The tone was warm and rich with an extraordinary resonance, as if it were humming along with the melody. I looked at her in amazement.

"I know," she said. "Crazy, isn't it? Sometimes my head gets to buzzing so strong it feels like my feet have left the ground."

I reverently laid the fiddle back in its box and handed her my violin. She played the same piece, almost note for note, then sat back and smiled.

"It's lovely. Dark and sweet, like chocolate."

She handed it back to me and I began to play the first of the melodies in "Joyner's Dream."

"Ah, 'The Downcast Lover,'" she said. "That's local, that is."

We played it together, stopping twice to discuss some point of technique, then continued with "Roll of the Dice" and "Rakehelly," finally lifting our bows to find we had an audience, Silas, standing in the doorway, and the inn's burly barman, his arms folded on the bar and tears in his eyes.

"I haven't heard that since my wedding day thirty years ago," he said, and offered us a drink on the house to play it again, but the moment was over.

I stood up and said with a bow, "Good night, Miss Cooper. It's a pleasure to know you."

Turning quite pink she replied, "Bye, Leslie. Sorry you won't be sticking around. Aunt Betty gave me this for you. Says it'll help you fight your devils." She placed a little plastic bag of tea in my hand. "Come back in July when we have the Cooper family gathering at the old campground by the river. We get folk from all over, a few caravans still and lots of music. You'd enjoy it." And then she was gone.

I picked up my violin, went to bed and dreamt of music and Old Nick.

I'd arranged to meet Sam the next morning at Saint Stephen to photograph John Joyner's saints. He had the work-lights on when I got there and by noon I had everything I wanted. I was more than willing when he invited me back to the farm for lunch. After hearty vegetable soup and biscuits hot from the oven we retired to the parlour once more.

"There's something that's always been a puzzle to me," Sam said. He hauled out a massive old bible, opened it to the record of marriages, births and deaths, and ran his finger down to the marriage of John Joyner and Molly Treadwell and the births of their three children, Gabriel, Frank and Clare. "Now here's what it is. You see my ancestor Gabriel bears the name Treadwell when it's written his parents were Joyners."

I was pleased to be able to explain the agreement between Thomas Treadwell and John and Molly Joyner regarding their first-born son.

Sam was silent for a moment, his frown reflecting the turmoil of his thoughts, and finally he said, "So by rights we should all be Joyners."

"Sam," I said, "you're as much a Treadwell as you are a Joyner and so am I though my name is Fitzhelm."

He considered this, then slapped his knee and declared, "Exactly right. We'll say no more about it." He poured two more glasses of his special tipple and we drank a silent toast.

Perhaps I was reassuring myself as much as him. In recent years I've relaxed enough to allow the Stantons back into my family equation, even returning the portraits of Archibald and Amelia to their former place on the dining room wall. Persy, an avid gardener, says it's a promising sign of late-blooming maturity.

I thanked Sam for his hospitality and asked if there was anywhere I could purchase some of his elixir. He led me across the yard to the old smithy and opened a big brassbound lock with an ornate key.

"Now that's Roland's work, that lock," said Sam. "Still breaks sweet as you please. These days there's some would steal the gold out of your teeth as soon as look at you, and besides, what Iris don't know can't ruffle her."

Adjusting to the dim light, I spied up in the rafters an odd contraption like a giant patchwork umbrella and a gaudily painted wooden horse's head. Then I caught a flash of copper. Sam switched on the light and all was revealed.

"When the old still gave up the ghost I was plotting how to build a new one, but a nephew of mine went on holiday to Portugal and found me this little beauty."

It was a simple apparatus, an enormous copper kettle that sat over the firepit of the old forge, capped with a sort of inverted funnel and a temperature gauge. The neck of the funnel was soldered to some copper tubing, first curved like the neck of a swan then coiled. The coil was immersed in a tub of water, which Sam said was piped ice cold from the well, and the end was poised to allow the alcohol to drip into a big glass jug. He then showed me the hand-hewn oak casks he aged it in.

"The mash is mainly Pippins and Pearmains from the old orchard with some windfalls thrown in to speed up fermentation and some rosehips for flavour. About three years does it, though it improves further with time." He carefully packed two of the earthenware jugs with straw in a sturdy handmade wooden crate and presented it to me.

"Sam," I said, shaking his hand, "you're an artist in everything you do."

"Not a bit of it," he replied with a final wink, "but I'm a champion journeyman."

No one saw me off when I left the following morning. I turned in the car at Fenton-on-Bliss and took the train to London as Beth and Nan had done. My journey couldn't have been more different. I shared a comfortable compartment with an elderly lady reading Ruth Rendell and a businessman immersed in the contents of his briefcase, while I reviewed my notes and studied my map of London.

At Euston Station I was met by a uniformed chauffeur holding up a sign with my name. He said he was David, and silently whisked me away behind tinted glass through the afternoon traffic to an enormous old building on the Thames near the recently completed Canary Wharf. I later learned it was the original Goldring warehouse, the same one where George Fitzhelm's career as a shipping clerk had come to its ignominious end. It presently housed the corporate offices of the Goldring Corporation, the ornate nineteenth-century charm ending abruptly with the facade.

I was greeted by a uniformed security guard with the name "Lonnie" embroidered on his jacket who escorted me by elevator to a modern top-storey addition. I followed him down a thickly carpeted hallway to a featureless double door. He unlocked it and handed me the key.

Coming from the Spartan amenities of the Kingsfold Inn to this palace of glass and steel was surreal. First off, it was warm. Even the marble floor of the foyer was heated. I descended three steps into the living room to be swept away by a panoramic view of the Thames. While there I'd sometimes go to the window to glance out and suddenly realize I'd been standing for twenty minutes or more mesmerized by the movement of traffic on the river.

Off the living room there was a kitchen with a full bar and wine rack and a well-stocked refrigerator. I found menu forms which one could attach to the outside of the door to have meals delivered from the executive dining room somewhere downstairs, and optimistically checked off a breakfast order for eight o'clock the next morning. I stretched out on one of the opulent leather couches, savouring the view and feasting on pâté and port, but couldn't overcome the feeling that at any moment someone would come to throw me out.

I chose the bedroom without a floor-to-ceiling window in the ensuite. Persy later told me the glass was treated so that no one could see in. I felt ridiculous hanging my meagre wardrobe in the huge walk-in closet. The bed was like a football field. Luxury aside, the place was overheated and airless and I slept fitfully, throwing off the bedclothes and wrestling with giant pillows until morning, when I was awakened by a gentle knock at the bedroom door. By the time I found a bathrobe, any human presence had disappeared. My breakfast had been delivered, and with it two letters.

One, I was delighted to see, was a reply from a man called Clarence Blackwood who was writing a biography of his illustrious ancestor and was also, he informed me, custodian of the Blackwood collection of rare nautical books. He wrote that Windward House had been sold to a London physician shortly after Lady Elizabeth Blackwood's death. He'd enclosed copies of some letters written by Lady Blackwood to her husband from the Covington Square address.

The second letter, embossed with the Fitzhelm crest, read as follows:

Dear Mr. Fitzhelm:

Welcome to London. Sir Henry apologizes that he's unable to greet you personally as he will be out of the country for about a fortnight. He's asked me to extend to you the full hospitality of the Goldring Corporation. I hope you find your accommodation satisfactory and will alert me if there's anything you require. I'll be happy to procure tickets to the ballet, opera or any plays you might like to see.

If you haven't already discovered it, there's a computer behind the bifold doors next to the hospitality area, and Lonnie has keys to a company car for your use, although David is available to drive you if you wish. Please contact me if I can be of any service.

Yours truly, Constance Beard
Executive Assistant to Sir Henry Fitzhelm

It concluded with phone and fax numbers and an e-mail address. Perhaps the formidable-sounding Ms. Beard could suggest where I might upgrade my wardrobe. My jean jacket definitely wouldn't cut it here. She answered on the first ring.

"Certainly, Mr. Fitzhelm. I can send up Sir Henry's tailor if you wish, or David can take you someplace suitable, if you'll pardon the expression." It was a promising hint of humour.

As I was starting to feel a bit claustrophobic I opted for the shopping trip. When I asked about researching London locations in the 1880s, she offered to do preliminary searches for me, saying she had resources that would speed up the process. I then went online to pick up messages and to check for any responses to my queries for Old Nick. There was one message about a fiddle with a carved head, but the head was female.

The next morning David delivered me to a modest-looking storefront called Gracey and Sons where an impeccably dressed man introduced himself as the grandson of the original Gracey. If he found my appearance less than prepossessing, he didn't bat an eye.

"Ms. Beard has suggested I provide you with whatever you'll need for your stay in London and for the country at Fallowfield. Let me introduce you to Cranwell, our tailor."

I couldn't help thinking of Beth's experience with Madame Felice, for, like Beth, it seemed all decisions were out of my hands. Shivering in my shabby boxers I was measured in every imaginable way, was embarrassed when asked if I dressed to the left or right, and gratified when assured that I'd made an excellent choice of suiting material from samples that all looked alike to me. I was to have what he called a lounge suit, a dinner jacket, a navy blazer and grey trousers, a light overcoat, and something called a hacking jacket, as well as all the accoutrements. Having worn Aunt Rachel's taste in ready-mades all my life, it was quite an adventure. After a final fitting, everything would be delivered and I looked forward to filling at least a tenth of my closet. The subject of cost never came up and I was too intimidated to ask. The next stop was a shoe store recommended by Mr. Gracey. Following his advice I picked out a pair of black dress shoes, some loafers and a sturdy pair of brogues, and then we were off to Marks and Spencer to replace my embarrassing underwear.

There was a stack of research waiting for me when I returned to the suite. The first pages were a property search on Windward House showing the purchaser as Dr. E.B. Candless and that the present owner was a Mrs. Alison Candless. I wrote immediately telling her of my interest in the history of the house and asking if she'd be so kind as to let me see it.

Graham's Hotel was no more, but the address proved to be a few blocks from where I'd arrived at Euston Station. Ms. Beard had found only one reference to the Cleary Academy, that being in the biography of a famous London hostess who had attended it from 1885 to 1887. Barker Fine Silver was still in existence but no longer associated with the Barkers or the Greens. She'd found no reference to Madame Felice or Fanny Gosling.

I'd been riding pretty high on my success in Kingsfold, but the prospect of a fruitless London search was really bringing me down. When I checked my supply of meds I was dismayed to discover I was almost out. I needed to find a doctor, but wasn't keen to expose my frailties to Constance Beard and thus to Sir Henry. I was fingering the stone around my neck when I recalled the sense of well-being generated by Old Betty's tea and Tina's words about fighting my devils.

An hour later I was propped up by a mound of pillows on the enormous bed giggling like a kid at a video cassette of some elaborately costumed martial arts film with bad Australian dubbing. After a series of wild dreams I woke up feeling more optimistic. Perhaps if I modified the dosage . . .

After breakfast David dropped me back at Euston Station. I'd drawn a rough map of the route Beth and Nan had probably walked. The farther I went, the more rundown and graffitied the buildings became. When I finally stopped at the correct street number, wide granite steps and a large arched portico with a keystone still bearing the soot-stained title GRAHAM'S HOTEL were the only remnants of its former respectability. To the left of the entrance was a tattoo parlour and to the right a shop selling lingerie and sex toys. A crudely lettered sign advertised rooms by the day or week. No locals with long memories here.

Next morning there was a note from Mrs. Alison Candless inviting me to tea at Windward House the following Monday, three days away. I occupied the time reading Tess's letters and transferring my handwritten notes to the computer. I made a hard copy to add to my printout of the journal, sent the file to my computer in Toronto, then deleted everything.

Monday morning my new clothes arrived along with an invoice for a figure that made me gasp. I had to remind myself that I now had money and everything I'd bought was made to last. I set out for tea feeling rather self-conscious in my new lounge suit, but got a much-needed boost when both Lonnie and David forgot themselves so far as to compliment me.

At Covington Square I found the name Candless atop a row of brass plates incised with an alphabet of medical degrees. I pressed the button and identified myself.

"Very good. I'll buzz you in. Top floor, elevator at the end of the hall."

I entered to find a vaulted ceiling, a checkerboard marble floor and a graceful curved double staircase which rose to a second-floor gallery dominated by a large rear-facing stained glass window portraying an entwined Venus and Adonis. I rode the tiny elevator to the top floor, where I was greeted by my hostess, Alison Candless.

She'd have been in her late seventies, silver-haired, frail and birdlike, conservatively dressed in a tartan skirt and twin set with pearls, although the effect was somewhat shattered by a pair of clunky trainers. I followed her into a cozy sitting room with an electric fire.

"Do make yourself comfortable, Mr. Fitzhelm. Let me take the covering off this chair. We have cats, you see, and the fur gets everywhere. My sister will be in with the tea in a moment." Right on cue a door swung open, propelled by an ample hip, and a stocky figure in a turtleneck sweater and baggy trousers swung 'round to reveal a loaded tea tray. "This is my sister Berenice."

"Call me Bernie," she said. "Everyone does." As she set the tray down, three fat tabbies emerged from the same door and solemnly faced me in a semicircle. "Let me introduce you to the girls. We call them the three Graces. This is Grace O'Malley, the famous female pirate, this is Grace Chisholm, the brilliant mathematician, and sitting at your feet is Grace Paley, whose brave stance against the Vietnam War we so admired." Grace Paley had sidled up to me and was eyeing my lap.

"Now, Grace, you're not to jump on Mr. Fitzhelm," said Alison. "She thinks that's her chair, you see. I wouldn't want her to spoil your lovely suit."

I swallowed my reaction, said not to worry and please call me Leslie.

"I'm sorry we couldn't see you sooner, Leslie, but we had a march on Friday and at our age we get a bit frazzled. We're protesters, you see, antiwar. I believe the last justifiable war was the Second World War. Lost my husband in that one. He was a doctor like his father. Specialized in tropical diseases. Army sent him off to Burma and he died of malaria in a Japanese POW camp. I was left with this enormous house and an inadequate pension, so I divided the place into consulting rooms. It was a bit of a wrench, but we're really quite comfortable up here."

"I'm so sorry."

"Oh, it all happened a long time ago, but I do miss him still."

"Ali's placard says, 'War No More,'" said Bernie. "Mine says, 'Stop the Violence,' so I can use it to picket against cruelty to animals as well. Ali took me in when my husband, Kenny, was institutionalized with Alzheimer's. He hardly recognizes me any more, poor old boy."

"Now, now, Bernie, Leslie didn't come to hear our tales of woe. What can we do for you, my dear? We've been dying of curiosity. The house isn't for sale if that's your interest."

I told them I was doing some research on Lady Teresa Blackwood, the famous world traveller whose home this had been, and spun them a romantic tale of love lost and the child that resulted. Their eyes glistened with tears as I described the pocket watch and the letter she'd sent to her lover along with the baby girl.

"And what became of the child?" asked Alison.

"Oh, she married well and had a long and happy life," I evasively replied.

Alison flashed me a knowing look and said, "Family history is always so fascinating, isn't it, my dear. I'm afraid I can't tell you anything about Lady Blackwood. My father-in-law bought the house before my husband was born and I didn't come here until I was in my twenties. The interior has changed completely, of course, and although I have keys for the suites it wouldn't be ethical to show you through them."

I assured her I understood and I'd presumed on her hospitality too much already.

Bernie said, "There's something about the name Blackwood that's nibbling away at the back of my mind, but I can't pull it up. If it comes back to me I'll give you a shout."

I'd mentioned my need to renew my prescriptions and Alison offered to arrange an appointment with one of her tenants. I was reluctant to leave such pleasant company, and it was after six when I said goodbye.

Alison phoned me early the next morning. She'd arranged a doctor's appointment for ten o'clock, and invited me up for coffee afterward. I heard a muffled exchange.

"Oh, and Bernie has something she's bursting to tell you."

Bernie came on the line. "Isn't that always the way? You go to bed trying to remember something, then wake up at two in the morning with a cry of 'eureka!' I told you about my poor old Kenny. Well, even though he doesn't know which end is up any more, he loves to have me read to him, uncomplicated things, newspapers, magazines, books with lots of action, and Ali said there was a box of old books and papers back under the eaves I could look through. There was some sort of manuscript about Australia and I recalled that the author's name was Blackwood. Ali says you can have the whole box if it's any use to you."

The doctor made no difficulty about renewing my prescriptions.

With great anticipation I took the little elevator to the top floor and had my coffee sitting cross-legged on the floor with one of the Graces in my lap, another sitting in the box as I dug through it, and the third watching us from her chair. What Bernie had discovered was the galley of Tess's book, *The World Beyond—An English Lady's Adventures in the Australian Bush*, complete with corrections and comments in her own hand. There were several old school textbooks, a coverless copy of Edward Lear's poems, worn editions of *Treasure Island* and *Two Years Before the Mast* signed "To Alex with love from Mama," and at the bottom, the two volumes of the gentleman pirate William Dampier's voyages that had so fascinated young George, a real treasure trove. I thanked Alison and Bernie profusely and left with my prize.

When I got back to the suite, Constance Beard had left a message asking if I could be ready to leave at six o'clock that Friday evening as Sir Henry was flying in from the Far East and David was to pick him up at the airport and go on to Fallowfield from there. I called her to say I'd be ready, then immersed myself in Tess's witty account of her travels. As thrilled as I was by this acquisition, I didn't feel right about keeping it and eventually boxed it all up to send to Clarence Blackwood. Persy says I'm too scrupulous by half and that the Dampier books were probably first editions and worth a fortune.

On Friday the airport was again shrouded in rain. My first impression of my cousin Sir Henry was of a tall, solid figure in a dark overcoat, his head obscured by an umbrella. Once in the car he proved to have a handsome, ruddy face, fair hair and a friendly but formal manner.

"Connie took care of you, I hope, and the suite was comfortable? Can't stand the place myself, too modern, no heart, but our foreign clients and business associates seem to like it. I don't stay over in London if I can help it. Can't wait to get home. You'll be comfortable at the cottage. It has a new furnace and modern plumbing, but other than that it's pretty much as it was in your great-grandfather's day. Hope you won't think it rude if I nod off. I can never sleep on aeroplanes and it's been a long day."

Almost three hours later his eyes opened as we drove through a pair of tall iron gates to stop at the front door of Fallowfield Cottage, where he wished me good-night. There was a warm light glowing from the deep-set windows and the scent of thyme rising from the damp earth of the front garden as I opened the door and stepped inside. I felt like I'd come home.

Too wound up to think of sleeping, I dropped my bags in the hall and went exploring. The study was my first stop. I scanned the bookshelves and was delighted to spot three ledgers identical in appearance to those in Sam Treadwell's workshop. There was the mantelpiece where Old Nick had rested in his casket, and on the desk by the ink-stained blotter sat the miniature portraits on ivory. I crossed over to the dining room, poured myself a generous brandy from a decanter on the sideboard, and ran my fingers over Beth's apostle spoons. A quick glance at the kitchen, then back out to the hall and on to the sitting room.

The first thing I saw was Marie-Claude Guérin's two watercolour sketches, the colours so fresh and the poses so natural they were like presences in the room, Beth as beautiful as I'd imagined her, and a marked resemblance between Rennie and Sir Henry. I much prefer these to the larger, more formal portraits I was later to see at Fallowfield Hall. In one corner, covered with a brightly embroidered Spanish shawl, sat Beth's pianoforte, and on it her collection of glass paperweights and a series of framed photographs. One in particular showed Beth seated at the keyboard and, standing beside her cradling Old Nick, an adolescent George.

The brandy suddenly hit me, and I never made it to a bed. I sank into the rose-patterned cushions of the sofa and woke up with the first light filtering through the French doors, trying to retrieve the details of a wonderful dream I'd had of Beth playing a lively melody on the pianoforte, but it wasn't George, it was me playing Old Nick, the first of a series of vivid dreams I was to have at Fallowfield Cottage.

I drifted off again and came to a couple of hours later with the room full of sunlight and the welcome aroma of coffee and bacon.

I headed for the kitchen, where I found an attractive woman in her thirties in jeans and a plaid shirt. As I ate my breakfast I learned her name was Harriet, that she was married to William, the Fallowfield handyman and mechanic and she helped out at the Hall whenever another pair of hands was needed. She'd make me breakfast and lunch until I was settled and give the place a lick and a promise when it needed freshening. Lady Julia hoped I'd have dinners with the family up at the Hall. The bacon was thick and smoky, the eggs fresh and full of flavour, and the toast, hallelujah!, was hot with melted sweet butter on it. The delicious bitter marmalade had to be home-made and the coffee had just a hint of cinnamon. I was in heaven.

By the time I'd settled into Nan's old room off the kitchen, showered and dressed, the kitchen was spotless and Harriet gone, having left substantial ham and cheese sandwiches in the fridge and soup on the stove for lunch.

I continued my exploration with the upstairs. The first bedroom had to be Beth's, full of light, with delicately flowered wallpaper, a tiled fireplace and a faint scent of lavender. At the foot of the bed was a simple wooden chest. A small bookcase contained a collection of popular novels from the '30s and '40s, Somerset Maugham, William Saroyan and Carson McCullers interspersed with some contemporary paperbacks, and on the bedside table, next to Jean-Paul Sartre's *Being and Nothingness*, sat a little inlaid wooden box. I attempted to open it, but concluded it must be one of Frank Joyner's clever puzzles. The other bedrooms were curiously devoid of character, as if the inhabitants had long since moved on.

I would create a routine. In the morning I'd explore the estate and its surroundings, the hillside graves of Rennie and Beth, the village of Edensgate and Saint Mark's church, then in the afternoon put in a few hours of reading or writing before changing for dinner.

On this first day, however, my solitude was interrupted just before six as I was preparing to find my way to the Hall.

"Hey, Leslie, it's your long-lost cousin Andy come to fetch you for dinner." A tall, fair young man about my age and obviously a Fitzhelm strode into the kitchen and gave my hand a firm squeeze. "Ma sent me over to make sure you didn't get lost. I'm the son and heir, by the way. There's no spare unless you count my sister Nell, who says she wouldn't have the title if you gift-wrapped it. She is going through an anti-aristocracy thing. Easy for her since she's not on the firing line." His upper-class diction was laced with slightly outdated American slang. From his appearance, jeans and a suede-patched jacket, I was overdressed for dinner.

"I think I'd better change."

"Good thinking. We're taking a shortcut and those shoes wouldn't survive it. We don't do the formal thing unless we're throwing a major wingding. We will be, by the way. My twenty-first birthday's coming up next month and the parents are pulling out all the stops. You'll probably have some company here as the Hall and annex will be stuffed to the attics with extended family."

I said I'd look forward to it, then went off to change, and as an afterthought uncrated a bottle of Sam Treadwell's brandy to give to Sir Henry.

As we walked Andy said, "I don't know what your politics are, but I should warn you Pa's on the conservative side. Nell says he's slightly to the right of Attila the Hun, but he's not really that bad, although he does still lament what he calls the 'retirement' of Maggie Thatcher. Otherwise he's pretty easygoing. It's just the five of us tonight. We chow down in the morning room. The dining room table seats twenty and we feel a bit silly huddled around one end of it."

We entered the Hall through the kitchen, where I shed my wellingtons for my new brogues and was introduced to the cook. Having Beth's gloomy picture of Fallowfield Hall in my head, I was pleasantly surprised at the lightness and airiness of the central hall and the warm, welcoming colours of the sitting room. Sir Henry greeted me with a clap on the shoulder, accepted the bottle of brandy with a nod and introduced me to Lady Julia and Andy's sister, Nell.

Lady Julia was slim and striking in tailored slacks, a turtleneck and a muted plaid jacket, with stylishly cut salt-and-pepper hair. She gave me a kiss on the cheek and said it would be good for Andy to have someone his own age around the place.

Nell was a surprise. Eighteen, very slender, dressed in black from head to toe, with multicoloured hair, several piercings in each ear, and exaggerated black eye makeup which gave her a sort of elfin, *Lord of the Rings* look.

She gave me a big grin and said, "Hi, cuz. Welcome to Manderley."

"Now, Nell, behave yourself," said her mother with an indulgent smile.

After drinks we filled our plates from a buffet on the sideboard and sat down to dinner. I noticed that Andy's use of Ma and Pa disappeared in their actual presence, and he addressed them as "Mother" and "sir." I decided to follow suit, calling Sir Henry "sir," but was at a loss as to how to address Lady Julia. Sensing my hesitation she insisted I call her Julia.

The main course was a perfect roast of beef, which Nell, a vegetarian, made a show of refusing, but I noticed she was well provided with alternatives. I assured them I was very comfortable at the cottage and asked if there was a computer at the Hall I could use. Sir Henry said he was sure Goldring could spare a computer and printer. The company name came up several times and I realized that despite its size it was still very much a family concern. Andy had taken a year off school to work with his father and would be attending the London School of Economics in the fall. Nell was studying photo-journalism and would spend the summer working in the Goldring publicity and promotion department. There was some discussion about the upcoming party and I learned that the annex Andy had mentioned was a recent addition built to accommodate visiting Goldring executives and business associates. We concluded with cognac around nine, then Andy walked back to the cottage with me.

"Hope that wasn't too much of an ordeal. It must be weird to be plunged into all this, coming from the colonies." He grinned to let me know he was joking. "Pa likes to work from home so I'll be around quite a bit. Do you ride? I get out two or three mornings a week when I'm here, and a horse is no problem."

I told him I hadn't ridden since I was a kid and didn't have the right gear, but I'd love to. He promised to hunt up some boots and breeches for me.

"You can ride Nell's old plug, Chauncey. He needs the exercise and she won't mind. Once you find your seat again we'll give you something more challenging."

That night I dreamed of riding with Beth.

I spent several days studying the two ledgers Beth had retrieved from George's professor and a third one on blacksmithing, lock-smithing and clockworks where I found the secrets of Frank Joyner's hidden drawers, panels and puzzle boxes. Yes, there it was, a simple little inlaid box he'd made for Beth on her tenth birthday. I rushed upstairs to try the key, which was the Latin word for "peace," *PACE—Pear, Apple, Cherry, Ebony*. Knowing which one was ebony, I identified the other woods and slid each inlay slightly to the right to release the lid. Nestled inside were two intertwined locks of hair, one fair and one dark, tied with a black velvet ribbon. I sealed it up again, embarrassed that I'd disturbed it.

The following week I discovered the music cabinet.

I had the use of one of the cars, an old estate wagon, and I'd started buying groceries in the village to make my own breakfast and lunch. It was raining that day so Andy and I didn't ride, and I spent the morning making copies of Frank Joyner's botanical notes. I was poking around the sitting room, sandwich in hand, when I spotted in a corner a cabinet almost invisible under the fronds of the giant fern which sat on top of it. Opened, it displayed several deep, indented shelves, and on each a stack of music. The top shelves were filled with popular songbooks and sheet music from the turn of the century through the '40s, but the real find was on the lower shelves—dozens of melodies, most notated in Frank Joyner's distinctive hand, but others with duplicate titles arranged for keyboard by Beth. I ran to get my fiddle and spent the rest of the afternoon going through them.

Imagine my astonishment when one of the sheets entitled "Bring the Glad Tidings" turned out to be the very tune I'd played on Old Nick in my dream. I have no explanation. I can only guess that I must have heard it during my night at the pub in Kingsfold. In fact, I've long since given up trying to rationalize anything that happened then.

It was a pleasure to be playing again and putting actual melodies to titles I'd found in the journal: "The Dancing Mare," two versions of "A Pair of Blue Eyes" with romantic lyrics added to the second by Beth, and "Columbine," the pretty little waltz that Beth and George had played to close the Saint Stephen's Day celebration, the same melody that had touched the heart of Berthe Stein and gained for me the very instrument I was now playing. I was totally transported and it wasn't until the phone rang that I realized I was late for dinner.

I arrived at the Hall full of breathless apologies and we sat down to eat. Everything seemed as usual until Sir Henry asked if I'd join him in the library after dinner. It was like being called to the headmaster's office. My heart sank to my toes and all my childhood insecurities rose up. I was convinced I'd worn out my welcome.

"Please sit down, Leslie."

"Yes, sir."

"Do call me Henry. We are cousins after all. First, let me say how much we've enjoyed having you here. Andy likes you tremendously, and Nell says you're a bit of a dish whatever that's supposed to mean." At this point I was resigned to the inevitable "but" so his next words didn't quite register. "I owe you an apology. That bottle you gave me on your first night here, I have to be honest. I'd assumed it was some sort of dreadful home-brewed concoction so I put it aside and promptly forgot about it. It was Julia who reminded me that I hadn't even acknowledged your gift let alone opened it, and she insisted we sample it together. What a revelation! We were quite dumbfounded. What is it? Where did you get it? Can I buy some?"

I was flooded with relief and told him about Sam Treadwell's still. I said I had no idea how much Sam produced or if he'd even be interested in selling it, but I'd certainly write to him and ask. Thinking the meeting was at an end, I rose to leave, but Henry wasn't finished.

"There is one more thing. The cottage."

I suddenly felt cold.

"As you know, the agreement was that the Fallowfield estate would maintain the place, but ten years ago we sold Fallowfield to the Goldring Corporation, so there is no longer an estate per se. Maintenance isn't a problem, but there is the matter of inheritance tax. With your father's passing, the death duties will be staggering. I've taken the liberty of having an appraisal done on the house and land, and it's come back at around 400,000 pounds. As a non-resident you can only deduct a third, which means you owe the British government in the neighbourhood of 100,000 pounds.

"Now I realize this comes as a shock to you, but hear me out. If you sell the place to Goldring I can promise you a price substantially above market value. It would still be available to you, of course, but you'd be relieved of the responsibility. I don't need an immediate decision, but those bastards will come after you sooner rather than later, and frankly I don't see an alternative."

It was devastating news. I told him I needed to think about it.

The next morning Andy and I rode. I'd graduated from Chauncey to a leather-mouthed bay gelding called Houdini who, true to his name, was tricky, but he behaved himself around Andy. We fetched up at the pub in Edensgate and sat outside with our drinks. We'd become very close and I openly confided my anxiety about the cottage.

"You have to understand about Pa," he said. "He lives for the company. You've only seen the easygoing parochial country squire, but Goldring is a substantial corporation and he's the youngest in the family ever to run it. He was only twenty-eight when my grandfather had his stroke. Goldring was holding its own back then but it wasn't going anywhere, and the cost of maintaining the estate was ruinous. It was Pa who convinced Granddad to break the entailment, sell the Hall to Goldring for a nominal amount and establish it as a corporate retreat and a secure facility for government conferences. That's why the annex was built. His business instincts are infallible, but he can be a bit heavy-handed on a personal level. His offer's well meant, but I can see this is very emotional for you. Just know that he likes you tremendously, and wants what he thinks is best for you."

I admitted I'd been surprised when Henry had accepted me based only on my letter about a tenuous family connection.

"Don't be daft. You must have run into Connie Beard when you were in London." I answered that I'd never actually met her but had been impressed with her efficiency. "That's Connie all right. Nell calls her Conan the Deployer because she has this army of researchers, spies, paid informants, and people in high places who owe her favours. You can bet Pa had a dossier on you within a couple of days of receiving your letter and knows your net worth down to the penny. Don't be surprised if he offers you a job. He's a great believer in nepotism. Says you can't buy that kind of loyalty."

It was all pretty overwhelming. I wrote to Sam and called Marion Gerston.

I just couldn't give the place up. Against all Marion's excellent advice, I decided to bite the bullet and pay off Inland Revenue with Gina's legacy. Sounds crazy, I know, but that money wasn't real to me. Fallowfield Cottage was.

We were well into April by then, and Andy's birthday party only a few days away. Preparations were at a fever pace. Julia was in endless consultations with event planners, florists and caterers. Henry and Andy decided to escape to London for a couple of days to see to the final fittings for Andy's new evening kit. Nell was off on a photo shoot, so it was only Julia and me at dinner and I was enjoying her rather motherly interest.

"You'll have a wonderful time at the party. Andy's considered quite a catch so there'll be lots of eligible girls. By the way, a couple of your cousins will be showing up late tonight. I hope you don't mind if they stay at the cottage. I'm sure you'll get along swimmingly."

I said I'd look forward to the company, kissed her on the cheek and wished her good-night.

I was in bed and half asleep when I heard voices in the hallway. Shortly after, I heard "Bring the Glad Tidings" being picked out on the pianoforte and realized I must have left the music out when I was practising. It was a pleasant way to drift to sleep.

The next morning I was up early and feeling confident enough to attempt my first solo ride. When I got to the Hall, Jimmy, the head groom, and his assistant were busy billeting horses imported from neighbouring stables to accommodate the imminent guests, so I saddled Houdini myself.

"You watch him, sir. He's a clever devil," said Jimmy.

I said I would, saddled up and rode off quite proud of myself. I hadn't been out twenty minutes before I realized I was in trouble. The saddle began to slip to one side and the minute my balance was off Houdini took off like a shot back to the stable. I was hanging on for dear life when someone galloped up behind me and grabbed the halter.

A female voice growled, "Pull up, you wicked old bastard!"

Houdini came to a jolting stop, damned near throwing me over his head. I more or less recovered myself, slid off and turned to thank my saviour, and that was when I met Persy.

It was like getting hit by a truck, love at first sight, although I have to admit I was half in love with her before I even met her. She was the virtual double of Beth's portrait. Yes, her colouring was different and she was certainly taller, but it was the same tilt of the head and little half-smile. She waved off my stammered gratitude.

"Jimmy must have been out of his mind to put you up on that devious bugger."

I defended Jimmy, saying I'd ridden Houdini before and should have been prepared.

"That bloody horse knows every trick in the equine book. He swelled himself up when you were tightening the girth. Let me show you. Once you get wise to him, just threatening him with a knee to the ribs will smarten him up. There you go. I'm your cousin Persy, by the way."

We finished our ride and headed back to the stable without further incident.

As we walked back to the cottage I asked about her name and she said it was short for Persephone, Persephone Daphne Fitzhelm to be exact, but she preferred Persy, saying it was infinitely better than her school nickname, which was Daffy. It's a joke between us now that when we argue I call her Daffy and she calls me Archie.

"You'll notice a theme to the names of my siblings and myself. My mother teaches classics and my father's an archaeologist. They met in Greece one summer when my mother was squiring a group of students through a succession of ruins and my father was part of a team unearthing a temple to Aphrodite. My sister Dite got saddled with that name. You'll meet my brother, Jason, when we get back to the cottage. We're twins, by the way. Runs in my mother's side of the family. If we'd both been boys we'd probably be Romulus and Remus."

She did most of the talking. I was in such a fog of infatuation I couldn't come up with anything remotely intelligent to say and it's a wonder she didn't write me off as a complete idiot. She claims she was equally smitten, but if so, she was certainly a lot cooler about it. I met Jason, a taller, more masculine version of herself, and the three of us squeezed into the front seat of the estate wagon to go for lunch and groceries in the village, with me struggling to appear normal, hyper-aware of Persy's thigh pressing against mine.

Henry and Andy had returned from London in time for dinner. The rest of the guests were arriving the following day, so we made it an early night, the three of us walking in companionable silence back to the cottage through the warm spring evening to the songs of the frogs and crickets. Jason discreetly disappeared. I would later discover that he and Persy shared that unspoken communication twins seem to have. I see it in our two as well. Persy and I, reluctant to say good-night, went to the sitting room for one last drink. She sat down at the keyboard and began to play "Bring the Glad Tidings." The photo of Beth and George and Old Nick jumped into focus as I picked up my violin and joined her, again experiencing that peculiar shift in the atmosphere I'd felt at Saint Stephen and in Old Betty's kitchen.

Persy said, "Something happened just then, didn't it?"

I said yes, but I couldn't explain it, then I kissed her.

It was Beth who wrote "Nothing is more yawn-inducing than someone else's happiness," and Persy concurs that young lovers bore the pants off everyone but themselves. She says it's a scientific fact that love is a form of temporary insanity. Something to do with blood being diverted from the left to the right brain. That about sums up our state at the time, although I'd argue the blood was diverted elsewhere. We finally surfaced and floated off to our respective beds, and I fell into a deep sleep, only waking from a dream of the two of us playing "Columbine" when I smelled coffee and found Persy sitting barefoot at the kitchen table, delicious in a T-shirt and jeans, her dark hair tumbled about her shoulders. We didn't speak, just sat smiling at each other. Jason appeared, poured a cup of coffee and beat a hasty retreat.

This made Andy's party something of an anticlimax. Tents had been erected and the conservatory doors were opened to the warm evening air with candles and torches everywhere. I sported my new dinner jacket and Persy wore a dramatic black and white dress. There were masses of people, most of them relations. Rumours of Persy and me had mysteriously spread and we were greeted with the kind of indulgent smiles usually reserved for infants and invalids. Andy kept digging me in the ribs with his elbow and Nell, like a Gorey drawing in claret velvet, gave me a big hug. Henry took me aside to assure me that there should be no problem as we were fifth or sixth cousins at most, all this before we'd done anything more than kiss.

I met Persy's sister, Dite, and their parents, her father tan and bearded, her mother disconcertingly like a photograph I'd once seen of Virginia Woolf. They seemed pleased enough about the two of us but I couldn't help feeling their minds were engaged elsewhere. Persy says that as much as she loves them they relate more to the ancient world than the modern one, and are so cerebral she has no idea how they conceived three children.

The evening was a blur of introductions, speeches and enormous quantities of food and champagne. I'm sure it was a wonderful party but we couldn't wait to leave. The distant murmur of the crowd and the strains of the dance band followed us all the way to the cottage. We slept together for the first time that night and we haven't been apart for more than a week since.

Jason drove back to London, and Persy and I spent the next few days getting to know each other, going for long rides and lingering over lunches in the village. She held my hand as I talked about my childhood, and my father's death. I sympathized with her attempts to understand her parents' emotional distance through reading psychology books, her failed ambition to be a concert pianist and her disastrous engagement to a much older man. I was disconcerted to discover that her grandfather was the same Nicky Fitzhelm who'd had a fling with my grandmother, Gina. I debated whether to tell her about it, but when I did she just laughed and said her grandfather's exploits were legendary and a family standard for bad behaviour.

My obsession with Old Nick and the journal had evaporated. I knew I'd share the journal with Persy eventually, but that time came sooner rather than later, when she levelled with me about what she did for a living.

She and Dite co-owned and operated an antiques and interior decorating shop called Tyme After Tyme. She admitted the name was chi-chi but it was perfect for the kind of customer they were targeting, mainly yuppies earning their first serious money and wanting a bit of instant history and ambience to go with it. What she hadn't told me was that genuine antiques were the tip of the iceberg, and the workshop where repairs and restoration were done was mainly employed with the manufacture of high-class fakes using just enough bits and pieces of the real stuff to fool the average punter. Persy claimed they practically begged to be taken advantage of anyway and she and Dite seldom bothered with any kind of provenance. The thought of putting something over on a dealer was too tempting for most people.

"Oh, it's something I picked up for a song at a country auction. Looks like Chippendale but I haven't had a chance to look it over properly. I was rather thinking of keeping it, but if you really love it . . ."

I guess she'd been expecting some shock or judgment on my part, but I couldn't stop laughing and I could see she was getting annoyed.

I managed to sputter, "No, no, I'm not laughing at you. You just don't know. My God, it must be in the genes. There's something you have to read."

I gave her my copy of the journal and Gina's letter and went for a very long walk. When I got back she was well into Beth's story, and was unusually quiet as we walked to the Hall. After we got back from dinner she curled up in the sitting room to finish it, and it was after two in the morning when she finally came to bed.

"I do look like her, don't I. Beth, I mean. She's my new hero. What a life! I'd love to see a portrait of Tess Blackwood. I felt sick when Old Nick was stolen. Do you have a photo of your grandmother? So Grandpa Nicky wasn't the aberration everyone claimed. Sweet Jesus, does Henry know? Of course not. I've never heard a whisper from anyone. This is brilliant! What are you going to do about it?"

"Nothing," I answered. I didn't want to share the journal with anyone else.

She disagreed, but didn't push.

Persy had to get back to London eventually. I went with her and stayed at her flat. London with Persy was a very different place. Ten days of theatre, clubs, gallery openings, and dinners in trendy restaurants was a whole new world. We attended a couple of antiques auctions, Persy taking photos and notes. Jason was just starting up his recording company, Salt Records, and we went to see some bands. We had Indian take-away dinner with the parents at their enormous flat cluttered with books and artifacts. The two of us were exhausted by the time we returned to Fallowfield. Parents aside, Henry was the acknowledged head of the family and we wanted to make it official. We were getting married.

We settled on a late-May wedding. Despite the short notice Julia was all for something lavish, but we wanted it to be small and informal with close family members and friends. We did agree to hold it in the conservatory. I phoned Junior and Grady and Teddy. They were thrilled to hear the news and would certainly come. I was going to buy a diamond, but Persy had her heart set on the little star ruby that Tess had given to Beth, so I had Teddy send it to me.

In the midst of all this, Sam Treadwell's answer to my letter finally arrived. He would be pleased and proud to provide Lord Fitzhelm with some of his brandy. Persy and I volunteered to go to Kingsfold to fetch it. I'd told Jason about the Cooper family, and he decided to come with us. We reserved rooms at the Kingsfold Inn, and drove down early on a Saturday morning.

I'd underestimated Sam. Intrigued with the idea of selling his brandy, he'd immediately gone to the Willows to consult Squire Bliss, who, it transpired, had been a solicitor before retiring to take over the family blood stock operation. He registered Sam's formula, and by the time we met, the two of them had formed a partnership to set up a small distillery. I agreed to approach Henry about a letter of endorsement and wished them the best of luck. Henry ended up putting a little money into it as well. Sam's gone now, but I still get my case of Treadwell's Own every Christmas.

We found a decent restaurant in Fenton-on-Bliss and got back to the Kingsfold Inn just in time for a musical evening at the pub. Tina called me up to play with her on "Joyner's Dream" to the noisy approval of the crowd. Persy and I performed "Bring the Glad Tidings" and "The Dancing Mare," and Jason surprised me by joining us on guitar to play "Yesterday." Everyone sang along and there wasn't a dry eye in the place. I proudly introduced Persy to Tina and Old Betty as my fiancée. Betty pursed her lips and raised her eyebrows as if to say, I told you so.

Tina said, "Oh, Leslie, she's lovely, but I'll never forgive you for not waiting for me."

It took me a minute to realize she was teasing and I was still trying to think of a smart reply when Jason asked if she'd ever thought of recording. The last we saw of him that night was in a tight huddle with Tina, Seth and Old Betty. (Tina and Jason got married in '98.)

Our wedding day was perfect. Julia had filled the conservatory with roses. Persy looked like spring with Tess's pearl pendant at her throat, a wreath of cornflowers in her hair and a little bouquet of wildflowers I'd picked for her from the hillside where Rennie and Beth were buried. Familiar faces drifted in and out. The moment of "I do" and the vision of Persy's face as I kissed her are the only things I clearly remember. If it weren't for Nell's photographs most of it would still be a blank.

I'd have been happy to stay in England forever, but Persy declared she was ready for a change and wanted to see what Canada was like. We flew out a few days later with Junior and Grady. Teddy had tactfully decided to stay in London for a couple of weeks to visit some old theatre cronies, so we had the house to ourselves.

We immediately set about making Gina's bedroom our own: new mattress, bedding, curtains and carpet and a fresh coat of paint. The '50s-era bathroom would be next.

It would have been somewhere in our second week of married bliss that I saw an article in the newspaper about the recent incorporation of Stanton, Midvale and Carven into a new municipality called New Watersfield. I had a good laugh imagining Rachel's reaction, then forgot about it.

Persy and Teddy had instantly hit it off. When he got back from London he introduced her to some acquaintances in the antiques and vintage furniture trade. She e-mailed Dite about setting up a Canadian account for Tyme After Tyme, rented a storage unit and started acquiring inventory. Teddy had a friend who owned a bed and breakfast in some little town outside Ottawa, and he and Persy decided to rent a van and go there antiquing for a long weekend.

I was fighting the inevitable letdown after the high of the wedding. I'd put up a good front as long as Persy was with me, but being alone with time on my hands was pure hell. I decided to get started on the bathroom, staving off the blues with mindless physical labour.

In the midst of this chaos I was contacted by the New Watersfield regional police with some shocking news. Rachel had shot Margarethe Jensen. Margarethe would recover, but she was in hospital. Rachel was there as well, confined to the psychiatric ward. I had to go and deal with it, but by God I didn't want to.

The shotgun belonged to Rachel's father and hadn't been fired in over seventy years. The recoil had dislocated her shoulder and propelled her across the landing, where she'd concussed herself on the newel post. The Jensens were reluctant to press charges, but with a gun involved they had no choice. If it had hit an artery Margarethe could have died.

I found her propped up on pillows, bandaged where the birdshot had peppered the side of her neck and the fleshy part of her upper arm. She gave me a tremulous smile, then began to cry.

"Oh, Leslie, she didn't mean it. She was just so worked up. You know how she gets. She was fit to be tied when they dissolved the old town council to elect the regional one and she lost her seat. Then those real estate people started hounding her with phone calls, ringing the doorbell at all hours. I was worried when she dug the old gun out of the attic, but she said she only wanted to scare them off. I was polishing the brass on the front door and hit the bell by mistake. She came charging down the stairs, yelling, 'You're trespassing. I'm not afraid of you!' and that's when the gun went off."

Ole Jensen heard the shot and found Margarethe bleeding and Rachel out cold. He called the police and drove his wife to the hospital. The police said Rachel was just coming to when they arrived, insisted she'd been attacked, claimed to have no memory of pulling the trigger.

The staff psychiatrist said that in his opinion, although Rachel might have some temporary amnesia, she was highly delusional and extremely paranoid and it was surprising that nothing had happened sooner.

When I was admitted to the room where she was being held, she was sitting up very straight on the edge of the bed. Her dress was torn, her hair had escaped its rigid waves and her right arm was in a sling. She also had the beginnings of two spectacular black eyes, but her manner was as autocratic as ever.

"Well, Leslie, I take it you've finally come to your senses. You can see for yourself what those animals have done to me. What has the world come to when a lady isn't safe in her own house in broad daylight? Call Ole to bring the car around. I'm ready to go home."

"Aunt Rachel," I said cautiously. "You can't go home. You've shot Mrs. Jensen."

"Utter nonsense! I never did any such thing. Slanderous! Turning against me after all I've done for her, and you as well, you conniving little ingrate. You won't get away with it. You'll pay! You'll all pay! Stantons are not to be trifled with!"

Persy once asked me if Rachel had ever struck me and I'd laughingly replied that no, she didn't have to. I was too scared to cross her. It was as if all the menace I'd sensed in her as a kid had boiled over. Her face was purple and her eyes popping as she lunged for me, her fingernails raking my face. I ran for the door and yelled for help.

I managed to drive home and immediately took a sedative, but it had no effect. I couldn't let Persy see me like this. I pulled myself together enough to phone Teddy, begging him to keep her away for a few more days, but he said they'd head right back and not to do anything stupid.

As I huddled in bed fingering Old Betty's talisman like a worry stone, I remembered that I still had her tea in the bottom of my backpack. In desperation I dug it out, stumbled down to the kitchen and brewed a whole pot. By the time Teddy and Persy showed up in the small hours of the morning I'd literally attacked the bathroom, demolishing the tiles with a hammer and pry bar, pulling up three layers of floor covering and finally attempting to rip out the vanity without detaching the plumbing—with Rachel's face in front of me the whole time.

Teddy was an old hand at dealing with my particular malady. He'd had a frank talk with Persy on the drive back so she was prepared for depression, but this manic madman was something else. Teddy took one look at me and forced neat whisky down my throat. Like a tire with a slow leak I gradually deflated, and between the two of them they wrestled me into bed, where I passed out for eighteen hours.

It was a grim-faced Persy who perched on the side of the bed with a glass of orange juice, making sure I swallowed the antidepressant she handed me. She informed me that the remainder of Old Betty's tea had been disposed of along with the debris from the bathroom.

"God, I'm so sorry," I mumbled. "I should never have asked you to marry me knowing this could happen."

"Oh no you don't, you bastard! You don't get off that easily. You felt this coming and you didn't trust me enough to tell me. 'For better or worse,' if you'll recall. If you ever pull a stunt like this again I'll have your balls for bookends!"

She does get graphic when she's upset or excited, a reaction, I suspect, to the dry discourse she grew up on. All that mattered to me was that she wasn't leaving.

"Look on the bright side. Half the work on the bathroom is done."

I could see a little tug at the corner of her mouth.

"Leslie Archibald Fitzhelm, don't you dare make me laugh!" she said, and I knew we were going to be okay.

Later, lying alone in the darkened bedroom I could do little else but think. At first it was black thoughts: my father's exile, imprisonment and death, anger at Rachel, frustration at not being able to confront her. Then I started feeling sorry for myself, poor old me saddled with the emotional downside of the family legacy. From self-pity I moved to what a nonentity and failure I was. Slowly I graduated to more hopeful thoughts: my one great adventure, the discovery of a real, living family, and then there was Persy. I did reach one conclusion. Other than Persy I had no focus. I was drifting. I needed to figure out what to do with the rest of my life.

The demolished bathroom was driving us all crazy and Teddy hired a contractor to finish the job. The noise and the guilt drove me up to the third floor. I loaded the old turntable with Hot League recordings and buried myself in the boxed remains of my father's life. I removed a few things, the honeymoon picture of my mother laughing on the beach, a photo of my parents proudly holding the infant me, my father and me in our waders displaying our catch with big grins on our faces, and my father's old address book. The name that jumped out at me as I leafed through it was Desmond Miller.

"I hope you get to meet Desmond sometime. He's a wonderful man," my father had said.

Desmond seemed genuinely pleased to hear from me. He taught during the week, so I arrived at his house at ten o'clock on a Sunday morning. His wife, Vangie, dressed for church, let me in and directed me to his basement studio, a large, low-ceilinged room lined with weathered barnboard, hung with what must have been a dozen different guitars. Sitting in the middle of the room holding a wasp-waisted old instrument with an exotic female face carved into the peg head was a small, wiry, coffee-coloured man of about fifty. The first things you noticed about him were his startling green eyes and wide smile, then his enormous long-fingered hands.

"Welcome, Leslie. Come meet the old lady who started it all. Elsie, this is Leslie. He's come to play with us."

I'd brought some of the Hot League arrangements with me and was nervous as a cat, spilling the charts out onto the floor, fumbling with the latches on my violin case.

He sat patiently while I collected myself, then said, "Your call, Leslie. What'll it be?"

I'd rehearsed it in my mind and then with my fiddle. I started with Blind France's old melody "L'Oiseau Bleu," then segued into George Fitzhelm's jazzy '20s adaptation, "Bluebird Blue." Desmond was with me all the way, picking up the melody almost from the first phrase, adding changes I would never have dreamed of, and by the time I made the transition he was supporting me with a syncopated rhythm. We ended in a two-part harmony. It was joyful, transcendental. We laughed out loud as we laid down our instruments.

"Your great-granddaddy would be so proud of you," he said, "and your daddy too. He loved music so much. It made me sad he never found it in himself."

We played and talked until well into the afternoon. I promised to send him George Fitzhelm's memories of the Hot League from the journal. When I asked if he'd ever gotten to perform "Night Train to Harlem," he shook his head, saying he'd played a bare-bones version of it with friends, but still hadn't realized his dream of performing it with full symphony orchestra. We parted with plans to meet again and I returned home in a peaceful and optimistic mood.

What we'd done with "Bluebird Blue" had planted an idea in my head. What if I combined melodies from the old manuscripts and charts into a sort of family history in music? I could call it "Joyner's Dream—The Kingsfold Suite." It worked in principle, but I knew I didn't have the skill to pull it all together. I decided to go back to school to study composition and arrangement and to improve my technique. Persy was delighted. She'd built up enough stock to rent a booth at an antiques market, and had been worried about my hanging around the house with nothing to do. I looked forward to the routine and discipline, and the luxury of following my own agenda.

Around this time I got a call from a man called Rayburn Hawkes the Third. His father, Rayburn the Second, had been the Stanton family lawyer for over fifty years and when he retired, the Third had inherited the job. A few weeks before the shooting incident, Rachel had fired him for suggesting she sell off some property to cover the higher taxes demanded by the new municipality, but she hadn't asked for the Stanton file and as far as he knew she hadn't appointed anyone else. I got the impression he wanted to distance himself from the whole mess, so Junior and I drove up to Stanton to collect the stuff.

We made some startling discoveries. From my father I knew that Rachel had had no legal claim to the estate. Everything had been left to my mother and on her death came to me. Rachel had been authorized to act on my behalf until I turned twenty-one, but Junior found a letter dated shortly after my father's funeral, supposedly signed by me, stating that I placed control of all my assets in the hands of Miss Rachel Stanton. It wasn't even a forgery. The signature was nothing like mine. Unbelievable! She could have lived out her miserable life in that house without any interference from me. We also discovered she was almost as good as her word about my not getting a penny of Stanton money. Under her stewardship the estate had dwindled to little beyond the real estate, and the rents from the row houses. Higher taxes had been the final blow. Junior, reading between the lines, suspected that Hawkes had been at the very least indiscreet with the information and might even have had a stake in the outcome, because that's when the real estate developers smelled blood.

Rachel had been declared unfit to stand trial and committed to a psychiatric care facility. I should have felt relieved, even liberated, but instead I was angry, conflicted. I didn't want her to be crazy. I wanted her to be accountable for the litany of childhood injustices that played over and over in my head like a tape loop. Persy finally snapped.

"That's it! I don't want to hear any more about it. Yes, she was a sociopathic old bitch. Yes, she treated you abysmally, but that was then and you're still reacting like an eight-year-old. Let it go. The woman is gaga. You want an apology? Forget it. You want revenge? Nothing you can dream up could top what's happening to her now. Think of her as just some crazy old lady who, if you didn't share this history, you might have some compassion for."

It was hard to swallow, but she was right, as usual. The last time I saw Rachel she had no idea who I was, but was pleased to have a visitor to complain to about me. She died two years later.

We spent that Christmas at Fallowfield, the first of many. We passed Christmas Day with the family at the Hall, everyone retiring early to be ready for the main event, the Saint Stephen's Day celebration. We were awakened at the cottage early the next morning by the rumble of vehicles, for it was still very much a community affair, and there were decorations to be hung and buffet tables to be set up for the mountains of food prepared with fierce but friendly competition by the ladies of the parish. By the time we appeared the conservatory was a feast for the eyes, ears and palate, everyone dressed in their party best. It was crowded, crazy, noisy beyond belief, and absolutely wonderful.

In the brief lull between the feasting and the dancing, parish announcements were made. The big news was that Andy was engaged, and to a local girl, Annalee Best, just graduated from veterinary college. They'd played together as children, had met again and fallen in love. We had our own announcement. Persy was two months pregnant. I think I still have bruises from all the backslapping. We played "Joyner's Dream" and "Columbine" to close the evening, Henry and Julia leading off the traditional waltz, followed by Andy and Annalee, then everyone else joining in. I didn't see any ghosts in the room, but I'm sure they were dancing as well.

I'd still found no trace of Old Nick, although my hopes were momentarily raised when I received photographs of a similar instrument in the hands of a famous Nashville fiddler.

By March of '93 Persy's belly was very round and firm. We knew it was twins and we'd set up a nursery with two of everything in the small back bedroom at McCaul Street. They were born in July of '93. We named them Teresa and Gerald thinking we'd avoid the usual rhyming names, but of course they became Teri and Gerry almost immediately. We feared it might be a little rough on Teddy having not just one, but two babies in the house, but he became quite the doting grandpa, proudly parading them around the neighbourhood in their double stroller, and they adored him.

We lost him in January of '97. We'd returned from Christmas at Fallowfield to find him gravely ill with pneumonia and refusing to go into hospital. He seemed to be improving, but it was too much for his heart. We found him early one morning sitting on the living room couch in front of the Hans Poelman portrait of Gina, half a glass of Scotch still on the table beside him. We thought he was sleeping, but he was gone. We'd planned to buy a bigger house, something in the area to be close to him, but without him it was just too sad, so we decided to sell the place and move out of the city before the twins started school. I'd never considered Stanton

House, but Persy prevailed, and after six months of renovations we moved in.

In '99 I accepted a full-time teaching position at my school. I'd noticed a familiar name listed for one of the upcoming student recitals, Gregory Vatisblank. Not only was it the same family, but there were eight siblings and cousins cheering him on, and they all played one instrument or another. It's been fun getting to know them.

It was only a year ago I came back to the journal with a view to publishing. I hadn't listened to my father's tapes since I'd recorded them. Hearing his voice and his story again I was overcome by the tragic irony that in this long line of thieves and cheats, liars and con artists and even a murderer, however charming they might have been, it was my poor, honest father who'd gone to prison for a crime he didn't commit. I got so depressed I nearly dropped the whole idea, but Persy convinced me to get on with it.

"Time to stop running away from the tough stuff, old chum. It always catches up to bite you on the arse" was how she put it.

The last hurdle was Henry. I sent him the manuscript and was prepared for him to reject it absolutely, but he finally called to say that he and Julia had thoroughly enjoyed it, and that it certainly added some spice to an otherwise undistinguished family history, with the added surprise of Sam Treadwell as another cousin. His one request was that I change the names of people and places to preserve the privacy of the family. My reaction was to publish and be damned, but Persy said I should think on it. Serendipity made my decision.

We were going to New York City on holiday. We'd gotten tickets for the Philharmonic and there were several galleries and museums we wanted to visit. Persy had just discovered a Russian artist and calligrapher who could create exquisite copies of illuminated manuscripts which she felt would be very saleable to interior designers. She knew that the collection at the Morgan Library was superb, and I was looking forward to seeing the Mozart scores, but it was a simply framed letter and its wonderfully convoluted explanation that captured me.

The letter was composed in 1726 by Jonathan Swift, but written by his friend John Gay under the pseudonym of Richard Sympson, a fictitious literary agent. It represented Lemuel Gulliver's book, *Travels into Several Remote Nations of the World*, as a true travel memoir, and was intended to promote the book to publisher Benjamin Motte. Motte saw through the subterfuge, guessed the true identity of the author, and bought the manuscript, thus producing an early best-seller. It occurred to me that if Swift could pass off his brilliant fictional satire as true, why shouldn't I publish my family's remarkable true story as fiction? It's been a simple matter to make the changes Henry requested, and my publisher is just as happy there's no likelihood of litigation with someone as wealthy and powerful as the real Sir Henry. As an added plus, if the fiction is successful we'll all be spared bus tours of historic Kingsfold, Fallowfield and Stanton.

New Watersfield has become one of Toronto's growing number of satellite communities. I sold the mill a few years back and it's now a high-end restaurant, brew pub and banquet facility. The old row houses are very much in demand by those wanting the illusion of village life in the heart of the suburbs. Stanton House has become quite a showplace with its red tile roof, green gingerbread and dragon weathervane, framed by the glorious garden Persy and Cam Mitchell have created.

My office-cum-studio is in the cupola, high above the chaos of the household. It's my little revenge against Rachel that Gina's nude portrait presently hangs over the fireplace in the parlour. The twins cheerfully refer to it as "Great-granny." They're an engaging pair of hellraisers, formidably bright (if I do say so) and musical. Teri takes guitar lessons from her uncle Desmond. She loves Harry Potter and is fascinated by her aunt Tina's tales of Old Betty. Gerry's more of a Bart Simpson fan. He plays piano and does a hilarious impression of

Jerry Lee Lewis, but I still have hopes he'll take up the violin. If not, maybe Persy and I will have another try. We have two horses, a dog, three cats, a nasty tempered parrot who swears (thank you, Persy), and at last count, nine rabbits.

I've saved the most stupendous news for last.

About six months ago while editing my notes for the journal, I revisited my ghostly encounter with Gerry Joyner in Old Betty's kitchen. It was almost as if he'd been nagging me from somewhere in my subconscious. I subsequently spotted an advertisement for a private collection of old and rare musical instruments on one of the Internet auction sites Persy follows, and among the photographs was one that took my breath away.

Old Nick. I recognized him instantly from John Joyner's carving at Saint Stephen and the photograph of Beth and George at Fallowfield Cottage.

I attended the sale prepared to bid whatever it took, and he's presently resting in his casket with his old bow once again. Actually holding him in my hands for the first time and producing the bright sweet voice I'd only read about was a moment of pure joy. He'll raise that voice when we perform "Night Train to Harlem" with the orchestra at my school in ten days' time, Gregory Vatisblank on piano, Desmond Miller playing Elsie, and me with Old Nick. I'll never be a virtuoso, but I flatter myself that I have a feel for the music which virtuosity alone can't express. "Joyner's Dream—The Kingsfold Suite" is complete.

Through the collector's provenance I've been able to trace most of Old Nick's journey since leaving George Fitzhelm's hands, but that's another story . . .

—LESLIE ARCHIBALD FITZHELM, 2006

My heartfelt thanks to Bill Whitehead, who encouraged and mentored me when I didn't know how to begin, to Suze Rotolo for being my constant reader, and to my agent, John Pearce, for his faith and persistence. Thanks also to my editor, Jennifer Glossop, and copy editor, Allyson Latta, for their help with the formidable cleanup. My gratitude goes to Jennifer Lambert for seeing a viable novel despite the initial chaos, to Alex Schultz for his encouragement and guidance (and the title), and to everyone else at HarperCollins for their support.